From the Journal of Tanis Half-Elven, Aboard the *Castor:*

Day and night the weather worsens, and our peril increases. After a brief respite, the storm returned in full fury. Huge waves crashed into the ship, and violent rain soaked us to the skin. We were deluged by water. We had to shout into each other's ears in order to be heard over the deafening thunder. Though Captain Nugetre remained at the helm, I couldn't imagine his efforts had any effect. The Castor *seemed lifted and flung like a cork in the surf. We lurched drunkenly from the attack of the Blood Sea.*

The seething chaos did not let up. In the late afternoon, Captain Nugetre, his red-rimmed eyes burning, announced that we had crossed over into the Tightening Ring. Now, he said, it was mandatory that we break the grip of the current and somehow lead the Castor *east and north, back to the Outer Reach.*

Otherwise we would be sucked into the Maelstrom. . . .

The DRAGONLANCE® Saga

DragonLance® Saga

The Meetings Sextet
Volume Six

THE
COMPANIONS

Tina Daniell

DRAGONLANCE® Saga Meetings
Volume Six

The Companions

All characters in this book are fictitious. Any resemblance to actual persons, living or dead, is purely coincidental.

All TSR characters, character names, and the distinctive likenesses thereof are trademarks owned by TSR, Inc.

This book is protected under the copyright laws of the United States of America. Any reproduction or other unauthorized use of the material or artwork herein is prohibited without the express written permission of TSR, Inc.

Distributed to the hobby, toy,a nd comic trade in the United States and Canada by regional distributors.

Distributed worldwide by Wizards of the Coast, Inc. and regional distributors.

Cover art by Clyde Caldwell.

Interior illustrations by Valerie Valusek.

DRAGONLANCE and the TSR logo are registered trademarks owned by TSR, Inc.

TSR, Inc. is a subsidiary of Wizards of the Coast, Inc.

First printing: January 1993
Printed in the United States of America
Library of Congress Catalog Card Number: 91-66486

9 8 7

ISBN: 1-56076-340-X
T08345-620

U.S., CANADA, ASIA,	EUROPEAN HEADQUARTERS
PACIFIC, & LATIN AMERICA	Wizards of the Coast, Belgium
Wizards of the Coast, Inc.	P.B. 2031
P.O. Box 707	2600 Berchem
Renton, WA 98057-0707	Belgium
+1-800-324-6496	+32-70-23-32-77

Visit our website at **www.tsr.com**

**For my three sons,
Clancy, Bowie, and Sky**

ACKNOWLEDGMENTS

My thanks to the original DRAGONLANCE® saga novelists, Margaret Weis and Tracy Hickman. I am privileged to walk in their footsteps in the world of Krynn. Game adventures written by Harold Johnson and Douglas Niles were particularly crucial to my understanding of minotaurs and kyrie. Book Department head Mary Kirchoff gave me a chance with *Dark Heart*, then another chance with *The Companions*. Editor Bill Larson caught mistakes and polished my prose. Last but not least, I am grateful to TSR story editor Patrick McGilligan, who wouldn't accept any less than my best effort.

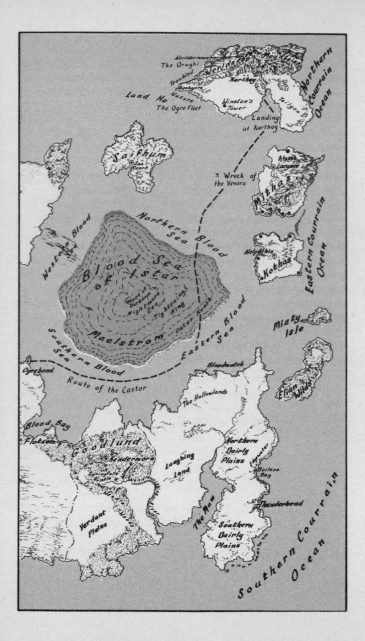

Chapter 1
The <u>Vanishing</u>

Tasslehoff Burrfoot was alone. Having for the moment reached the limit of exploration afforded by a midsize ship like the *Venora*, the kender had retreated to the cabin he shared with Sturm Brightblade and Caramon Majere. He couldn't help but notice that this somehow pleased the captain, whose shouted oaths and threats had followed him belowdecks. And after Tas had tried so hard to be helpful with the mainsail rigging!

In the cabin, really no more than a narrow room with three bunk beds virtually stacked on top of one another, Tas sat cross-legged on the floor. Topknot bobbing, he poked through his pack and the innumerable pouches he always carried, examining their contents as if he had never laid eyes on them before. His convenient memory assured him they were all "found" objects, although in most cases, he had quite forgotten how or where they were found.

Spread around him lay all manner of things—a tiny porcelain figurine of a unicorn, a brilliantly-hued feather, sparkling stones and pieces of jewelry, gnarled twine, rolled and beribboned parchment, a wooden flute, yellowed maps, favorite buttons, a ranger's tarnished badge, a scrap of hide with stringy, gray hair that Tas recognized and treasured, for it was, he swore, a souvenir of his fabled encounter with a great and rare woolly mammoth. ...

One shriveled item particularly drew his attention. Picking it up, Tas examined it in the imperfect light cast by an oil lamp sitting on a rough-hewn shelf screwed into the wall under the cabin's lone porthole. Outside, Tas could glimpse the blue waters of the Schallsea Straits as they rose and fell rhythmically in the late afternoon.

"Huh ... I don't remember that!" Tas said ruminatively, peering at the wrinkled possession. "Looks like an ogre's ear to me, although I don't recall cutting one off—an ogre's ear, that is. Maybe Flint gave it to me, although I don't remember him cutting off an ogre's ear, either. I do remember him cutting off an ogre's foot once, but that's different." He squinted at the thing, trying to decide. "No, definitely an ear."

He shrugged his shoulders, put the object down, and continued sifting through his cherished possessions. His search had started with a definite purpose that was now in obvious peril of being forgotten as this or that glittering bauble diverted the kender's attention. Finally, with a delighted grin, Tas recalled his purpose and reached for an ordinary-looking green glass bottle, small and round, with a long neck.

"Aha!" Tas exclaimed with satisfaction. After a momentary inspection, he placed the bottle on a shelf next to the lamp. In the lamplight, it took on a somewhat more unusual appearance, glistening with iridescent highlights. A quill pen and piece of rough parchment already rested on the shelf, which was low enough and wide enough to double as a desk.

Priding himself on being exceptionally well organized, Tasslehoff proceeded to scoop up his trove of treasures, distributing them among his series of pouches and his ruck-sack, promising himself that one of these days he would sit down and take a careful inventory of all his precious belongings.

* * * * *

On the deck above, back near the stern, Caramon Majere sat cross-legged amid a small group of rough-and-tumble sailors. Wherever he went, Caramon made friends easily. He, Sturm, and Tas had booked passage several days ago on the sloop. Although the *Venora* was only two days out to sea on its voyage from Eastport to Abanasinia, Caramon was already on a first name basis with everyone on board, from Captain Murloch—Caramon called him Jhani Murloch—on down. The scruffy group on deck was sharing raucous camaraderie and a jug of mead under the late afternoon sky.

Dusk approached, but the setting sun filled the sky with a bright, orange-red light. No clouds marred the vista. A light wind kept the sloop moving gently. None of the sailors gathered had the impending obligation of night watch. They seemed to flock around Caramon, drawn to his vitality and good humor. They egged the well-muscled young man on as he boasted about his numerous female conquests.

"Caergoth offers the finest females of any port on Krynn," asserted a burly, whiskered sailor at one point.

"They're portly, all right," countered one of his cohorts, a squinty-eyed seaman. He drew a round of derisive laughter. "I likes 'em lean and lively myself, and for that, you can't beat Flotsam."

"I'll never forget Ravinia," rhapsodized Caramon,

already wistful with drink. The sailors seemed riveted by his words. "Do you know the barmaid in Eastport?" One of the men grunted recognition. "She was stingy with her kisses," Caramon complained, then paused for effect. "But I was generous with mine!"

A roar of laughter greeted his remark. Caramon tossed back his head and joined in, laughing so hard that tears ran from the corners of his eyes. The jug of mead was passed to him, and he took a long swig before passing it on. The spirits circled the half-dozen others with surprising speed before ending up back in Caramon's hands.

Pleased with the impression he was making, Caramon brushed his golden brown hair from his eyes and took another deep, long draft. He hadn't noticed that for some time now he was the only one drinking from the jug.

* * * * *

Up on the foredeck, the ribald laughter made only the dimmest impression on Sturm Brightblade. Hands clasped, leaning over the ship's side railing, the young man whose ambition it was to become a Solamnic Knight was lost in a mood, staring down into the darkening water. No light was reflected in his limpid brown eyes.

For long minutes, Sturm barely moved. He could have been mistaken for a statue. The least sociable of the three companions aboard the *Venora*, Sturm kept his thoughts to himself in a manner that could be—and had been, on more than one occasion—construed as arrogant. But this twilight evening, standing in lonely profile, Sturm seemed less arrogant than a man apart, aloof not only from strangers but also from his friends.

The voyage had set him to brooding. Sturm's life had once taken a dramatic turn on a ship. As an infant, he, his mother, and her retinue had fled the family's ancient castle in Solamnia, leaving his father behind to deal with the angry populace that had risen against the knighthood.

Although he had been too young at the time to remember the tale himself, Sturm felt the experience keenly imprinted on his consciousness because his mother had often recounted the story. The image of his father banishing them from their home, though it was for their own safety, was burned into his soul. At an early age, Sturm had learned about the painful price of honor. Few in the world held the Solamnic order in high esteem these days, but Sturm was committed to living up to his father's noble ideals and to following the Oath and the Measure.

As if reflecting his dark thoughts, a canopy of clouds towered on the horizon. A sharp, cool wind came up, rousing Sturm from his contemplation. He noticed the cloud mass immediately but with no particular interest, thinking idly, as a child might, that it appeared to have a shape like some great, flying creature with outspread wings and groping talons. The cloud seemed to roil the waters before it. As he continued to gaze in its direction, Sturm became aware that the cloud mass was building ominously. It was approaching rapidly and would be upon the ship in mere minutes.

Sturm stirred himself, stepped back from the railing, and glanced toward the rear deck, which still echoed with the boisterous laughter of the crew. He ought to find Captain Murloch and make sure the ship was ready for a blow. Then he ought to check on Caramon and Tas.

* * * * *

Back belowdecks, Tas had been very, very busy, carefully phrasing his magic letter to Raistlin Majere, Caramon's twin brother. Wouldn't Raistlin be thrilled! Tas had been eagerly anticipating this occasion for a long time—well, at least since the night they had boarded the *Venora*, when the contents of one of his pouches had shifted and the magic message bottle had poked him in the side, reminding him of its existence.

That's when he remembered the magic bottle he had obtained some years ago in exchange for beads and perfume from a shop dealer in Sanction. Or maybe it had been from a cousin in Kendermore. It was so-o-o long ago.

At any rate, Tas had been assured that the bottle could be tossed into the widest ocean and would carry a message to anyone, anywhere on the entire continent of Ansalon. That was just the sort of mind-boggling feat that figured prominently in the stories Uncle Trapspringer used to tell him, and this was the perfect opportunity to use the magical device. Raistlin, practically a mage himself—he hadn't taken the Test yet, but he would someday soon—would be sure to enjoy such a special method of communication. Who knows? The young mage might even pass on a good word about Tas's creativity and general reliability to that grouchy old dwarf, Flint Fireforge.

But you had to be extremely judicious about what you wrote—or said—to Raistlin, Tas thought as he sat with the quill pen poised over his piece of wrinkled parchment. Raistlin had a tendency to be ill-humored, even downright dour at times. A message in a magic bottle might be the very thing to coax a smile to his lips, providing it was a well-scribed message.

For many minutes, Tas pondered the blank paper before him, his brow furrowed, his topknot uncommonly still. Finally Tas had begun writing:

Dear Raistlin,

Isn't this amazing? I'm writing to you on board the good ship Venora *... at least it's been a good ship so far (about two nights and two days). Caramon is upstairs ...*

Tas crossed that out.

Caramon is up on deck, having a good time with his new friends, the sailors, and Sturm is probably wandering around up there, too, thinking serious thoughts. You know Sturm. Well, I guess you know Caramon, too. Hi, Tanis!

The point of this letter is to tell you what happened after we arrived in Southern Ergoth. We made the two-day journey down the coast without any incident. Our little errand was successful. Asa was correct as to the whereabouts of the minotaur herbalist who sold the crushed jalopwort needed for the rare spell you are researching. I never had any doubts, since, like all kender, Asa is an expert with maps, and besides, he's my good friend of many years standing and certainly knows his herbal business. Don't worry. I have the crushed jalopwort safely tucked away in one of my pouches.

At this, Tas jumped up and patted one of the pouches on the bunk just to be sure, then slung the sack across his back, his eyes darting around vigilantly. Tas neither saw nor heard anything peculiar. No sound reached his ears other than the peaceful creaking of the ship and the padding of his own movements. Reassured, he sat back down at the makeshift desk under the porthole and resumed his magical missive.

You may already have guessed that this bottle is a magical one. I acquired it by shrewd and honest means during my period of wanderlust (I think), and when I noticed it a couple of days ago, I thought I would compose a letter to you and Tanis and Flint. Hi, Flint! Bet you thought I'd forgotten you!

If all goes well, this letter will be plucked out of the sea by some deserving fisherman who will cannily discern its significance and bring it to you in Solace for ample reward. The bottle will actually speak its message—my voice—to whoever uncorks it. Can you imagine that? Well, I guess you can by now.

Anyway, we're returning to Abanasinia by aforementioned ship and should be back in Solace within a week or two, depending on how often we stop to rest and have some fun. And you know how often Caramon likes to stop and rest and have some fun, so this letter will probably beat us back!

Here Tas paused and scratched his chin. That was a good beginning. He chewed the end of the quill pen before dipping it back into the inkwell.

Anyway, the mission was a success. Caramon especially enjoyed the town nearby, called Hyssop—Asa was right about that, too—and he seemed to make a lot of new friends there, especially female friends. Sturm kept Caramon company some of the time. Other times he explored the docks and the port of Hyssop, which is a much smaller place than Eastport but clean and friendly. They don't get many visitors from afar. I think Sturm enjoyed the novelty of the town, but it's hard to say with Sturm.

I did my best to keep an eye on both of them and also did some exploring of my own. Hyssop is filled with one-of-a-kind shops, but many of the storekeepers seemed to have never met a kender before. They became so overexcited whenever I stopped into one of their shops that Sturm finally suggested—insisted really—that I stick with him and stay away from the market district.

But there are certain strange and inexplicable parts of our trip that I would like to tell you about and which are the purpose of this letter, because I certainly wouldn't waste a magic letter on a boring trip.

The minotaur herbalist's shop was unlike any I've ever been in. For one thing, it was in a cave, and if you didn't have Asa's map, you'd never be able to find it. Also, the minotaur herbalist was just as polite and pleasant as can be. He didn't smell as bad as most of them usually do, either. Sturm said he actually detected the scent of soap on the horned beast, whose name is—I guess I should say was, but that's getting ahead of myself—Argotz.

The rhythmic creaking of the ship suddenly changed, its gentle motion interrupted by a sudden lurch. A gust of wind slammed open the porthole over the desk. Tas jumped up and peered out, happy for the distraction. Good! A storm was brewing! Tas had never been at sea during a storm. He felt certain it would be fascinating and enjoyable.

Tas sat back down at the desk and began to scribble faster in order to finish before going up on deck to watch the storm.

* * * * *

Sturm had barely started to make his way toward the rear deck when the first hailstones pelted him with the force of a thousand tiny, hurtling missiles. The deck shifted beneath his feet, and he momentarily slipped on the icy pebbles before catching his balance. Glancing up, Sturm saw that the ominous mass of clouds had come upon them so swiftly that the sky was suddenly blackened around them. Lightning crackled above. Flames flared from the masthead of the *Venora*. Grabbing the side railing, Sturm leaned into the wind and began pulling himself toward the Captain's post in the stern.

An instant later, Sturm was nearly blinded by stinging rain that poured down with awesome intensity. Shielding his eyes with one hand and clutching the rail with the other, Sturm was barely able to lurch forward.

What he saw as he approached the stern left him with a sick feeling in the pit of his stomach. A group of sailors were bunched ahead of him, working frantically to lower a small boat into the heaving waves. Sturm fought his way toward them. As he did, the ship pitched and he fell backward. By the time he succeeded in pulling himself upright, the lifeboat and the sailors had disappeared over the side.

As Sturm looked on in astonishment, several other members of the *Venora*'s crew slipped furtively over the side, carrying what looked like makeshift life buoys under their arms. Sturm called out to them, but against the raging tumult of the storm, he could barely make out his own voice. When he reached the railing where they had jumped, Sturm peered downward but could see nothing except the dark waves thrashing the ship.

Their desertion was a cowardly act and strange as well.

Did the deserters expect to fare better in the wild sea than on board the storm-tossed *Venora*? Was it some kind of mutiny? Sturm glanced up at the steering deck, where Captain Murloch usually stationed himself. Sturm's perplexity deepened into outrage and fear. Murloch wasn't there. Not a soul stood by the wheel, which was spinning dizzily.

Strange indeed. Captain Murloch didn't seem to be the type to abandon his duties. It was Sturm who had picked him out from among the sea captains whose ships were moored at Eastport. Murloch's mournful, craggy face bespoke experience. Tas had dubbed the captain "Walrus Face" because of the pronged teeth that stuck out over his lantern jaw.

A punishing crash drew Sturm's attention upward. With the peculiar grace of a ballet, the top half of the *Venora*'s mast broke off and toppled slowly into the violent sea. Nobody had bothered to furl the sails as the storm approached, and now there was no one to respond to this latest crisis.

Sturm's worried thoughts turned to his companions. He started to pull himself along the rail toward the back of the small cabin where he had last seen Caramon drinking with a group of sailors. The *Venora*'s deck seesawed wildly back and forth beneath his feet. The ship seemed to be spinning around in circles that left Sturm's head swimming. Wind and rain whipped around him, creating an overwhelming cacophony.

Finally, after what seemed an eternity, Sturm lunged from the side rail to the small cabin and pulled himself around to the rear, which offered some small shelter from the battering of the storm.

With dismay, Sturm shook his head at what he beheld. Caramon was sprawled on the deck, eyes dreamily closed, an overturned jug of liquor rolling around at his side. Drunk, thought Sturm with exasperation. Sturm had developed an abiding respect for his friend's fighting skills and bravery, while acknowledging privately that Caramon's judgment, due to his overly generous nature, could not always be relied upon. But this lapse, at this particular time, seemed almost inexcusable.

And where were his drinking companions? Clearly, Caramon had been left behind.

The deck shifted violently beneath Sturm's feet. He braced himself against the side of the cabin, gauging how difficult it would be to drag Caramon into the slight shelter offered by the interior of the cabin, then shake him awake. After that, Tas still needed to be found, Sturm thought to himself grimly. And this all presumed there were still enough crew members aboard to bring the *Venora* under control.

Keeping one foot braced against the cabin wall, Sturm leaned over to grab his friend. Although the deck was slick from the rain, it would be difficult to budge Caramon's bulk. It was then that Sturm noticed that Caramon's weapons were missing. Before he could contemplate this odd fact, he heard a scuffling sound. Sturm looked up, but it was too late. The young Solamnic felt a thump on the side of his head, followed by the sensation of falling down a deep, dark, bottomless hole, with the wind shrieking in his ears.

* * * * *

Tasslehoff had been absorbed in finishing his letter to Raistlin. When the ship's increasingly turbulent motion caused the oil lamp to slide off the writing desk and shatter, the cabin was plunged into darkness. Tas looked up expectantly, just in time to grab the magic message bottle before it rolled off the desk.

"Oh ... the storm. I forgot," the kender muttered to himself. Quickly he rolled up the parchment and stuffed it into the bottle. He pinched off a piece of the cork and crumbled it inside, then watched as the letter took on a golden glow before it vanished. Following the instructions he recalled, he swiftly corked the bottle and held it up. It appeared to be empty.

Standing on his tiptoes, Tas pressed his face against the porthole. In the dim light, he could make out little except that this was certainly a fine storm. He tugged the porthole open, and with a mighty effort, hurled the bottle into the churning sea.

As he stepped back from the porthole, the cabin tilted at a crazy angle, and the chair Tas had been sitting on crashed into his shins. Flashes of lightning filled the porthole with brilliant white light, extinguished almost as soon as it appeared. Loud cracks of thunder followed. In between two thunderclaps, Tas heard something else up on deck.

Trying unsuccessfully to ignore his throbbing shins, Tas began hopping around the cabin, gathering up the rest of his pouches and shoving them into his rucksack. He had no intention of leaving any of his treasures behind. "No telling what might happen in a storm like this," Tas mused aloud. "Sounds like it's even more exciting up on deck. Sturm and Caramon must be having a great time up there. I bet they can't wait for me to join them." He took a moment to strap his hoopak, the fighting weapon prized by kender, to his back.

Tas paused at the door to the cabin, casting a quick glance behind him. Another flash of lightning at the porthole momentarily blinded him.

"I wonder if it's okay to use the magic message bottle during a storm," he reflected. "Oh, well. Too late now." He turned and bounded through the narrow passageway leading to the cabin, then up the stairway to the deck.

Prepared for a warm greeting from his friends, Tas was disappointed when he didn't see anyone. There was no sign of Sturm or Caramon, or even Captain Murloch. With typical kender agility, Tas managed to keep his footing on the rolling deck as he looked around. The mainmast appeared to have broken and toppled into the sea. The sails left attached to the stub of the mast whipped around wildly. The *Venora* careened dizzily. Where were Sturm and Caramon, not to mention everybody else?

Sensing some movement behind him, Tas whirled around and came face to face with Captain Murloch ... old Walrus Face. The captain grinned at the kender, his yellowed teeth sticking out over his lower jaw. Swell, thought Tas. Despite his ship's dire predicament, the captain was managing to keep in good humor.

"Hi, Captain Murloch," Tas shouted into the wind and rain that lashed his face. "Quite a squall we're having. I bet it's going to give the ship a bit of trouble. I'll stay by your side and help you out. I've been on many ships in such circumstances ...well, not too many, actually. Seven or nine, not counting this one. But Sturm and Caramon can be a big help, too. Do you know where they are? Good thing our friend Flint isn't along, because ..."

Tas took a few steps closer to Captain Murloch, to make sure he was being heard. Somehow nothing seemed to be registering on the captain's grinning face. Perplexed and distracted, Tas failed to see the captain's arm swing up or notice the club arcing toward his head until it was too late.

"Damnable kender! They'd talk your ears off in the middle of a hurricane," Captain Murloch muttered to himself. But the captain's club had put a stop to the kender's chatter. Tas lay unconscious at Murloch's feet. The captain seized him by his topknot and dragged him toward what was left of the main mast. Beneath the shredded sails lay the unconscious forms of Sturm and Caramon.

Captain Murloch dragged the limp bodies closer to the mast and began to rope them to it as he had been instructed. He worked as quickly as he could in the fury of the storm. Finally, when he was finished, he stood for a moment to survey his handiwork. Heavy, purple-black clouds blotted out the sky overhead. The *Venora*'s timbers creaked loudly.

Captain Murloch had kept his part of the bargain. The generous payment he had received meant he would be well compensated for the loss of the *Venora* and the risk to his own life. Like many old sea hands, Murloch loved his ship and regretted losing it. He would almost rather have lost his life.

"Well old girl, we had a good run," the captain murmured, licking his lips.

Murloch bent down and pulled a thick ring of cork from a hatch near the mast. He slipped it over his head and secured it with a rope at his waist. Looking back at the three unconscious bodies, then down toward the dark, turbulent waters, he climbed over the rail and plummeted toward the sea below.

He had managed to thrash his way through the high waves and swim several hundred feet away from the ship by the time the angry cloud that hovered above the *Venora* lowered itself upon the ship, spitting fierce blasts of lightning and hail.

Then, with a fearful, rushing clamor, the cloud began to rise slowly, carryinging the *Venora* with it. From his distant vantage, Murloch could barely make out the ship's bow and stern as the *Venora* spun around like a top and was sucked up into the vortex.

* * * * *

Half a day later, the treacherous Captain Murloch, drifting with the tide, spied the distant shore of Abanasinia. He was nearly home free.

Tired and hungry, he was nonetheless comforted by the prospect of being a rich man for the rest of his life.

His cork preserver fitted snugly around his middle, Captain Murloch reached out and stroked the water, paddling in the direction of the coastline.

An odd sound drew his attention skyward. The sun was so bright and hot that he had to shade his eyes. Specks appeared to be dancing in the air.

Suddenly Captain Murloch stopped paddling and stared in shock. What appeared to be specks was actually a cone-like swarm of flying insects. As he watched in terror, he realized that they were hovering above him, moving along with him. At that moment, the swarm dipped and came diving downward.

They were giant bees—hundreds, thousands of them, swirling, buzzing, stinging. Captain Murloch reached up futilely with one arm, trying to bat them away. His arm was quickly covered with the savage creatures.

The scream that issued from Captain Murloch's mouth was a cry of utter helplessness. The giant bees swarmed into his mouth, covered his face, went for his ears and his eyes. They formed a living carpet over Captain Murloch, twitching and bristling as they went about their deadly business.

Within seconds, his heart ceased beating, and the bees flew up and into the sun.

Below, the captain's face was a mask of red welts. His tongue hung out, black and swollen to five times its normal size. His arms hung limp and useless in the water.

Captain Jhani Murloch drifted toward shore.

* * * * *

Thousands of miles away, in a rugged and desolate place—a salt-encrusted land parched by the sun, scoured by the wind, and surrounded by an inhospitable sea—a hulking figure bent over to read the signs of the shiny objects he had carefully arranged on the high table of a mountain plateau.

It had taken half a day's climb from his camp on the dry, ravaged lowland to get here. Nevertheless, twice a week he made the trek in order to commune with the gods—one god in particular.

The looming figure tilted his head upward, observing the manner in which the light of noonday was refracted in the colored glass, prisms and crystals, and silver shards of mirror.

Some distance away, grouped in a triad, stood his three most trusted and highly-attuned disciples, known simply as the High Three. Once the figure they watched had been one of the High Three. Now he was their unquestioned leader. It was inevitable that someday one of them would succeed him and carry on the sacred duties.

Beyond the High Three, ringed around them, behind turreted rocks and craggy formations, stood dozens of lesser acolytes, their features monstrous and contorted, their weapons brutal and deadly, glinting in the sun. Their animalistic faces betrayed no emotion; their huge, round eyes stared, dull and trancelike.

Beyond the acolytes were arrayed dozens of others, these mere guards and soldiers, but equally loyal and fearsome, waiting for but a signal from their leader.

Whatever was asked of them, they would do. They lived only to serve the Nightmaster.

The Nightmaster circled the shiny glass objects, stooping and peering at each of them, fascinated by the glimmers and swirls of light. Shading his massive brow, he gazed up at the sun and the hot white sky, assessing what he had observed and what he had learned.

Feathers and fur dangled from his great horned head. Bells jingled when he moved. In his huge hands, he carried a long, thin stick of incense, which trailed smoke and a sickeningly sweet scent. From object to object he stepped, pondering the signs.

Certain precautions had yet to be taken, certain preparations carried out. Renegades and interlopers had to be dealt with. Resources had to be marshaled. Nothing must interfere with the casting of the spell.

Sargonnas waited.

The Nightmaster looked deep into the patterns of light in the colored glass and knew that soon it would be time.

Chapter 2
Message in a Bottle

"Twenty to five," said Tanis glumly, scratching a new figure into a table in Flint's workshed. The grizzled dwarf, with evident cheerfulness, rolled a smooth, round black stone into the center of a circle marked in chalk on the floor of the shed. The circle held a clutch of smaller, multicolored pebbles. The instant the larger stone made contact, Flint skipped over with surprising nimbleness and snatched up as many of the pebbles as he could as they scattered outside the circle.

"Twenty-eight," Flint pronounced with satisfaction, once he had counted the stones he held in his hand. "But we don't have to keep track, my boy. After all, it's only a silly game." He tried hard to tamp down the smile tugging at the corner of his lips.

"Twenty-eight to five," said Tanis, scratching out the old figure and marking in the new one.

Although it was the middle of a workday, Flint was semiretired and opened his shop only when he cared to deal with bothersome customers. He kept his tools clean and well sharpened, but some of them hadn't been taken down from their pegs in weeks. No longer did the grizzled dwarf have the passion for metalsmithing that had driven him to become a master of the craft, so skilled and inventive that even the elven race prized his work. It was the metalsmithing trade, in fact, that had first brought Flint and Tanis together years earlier, when the half-elf was a mere boy in Qualinesti.

Today Flint had proposed a little game of roosterball to prod Tanis out of his sulking mood. It wasn't succeeding. All Tanis could think about was Kitiara, who had left Solace a few months back without telling the half-elf where she was going. Flint, on the other hand, was in a whistling mood lately, because that irrepressible kender, Tasslehoff Burrfoot, had also been away, on a journey with Caramon and Sturm, for weeks now.

It was so peaceful when Tas wasn't around, Flint thought to himself at least once a day.

Tanis stood and walked over to the chalk circle, arranging the pebbles in the center. Then he paced back the required distance before turning to face the target. His tall, slender form seemed almost to contract with concentration as he swung the black stone forward and released it with a distinctive flick of the wrist. Despite his admirable technique, the stone rolled wide of its mark, glancing off the clutch of pebbles. Tanis hastened to the circle, but none of the pebbles managed to roll beyond the perimeter.

"Aw, too bad," said Flint, bringing his thick white eyebrows together in a semblance of a frown. Amusement danced in his eyes, however, and Tanis was not deceived.

"I cede the win to you," the half-elf said with irritation, his face wearing a sour expression. "There's no point in continuing with you so far ahead."

"Fine, fine," soothed Flint, walking over and picking up the stones, which he placed carefully in a wooden cup. Clearly pleased with himself over his margin of victory, the old dwarf nonetheless cast a sympathetic look at his young friend. "All this fretting over a woman!" he muttered, loud enough, he hoped, for Tanis to overhear. He took the cup and put it back in its place on one of the many neatly ordered shelves that lined his metalworking shop. "In more than one hundred years, I've never seen you carry on so. I've seen you fight and defeat ogres and brigands. I never thought you would be bested by a woman. ..."

He stole a glance at Tanis, searching for a reaction. But the half-elf remained lost in thought, brooding, with his arms folded across his chest as he sat on one of Flint's high stools.

Flint turned back to the half-elf gruffly. "You owe me a copper all the same," he said pointedly.

That got Tanis's attention. "But we didn't finish the game," he protested.

"All the more reason," declared Flint huffily. "You said yourself that you ceded the win. Serves you right, grumping around about a woman so much you can't even finish a game of roosterball."

Peevishly Tanis reached into his pouch, felt around with his fingers, and came up with a shiny copper piece. Flint grabbed it greedily and inspected it closely, almost suspiciously, before stuffing the coin into his pocket. His little act was almost enough to bring a grin to Tanis's face.

A knock sounded at the door.

Opening it up, Flint saw one of Solace's many ragamuffins, a freckled ten-year-old named Moya, holding out a folded note while rocking back and forth on his heels.

"Message for Flint Fireforge," said Moya importantly, although of course he knew Flint Fireforge, as did most of the citizens of Solace.

Flint took the note, but before he could open and read it,

Moya snatched the paper back and said, "That'll be one copper, puh-lease."

"One copper!" Flint fumed. "That's highway robbery."

"Going rate," declared Moya flatly, stuffing the note into his back pocket beyond Flint's reach.

"One copper!" Flint railed. "I should read it first, and if I like what it says and who it's from, then maybe I'd pay one copper! But why should I pay a copper for something I might not even want?"

Moya stood firm. Grumbling, Flint reached back into his pouch and gave the young messenger the copper that he had just won from Tanis.

Fuming, Flint slammed the door. He turned back toward Tanis and opened the note, which he already knew from the unique way that it was folded, in crisscrossing triangles, came from Caramon's twin brother.

Tanis read over his shoulder.

Flint,

I have reason to believe that Caramon, Sturm, and Tasslehoff are in great danger. Meet me at the place by Crystalmir Lake. Bring Tanis.

Raistlin

Tanis's brow furrowed with curiosity. He wasn't sure what to make of this missive from Raistlin. With Caramon and the twins' half-sister Kitiara away, Raistlin had withdrawn from the remaining companions, becoming even more aloof than usual. Tanis knew that he rarely had been separated from his twin brother for very long, and the half-elf supposed Caramon's absence put Raistlin in a solitary and perhaps agitated mood. The robust Caramon normally cast a protective shadow over his weaker brother, but when Flint and Tanis had chanced to meet Raistlin at Otik's tavern several days ago, the situation had been reversed. It was the young mage who seemed preoccupied with the welfare of Caramon, whose return to Solace was overdue.

"Caramon said he would be back within a fortnight," Raistlin had insisted. "This isn't like him to stay away, without sending any word to me."

"It's just like Caramon," Tanis had argued, adding thoughtfully, "but it isn't like Sturm."

"I'll tell you who it's like—Tasslehoff. And Tasslehoff is in charge," stated Flint. He drained his ale, signaled Otik for another, and leaned toward the other two conspiratorially. "He just lets you think you're in charge, but wherever you decide to go, it's him that's leading you by the nose. No, it's probably all Tas's doing, and it's just like that doorknob of a kender to be gallivanting around Southern Ergoth without the slightest thought of his friends back home. I don't see the point of needless worrying. Tas always turns up, and Sturm and Caramon will turn up with him. Enjoy the temporary lull, I say."

That was about as long a speech as the customarily taciturn Flint ever made. The dwarf drank deeply of another tankard of ale, wiping the foam from his lips with his sleeve. Beaming and looking around the place, Flint didn't notice that Raistlin gave no response. The young mage had sat there, keeping them company but saying little. Indeed, as afternoon became evening and the hours wore on, Raistlin took scant appraisal of his friends. After shifting his chair, he stared beyond them, seemingly mesmerized by the pile of wood that Otik had coaxed into flames, the flickering fire reflected in Raistlin's intense hourglass eyes.

Now there was the cryptic message to meet Raistlin at Crystalmir Lake.

"What do you think?" Tanis asked Flint.

Dismay was the answer on the dwarf's craggy face. The message was unwelcome. He regretted even more the copper he had paid to receive it.

Southern Ergoth was only about a month's journey, round trip. Almost three months had passed since the day when Sturm, Caramon, and Tas had departed. "Aw," the dwarf said, waving his hand, "that Raistlin is such a worry-wart. It's probably nothing. But," he added with a sigh, "I suppose we'd better hurry on over to Crystalmir Lake."

Much as he once had with Tanis, Flint had more or less taken the Majere twins under his wing some years back when their mother died and they were still teen-agers. Through the dwarf, the half-elf had grown to know and like the brothers—with reservations. Caramon was stalwart and good-natured, yet his easygoing habits sometimes led him astray. As to Raistlin, the pale young mage with the intense gaze, Tanis admitted to himself that he found it difficult to strike up any rapport with Raistlin when Caramon wasn't around.

"Come on," said Flint, putting an arm around his friend and leading him toward the door. The dwarf stopped for a moment at his worktable and used a broken bit of charcoal to scribble something on a smooth piece of bark. He winked at Tanis, hanging it on the door as they walked out. *Gone hunting*, the sign read.

The two friends had to proceed along the elevated walk-ways strung between the giant vallenwoods toward the eastern edge of town. If the people of Solace hadn't already been accustomed to seeing the pair together, the dwarf and half-elf would have attracted some stares. Flint, stocky and short, with his rolling gait, hurried to keep up with his much taller companion, who glided down the walkways with the easy grace and surefootedness of his mother's race, the Qualinesti elves.

On this occasion, the picture was made even more comical by Flint's constant gesturing and exclamations as he spouted abominable tales of Tasslehoff, intended to draw Tanis out of his melancholy mood. But Tanis remained mostly silent, taking long strides as Flint endeavored to keep up.

It wasn't Raistlin's urgent summons that darkened Tanis's thoughts as they walked to Crystalmir Lake so much as it was Raistlin's half-sister, Kitiara Uth Matar. For Tanis, Kitiara was never far from his thoughts.

Her laughing face and crooked smile teased his mind by day and his dreams by night.

Tanis and Kitiara had been quarreling more than they had been getting along. Then one day, several weeks ago, Kitiara had informed Tanis that she had an offer to travel in the north with a band of mercenaries hired by a certain lord for some mysterious, no doubt illicit, purpose. Tanis denounced the expedition as unworthy of her. Kitiara had retorted that it was better than dying in her sleep in dull old Solace.

Upset by the idea of Kit leaving, Tanis had switched tactics and offered to accompany her. This had sparked a fit of laughter on Kitiara's part. She recovered, but a glint of anger lit her dark eyes. "You wouldn't fit in," she said with more than a hint of insult.

The next morning, Tanis had risen early to see Kit off. She was already astride her horse when he reached the stable. He had to run and grab the bridle to stop her for a moment. Kitiara had smiled vaguely down at him, then bent her dark, curly head and kissed him hard on the lips, before riding off without a word.

Even now Tanis could conjure up the sensation of that kiss. "Flint," he said to the dwarf as they hurried along the high walkways, "have you ever been in love?"

Astonished by the impertinent question, the crusty dwarf stumbled and grabbed the rail of the walkway.

"Not saying that I ever was," recovered Flint, resuming his pace. "But if I had been, I sure would have been more careful about who I happened to fall in love with than some people I know!"

"What do you mean by that?" the half-elf demanded hotly.

"I mean, you young pup, that Kitiara Uth Matar is hardly my idea—or anyone else's idea, for that matter—of the ideal female," Flint said firmly. "I've seen the way you moon at her and the way she looks back at you. Two different things. Nothing in common, if you get my drift."

Flint shook his head with exasperation as they rounded a curve and headed toward the bridge that would take them down onto the forest path leading to the lake. "Besides," the dwarf muttered, "I seem to recall you two having big arguments practically every day before she lit out of here. To my way of thinking, it was half the reason she left."

Tanis stopped and grabbed Flint's arm. "You haven't answered my question," he said tersely.

"Well," said Flint, halting in midstep. His eyebrows shot up and down like a pair of wriggling caterpillars. "There may have been someone once. Another hill dwarf like myself, of course. I don't know that you'd call it love. It was sort of ... a romance."

Flint stumbled over his words, the color rising to his cheeks. He looked at his feet, shifting his weight back and forth. Tanis waited for him to go on.

"Well?" queried Tanis at last, leaning closer to his friend, "Go on, what happened? Tell me."

Flint's expression was pained. "She was a huntsman's daughter," he said hesitantly. "Our families had pledged us to be married since birth. Times were hard in those days." He snorted. "Still are ..."

Tanis listened with fascination. The dwarf was normally stingy with personal information. Maybe his good mood had put him off guard, allowing his natural reserve to slip.

Flint paused, seeming to watch something in his mind's eye. Abruptly he shook his head as if to clear it of cobwebs.

"She was just ... someone! Back when I was young and foolish like you!" he said gruffly. "You know how it is with dwarves. Marriages have to be arranged and approved by the clans. Or do you know very much about the history of the hill dwarves and mountain dwarves? Now there's an interesting tale. ..."

Tanis coughed. "What was her name?"

Flint glared at him. "Lolly Ockenfels."

Tanis broke out into a grin.

"A respectable clan, the Ockenfels," Flint said defensively. "They were exceptional huntsmen. But the point is, I didn't think that it was a good time to get hitched, married, and take on family responsibilities. I was just a sprig of a lad, and although I'd seen her around, I didn't really know Lolly all that well. That is, until we had a secret rendezvous to talk it over, and I found out that she was a lot like me."

Tanis raised his eyebrows questioningly. "Pigheaded?" he ventured.

"Strong-minded," Flint said, irritated. "And when we had our secret meeting, why, I found out she was just as eager as I was to scotch the whole thing. Only ..."

"Only what?"

"You ask a lot of bothersome questions," Flint snapped. "I don't know why I'm telling all this to you." He broke off and moved toward the bridge, but Tanis stepped in front of him, blocking his way.

"Only what?" the half-elf repeated.

Flint spoke in a quiet voice. "Only, meeting with her, all alone like that, I got to know her better and see what she was like. Strong-minded, like myself ..."

"You said that."

"And kinda pretty. Long pigtails, good, strong shoulders ... dark brown eyes that were, uh, deep." His voice trailed off. Flint chanced a glance at Tanis, who was waiting eagerly for the rest of the story.

"Well?"

Flint set his jaw. "That's one too many questions, boy." The dwarf swatted Tanis on the shoulder, knocking him off balance. "I've said too much already, and Raistlin's waiting."

Flint clomped off toward the bridge. Tanis looked after him thoughtfully. Then, with a couple of long strides, he caught up.

Coming across the bridge from the opposite direction sauntered a couple of seedy farmhands heading toward the marketplace in Solace. One, dressed in an ill-fitting tunic, pointed at Tanis and made a loud remark about "pointy elf ears," provoking a guffaw from his companion.

Flint could feel Tanis tense as they approached. Considering the mood Tanis was in, Flint thought, the half-elf might get himself into trouble.

The dwarf moved quickly, deftly unbuckling a mallet from the belt around his waist and seeming to drop it accidentally to the ground. He managed to kick it with his boot so that it slid toward the scruffy pair and stopped, spinning, at the feet of the one who had made the crude comment.

The man stooped to pick it up, but Flint was already there. When he lifted his mallet up, the dwarf "accidentally" smacked its hard, rounded end into the chin of the man in the tunic. The farmhand collapsed in a heap.

"Oops," said Flint as he and Tanis continued on their way. The other fellow, slapping his friend's cheeks, looked after them in slack-jawed amazement.

* * * * *

By the time Tanis and Flint reached the wooded path along the shore of Crystalmir Lake, their moods had switched. Wondering with some relish what adventure might lay ahead, Tanis's spirits had buoyed considerably, while Flint, who had kept up a monologue about what a nuisance Tasslehoff could be, had worked himself into a fretful temper.

The summer had come in with a blaze of scarlet, purple, and gold wildflowers that lined the path. Tall trees ringed the lake. The sky was cloudless, and there was no hint of wind. Placid Crystalmir Lake stretched out before them like shiny blue glass.

Gazing at the lake's smooth surface, Flint's spirits revived somewhat. He was pretty sure he could beat Tanis at rock-skipping. Maybe he could win that copper back.

Ahead of them they spotted Raistlin, his back to them, perched on a large flat rock overlooking the lake. The aspiring mage wore a rust-colored robe that covered his thin frame and spilled over onto the stone. Tanis and Flint knew the Majere twin liked this place. It had something to do with an adventure he, Caramon, and Kitiara had here when they were kids. Now he often came here to be alone for hours at a time—"to ponder the imponderable," as Flint put it, "which, fortunately for the rest of us ordinary folks, is a job for mages."

Raistlin turned and stood to greet them, his grave smile quickly evaporating. His face was tightly drawn. The mage motioned for them to sit next to him on the rock.

Flint grew silent. He felt Raistlin's eyes rake his face. Not for the first time, Tanis thought that Raistlin's eyes, with their pale blue irises, seemed to bore right through people.

"What's all the mystery?" Tanis asked mildly. "Why couldn't we meet at Otik's?"

From a deep fold in his cloak, Raistlin produced an ordinary-looking green bottle with a long neck. "Because I don't think anyone should know about this except for the three of us," he said mysteriously.

Flint bent his head to take a closer look at the unexceptional bottle and made a sound that was halfway between a harrumph and a guffaw. "Doesn't look so interesting or important to me," the dwarf snorted, with a tinge of disappointment.

Raistlin shot him a piercing glance. "Watch!" said the mage tersely.

He pulled out the cork that stoppered the bottle. There was a slight hiss and an escaping aroma of salt air. As the dwarf and half-elf watched, the body of the bottle began to glow brightly. Motes of light swirled within, then began to shimmer and form a recognizable shape. The lights were like tiny, brilliant stars, dancing and swirling, almost hypnotic in their effect.

The shape they formed was that of Tasslehoff Burrfoot,

the very image of the kender, reduced to miniature and animated by the sparkling points of light. The kender was gesticulating. Not only that, but Tasslehoff's utterly distinctive voice also piped eerily out of the long neck of the bottle.

"Dear Raistlin,

"Isn't this amazing? I'm writing to you on board the good ship Venora ... at least it's been a good ship so far (about two nights and two days). Caramon is up on deck having a good time with his new friends the sailors, and Sturm ..."

The trio listened in silence to the first half of the magic message. Tanis was amazed. Flint's jaw sagged open.

"Incredible," said Tanis. "Where did you get it?"

"A kender in a bottle," mused Flint wryly. "Not a bad idea. Not a bad idea at all."

"Shhh!" said Raistlin, "Here comes the important part."

The kender image continued its tale:

"... He didn't smell as bad as most of them usually do, either. Sturm said he actually detected the scent of soap on the horned beast, whose name is—I guess I should say was, but that's getting ahead of myself—Argotz.

"As I said, Argotz had the crushed jalopwort, and I haggled a fair deal out of him, and I guess he threw in some extra out of gratitude because when I got back to the inn where we were staying in Hyssop I noticed that I had about twice what I paid for.

"Anyway, that's not the strange part—remember, I told you there was a strange part. Although I guess you could say that it is plenty strange when a minotaur runs an herbal shop in a cave. At least Asa said so, and I seem to recall that you said so, too. But the really strange part ..."

"The kender isn't even here and he's talking nonstop," muttered Flint, rolling his eyes.

"But the really strange part is what happened next. Oh, did I mention that Argotz was packing up all of his herbs and seemed to be in a big hurry to go somewhere? Of course, we didn't think anything of it until two days later when we woke up on our last morning at Hyssop. That was the day we had planned to leave, and we did leave, too, but before we left, a man came rushing into the inn to tell everyone about what had happened to the minotaur herbalist at the edge of town.

"We went out there ourselves to see, and sure enough, what the man said was true: A great big explosion had ripped through the cave and blown out the side of the mountain. Bits of the minotaur's goods and belongings were scattered in all directions. 'Argotz probably made a mistake and mixed some of the wrong herbs,' one of the local geniuses said. But if that were true, I answered, then why was his head, neatly severed and dripping blood, stuck on a pike at the edge of the path leading off the main road to the cave?

"Sturm and Caramon and I thought it was darned curious, but probably none of our business, and we were ready to leave anyway, so we made the boring journey back to Eastport and hired Captain Murloch and his ship to take us to Abanasinia. Captain Murloch reminds me of Flint, although he's much burlier and human, of course, but Captain Murloch thinks he knows the right way to do everything and doesn't always appreciate my advice.

"Anyway, that's the story of the minotaur herbalist and the crushed jalopwort, which I hope you like, since it cost me the use of this magic message bottle. I have to hurry now because there's a powerful storm brewing—rather unusually dark and fearsome, if you ask me—and I want to toss this into the sea while the waves are crashing high.

"P.S.: To anyone who finds this bottle and uncorks it, you will hear this message, but that's okay. Bring the bottle to Raistlin Majere of Solace, and he will give you at least fifty coppers for it, or even more because he's generous and doesn't care a whit about money anyway. Ask around town. Most everybody knows him.

"Truly yours,
"Tasslehoff Burrfoot of Kendermore,
"lately of Solace"

Swiftly Raistlin replaced the cork in the bottle and dropped it back into the folds of his cloak. The mage peered at Flint and Tanis, watching their reaction. "The magic is in the cork," the young mage noted for their benefit, "more so than in the bottle."

Still entranced by the idea of Tas in a bottle, Flint could only shake his head in wonderment.

"Where did you get it?" Tanis, his eyes narrowed, repeated his earlier question.

"A lucky stroke," replied Raistlin. "An honest peddler scooped it out of the water near the docks when he disembarked at a small port called Vengeance Bay on the coast of Abanasinia. After uncorking it and hearing the message, he decided to seek me out. He was planning to travel in this vicinity anyway, but fortunately he came to Solace directly. He arrived yesterday and inquired about me at the Inn of the Last Home. Otik located me, and," the mage added pointedly, "I paid the peddler seventy-five coppers just to prove the kender right."

"Seventy-five coppers!" exclaimed the notoriously thrifty dwarf.

"The message bottle is quite unique," agreed Tanis, standing and stretching. He gazed out over Crystalmir Lake, remembering a picnic he and Kitiara had had once on its shores. "But I don't understand why it puts you in mind of danger. It's just Tas on a boat writing one of his rambling letters. The part about the minotaur herbalist is a little odd, but—"

"The peddler brought other information with him," Raistlin cut in. "He had come from Eastport himself, where the talk of the docks was that the *Venora* had been lost at sea in an unusually sudden and violent storm. The peddler has made the trip between Southern Ergoth and Abanasinia many times, so he knows Captain Murloch by sight, and he swears he saw some of the captain's mates drinking in the taverns of Vengeance Bay. And they were paying for their celebration with minotaur coin."

"Curious," agreed Tanis, running his fingers through his reddish brown hair.

"Even more curious," added Raistlin, "is that the corpse of Captain Murloch washed up on the rocks within the week. His body was bloated, his features erased. His face was eaten away, covered by strange burns and punctures. Despite that, the crew recognized him as their captain, and immediately they collected what remained of their minotaur money and scattered to the winds."

Tanis sat down heavily. Flint's brow furrowed.

"It's been over seven weeks since the *Venora* left East-port," added Raistlin significantly.

"How do you know it isn't some kind of trick, or one of Tas's pranks?" barked Flint suspiciously. "How can you trust this peddler?"

"It's no trick!" responded Raistlin impatiently, "The peddler only wanted to do the errand and get his coppers. I could see that. He was well-meaning. The message in the bottle held no augury for him."

Flint sighed. He stood and skipped a stone across the surface of placid Lake Crystalmir. Seven skips. Not bad, the dwarf thought to himself with some pride.

Sturm and Caramon—those big oafs were nothing more than overgrown kids, really. They couldn't be counted on to behave sensibly, Flint thought. Why, he had spent hours with them in the woods along these very shores, and all around Solace for that matter, teaching them the lore of the forest. Willing enough pupils, but put them together with Tasslehoff, and …

"So they're a few weeks late," said Flint cautiously. "I don't see what all the bother is."

Raistlin grew solemn. "There's something else … something I should have realized before. You remember that I happened to be with Tasslehoff when his friend Asa told him there was a minotaur herbalist on Southern Ergoth who sold crushed jalopwort in his shop.

"As unlikely as that information seemed, I paid special attention because of an ancient spell I had come across once in one of Morath's spellbooks. Although the pages were crumbling and I couldn't decipher all the phrases, the spell intrigued me."

Tanis watched Raistlin closely. As he had when he first heard this story, the half-elf thought there was some part of the account that Raistlin was keeping to himself.

"I knew that the spell required jalopwort," Raistlin continued, "and that jalopwort is rarely found in these parts. Here was an opportunity to obtain some. Sturm and Caramon volunteered to accompany Tas on a journey to Southern Ergoth to purchase a quantity for me."

"And?" prompted Flint, who was beginning to think that Raistlin was getting awfully long-winded these days. The dwarf knew all about the crushed whatever-it-was and the reasons behind the trip to Southern Ergoth. He took aim and skipped another stone. Nine skips, the dwarf counted with satisfaction.

Raistlin templed his fingers, staring at both of them with that intensity that so unnerved Tanis. "After receiving Tasslehoff's message, I made the journey to Poolbottom yesterday and consulted with the Master Mage. He reminded me of something that I should have taken into account. Jalopwort grows in abundance only on the island of Karthay, a remote and desolate part of the minotaur isles. According to minotaur law, it cannot be transported or sold outside the realm. Minotaur society deems jalopwort sacred. That indicates whoever killed the minotaur herbalist—"

"Argotz," murmured Tanis, remembering.

"Whoever killed Argotz," continued Raistlin, "may have followed Sturm, Caramon, and Tasslehoff and tried to kill them."

Tanis jumped up, eager for an adventure, eager to be

doing something, anything but mooning around in Solace.
"Then we must go to Vengeance Bay, track these seamen,
and force them to tell us what happened to the *Venora*. If
necessary, we'll go to Eastport and look for clues."

Flint looked at his elven friend in horror. "Go to
Vengeance Bay ... Eastport?" the dwarf sputtered. He was
worried about his friends, but this seemed a little hasty.
Flint had been thinking of taking a summer trip, but somewhere nice and quiet and alone up in the mountains, not to
the rowdy, crowded towns of the seacoast.

"No," Raistlin said flatly. "It has been over ten days since
the peddler was in Vengeance Bay. And Eastport would
yield nothing. It would be a fruitless chase."

"Listen to Raistlin," agreed Flint hurriedly. "It wouldn't
make any sense."

Raistlin gestured impatiently. "And remember, the
sailors were celebrating with minotaur coin," the mage
said. "No, it wouldn't make any sense to head to the west,
because if I am right, the danger to my brother and our
friends lies far, far to the east. That is where we must go as
quickly as possible. To the Blood Sea and the minotaur
isles."

"To the Blood Sea?" gasped Flint. His face lost color. He
had to sit down to absorb the shock.

"The minotaur isles?" asked a surprised Tanis. "But
they're thousands of miles away, several months of arduous land travel. Even if Sturm, Caramon and Tasslehoff
have been taken there, if they're in danger, we could never
hope to arrive in time."

"How the devil would they get from the Straits of
Schallsea to the minotaur isles in so short a time?" asked a
bewildered Flint.

"I don't know how," admitted Raistlin. "Probably by
some highly evolved magic. But if they are alive, that is
where they are. This I believe. And I am going to go there
and try to find them. The only thing I want to know is are
you going to come with me?"

"How?" asked Tanis again. "How can we possibly hope to cover such a distance?"

The mage's eyes glittered excitedly. "When I spoke with Morath, he told me of an oracle who lives near Darkenwood and knows of a portal that could take us, in the matter of heartbeats, to Ogrebond on the coast of the Blood Sea."

"Ogrebond!" muttered Flint disconsolately.

"From there, we would have to make our own way by hiring a ship and crossing the Blood Sea to the minotaur kingdom."

"Oh, no!" Flint threw up his hands. "I'm not crossing any Blood Sea! I've heard all about the Blood Sea!" He pointed out across peaceful Crystalmir Lake. "Maybe," he continued, "just maybe, I'd cross Crystalmir Lake to rescue my friends, but maybe I wouldn't, either. It would depend on my mood and which friends they happened to be. But you're not going to get me into a boat to cross the Blood Sea no matter what portal or which friends or how many coppers you gave some shrewd roving peddler!"

Raistlin paid little attention to the grizzled dwarf, who was making a great show of stomping around kicking rocks and tree stumps. He stared intently at Tanis. The half-elf shifted uncomfortably under Raistlin's gaze. Tanis guessed the mage knew more than he was telling them, but he didn't doubt his genuine purpose. He knew that if Raistlin believed it to be so, then Sturm, Caramon, and Tas were indeed in trouble.

After a long silence, Tanis stood and extended his hand in agreement. "They would risk their lives for us," said the half-elf solemnly, "and we owe as much to them."

Raistlin gave him a nod of thanks.

"What about Kit?" Tanis asked, thinking of her all of a sudden. "Don't you think one of us should make an effort to contact her?"

"I have already sent her a message," said Raistlin. "Don't worry about Kitiara. If she can meet up with us, she will."

"But where is she?" persisted Tanis. "Maybe I—"

Raistlin cut him off with a look.

Flint stood near the shore, glowering, holding a perfectly round, flat stone in his hand. He sailed it out over the water. It skipped once, twice, then sank. A bad omen, he was certain.

The stocky dwarf came over to Raistlin and Tanis, who were waiting for his decision. He looked them both in the face, certain he was staring at two fools.

He extended his thick, right arm and laid his knotty hand over Tanis's and Raistlin's. "I just want to make one thing clear," the dwarf growled to the mage. "I'm doing this for Sturm and your brother, not for that blasted kender!"

* * * * *

Raistlin had told them to pack food, weapons, clothing, climbing equipment, and other essentials. Flint got little sleep that night, packing and repacking his haversack, sharpening his axe and knife, and muttering to himself about what a fool he was. Just before dawn, a knock sounded at the door, and there stood Tanis, all packed for the trip and grinning broadly. What put the half-elf in such a blasted good mood? Flint wondered.

They were supposed to meet Raistlin at a bend in the road leading out of Solace. Hurrying out the door, Flint remembered something, then raced back in and brought out the piece of bark. With a stub of charcoal, he scribbled something and hung the sign on his door as he and Tanis hurried out into the gray dawn.

The sign read, *Gone Hunting—Indefinitely.*

Chapter 3
Uncle Nellthis

For six days, Nellthis's hired men had been trying to pick up the trail of the elusive leucrotta that was rumored to be preying on denizens of the forest east of Lemish near the foothills of a small, saw-toothed mountain range.

Of all the unusual creatures of Ansalon, the leucrotta was one of the most rare, so rare that Nellthis doubted the reports of its existence so near his fiefdom.

He sent a loyal subordinate, a broad-shouldered worthy by the name of Ladin Elferturm, his best hunter, to lead the band of a dozen stalwart men who would stalk the creature.

Around women and at feasts and small gatherings, Elferturm seemed a bumpkin whose thick tongue was somehow stuck in his square jaw. But in the forest or the mountains he was in his element, his senses alert to the slightest nuance of sound or smell. No one had better aim with a longbow—no one except Nellthis himself, that is.

Even accepting that the rumors were correct and a leucrotta was in the vicinity, tracking it would be tricky. A leucrotta's hoofprints were virtually identical to those of a stag, and the woods in these parts were rife with mature deer. By the second day, Ladin Elferturm believed the peasant accounts because he had found several carcasses of doe and stags, ravaged and torn by sharp, jagged teeth, then left half-eaten. By the fourth day, he felt certain that he could distinguish the tracks of the leucrotta from the other wild animals in the area, and that he and his men had the huge, dangerous creature on the run.

On the morning of the sixth day, Ladin Elferturm squatted on his haunches and, with his fingertips, felt the moistness of the spoor on the ground at his feet. His almond eyes, framed by short black hair and a well-trimmed beard, lifted up to note the steep, winding gorge ahead. He knew that the gorge, a narrow, straight-walled canyon with a seasonal streambed, had only one other opening, less than a mile to the north.

With a signal, Ladin Elferturm separated his men into two groups and sent the splinter group around to the other end of the gorge, through a sloping forest, to guard the way out. Then he gave one of his men a message to take to Nellthis. After that, Elferturm and his men made temporary camp. With some pride, the hunter waited for his lord.

Nellthis arrived at the camp less than four hours later, accompanied, as Ladin Elferturm knew he would be, by his niece, Kitiara Uth Matar and several loyal retainers. All wore jerkins and carried assorted hunting and trapping gear. With her cropped, raven hair and easy swagger, Kit was virtually indistinguishable from the men who hurried over to confer with Elferturm.

Impatient these last several days, Nellthis had ridden out from his small castle immediately after receiving word that the leucrotta was trapped. Now his manner was brisk and authoritative. He barked out orders. The men hastened to take their positions, some near and others distant, posting sentries at several points above the gorge.

Elferturm's job was done and done well. The hunter stole a glance at Kitiara, her face flushed and eager, her dark eyes watching her uncle as he hurried about, readying his men for the kill. Kit did not so much as give Elferturm a nod.

Within minutes, the hunting party was ready and mounted again. Nellthis had chosen two men, as well as his niece, to accompany him below. The four cautiously began to descend into the gorge.

Elferturm's task was to keep watch from the high ground. He wasn't surprised to be left behind, but he couldn't help being annoyed. Elferturm fancied himself a better shot than his master, although everyone knew otherwise, and he had hoped against hope for a chance to demonstrate his skill in front of Kitiara by slaying the leucrotta.

* * * * *

Nellthis and Kitiara, followed by two others whose principal responsibility was to carry weapons and supplies, eased their horses down into the narrow gorge. As Kit watched, her uncle dismounted and checked a trail of hoofprints, still fresh in the sand next to the shallow stream. He grinned up at her with fierce satisfaction. Nellthis signaled Kit and the others to tie up their horses and to proceed, as stealthily as possible, on foot.

Nellthis of Lemish carried only his favorite ornamented longbow, made of hemp and yew, its width the equal of his height. Over one shoulder he wore a sling of arrows, their shafts of birch with feathers of goosewing and arrowheads of poison-tipped iron. Kitiara carried the longbow with which she had been practicing, shorter than her uncle's for easier handling, with a heavy leather grip.

They stepped lightly among the stones, moving along the gorge, doing their best to stay hidden, weaving from clumps of bushes to outcrops of granite. Nellthis and Kitiara split up, one on each side of the gorge, each followed by one of the retainers.

Nellthis kept slightly ahead of the others. As they moved down the gorge, they could spot the other men, far above, posted at intervals. Kit knew that her uncle relished this moment. A great hall in his castle was set aside for his animal trophies. Nellthis prided himself on his vow to have assembled one day a perfect stuffed specimen of every beast on the face of the continent. His eagerness for this hunt was all the keener because months had passed since Nellthis had been able to add to his already impressive collection.

Now Kitiara watched as her uncle pressed against the wall opposite her, straining his eyes and ears for any indication of the creature trapped in the gorge. To kill a leucrotta, Kit knew, would keep her uncle satisfied for many months.

In some respects, Nellthis was a comical man. Hopelessly short and chunky, with an incongruous rapier mustache, he was nonetheless vain and fussy about the way he looked. Like a spoiled princess, he would spend hours choosing the color and trim of his garments. He kept a seamstress on the payroll solely to provide him with the latest in fashionable wear.

Kit knew that, behind his back, Nellthis was mocked for his temper tantrums, his gluttony, and his habit of drinking too much, falling asleep early, and staying in bed most days until early afternoon. Nellthis was wealthy enough to be able to afford anything he wanted, not only the best food and drink and a vast retinue, but also a routine of comfort and indulgence.

No admirer of sloth, Kit still respected her uncle's power and ability to exercise his slightest whim. Even more, she prized Nellthis as a link to her father, even though he wasn't a blood relation. Nellthis was the husband of Gregor Uth Matar's sister. Kit had never known her aunt, who had died in childbirth along with the baby. But she knew Nellthis had maintained loyal contact with Gregor while he was in Solace, and she suspected that her uncle was one of the few family members Gregor had been able to call on for "temporary loans" on behalf of his wife and young daughter.

After Gregor disappeared, Nellthis had kept in touch with Kit through the years. And now, bored with Solace and disenchanted with Tanis, Kitiara had come to stay with him for the time being.

As Uncle Nellthis edged cautiously ahead, flattened against the wall of the gorge, Kit marveled at his skill as a marksman and master hunter despite his profligate lifestyle.

A crackling sound put them both on alert. Waving one arm, Nellthis gestured to Kit. Like him, she notched her bow. Slowly, moving on opposite sides of the gorge, they edged around a zigzag bend that opened into a broader section of the canyon marked on Kit's side by a large needlebush.

Almost simultaneously, both saw the deep cut in the ochre-colored rock that formed a cave. From the shallow depths, two feral red eyes bored out at them. Nellthis, on the same side as the dark opening, froze. Kitiara crouched low to the ground.

The two watched, half in awe, as a giant creature stepped out into the daylight, seeming to dare them. The leucrotta stood over eight feet tall and nine feet in length, its body similar to that of a great stag, its head like that of a monstrous badger. The head was as black as tar, while the rest of its body was a deep tan. Its hooves were cloven. Its tufted tail was like a lion's.

Its jaw hung open, drooling slime and revealing bony ridges of pointed teeth. Even from a distance, Kitiara could smell its fetid breath. The breath of a leucrotta was as notoriously foul as its appearance was ugly, perhaps one of the reasons why it lived a solitary life, preferring desolate places.

As the leucrotta stood there, watching them ominously, Nellthis beckoned the two men behind them to move forward on Kitiara's side. One of the men stayed near Kit, holding swords and various hunting paraphernalia at the ready. The other had the perilous task of crawling forward on his stomach, clutching a large, thick net that could be thrown over the creature to ensnare it.

The leucrotta appeared to take note of all four of its adversaries, but surprisingly it didn't make a move to charge. With its overwhelming size, it probably could have bounded past them in either direction and escaped. But instead it just stood there, waiting for the human predators to make the first move.

In one swift, liquid motion, Nellthis rose, nocked an arrow, aimed, and loosed it at the leucrotta. As he did so, Kit rose also, nocking one of her arrows, while the man with the net started to rush forward to toss it over the dangerous beast.

Everyone was a half second later than the leucrotta, which had already chosen its first prey. With a startlingly sudden movement, the beast leaped forward and caught the man with the net as he threw it and turned to retreat. With the net half-draped over its head, the leucrotta loomed over the man, opened its huge, powerful jaws, bit through the net, and severed the man's head with one brutal snap. The body gushed blood, spattering Kit and Nellthis, as the leucrotta shook its victim wildly and tossed the body like a rag doll against the wall of the gorge.

Nellthis's arrow stuck out of the creature's left flank, looking puny and inconsequential. Kitiara's shot had missed. Both of them had nocked second arrows by the time the leucrotta ducked behind the needlebush, partly protecting itself from attack.

Nellthis and Kit hesitated, warily watching the huge animal, whose eyes bore down on them.

Suddenly the creature opened its maw and made a loud, chittering, high-pitched noise that blocked out all other sound and was almost painful to Kit's ears. Working its jaws rapidly, the leucrotta continued the shrill sound for several long moments without budging from its sheltered position.

"What is it doing?" Kit hissed to Nellthis, across the canyon.

"It's taunting us," Nellthis replied in a low voice. "Bragging about its victims." Crouched low, Nellthis spoke without a trace of fear.

"You understand its tongue?" asked Kit, startled.

A merry light danced in Nellthis's round eyes. "No," he admitted, chuckling. "Just guessing."

The leucrotta worked its jaws again, emitting another long blast of high-pitched, unintelligible sounds. High above, Kit could see Nellthis's archers, drawn by the sound, taking up positions on the ridges of the gorge. Although they took aim with their weapons, they knew better than to shoot unless absolutely necessary. This was to be Nellthis's kill.

"I think it said, 'I'll eat the fat man first, then the tasty female,' " Kit hissed to Nellthis, wrinkling her face into a crooked smile. Nellthis grinned back.

Suddenly, from the top of the ridge, a stream of screeches sounded, echoing the leucrotta's.

Eyes wide, Kit scanned the ridge, certain a companion beast had appeared on the scene. Nellthis, too, his concentration thrown, started up. The leucrotta itself paused in its tirade and raised its head, sniffing the air for the scent of an intruder.

Kit's gaze finally latched on to Ladin Elferturm, grinning proudly at his imitation and motioning Kit and her uncle to move in for the kill while their quarry was distracted.

Unfortunately, the beast had already shifted its focus back to the hunters. And before Kit or her uncle could collect their wits, the leucrotta leaped from its hiding place.

Nellthis knew his timing was off when he pivoted to shoot an arrow up into the huge, shadowy form that was crashing over him. He aimed upward, rolled under and forward, surprisingly quick for such a chunky man, and felt the shock of the leucrotta's claw as it smote him heavily on the back. Momentarily confused, Nellthis struggled to his knees, lurched against the canyon wall, and nocked another arrow.

Scrambling to his feet, he saw the leucrotta lying on its side several feet away, twitching and spasming, slime and odorous blood gushing from its thrashing head. An arrow —his arrow—stuck in the creature's belly, while another, Kit's, protruded from the leucrotta's neck. Kit slumped against the opposite wall, obviously dazed but unhurt. With some effort, she gave him a nod of assurance.

Nellthis walked over to the beast. Pain seared his back, yet with it came the exhilaration of the kill. He stood for a moment, lording it over his fallen prey, then shot an arrow into its brain. Almost instantly the leucrotta expelled its final breath and lay still.

Kit came over to stare down at the monstrous creature, every bit as formidable and ugly in death as in life. The surviving retainer hastened to their side. He raised his peaked cap, a signal to those above to raise a raucous cheer.

"I suppose I should thank you for saving my life," said Nellthis almost wistfully.

"Are you disappointed, Uncle?" asked Kit. "I don't think my arrow killed him. I think it was both at once ... yours and mine."

He looked at his young niece, with her dark eyes and solemn expression, and knew that she wouldn't be saying so if she didn't believe it to be true. "Yes, both," he said, with a glow of satisfaction.

Elferturm scrambled down the side of the gorge, the first of the hunting band to join them. His chest puffed out importantly. "A good kill," he offered.

Nellthis's glow disappeared. He turned on his chief

tracker with a snarl. "No thanks to you. The next time you think you've come up with a useful bit of strategy, make certain I know about it first, or it will be the last hunting you ever do in Lemish."

Elferturm flushed an angry red, as Kit and her uncle turned their backs on him and walked away.

Hours later, after hauling the heavy creature out of the gorge, tying it on a travois behind the horses, and burying the luckless man who had lost his life to the leucrotta, Nellthis, Kit, and the band of hunters rode triumphantly into the castle courtyard.

All of Nellthis's servants and workers gathered 'round to congratulate their master, who ordered a celebration feast for that evening. He stood there, comically squat and bristling with pride, shrugging off concerns for the bruises on his back. To all who listened, he gave his niece equal credit for the trophy.

On the sidelines, Kit observed him with a mixture of affection and amusement. She was about to return to her room when she saw Nellthis take notice of a shadowy figure behind a curtain in one of the windows above signal down to him. Kit couldn't make out who it was, but Nellthis briskly gave orders for the preservation of the trophy and excused himself from Kit and the others. Quickly he walked toward the nearby kitchen entrance of the castle and disappeared behind the oaken door.

This wasn't the first time Kit had noticed such behavior on the part of her uncle. Nellthis seemed to be full of mysterious doings these days. Kitiara tried to figure out what he did with most of his time, where he disappeared to, sometimes for days on end. She had attempted to wheedle the information out of him, but to no avail. That was one of the things she liked about her uncle, his perpetual air of conspiracy. And if he chose to be secretive, that was his business, even if Kit thought that at some point she might try in earnest to make it hers.

"It was your arrow that done it, Kitiara Uth Matar," said

Ladin Elferturm, coming up behind her and touching her arm awkwardly. The hunter searched Kit's eyes for some encouragement.

"It was both arrows," Kit said tersely, shaking his arm off. "And even if Nellthis weren't my uncle, I would vow that it is disloyal of you to say that behind his back when you know the trophy is so important to him." She started to stride away.

Elferturm grabbed her strongly by the wrist, holding her back. "What's come over you, Kitiara?" he tried to whisper, knowing his voice was clumsily loud and his words all wrong for this high-spirited woman. "I thought … I thought there was, uh"— his tongue was all in knots—"something between us."

Kitiara was about to reply witheringly when someone grabbed Elferturm from behind, whirling him around. Kurth, the castle smithy, stood there glowering at the hunter. The tall, broadly muscled smithy clenched his fists nervously at his side as he spoke. Having come directly from the forge, he still wore his apron.

"I warned you to stop pestering Kitiara, Ladin," said Kurth forcefully. "She's mine and couldn't care a whit about the likes of you."

"I'm sick of your interfering," said Elferturm, thrusting his chest up against Kurth's, their gazes locked murderously.

Elferturm had abandoned his grip on Kitiara. She inched backward. They had all but forgotten her, pushing and shoving and threatening each other.

Let them have it out, she thought. She was tired of both of them. They were as dumb as cheese, shouting her name and proclaiming their love. Kitiara glided away and was just vanishing behind kitchen doors when Kurth took his first swing, missing, and Elferturm reacted, landing a roundhouse to the smithy's outthrust chin.

* * * * *

Deep in the bowels of Nellthis's castle, in a small basement room where the most expensive wines were stored, a room bolted from the inside although it was off limits to the castle help, Nellthis of Lemish was holding a parley. Nellthis sat at a wooden table in the room, illuminated by a single candle that burned with a blue flame. The room was dank, and the candle sputtered as if gasping for air. Spiders crawled over the racks of bottles.

Nellthis was joined at the parley by three companions, or it might be more accurate to say three murky figures. Their humanity remained in question, since they were swaddled in clothing and kept to the shadows even in the dim illumination cast by the candle.

One, tall and lean, wore a cowl that drooped over his forehead and around his face so that little but his eyes, mere slivers of green, could be discerned. It was this one, a male by the sound of his sonorous voice, who took the lead in discussions with Nellthis and who seemed to have authority over the other two.

One of these, a stooped, almost hunchbacked figure, stood next to the cowled one but said nothing other than an occasional sharp word in a northern dialect that Nellthis himself could not interpret.

The third was the most peculiar, and the one that, judging by the watchful movements of the others, was the object of both curiosity and fear. This one stuck to a corner of the small room, a corner that was darkened and cobwebbed. Nellthis knew he ought not to stare, so instead he stole unobtrusive glances at this third member of the trio, who wore long dark robes, a hood, and a mask.

The back of his robes fluttered with evidence of some appendage whenever he moved or shifted position. Oddly, when the robes shifted to reveal glimpses of his body underneath, he seemed to give off fissures of light, like mottled scales reflecting the candlelight. Despite the darkness, this one's eyes shone blood red. Nellthis couldn't make out the face, but he couldn't help flinching every time he heard the telltale sizzle, followed by the sulfurous smell, occasioned by the acidic drool from the evil being.

Nellthis took his time studying the messages and reports spread out on the table in front of him. Carefully he read each of the directives, and then reread them to be certain of the contents. The others had to be patient with his fussy caution, although after almost half an hour of waiting, the figure in the corner stirred and rumbled ominously. More of the spittle pitted the floor, sending acrid fumes into the moldy basement air.

Nellthis finally seemed satisfied and, with a theatrical flourish, put his signature to each of the documents in turn. When he was finished, he picked them up, rolled them together, and handed them over to the tall, cowled figure.

"Our mistress will be pleased," the cowled figure said without emotion, "and you will be rewarded."

"My reward," said Nellthis grandly, "is to serve."

The three, even the sinister one in the corner, bowed respectfully. Nellthis went over to one of the wine racks, and tugged at two bottles on an upper shelf. The rack slid forward soundlessly. Behind it, the wall opened, revealing a narrow passageway that led under the castle courtyard and came up several miles away in an isolated patch of forest. The three ducked under the archway and headed down the dark stairway. The one from the corner was the last to leave. As he passed, Nellthis, noting the creature's fangs and spiny tail, couldn't stifle a shudder.

But the moment passed. Minutes later, Nellthis had closed the wine room and was rubbing his hands together cheerily while trotting up flights of stone steps to his quarters.

*　*　*　*　*

Kitiara lay on her back on a huge bed in the plush room Nellthis had set aside for her at the top of the north tower. Idly she surveyed the finely etched grillwork of the ceiling.

For the nearly three months she had been visiting Uncle Nellthis, Kit had been uncharacteristically inactive, though she had fought one duel and taken three or four lovers. She had also taken the time to hone her skills at archery and with the bullwhip. But Kit hadn't ventured outside of Nellthis's domain and had put off her customary mercenary activity.

She was discontented. At moments like this, despite herself, she wondered what Tanis was doing. Damn the self-righteous half-elf! Yet somehow he often managed to worm his way into her thoughts.

Kit wondered about Uncle Nellthis, too, and this concern was more immediate. Although Nellthis had neither seen nor heard from Gregor in years, he still benefited from that connection, to Kit's way of thinking. The two men hadn't known each other especially well, but Nellthis liked to hint that they had been involved together in at least one extralegal escapade. At one time, the two families had lived side by side. Decades ago, Uncle Nellthis, brash and independent, had broken the family bonds and settled his own estate on the outskirts of Lemish.

There was something about Nellthis, something slippery and intriguing. He had rich furnishings and many servants, yet he did little work, and his fields produced only a modest harvest of corn and seed. Kit couldn't discern how he supported his luxurious lifestyle.

Lately, she knew, Nellthis had been traveling a good deal, making many short trips to nearby villages and towns. When he returned, Kit noticed, inevitably he brought back a sturdy peasant or two whom he added to his growing household staff. By now there were dozens of them—Kitiara had lost count—and they seemed to have very little to do in the way of actual work during the daylight hours.

Sometimes Nellthis would all but vanish inside his own castle. It was a rambling old structure, with several small buildings attached, including a barn and a stable. Yet there were times when Kitiara would roam the place by the hour in a futile search for Nellthis, until suddenly, turning a corner, she would burst upon him, standing there as if he had been waiting for her and grinning mockingly.

Kit knew better than to pry. She bided her time, watching and waiting. Nellthis had always been good to her. He had always extended generous hospitality whenever, without warning, she dropped in for a visit. Kit had found his home a comfortable refuge when it suited her.

A knock sounded at the door, startling Kitiara out of her reverie. She jumped up and opened it, her attitude brusque. She half-expected to be pestered by one of her rival suitors, the victor of the shoving match, his face smudged and clothing heroically torn.

Instead, a kender stood there, and in the background, watching the kender nervously, hovered one of Nellthis's servants, the beetle-browed Odilon. The kender's topknot was worn on the side of his head and dangled down to his knees; he was fair-haired, shorter and older than Tasslehoff Burrfoot. She didn't recognize him.

Beaming, the kender held out a small, rolled parchment, sealed with wax. The seal was unbroken, Kitiara was surprised to see, given the notorious curiosity of kender. So he must be one of the breed of kender message bearers, whose reliability was as unpredictable as their curiosity was famous.

Kit reached for the letter, but the kender, switching to a serious mien, withdrew his hand so that she grabbed air.

"Kitiara Uth Matar?" asked the kender importantly. "Because if you are Kitiara Uth Matar, born of Solace but late of anywhere—at the present moment, Lemish—then I bear a message of the utmost urgency."

Kitiara nodded impatiently, holding out her hand.

The kender resumed beaming and held out the scroll a second time. This time Kit was quicker and had the message in hand and pulled close before the kender could withdraw it. Undaunted, the smiling kender started to edge inside the room, but Kit stepped forward, standing in the doorway and adroitly blocking his path.

"Duty done," chirped the kender cheerfully. "My name's Aspendew, and I've traveled a couple of hundred miles just to deliver that particular message, although of course I have plenty of other things to do in this neck of the world. I've got a sister who lives just a day's hike to the east. At least I think of her as a sister, I do love her as a sister, but actually she's a cousin. And there's this notorious haunted cavern I've always wanted to visit; it's marked on one of my maps. It's a big secret place; I never tell anybody about it, but I think I might tell you, especially if you happened to let me read that letter, which has me kind of curious after bearing it all this way. ..."

Aspendew shuffled back and forth, looking for some opening past Kitiara. Nellthis's servant, Odilon, moved forward and grabbed the kender by the collar, hauling him backward. As he disappeared down the winding stairs, firmly in Odilon's clutches, Aspendew held up a gem on a chain, chattering.

"Oh, don't worry. You don't have to pay me anything! The young mage—at least he said he was a mage, but he was pretty young for it—paid me handsomely in coin and then threw in this rare and dazzling necklace to boot. I hope it's magical, but with mages, you never can tell. I happened to meet a mage once who had this very peculiar sense of humor, and ... Oops, gotta go! I'll be in the kitchen for a while, having a bite to eat, if you have any message you want to send back to Solace. Although I won't be going back in that direction right away—not until next year actually, but ..."

Kitiara shut the door, half grinning at the necklace, which she recognized as a common and inexpensive one of her mother's that Raistlin had kept stored among his possessions as a keepsake. Raistlin possessed an odd fondness for kender, and he was one of the few people she knew who would trust one to deliver any message, much less an important one. In this instance, at least, his trust had been rewarded.

Sitting down on the edge of the bed, Kit opened the letter and began to read. Her half-smile quickly turned to a look of dismay. Kit reread the short message, then sat there for a long time thinking without coming to any definite plan of action.

* * * * *

Moonlight was silvering into the room when Kit finally rose, determined to seek out Uncle Nellthis and ask his advice.

This time she found him easily enough in his living quarters, sitting at a large desk surrounded by a pile of letters and reports. An oil lamp cast a golden glow. Though the hour was late, Nellthis seemed hard at work in one of the confounding ways he had of busying himself. Yet he looked up as if he had been expecting her and put aside his quill pen. Childless himself, Nellthis liked to look upon Kit as a daughter and never failed to greet her warmly.

Kitiara told him about receiving a letter from Raistlin delivered by the kender Aspendew. Nellthis had already heard about Aspendew, who had invited himself to stay for supper. Proving himself a good salesman, Aspendew had convinced the castle cook to write letters to his kin for delivery to various parts of Southern Ergoth. In spite of the late hour, the cook was still down in the kitchen, diligently composing his letters, which took some time and a good deal of assistance from Aspendew, since the cook was unschooled and practically illiterate.

"I suspect our kender guest will still be around for breakfast tomorrow morning," chuckled Nellthis.

He asked to see Raistlin's letter. Kit handed it over and waited as Nellthis read the communication, wrinkling his brow.

Nellthis had never met Raistlin, though Raistlin inter-

DRAGONLANCE Meetings

ested him indeed. He always asked Kit about him and Caramon, her half-brothers, when she visited. Nellthis didn't know any of the other companions mentioned in the letter, although he had heard bits and pieces about them, too, especially the half-elf named Tanis. His expression, in the glow of the oil lamp, showed that he was as concerned by the letter as his niece.

"Can this be so?" Nellthis asked finally, setting the letter down. "Is it possible your brother is wrong?"

"Quite possible," Kit said grimly, "but he has an annoying habit of being right. And what he says adds up. Don't you agree?"

Nellthis nodded.

"What can I do? I was contemplating leaving here to attend to my own business. Now I suppose I will have to deal with this," Kit said with a show of annoyance that didn't entirely mask the concern she felt. A lifetime of caring for her younger brothers couldn't be shrugged off so easily. "Caramon would lay down his life for me; I know that. I must do something, but how can I go to them? If Raistlin is right, the answer lies thousands of miles from here, a protracted journey by horse, and not much faster and ten times as treacherous by water. By the time I arrived, even assuming Raistlin is right and I can hook up with them …"

She paced back and forth in front of Nellthis, boiling with frustration. Nellthis drummed his fingers on his desk. His mouth compressed into a thin line. Slowly an enlightened expression dawned on his face.

"If only there was a way," Kit repeated, pounding a fist into the palm of her hand.

"There might be a way," said Nellthis in such a cunning tone that Kit stopped and stared at him. His eyes were narrowed, his fingers had stopped drumming, and his hands were templed together.

She leaned across the desk. "How? What do you mean, Uncle?"

"There might be a way," repeated Nellthis, "but it will be difficult to arrange."

"Money? I have some, but I can get more. My word can be my guarantee."

Nellthis waved his hand to indicate that money was not the problem. "I have plenty of money."

"Time? Isn't there enough time?"

Again Nellthis waved his hand in dismissal. He was looking past her, up at the ceiling, making a show of thinking.

"What, then?" demanded Kitiara.

"Difficult," Nellthis said, pursing his lips. "But perhaps it can be arranged. The journey itself will require no money, only courage and good luck."

Although Kit had no idea what Nellthis had in mind, she could tell by his demeanor that he was serious. And in matters to do with family, she trusted Uncle Nellthis as much as Kitiara Uth Matar trusted anyone. Even though the trip seemed impossible, and Kitiara could think of no conceivable way that such a journey could be completed within a short frame of time, she found herself believing him when he said that it might be arranged.

She flashed him a warm, crooked grin. "I have the courage," she said, "if you can supply the good luck." More earnestly, she added, "I'll do whatever needs to be done and repay you in any way I can."

"Tut-tut, Kitiara," replied Nellthis. Staring at her fixedly, he lowered his voice. "I expect nothing but your gratitude. Oh, before I forget," he added nonchalantly, reaching for a tiny bottle of colorless liquid on his desk and holding it out toward her, "here's a memento of the part you played in bagging that leucrotta. I had the man who preserved the head set it aside—especially for you."

"What is it?" Kitiara asked, peering suspiciously at the thick liquid that floated in the small, innocuous-looking glass container.

"A vial of the creature's saliva," explained Nellthis.

"According to legend, it makes an effective antidote to love philters. Judging by that amusing episode in the courtyard, I think you might have more use for it than I."

Skeptical, Kit's eyes flicked back and forth from Nellthis to the vial. His expression was unreadable. "Take it," he urged. "It might come in handy someday."

Kitiara gave him another crooked grin as she pocketed the small vial.

"Now we must hurry," Nellthis added, taking up the quill pen again and scribbling a note. He folded the note into his pocket and rose from the desk. "We have things to do ... friends of mine that you must meet. You must pack your belongings. You have to hurry if you want to be on your way by sunrise."

Chapter 4
Across the Blood Sea

The first to awaken was Caramon, his head throbbing painfully. He had a vague sensation of having dreamed something— of being up in a high stone tower, buffeted by strong winds and driving rain. Only it wasn't a tower; it was the tallest tree in a forest, bending and swaying, with Caramon clinging precariously high in its branches. Lightning struck the tree, and it snapped in the middle, and Caramon was falling. But he could save himself. All he had to do was grab the anchor of a silver ship flying by, an anchor that bobbed and dangled mere inches from his fingertips. …

"Unh," he grunted. That sailor's mead was worse than dwarf spirits. Caramon reached up to massage the bridge of his nose, but something held his hand down. Opening his eyes painfully, he realized that, for some reason that escaped him, he was roped to a post along with Sturm and Tas, who were still unconscious. Caramon closed his eyes again and relaxed. It was just a bad dream. It would all go away when the mead wore off.

The sounds of the storm faded and were replaced by the cries of gulls, the sighing of the wind, and the gentle rocking and swaying of a ship. Then, after some time, other sounds became gradually audible ... low grunts and scraping noises and the squeaking of oars.

Caramon's bleary eyes opened again, and he tried to assess the situation. Where was he, anyway? What had happened? Why were he and Sturm and Tasslehoff roped to the ship's mast?

Sturm leaned against him, his head thrown back and his mouth agape. Behind them, if Caramon twisted his shoulder, he could make out Tas, an ugly purple bruise spreading across his forehead. Caramon elbowed Sturm, but got no reaction. He could hear Tasslehoff as the kender began to stir and groan.

All three were bound and shackled to the center post of the *Venora*. As far as Caramon could see, nobody else was aboard the ship, which seemed to be drifting gently with the current.

Caramon combed his memory, trying to recall how he got there. The last thing he remembered, he had been on deck, swapping yarns and sharing mead with some of the sailors. They were on their way back from Eastport. It was a beautiful clear night, one of those times when all seemed right with the world.

Straining his eyes, he couldn't place the sun, but Caramon felt that it must be daytime. It was hot and humid. The sun must be up there somewhere, behind the filmy gray clouds. Not clouds ... more like a warm-weather mist, which cast its pall over everything, so that Caramon could see only a short way ahead of him on the ship.

All of a sudden, the sounds that he had been hearing stopped and were replaced by other, closer, more distinct sounds. Footfalls. Clanking weapons. Voices.

"What is it?" whispered Tas groggily. "What has happened?"

"Shhh."

The mist cleared slightly. Caramon saw hands gripping the side railings of the *Venora* and figures climbing over the rail onto the ship. In twos and threes, they began to creep forward, coming closer, closer, so that soon Caramon knew he would be able to make out their features.

Over his shoulder, Caramon whispered vehemently, "Sturm, wake up!" He could feel the Solamnic move his head and begin to stir.

As the figures approached, Caramon saw that they were a motley assortment including several human ruffians, a few ogres, a phalanx of minotaurs, and a mysterious caped, cowled figure, hunched over, who stood almost out of view toward the rear. Caramon couldn't get a good look at this furtive figure, who occasionally hissed orders at the rest, unaccountably creating the impression of some slithering, serpentine creature.

Caramon shifted his attention back to the ogres. He felt certain they were ogres, yet they were strange and unlike others of that ill-begotten race. They were shorter and fatter, with stringy flaxen-colored hair, greasy gray skin, and webbed hands and feet. Caramon was taken aback by the sight of ogres alongside the minotaurs, for in olden times, the minotaurs had been slaves of the ogres, and the two brute races were usually regarded as dire enemies of each other.

The humans were dressed in ragged if colorful patchwork clothing. They were lean and sun-parched, but obviously rugged. From their waists dangled cutlasses and assorted seagoing utensils. The ogres and minotaurs likewise carried conspicuous tools and weaponry.

Caramon jerked his shoulder again, and this time he felt Sturm's head rise groggily. He sensed Tas struggling with his bonds, but the warrior knew from experience that the kender's efforts were in vain.

The minotaurs took charge of the boarding party, elbowing their way to the front of the group. Though there were only four or five of them, the bullish creatures, garbed in harnesses and skirts with gemmed rings through their ugly snouts, dominated the group. Short, rust-colored fur carpeted their massive bodies, and horns curved sharply upward from their wide brows. Their cloven hooves made a harsh clatter on the deck.

Two of the minotaurs stepped toward the trio of prisoners, pausing a few feet away. They spoke to each other in voices that were muted for minotaurs but whose deep, gravelly tones carried easily to Caramon's ears.

"Be these the three?" rumbled one. He carried several axes and a wicked-looking knife stuck into his leather straps.

"Fool! Of course they are. Do you think the Nightmaster would make such a mistake?"

The creatures' foul smell acted like powerful smelling salts for Caramon, clearing his senses of their previous grogginess.

The second one must be the leader, Caramon thought. Around the minotaur's thick, muscular neck gleamed a tight collar of polished stones. At his waist, he wore a loincloth of girded metal. He carried only a barbed flail.

"They look pathetic. What threat could they possibly pose?"

"I only do the master's bidding, Dogz. I do not read his thoughts."

"Which is the one?"

"That's what we must find out."

The others hung back in a circle like wolves cringing at the edges of a blazing campfire. With their huge bulk and seven foot height, the minotaurs loomed over Caramon, obscuring his view. The cowled figure remained in the background, enshrouded by fog, so that Caramon couldn't be sure of its outline. Only occasional hisses and swishing utterances reminded him that there was someone, or some thing, back there.

Struggling to sit erect, Caramon noticed another vessel through the mist, a sleek longship off in the distance. He could just make out the topsail poking through the curls of mist. He guessed the ship was about three hundred yards away.

"Caramon! What's going on?" That was Sturm's voice.

From his angle, the Solamnic couldn't see much, and from the sound of his voice, it was clear that he was still dazed.

"Minotaurs and some human rabble," whispered Tas, although he could see even less than Sturm.

"Pirates," muttered Caramon.

"Silence!" barked the leader. The minotaur lashed out with his flail, catching Caramon on the side of the face and making a deep strawberry cut on his cheek. "We're no pirates, fool!"

At that, the two minotaurs retreated back into the fog to where the caped figure stood. From the muttered growls that floated through the air, it appeared that the minotaurs were consulting with this peculiar specimen. The others moved closer to the mast, tightening their circle around the three prisoners. They had bloodthirsty looks in their eyes that left Caramon distinctly uncomfortable.

"Where are we?" asked Sturm in a low voice, sounding more clearheaded now.

"I was hoping you'd have an answer to that question," replied Caramon grimly.

"If only I could consult my maps," chimed in Tasslehoff.

Caramon said nothing. Best to keep silent, he thought to himself. No sense letting this piratical band know how confused they were. The big warrior had a feeling that any signs of weakness would only add to their trouble.

The two minotaurs who had been conferring with the cowled figure returned, towering over him. The one called Dogz reached toward Caramon with thick, wide hands, and ran them over the front and back of Caramon's body, searching for something. Caramon struggled, but he could do little to resist. He spat defiantly into the face of the huge, smelly minotaur.

He heard chuckling from the onlookers as the minotaur reared back in surprise and, with the force of a sledgehammer, kicked the Majere twin in the face. Caramon spat out a bloody tooth and doubled over in pain as Sturm cried out, "By my honor, you will live to regret that cowardly blow!"

"That goes double for me!" shouted Tasslehoff. "When his brother hears about this, you'll be lucky if you aren't turned into a horny toad. He'll—"

"Leave off, Tas!" Caramon managed to gasp.

But the minotaur paid no heed. Already Dogz had moved on, bending over Sturm and groping through the young knight's clothing and gear with his rough hands. This is not the one either, thought Dogz. This human carried nothing on his person, no weapon or purse.

"Hunh," Dogz grunted, holding up one hand, which dripped blood from the matted wound on the back of Sturm's head. In disgust, he slapped Sturm across the side of the face. The Solamnic took the blow stoically, as he had the search, saying nothing.

"That's it!" Tasslehoff cried, struggling in vain against his bonds. "Now you've crossed the point of no return! Sturm never hurt an unarmed person in his whole life— well, at least as long as I've known him! Which is years, or certainly a year or two by now. And he is about as noble and well-meaning a fellow as you will ever meet, quite apart from myself."

This time the kender's voice seemed to surprise the minotaur, as if he hadn't quite deigned to notice Tas before. Caramon heard a sharp intake of breath as Dogz stepped back to speak, in his low rumbling voice, with the leader.

"The third one is a kender, Sarkis."

"So?"

"Kender are unclean. They roam the earth, living by

stealth and dishonor. To touch one, it is said, is to invite scorn or, worse, disease. I do not think it is necessary to search this one."

From behind the two minotaurs came an angry hiss. From behind Caramon rose Tas's indignant voice.

"Unclean! Why, you big horny cow! I'll have you know that I bathe regularly. I washed my face just yesterday, to be exact—that is, assuming this is the day after yesterday, which I don't know for sure because I have no idea where I am or how long it took me to get here. But if you want to bring up personal hygiene, I suggest you take your two moon-sized nostrils, bend over, and take a whiff of yourself!"

Sturm bit his tongue.

Caramon rolled his eyes.

The human scum and webbed ogres snickered.

The one named Sarkis stepped away from Dogz and faded into the gray mist toward the cloaked figure. This time Caramon couldn't make out any words, only bestial snorts interspersed with guttural syllables and hissing sounds. The leader was obviously conferring with the mysterious figure.

Caramon's thoughts whirled. They stopped at the thought of his twin. Raistlin and he had become expert at pairing up to seize the advantage in many tight situations. With a fierce longing, the young warrior wished he had his brother at his side now. What would Raistlin do in such a spot?

Sarkis returned and addressed Dogz contemptuously. "Pah, Dogz! It is true that kender are dishonorable, but it is well known they are impervious to common or uncommon illness. You are as likely to catch disease from a tree stump. Let me do the job, you superstitious fool!"

Tasslehoff was able to twist around to see Sarkis descend upon him, huge hands outstretched. "You ugly, wart-faced, pig-snouted, dun-colored cretin! I'm as honorable as they come—well, maybe not as honorable as Sturm, or even Caramon, who is honorable in his own humble way—but twice, ten times, one hundred thousand times as honorable as the likes of you! And let me warn you that I could give you any disease I wanted if I only cared enough to bother. ... Hey, stop! Quit that! That tickles! Heh-heh! Hah-ha-ha-ha-hah!"

That crazy kender talks too much for his own good, thought Sturm. He saw from his vantage that Sarkis had discovered Tasslehoff's packs and pouches. The minotaur leered, showing yellow teeth in his brutish face.

Sarkis stomped over to his second-in-command, holding up Tas's pouches. He glared savagely at his subordinate.

"Well, what is it?" asked the chastened Dogz.

The humans and webbed ogres tittered until Sarkis silenced them with a glance. Sarkis strode back to the figure in the fog. Their conversation consisted of more hissing and muffled grunts. He returned to Dogz.

"He is the one," Sarkis announced.

Dogz started forward, but Sarkis grabbed him by the shoulder. "Do not harm him! Bring him and"—he handed over the kender's belongings—"his pouches."

Dogz hurried over to Tasslehoff. A high-pitched shriek filled the air. Caramon and Sturm strained against their bonds, but there was nothing they could do.

Dogz came back around the mast, carrying Tas, holding the squirming, ranting kender as far away from him as he could, dangling him by his topknot. It looked as if the huge minotaur was carrying a rabbit by the ears, but the rabbit, in this instance, was cursing a vile streak.

"Ouch! Of all the— You clod-footed, garlic-breathing pokehead! Watch what you're— Ouch! Where are we go— Ouch! You overgrown, thickheaded, milkless cow! Ouch! That's my hair you're pulling! Hey, what about Caramon and Sturm? Yeeeow!"

As Caramon and Sturm watched, the minotaur passed the kicking kender to two of the humans, who climbed over the rail and disappeared, presumably into a dinghy below. Smirking with satisfaction, Dogz turned to face Sarkis.

Caramon heard a scuttling sound and could just make out the cowled figure retreating toward the ship's railing, then being swallowed up by the fog as he went over the side. Other humans, webbed ogres, and minotaurs hurried to do likewise.

Stepping forward, Dogz asked menacingly, "What about these two?"

Sarkis shrugged indifferently. "They are unimportant. Throw them overboard and set fire to the ship."

The few remaining humans edged forward. One of them, a lumbering hulk of a man with a red beard and bearing a rope scar on his neck, gave Dogz a look of eager pleading. Dogz nodded to him.

The two bull creatures turned away and also disappeared over the side of the ship.

The humans swarmed over Caramon and Sturm, punching and beating them with short clubs. Unable to defend himself, Caramon tried to protect his eyes by clamping them shut. Next to him, Sturm moaned, then grunted as the first blows landed, but after that the Solamnic took his punishment in silence.

The huge man with the rope scar began to kick at the mast. After several kicks, it snapped at the bottom, and he and the other humans lifted it, dragging Sturm and Caramon over to the side of the *Venora*.

Sounds of the ship being wrecked surrounded them. Then came a sloshing noise, followed by a whoosh and a sudden rush of heat and fire.

Still bound to the jagged section of mast, Sturm and Caramon were hefted into the air. The men began a crude chant, lofting the prisoners in an arc over the water, then swinging them back to the ship several times before letting go with a final shout. Sturm and Caramon and the mast section sailed through the air before plummeting toward the water in a twisted jumble.

As he smacked the water, Caramon struggled to react. His arms seemed all tangled up with the wooden mast, and his hands were tied tight. Even without these disadvantages, swimming wasn't Caramon's strong point. He would have drowned in Crystalmir Lake some months ago if Sturm hadn't rescued him. He had made some modest strides since that day, but now he kicked for all he was worth.

Because of the way in which they had hit the water, Sturm was briefly pinned under the mast and took a few seconds to surface. Gasping for air, Sturm struggled to free his arms, but like Caramon, he couldn't. He scissored his legs, kicking strongly. Fortunately for the two of them, the wooden mast section helped keep them afloat.

"Don't kick so hard!" Sturm managed to wheeze at Caramon. "You'll use up all your strength. Take it easy for now."

The water was strangely warm and murky, brown rather than blue-green and swirling with sediment. Their kicking churned up bubbles and slimy, clinging vegetation. The water had a decidedly stagnant smell.

Suddenly a tremendous explosion rocked their ears. Both men twisted their necks around in time to see, through the mist, the *Venora* explode in a great plume of smoke and fire. The current had already carried the ship several thousand yards off. The other ship, the one Caramon had barely glimpsed, had vanished into the haze.

Caramon and Sturm watched for several minutes as remnants of the ship burned and sank into the waves. Almost as if by signal, then, the warm fog descended heavily, obscuring everything but the rolling infinity of the ocean.

As they struggled to keep afloat, both Caramon and Sturm had the same unspoken thoughts.

Where were they? Why had this happened to them? How in blazes would they ever find and rescue Tasslehoff? Or save themselves?

* * * * *

Although he certainly missed his good friends Caramon and Sturm, and although he certainly needed rescuing, Tasslehoff Burrfoot was having a pretty good time.

It was true that he was stuck in a small iron-barred brig in the lower deck of the minotaur ship, which stank worse than a mountain of dead skunks. It was also true that he was a prisoner of the minotaurs, the webbed ogres—which he had learned were called orughi—and human seafaring rabble who might at any moment put him to death.

But so far he had been treated rather well, all things considered. Sarkis had given him back his packs and pouches. Indeed, the commander of the ship acted as though the kender's possessions were sacrosanct and would be safer under the protection of Tas. Tas could spend hours poring through his various belongings, and now he had no shortage of hours to kill. He wished he hadn't sent the magic message bottle to Raistlin, since this would be an even better time to use it.

Tas got plenty of sleep. And his captors fed him reasonably well under the circumstances, mostly a greasy, lumpy meat stew that once you got used to it tasted just fine. The bowls of stew were sometimes brought to him by monkeys, who were on the ship in droves and acted as the cook's helpers. One of them in particular, a pear-shaped woolly monkey, Tas got to know rather well. He dubbed him "Oh-Tick," after a certain innkeeper he remembered fondly, and when he conversed with Oh-Tick, Tas felt the monkey, tilting his head in a listening kind of way, almost understood him.

Tas had plenty of interesting visitors. Very few of the ship's denizens had ever met or even seen a kender before. So they trooped down, by ones and twos, to gawk at him, in some cases to taunt him, and in a couple of instances to throw fruit cores and dirt clods at him.

Tas threw the fruit cores and dirt clods right back, but he liked it best when they came to taunt him. The human rabble really knew some good insults, and this in turn stimulated Tas's imagination. He came right back at them with some of the most totally offensive things he had ever thought of. It made several of his visitors so angry that their faces got all purple before they stomped away.

The minotaurs had more dignity, even if they smelled worse. They would approach almost respectfully and gaze at him in his solitary cell. Tas only saw Sarkis once again, when the leader came down all alone and spent several minutes standing impassively, watching Tas, his eyes taking note of every detail of the kender from topknot to soft leather boots. Tas couldn't manage to get a word out of the huge, ugly beast.

Dogz was different. Scornful and arrogant, he, too, came to take a leisurely look at Tasslehoff. After their first encounter, which was marked by a nasty exchange of barbed comments, Dogz returned again and again. Tas began to have stilted but edifying conversations with the huge beast, who seemed in some ways to be as curious about him as Tas was about everything, and indeed more fearful of Tas than the other way around. Gradually the two developed an awkward, almost friendly relationship.

Dogz was Sarkis's cousin, as it turned out, and utterly in awe of and loyal to his higher-ranking relative. Sarkis regarded Dogz's friendship with the kender to be another sign of a pathetic weakness, so Dogz had to steal his opportunites to see the kender.

"So you really like being a minotaur, huh?" asked Tas, amazed at the fierce pride exhibited by the strutting bull creature. Tas found Dogz fascinating, but the kender couldn't help but know, even if Dogz seemed oblivious to it, that minotaurs were a race widely scorned on Krynn.

"It is ... a great honor to be a minotaur," rumbled Dogz uncertainly.

"What's the good part?" asked Tas, intrigued. "I mean, when you're a kender, the whole world's your oyster. You've got friends and relatives everywhere, except maybe in Thorbardin among the Theiwar, although I'm sure even they would warm up to me eventually. You know how to make the very best maps, and if you're lucky, you've got a handsome topknot. …"

Tas paused, realizing that this minotaur wasn't going to interrupt or answer until Tas shut up. So Tas did something he rarely did. He shut up, giving Dogz the cue to speak.

"We fight to live, live to fight," said Dogz after a long pause. He spoke haltingly but impressively. His wide-set eyes, Tas thought, looked almost mournful. "We bow down to no one. Our destiny is to rule."

"Pretty heavy burden," said Tas thoughtfully. He was tempted to add "even for a beast of burden," but he thought perhaps he'd better not say that.

"Yes," said Dogz, raising his eyes to meet Tas's gaze.

After about a week, Tas realized that he hadn't seen his favorite monkey, Oh-Tick, for several days, and he asked his regular visitor about it.

"Monkey stew," said Dogz, pointing to the bowl of stew in Tas's hands. "That is why the disgusting creatures are on board. Did you think they were pets?" Dogz gave a snort of laughter.

Oh-Tick's demise made Tas feel lowly and ashamed. Suddenly he lost his appetite for the stew. Dogz noticed that he had stopped eating and said, rather gently considering his rumbling tone, "Kender don't usually eat monkey?"

"Not usually," Tas replied disconsolately.

"What do kender eat?" asked Dogz thoughtfully.

"Almost anything," said Tas, "except monkey. Especially a monkey friend," he added diplomatically.

"We always eat monkey stew," said Dogz. "They are silly animals." Then, more sympathetically, "I'm sorry."

"Me, too." Tas shoved his face between the bars to peer at Dogz. "I suppose I could pretend it was bran meal or something. I love plain old bran meal. I dream of hot bran meal with currants and honey! You wouldn't happen to have any plain old bran meal on this ship, would you?"

Dogz shook his head. Tas sighed and pushed away his

bowl. Several minutes passed in silence before Dogz asked tentatively, "If you aren't going to eat your monkey stew, would you mind if I ate it?"

Tas pushed the bowl between the bars.

When Dogz's shipmates came down to observe Tas, he got a chance to observe them, too. The kender was thrilled by the close-up view of minotaurs, and especially the webbed ogres, who waddled up to spy on him. Short, fat, and dull-witted, they shouted their insults at him in orughi, so Tas could only do his best to match their tone and decibel level in Common.

Tas had to look quick at some of the orughi, who after clucking their insults would scoot away before the kender could respond. Tas liked it when they stayed around awhile so he could study the ancestral weapon many of them carried over their shoulder, an iron boomerang with a long metallic cord, which Dogz told him was called a tonkk. It was used to hunt flying creatures. Tas would have liked to try using a tonkk, which reminded him of his own favorite weapon, the hoopak.

Tasslehoff still had his own hoopak, which had been strapped across his back when he was taken off the *Venora*. Sarkis hadn't shown any interest in taking it away, and besides, it was no help to Tas in his cramped prison quarters.

One afternoon, after about a week, Tas felt the ship slowing down. There was a good deal of commotion on deck above as the ship shuddered to a halt. Tas heard the sounds of cargo being unloaded, and then the muffled tramping of the crew disembarking. For several hours, Tas heard sounds of activity above, but during the entire time, no one came to check on him.

The kender was beginning to think they had forgotten all about him when at last Dogz and Sarkis came below, speaking to each other in their low, guttural voices. They carried a small wooden cage that smelled of monkeys and made Tas think forlornly of Oh-Tick.

They entered Tas's cell, squeezed the kender inside the cage, and then slid the cage onto two poles, which they hefted and balanced on their shoulders. Then the two minotaurs carried Tas up on deck and down the gangway, where the kender got his first glimpse of the fabled minotaur island of Mithas.

With the cage bobbing on their shoulders, Dogz and Sarkis paraded Tas through the streets of the minotaur city of Lacynos. What an amazing place, Tas thought. He could hardly wait to tell all his friends about it … if he was lucky enough to live through the experience!

The harbor was crowded with war galleys, cargo ships, and fishing boats. A system of ropes and pulleys unloaded huge bundles of lumber and other vital goods from cargo ships. Human slaves supplied the power, overseen by whip-wielding minotaurs. Fierce-looking merchants and human pirates argued with each other on the docks. The water was thick with floating seaweed and garbage.

The city proper began where the wharf ended. Lacynos's rutted lanes, filthy alleys, and busy streets were paved with dirt that, as a result of rain and heavy traffic, had been churned into thick, gooey mud. Crude wooden buildings, larger than any Tas had seen in all of Southern Ergoth, were organized into block patterns. Outside ladders took the place of inside stairways; square holes in the rooftops provided egress.

Tas had to twist around repeatedly to glimpse all the strange, marvelous activity. There were plenty of humans, who seemed to have a monopoly on the corner taverns. Many of them looked like armed brigands, flaunting their plundered gems and rings. They carried wicked, curved swords and hooked weapons. The outnumbered humans mixed with the minotaurs, but Tas noticed that occasionally loud arguments took place between members of the two races and fights broke out.

So frenetic was the atmosphere that not everyone noticed Dogz and Sarkis carrying the caged kender, but others did.

The human ruffians pointed and guffawed. The minotaurs peered curiously and growled with contempt. Tas pointed and guffawed and growled right back, trailing laughter in his wake.

They turned down a wider street, carrying Tas toward a bustling square of stalls, tents, and booths where the smell of fish and sweat was overpowering. The sounds of loud haggling drowned out other noises.

"Our marketplace," Dogz boasted, inclining his head toward Tas. "Here you can buy the finest silver pieces in all the minotaur isles. But you have to be careful. There is also an abundance of worthless items."

Sarkis barked a command at Dogz. "Stop talking to the kender!" he ordered. "It is a sign of weakness."

Bouncing around in the cage, Tas decided to say nothing, sorely tempted though he was.

Here in the market square, with only a few more hours of daylight remaining, business was conducted in a colorful and chaotic manner. Few noticed Dogz and Sarkis as they shoved and elbowed their way through the crowd. Tas spotted exotic jewelry and weapons for sale, wool and clothing, and every variety of fish in the sea, smoked, canned, fresh, and not so fresh.

Up another, more deserted street they turned toward the most impressive building in the city of Lacynos, the seasonal residence of the king of the minotaurs. This was an elaborate, marble-columned mansion with spacious gardens and adjoining buildings set on high ground overlooking the teeming minotaur metropolis.

They passed a contingent of human slaves, disfigured with cuts and dried blood, digging ditches for runoff under the supervision of whip-wielding minotaur guards. These humans, in many cases gaunt and jaundiced-looking, were objects of pity in Tas's eyes. They slaved under the lash and didn't even dare to glance up at the kender as Tas passed.

When they arrived at the front gate of the palace's outer wall, Tas saw well-ordered formations of minotaur soldiers drilling outside the grounds. Sentries were posted at intervals along the wall, and everyone seemed to know Dogz and Sarkis. The guards quickly hailed and admitted them.

To tell the truth, Tas was getting a little tired of his cramped sightseeing trip and more than a little curious about where he was going. Consequently, the kender was perfectly happy when, after descending a long flight of steps to a lower level of one of the buildings, the minotaurs finally stopped. Sarkis unlatched the cage and Tas tumbled out. He barely had time for a good stretch before Sarkis pushed him into a dim and dank, if much roomier, jail cell.

Without further comment, Sarkis gave a snort, turned, and climbed back up the stairs. Dogz stalled, glancing at Sarkis's retreating form before turning back to Tas. "Goodbye, friend Tas," the minotaur said sadly and turned to leave.

"Wait! What's going to happen now?" Tas shouted, but it was too late, for Dogz had hurried back up the stairs.

An hour or two went by. It was hard to keep track of time in the boring cell. It wasn't that it was so dirty, although it was dirty enough, or that it was so smelly, considering that Tas was almost getting used to the stench of minotaurs. It was just that the complete furnishings consisted of a bunk and a bucket, with nothing else to see or do, and Tas was so uncharacteristically dispirited that he didn't even feel like rummaging through his pouches. By comparison, the minotaur ship had been a carnival of entertainment.

Things began to look up when footsteps sounded and two minotaurs he hadn't seen before came down the stairs with Sarkis, who carried a flail. One of the minotaurs wore a crimson cape and a thin gold band around his forehead. Tas wondered if it was truly gold and wished he could hold it in his hands for just a minute to see. The other minotaur was ugly and horned like most of them, but wore a kilt and didn't bear any weapons.

The one with the gold band bore an air of authority. He stepped in front of the others and looked at Tas. The expression on his snout face was blank. His foul breath made Tas retreat to the back of the cell. His yellow teeth glistened.

"So this is the kender mage," said the caped minotaur.

"Yes, King," answered Sarkis.

Kender mage? Tas thought. What in blazes were these dumb bullheads talking about?

"The Nightmaster will be very pleased," the king said, then spun on his cloven heels and started up the steps.

So astonished was Tas by the brief exchange that he barely had time to say anything. "Nightmaster who?" he shouted after the retreating figure. "King who? If you're the bull in charge, then you'd better let me out of here before my friends find out where I am! And I've got plenty of friends—numerous—lots! If they chose you for king, it must be because you have the worst breath in all of Lacynos—no, make that all of Mithas. Make that all of Ansalon, you overdressed, forked-tailed, bulging-eyed lardhead!"

If only he had room to toss his hoopak. If only iron bars didn't stand between him and the minotaurs. Tas grabbed his hoopak and waved it threateningly.

Sarkis and the other minotaur, the one who wore the kilt, stood there, watching Tas indifferently, waiting for him to shut up. Eventually he did.

"I have never seen a kender before," rumbled the kilted minotaur in a surprisingly civilized tone. "And I have certainly never seen a kender mage."

"Yes, Cleef-Eth," said Sarkis. "As ordered, I have delivered him to your keeping."

Tas waited to hear what Cleef-Eth was going to say next. Sarkis deferred to him, that was plain. And Cleef-Eth appeared to be a minotaur of some intelligence and standing.

"Torture him until he reveals to us his secrets," said Cleef-Eth, leveling his big, round bullish orbs at Tasslehoff.

"Don't kill him, though ... not right away, at least. But hurt him so he knows that we mean business."

Sarkis snapped his flail against his palm. "It will be my pleasure, Cleef-Eth," he said with relish.

Chapter 5
The Oracle and the Portal

Fallen tree limbs overgrown with twisted vines and a sponge-like, mossy vegetation crosshatched the dense forest, making the going difficult. Sudden torrents of water, evidence of some vast underground river, surfaced, rushed by, then vanished back beneath the wooded maze.

The land sloped gradually upward. Peaks ringed the forest where the terrain broke into abrupt escarpments and promontories. Here and there, shafts of pale sunlight pierced the greenish-blue atmosphere that enveloped the woods.

Slowly the three friends made their way through the junglelike forest. With blunt swings, Flint and Tanis hacked away at the lush greenery, clearing a path. Tanis grumbled at having to use his sword for such activity, while Flint, who had been the grumbler for most of the morning, could find some pleasure in wielding the sharp-edged shortaxe he usually kept slung at his side. Behind them, Raistlin waited wordlessly each time they halted, leaning on the stout cedar walking stick that had been carved for him by Flint some months ago. His pale face was lined with tension, but he was more patient with delay than either of his two companions.

The Master Mage's directions had been very precise. Although well-concealed, its whereabouts known only to a small, privileged number of magic practitioners, the cave of the Oracle lay only slightly more than half a day's trek from Solace. Morath had warned Raistlin to beware. In spite of deceptive appearances, the Oracle had fantastic powers and did not welcome uninvited strangers.

Outside Solace, the crushed gravel road that led to the southeast cleaved into two smaller pebble roads, one leading deeper into the mountainous south and the other curving to the east. Following Morath's instructions, Tanis, Flint, and Raistlin took the eastern fork. After a half-dozen miles, the path spidered off in numerous directions, giving a traveler the choice of several well-trodden dirt paths. Without the Master Mage's counsel, they never would have chosen the least of these, a northeasterly trail of dirt and mud that led, after a few miles, to a seeming dead end, a thick canopy of low-growing plants surrounding a grove of immense, broad-leafed trees with low-slung branches and huge trunks.

For half an hour, they slashed their way through the smothering undergrowth, then maneuvered past a cluster of formidable trees with outstretched branches. On the other side of the barrier, as the Master Mage had foretold, the faint traces of the old trail resumed.

Sometimes stooping, at other times crawling over or under obstacles of boulders and fallen trees, the trio spent an hour laboring on the wending, debris-ridden trail.

Raistlin kept a dogged pace. His determination to reach

the Oracle impressed Tanis, who had banished Kitiara from his thoughts and was occupied with the task at hand. Flint took every opportunity to gripe and grumble.

"This mage of yours better know what he's talking about!" Flint complained at one point, mopping his brow with a handkerchief that was by now mottled with dirt and sweat.

Raistlin fixed him with a stare. "If you have any doubts, then turn back," rasped Caramon's twin, who was every bit as road-weary as the dwarf and furthermore less accustomed to such exertion. His face was pale and shiny. "Although I thought someone with your forest skills would find this outing a lark."

Flint scowled furiously but held his tongue, turning his back on Raistlin and continuing to clear the trail. Tanis would also have liked some assurances, but he saw the glint of anger in Raistlin's eyes and chose to say nothing.

Finally the elusive trail appeared to end in a small grassy clearing. At one end of the clearing stood a mammoth fir tree with a trunk that seemed welded to other trees and huge rocks wedged up behind it. At the base of the great fir was a black, hollow maw. This was obviously the place, for out of the cavity spewed tendrils of mist, accompanied by a strange brackish smell.

Both Flint and Tanis hesitated, but Raistlin moved ahead of them, peering cautiously. With his staff, he beckoned the dwarf and half-elf forward. The young mage led the three of them up to the mouth of the forbidding cave.

"Hallo!" cried Raistlin boldly, leaning into the darkness, his voice harsh and loud in the forest calm. "Three friends have come to call! We have greetings from Morath, the Master Mage!"

The only reply was silence. As Raistlin spoke, cold, white fingers of mist curled around his feet and spiraled upward, encircling his legs and his body, not quite touching the young mage, but oscillating and pulsating as if responding to the warmth of his blood.

With widening eyes, Tanis observed the eerie mists and glanced over at Flint, who nodded grimly. A few paces behind Raistlin, the two of them pulled weapons. Over his shoulder, the young mage cast a stern glance. Reluctantly the dwarf and half-elf sheathed their fighting tools.

After several long moments, Raistlin shook his head with irritation and came to a decision. Without a word of warning to his companions, he lowered his staff, ducked his head, and plunged into the black cavity. Almost instantaneously the mist broke up and was sucked inside the cave with him. Flint and Tanis had to hurry to catch up.

Just inside the opening, the three collided. Raistlin had paused beyond the entrance to allow time for his eyes to adjust to the dim light. At first, none of them could see very much through the murky darkness. The bone-white mist swirled about them, undulating and changing shape. Even using his elven night vision, Tanis could see little. The mist, while seemingly insubstantial, created a barrier impenetrable to sight. It did not hinder hearing, however. After a moment of utter silence, Tanis and the others picked up the sound of voices, wailing indistinguishably from farther ahead in the darkness.

Nor were their senses of smell blocked. "It smells worse than a dead troll in here," Tanis whispered to Flint, who clutched a rag to his nose and mouth in an attempt to ward off the stench.

"Silence!" hissed Raistlin.

Reaching upward with his staff, Raistlin touched the ceiling and informed the others that they were in a low tunnel. He edged forward, feeling his way with his right hand, his companions following. Bunched together, the trio stumbled forward for several minutes until they rounded a narrow bend. Then a spot of dim illumination directly ahead of them made their progress easier.

The light gradually grew brighter until they emerged into a living quarters of some type, round rather than rectangular, walled on all sides except for the tunnel entrance.

The room was free of weird voices and dark augury. Looking up, Tanis saw sunlight filtering down. The dirt floor was dry, hard-packed, and swept tidily. A chair, a cot, and a large rope trunk gave evidence of habitation.

At the far end of the room, a huge caldron steamed and bubbled. The mist retreated, hovering over the caldron. There was no sign of owner or occupant. The overpowering, putrid smell still hung in the air.

Relaxing somewhat, Tanis reached out to touch the walls, which intrigued him. Streaked with muted colors, they appeared to be neither wood nor stone. Nevertheless, they felt hard to Tanis's touch.

"Some sort of petrified wood," muttered Flint admiringly, stroking his gray-flecked beard. He nudged Tanis with his elbow, hooking his eyes toward Raistlin.

Both watched with some bewilderment as the young mage, oblivious to his companions, edged forward and dropped to a squatting position in front of the cot, seeming to speak in a low voice to the very ground at his feet.

"We do not come as enemies ..." Raistlin was murmuring, his gaze cast downward. Tanis and Flint could barely pick up his words. "... and if we did, surely you could easily defeat us, Chen'tal Pyrnee."

Peering closer, Tanis saw a white shrew cowering under the cot, its whiskers twitching furiously. Flint spied the tiny creature at the same time. The shrew, which had red pinprick eyes as hard as darts, was scurrying back and forth, squeaking and squealing.

"You do not need to be afraid of us," Raistlin added hastily, still crouching close to the floor. "We are here to show our respect and to beg a favor. I know that we have intruded upon your abode, but hear us out. If you choose, you may banish us, or even destroy us. My teacher, Morath of Poolbottom, tells me that you can do either, for you have truly extraordinary powers."

A boom split the air, followed by a sizzling and crackling noise. The shrew vanished. Materializing next to the heavy caldron, as if emerging from a jagged opening in the air that immediately closed behind it, stood an ancient ogress ... the Oracle. She stirred the pot, one venomous purple eye appraising Raistlin. The other seemed to be sewn shut, oozing pus.

Watching warily, Tanis took a step backward. Flint fingered his axe handle nervously. Raistlin straightened to a standing position.

"I would just as soon have your bones for soup!" cackled the ogress. "Don't think I can't; I need but lift a finger!" Her voice was hoarse and shrill. She stirred vigorously, cocking her head in Raistlin's direction. "How is that old fool Morath, anyway? I never hear from him unless it's for a favor. Who are you to flaunt his name?"

Chen'tal Pyrnee was an incredibly ugly ogress. It would have been impossible to guess her age or weight. Swaddled in loose clothing and numerous scarves of various, mismatched, faded colors, she was as bulky as a bear. Her presence seemed to fill the cave, casting an ominous shadow over the three companions.

Her face was mottled with warts and bumps. Her nose and chin sprouted long, curling hairs. Her mouth showed missing and blackened teeth. Stringy, corn-colored hair fell beneath a plaited cap. The hideous effect was topped off by the hooded eye, which looked to be the result of accident or disease. The nauseous odor emanated more from her than from the contents of the mist-shrouded caldron.

"I was his pupil," said Raistlin, facing the ogress and bowing slightly. "Morath trusts me, and that is why he told me how and where to find you. There wasn't time or means for me to send any message in advance. We are on a mission of some urgency."

The ugly ogress lifted a dipper of whatever foul liquid she had been stirring and tasted it, frowning. As she did so, her one good eye squinted disdainfully at Raistlin. Tanis marveled at the young mage's composure. Caramon's twin brother met the hostile gaze of the Oracle without flinching and without any apparent distaste.

"That mage is a blabbermouth, if you ask me," Chen'tal Pyrnee muttered. "He's always sending young know-it-alls to connive and bargain for my spells. They line up by threes and fours outside my door, begging my assistance. I take pity on a few of them and help 'em out, just to be nice on account of Morath. But most I turn into warthogs or grass snakes. If they can't change themselves back, why they ain't worthy of being mages in the first place!"

"The master told me that he hasn't sent anyone to you for several years," replied Raistlin blandly. His eyes met her rheumy, solitary gaze.

"Ha!" Chen'tal Pyrnee made chewing motions with her lips. She glared at Raistlin. "Mebbe so, mebbe so. I lose track of the years. But does that give you any excuse to contradict me? You young, pious, snotty know-it-alls are all alike. Who are the other two? I can't imagine the Master Mage is taking in dwarves and elves these days." With a long, wrinkled finger, she contemptuously indicated Tanis and Flint.

Flint was of a mind to conk the ugly Oracle on the head with the butt of his axe, but Tanis held him by his tunic. Tanis glanced quickly at Raistlin, who, with a small frown, indicated they were to treat the ogress with respect. Tanis lowered his head humbly, managing to elbow Flint into joining him in the gesture.

Raistlin had made it clear how important this cave-dwelling ogress was to their quest to rescue Tas, Sturm, and Caramon. He had also made it clear how dangerous Chen'tal Pyrnee could be if crossed.

"They are my friends," Raistlin said.

The ogress's gaze flickered back to the young mage. "Friends, pah! It is easy to know an enemy," Chen'tal Pyrnee said cryptically, "but not as easy as it is to mistake a friend. An enemy can prove himself by a single deed. A friend must prove himself over and over again."

"I quite agree," Raistlin said, nodding.

Watching the young mage suspiciously, Chen'tal Pyrnee scooped another dipperful from the caldron and then unexpectedly threw the liquid against the wall of the cave so close to Raistlin that he had to step aside quickly to avoid being splashed. The liquid scorched the rocklike wood and drizzled down the wall, burning away an outer layer to reveal brilliant patterns of copper and turquoise. For a brief instant, the room was flooded with light and color. Then it flickered and faded.

Tanis had all he could do to restrain Flint. Raistlin, his face taut, said nothing. The young mage knew the ogress was trying to intimidate him. In truth, he was impressed and more than a little afraid. Morath had warned him that Chen'tal Pyrnee could be volatile.

The Oracle kept stirring her brew, gauging Raistlin's reaction. The mists pulsed above the steaming caldron. The wall sizzled. The ogress's solitary eye roamed the cave, surveying the companions.

Finally she spoke. "I could perform tricks like that all day," boasted Chen'tal Pyrnee, breaking the tension. In spite of herself, she was satisfied by the respectful demeanor of these three unlikely companions. Suddenly she stopped her incessant stirring. "But," the ugly ogress added, giving Raistlin a placating wink with her purplish eye, "you are in a hurry and have business to conduct. What brings you here to see old Chen'tal? It had better be important, or at least interesting. I don't entertain dull visitors. Not for long, anyway." She gave a dissonant cackle.

Raistlin took a step forward, digging into his pack and offering a thick wedge of speckled cheese wrapped in rough white paper. "We brought you a gift," he said politely.

Reaching out, Chen'tal Pyrnee grabbed the offering and swiftly unwrapped it. Her lone eye gleamed with obvious pleasure as she held the thick wedge of cheese in her gnarled palm. All Flint could think of as he watched her was how hungry he was all of a sudden and what a waste of fine cheese this was. The dwarf hoped the ogress couldn't hear his stomach rumbling.

Chen'tal Pyrnee plucked at the cheese and stuffed a chunk into her mouth, grotesquely dribbling bits of it as she chewed ferociously. "Mmmm ... tasty," the Oracle said grudgingly. She held her hand up high and let the rest of the cheese plop into the steaming caldron.

Flint gulped with disappointment. Reading his thoughts, Tanis could barely repress a smile.

"Morath remembered how much you like the cheese from town," Raistlin continued smoothly. "And this"—the young mage held out a pouch tied with a ribbon, obviously stuffed with coins—"is what I brought as payment for the favor we ask of you."

"Which is?" asked Chen'tal Pyrnee with curiosity, taking the pouch and hefting it in her hand. It jingled, obviously heavy. She didn't need to empty and count the pouch to know that it was sufficient payment for the services she was usually asked to perform.

"From the Master Mage, I have learned that you possess the key to a portal that could transport us to Ogrebond at the edge of the Blood Sea. Our friends, including my brother, have been taken captive in that part of the world and are held in dire jeopardy. We do not have enough time to journey there by land or sea and are desperate for swifter means of travel. We come to you, trusting that you will appreciate the urgency of our quest."

The ugly ogress made a reproachful face and wagged a finger at Raistlin. "Morath shouldn't be telling folks that I have knowledge of a portal. He should know better."

She lowered her voice conspiratorially and leaned closer to Raistlin, so that their faces were an arm's length apart. Her mouth twisted, as if she were attempting a rare smile. Her breath smelled worse than any horse's. The purple eye bulged in its socket. "Portals exist through the benevolence of the Hulderfolk. They are not to be used for purposes of mere expediency. The Hulderfolk set certain conditions. The magic involved is of the highest potency."

"But do the Hulderfolk truly exist?" interjected Tanis from behind Raistlin. "Are they not simply legend?"

The purple eye swiveled to scrutinize Tanis, who had spoken without thinking. The half-elf braced for some type of abuse from the Oracle, but Chen'tal Pyrnee seemed amused rather than angry at his outburst. "Oh, I should think the Hulderfolk do exist," the ogress cackled. "There's no real proof, of course, as there is no real proof of many things. People say the Hulderfolk are invisible during the day and shy at night. Yet I believe they are always with us, watching and waiting. You must live according to what you believe." She shrugged. "I, for one, believe in the Hulderfolk."

Here she endeavored another rare smile. Two smiles in one day, probably a record, thought Flint to himself.

The ugly ogress turned back to Raistlin, hefting the money pouch once again. Her smile vanished. With a flick of her hand, she tossed the pouch back in his direction. It landed at his feet.

"A cartload of coins would not be enough for me to tempt the Hulderfolk," she said flatly. "I would be risking my very existence."

She leaned toward Raistlin again, speaking softly with her stinking breath. "Magic would raise the stakes. Now, I'm not saying I know the whereabouts of a portal, and I'm not saying I don't. If I did, it would take a magic artifact to grant your request. No amount of coinage would make the slightest difference. If you had a magic bauble to trade, we might have something to talk about. Being a noteworthy pupil of Morath's and all, you might happen to have such a bauble. If so, you'd be well advised to barter with it."

With a smirk, the unpleasant hag resumed stirring the hot, bubbling caldron. She cackled and muttered to herself, her purple eye remaining fixed on Raistlin.

The young mage stood with a wan, defeated expression. He started to say something, then thought better of it. The silence in the room grew oppressive.

"Raistlin!" whispered Tanis, beckoning him to his side.
The mage turned to confer with his friend. Flint, who was
weary of the ogress, sidled up next to them, listening.

"What about the message bottle from Tasslehoff?" asked
Tanis, "That's a magical artifact, isn't it?"

"You've got it with you, don't you?" put in Flint.

"Yes," said Raistlin tersely.

"We have no further use for it," added Tanis. "She might
want it."

"You don't understand," said Raistlin stubbornly.

"I can hear practically every word you are saying!" crowed
the ogress. Chen'tal Pyrnee cupped one hand to her ear, bent
her head toward them, and cackled. "Practically every
word," she muttered to herself grumpily, stirring the caldron.

The three companions moved away from her and huddled
closer together. Raistlin lowered his voice. "The bottle means
nothing to me," the young mage whispered, "but to give it to
Chen'tal Pyrnee goes against my teaching. This ogress traf-
fics with whomever will pay her price. In the past, she has
allied herself with evil. She may do so again. No magical artifact, however innocent, should fall into her hands."

"But she already has at least one artifact—the magical
key or whatever it is that unlocks the portal," puzzled Flint.
"Therefore, wouldn't it be acceptable to give her ours in
exchange? That way, she's not really gaining any power."

"That's true," admitted Raistlin hesitantly.

"After all," added Tanis, "it may be a question of Caramon's life."

"Sturm's, too," chimed in Flint, "not to mention Tasslehoff."

Raistlin frowned. "I suppose you're right," he said. The
mage turned back to Chen'tal Pyrnee, who had been
observing the huddle and trying to eavesdrop. Her purplish orb gleamed with interest.

Fumbling in his pack, Raistlin pulled out the message
bottle. Immediately Chen'tal Pyrnee grabbed it and held it
up in two hands, her hideous face alight with pleasure.

"A message bottle!" she exclaimed. "It's so pretty! I haven't seen one for eons! They're not very practical, however. Each owner can use it only once. But they do come in handy." Suddenly her brow furrowed. "I hope there's a good message inside, so I don't get bored with it in the meantime."

"If you like kender, you'll love—" Flint began before Tanis clapped his hand over the dwarf's mouth.

Chen'tal Pyrnee turned to stare suspiciously at the dwarf, but Raistlin cut in, waving his hand reasurringly. "It's from a kender on an ocean voyage, and—"

Listening to Raistlin, she nodded excitedly. "Oooh! A kender!" Chen'tal Pyrnee squealed with delight. "I couldn't be more pleased. They are such diverting creatures. I hired one to clean and sweep for me over seven years ago, but it didn't work out, because one day … Oh, never mind. It's a long story—kender stories always are—and as I recall, you're in a bit of hurry."

Moving with surprising speed, the ogress bustled over to the large trunk and opened it, with her copious backside carefully screening the interior from her visitors' view. She rummaged among the contents, noisily shoving things aside, until at last she straightened up and turned around, triumphantly clutching a shimmering black gem dangling from a silver chain.

"Here it is!" the Oracle proclaimed, handing it over to Raistlin. "It is very powerful, so use it wisely."

"The Amulet of Darkness," said Raistlin wonderingly, holding it up for the others to see. The gem spun slowly on its chain, catching the pale light in the room.

Flint thought it looked like a lot of other black gemstones he had seen in his life. Tanis could tell that Raistlin recognized it as unique.

"Of course," Chen'tal Pyrnee added wistfully, "I have never had an opportunity to use it myself, so I can only suggest how best to make use of it."

"I thought the Amulet of Darkness had been lost forever," mused Raistlin.

"Lost, perhaps," said the ogress, "but not forever. Besides, I didn't say it was the one and only Amulet of Darkness. You did. All I guarantee is that it will take you through the portal to Ogrebond. It will do that, I know. You can call it the Amulet of Mustard Pie, for all I care."

"How do we release the magic?" asked Raistlin.

Looking around warily, the ugly ogress leaned over and whispered into Raistlin's ear. The mage nodded, giving a sign to the others that he was satisfied. He pocketed the amulet.

"Where do we find the portal?" asked Tanis.

"Easy enough," said Chen'tal Pyrnee. She launched into a shrill recital of directions that were so elaborate they left Tanis dizzy. Something about due east, sharp left at dog rock, follow the tree line up to a high precipice, a gusty overhang, and then ...

"I know the spot," said Flint.

The ogress stopped talking and turned her suspicious stare to the dwarf. The other two companions also looked at the dwarf in surprise. "I've hiked around these parts for thirty years," he said proudly. "You can't name a peak I haven't climbed or at least seen."

Tanis looked at Raistlin. "Then let's go," the half-elf said eagerly.

"Yes," Raistlin agreed. He made another slight bow to the Oracle. "Thank you for your help."

All three of them backed out of the cave, keeping their eyes on the one-eyed hag who was stirring her misty caldron with one hand and, with the other, happily holding the message bottle aloft.

"Thank you for the kender message bottle!" Chen'tal Pyrnee called to them as they retreated from sight. "Good luck with the portal! One never knows about portals. And if you happen to run across that old grump Morath, tell him not to send me any more visitors for at least a decade! I'm all done in!"

* * * * *

Tired and ill-tempered, the three companions made camp only a few short miles from the Oracle's cave. The strange, smelly ogress hadn't put any of them in a better mood for the adventure ahead. Tanis collected sticks and fallen branches for a fire, while Flint made a flaxweed broth for supper. Raistlin stayed apart from the half-elf and dwarf, eating placidly, his face drained, his eyes preoccupied as they stared into the dancing tongues of flame.

Finally Flint's cranky muttering got to the mage. "If you want to turn back, then turn back!" snapped Raistlin. "Both of you! If necessary, I'll find the portal and go to Ogrebond myself!"

"I didn't say anything about turning back," retorted Flint. "I was talking about where we're heading tomorrow!"

"Flint says it's a remote ledge at the top of a sheer cliff," explained Tanis diplomatically. "Very difficult to climb."

"How far away?" asked Raistlin, having regained his customary composure.

"Not far," huffed Flint, sipping his brown broth. "That's not the problem. I can climb it, and probably Tanis. But," he added, eyeing the young mage's less than impressive physique, "it may not be, uh, practicable for a fellow in your, uh, condition."

"How far away?" insisted Raistlin.

"One, maybe two hours only," said Tanis.

"Good," said Raistlin.

"How do we know the Oracle told the truth? How do we know there's a portal up there? How do we know it's not a waste of our blasted time?" Flint's voice rose vehemently.

"She told the truth," muttered Raistlin. "Morath said if Chen'tal Pyrnee chose to bargain, she would bargain fairly."

"But how do you expect to climb a precarious rock face?"

"Stop worrying about me," ordered Raistlin, "and get some sleep!"

Snorting angrily, Flint said nothing further. He hauled out his bedroll, lay down on it with his back to the others, and within minutes was snoring loudly. No words were exchanged between Tanis and the young mage during this awkward interlude.

Lunitari and Solinari shone at opposite ends of the sky, rising slowly toward each other, twin paths that at this time of year, late summer, would not intersect. The night was bright with stars at this elevation. The foliage had thinned considerably. The slope was strewn with sculpted rock. The light of the stars and moons revealed sparse, stunted trees rimmed by nearby peaks frosted with shining snow.

The serenity of the night echoed with the furtive sounds of nocturnal creatures. A gentle wind rustled the treetops. Tanis breathed deeply of the pine and earth and crisp mountain air.

He ventured to glance at Raistlin who sat, hands cupped together, still lost in thought, looking so worried and worn that a sharp breeze could knock him over. As Tanis watched, the young mage sighed, stood, and began pacing around the campfire. The half-elf was well aware of Raistlin's physical limitations, especially compared to his more robust twin. But he also knew that the young mage regularly adventured side by side with Caramon. And on more than one occasion, Tanis had seen a flash of the same fire that animated Raistlin's half-sister, Kitiara. No, Flint was wrong to underestimate the young mage, Tanis decided, physically or otherwise.

At that moment, Raistlin looked up and met Tanis's gaze, returning it defiantly.

"What's really bothering Flint," offered Tanis gently, "is the idea of the Blood Sea. He knows you'll make the journey all right. But he himself has a deadly terror of crossing any body of water, dating back to that unfortunate camping trip on the shores of Crystalmir Lake."

Raistlin gave a low chuckle and sat back down. The weariness of the day's effort settled on him like a great weight. "Perhaps," the young mage said softly.

Some months back, Flint and Tasslehoff had arranged an overnight expedition on the far shores of Crystalmir Lake.

Caramon and Sturm had come along and spent the day learning hunting and tracking skills from the grizzled dwarf. Tasslehoff tagged along with Raistlin, who busied himself searching for herbs and flowers for his spell components. It was on that day, ironically, that Tasslehoff had told Raistlin about his good friend Asa and the unusual minotaur herbalist from Southern Ergoth Asa had spoken of.

It had been a glorious day, one of their first extended experiences as companions, marred only by an incident on the following morning. Tas had "found" a boat, then persuaded the rest of them to launch it on peaceful Crystalmir Lake. Some distance from shore, Caramon had spotted a large green dart-eel lazing about, and with typical ebullience, he had boasted he could catch it by hand. However, Raistlin's twin had leaned over too far, and the boat capsized.

Quick thinking by Raistlin led him to bob up underneath the boat in the air pocket entrapped there. Tas and Sturm were good swimmers and succeeded in righting the boat. Flint dove to rescue the burly Caramon, who couldn't swim and had sunk to the bottom. The long seconds stretched into minutes as the trio waited anxiously. Finally Sturm and Tas jumped in again. Sturm hauled a sputtering Caramon to the surface, and shortly thereafter, Tas came up holding on to Flint's collar. The half-drowned dwarf, choking and chilled to the bone, vowed that nobody would ever coax him into another boat for the rest of his life.

"Considering what a weak swimmer Flint is," said Tanis, "it was rather heroic of him to try to save your brother."

"Heroic and foolish," grunted Raistlin. But his tone had grown milder. Tanis, his gaze diverted by the rhythmic swaying of the treetops, didn't notice the young mage as he slumped down on his blanket and wrapped his cloak around himself.

"Yes," chuckled Tanis. "Heroic and foolish. Two words that go well together." He gazed up at the beauty of the moons and stars, drinking in the peacefulness of the place.

"Flint has mentioned that incident several times," he mused softly. "It's engraved on his consciousness. Worst of all, for him, may be the fact that he was rescued by Tasslehoff. Any way you look at it, he owes his life to the kender—at least that time. Repaying that debt might be the only thing that gets him back onto a body of water—even one as accursed as the Blood Sea."

Tanis paused, his thoughts returning for a moment to Kitiara. A rush of confused emotions swept over him. The half-elf had never been able to bring himself to speak to Raistlin about her. This might be a good time.

"Tell me, Raist," Tanis began. Then he heard soft breathing, turned, and saw that the young mage was deep in slumber.

He crossed over to Raistlin and dropped an extra blanket on him. The air was turning cold. Tanis sat back down, pulled his own cloak over his shoulders, and sighed. Although they should be in safe territory, he decided that he'd better keep watch for a few hours before catching some sleep himself.

* * * * *

By late morning of the next day, after following a rugged, steep path up the mountain flanks, the companions came to the place that the ogress had described and that Flint knew from his previous journeys. Standing in a narrow ravine, he pointed upward to a cluster of eroded sandstone crags that rose like a fortress high in the sky. At the top of one of them, they could see a shelf of stone that jutted toward the east, where the spectacular configuration was dwarfed by even more imposing mountain ranges.

Flint took the lead, climbing up the sheer rock face, following the line of crooked trees that clung stubbornly to cracks and crevices. Tanis came next, trailed by Raistlin. Each was roped to the other around the waist.

The crag they were scaling must have been four hundred

feet high. It was slow going, made slower by the fact that
Flint insisted on leading and doing things his own way.
Meticulously he inched upward, pounding short iron
stakes about an arm's length above his head and tying himself firmly before finding a new foothold. Raistlin had been
prescient with his suggestion that the dwarf bring along
everything necessary to survive a mountain expedition.

Tanis and Raistlin had an easier time of it, thanks to
Flint's trailblazing. Still, even for an experienced climber, it
was arduous work. The footholds that provided a secure
respite were few. Tanis and Raistlin had to claw and cling
to pitted rock while hoisting themselves ever upward.
Toward the top, the temperature cooled noticeably, and
unexpected gusts of wind buffeted their backs.

Flint had to admit that Raistlin posessed grit. The young
mage didn't complain.

Only once did Raistlin weaken and slip. Ahead of him,
Tanis was alert enough to pull the rope taut, breaking the
young mage's fall, while with his other hand, he gripped
the link to Flint above. Raistlin managed to pull himself up
and grab hold of the rock face. Fluttering his hand, he signaled Flint to continue. The dwarf had been right in thinking that his sinewy friend Tanis would have no trouble
safeguarding Raistlin.

After nearly two hours of hard climbing, the three of
them attained the summit of the precipice. They slumped
on the ledge, out of breath, before turning their eyes to
behold what lay beyond. The shelf was just large enough
for the three of them. As the precipice rounded to the east,
it revealed massive mountains with dramatic escarpments
and snowcapped domes.

Directly below them was a deep, jagged gorge. Steam
from fissures in the rock obscured its bottom. A plunge
down that craggy face would mean certain death.

As Flint stood on wobbly legs, he realized that the strong
gusts of wind were coming at him from two directions, east
and west, the ledge caught in a crossfire of physical forces.

The strong winds tore at him. He motioned for the other two to wait and crawled unsteadily to the far side of the ledge, where he pitted one of his iron stakes. While Tanis and Raistlin watched, he pitted several more, and then rigged his rope so that they might all stand, anchored to the crag, without being blown off into space.

They stared below.

"Is that where the portal is supposed to be?" asked Tanis skeptically. He had to repeat his question more loudly before it was heard over the rushing cry of the wind.

"Yes," shouted Raistlin, his voice hoarse.

"I wouldn't want to trust in it," said Flint. The other two said nothing in reply, because they would rather not depend on it either. But what choice did they have?

Flint picked up a loose rock and held it over the side. Tanis nodded. He let it drop.

They waited for several minutes, straining against the noise of the wind to hear it hit bottom. Finally Flint thought he heard a ping off the rocks below.

"No portal," said Flint disgustedly.

"Inanimate object," disagreed Raistlin, shouting again. "The portal won't accept an inanimate object unaccompanied by a mortal being, and in any case, it won't open until I cast the proper spell!"

After a long pause, Tanis asked, "How can we be sure?"

Raistlin didn't reply immediately. The three of them stood on the rock ledge, high atop the crag, leaning out over the craggy gorge that extended hundreds of feet below. The wind blasted around them, tearing at their hair and clothing. Flint's ropes kept them from toppling off, but even so, they had to struggle to maintain their balance.

"We don't know," yelled Flint finally.

"Is that right?" Tanis asked, turning toward Raistlin.

"Yes."

Tanis and Flint looked at each other. Flint rolled his eyes. Tanis unsheathed a knife.

"Then say the spell," the half-elf said.

Raistlin closed his eyes briefly, concentrating, then opened them. He murmured some ancient words that sounded incomprehensible to Flint. Then, in common language that both of them understood, he shouted, "Open portal!"

With his knife, Tanis slashed at the ropes that held them to the stakes. Swiftly he jammed it back in its sheath. As he did, the three of them moved forward, leaping off, Flint and Raistlin linking arms with Tanis in the middle. An unintelligible shriek escaped their lips.

Whether because of the wind or their lack of coordination, the three companions got all tangled up as they plunged, heads first and feet splaying, toward the jagged rocks below.

Chapter 6
Captive and Adrift

For days they drifted. Since Sturm and Caramon had no idea where they were, it didn't make sense to try to swim in any particular direction. Besides, the ropes that bound them to the splintered mast were shrunk by the salt water. It was all they could do to keep their chins above the waves and kick out with their legs.

The sky remained gray and leaden, and a haze blanketed everything. The shroud was impenetrable. They could see nothing.

Although the sun never shone, a diffuse light permeated the haze, and it was hotter than deep summer in Solace. The heat smothered them like a sodden blanket, burning their skin and eyes, relentless in its constancy.

Night offered only slight improvement. They would

have welcomed nightfall and relief from the heat, except it plunged them into utter darkness. They could barely discern each other, much less the twin moons, Lunitari and Solinari. In this part of the world, wherever it was, the sky was monolithic, oppressive.

The water itself offered little comfort. Brackish and brown, almost muddy, the sea remained uncomfortably warm even at night, carrying a pungent smell. The waves heaved and roiled, though there was little wind. It was almost as if some turbulence beneath perpetually agitated the surface.

For two days, they saw no signs of life, no ships on the horizon, no sea birds, no fish. For two days, they had nothing to eat or drink, nor any sleep. For two days, they kicked and paddled as best they could, draped over the mast, gradually losing strength and willpower.

"It could be worse," Caramon had said the first day.

"How?" questioned Sturm.

"It could be Flint instead of me," replied Caramon. He managed to force a grin. "He's the only poorer swimmer I know."

Sturm returned the grin. He was determined not to think about his body, weakened by hunger and pain. In spite of that, he began to doubt how much longer either of them could survive.

"I wonder ..." began Sturm.

"What?" asked Caramon.

"Where are we?"

On the third day, the haze gradually grew even thicker, so that by midday, they could hardly see a dozen feet beyond where they floated. Sturm and Caramon glanced at each other nervously as they began to hear creaking and groaning. High-pitched shrieks rent the air. Broken beams and pieces of planking and heavy, waterlogged clumps of kelp materialized, bumping up against them in the water.

Sturm leaned away from the mast and was able to snatch some of the seaweed in his mouth.

"What are you doing?" asked Caramon, aghast.

"It's quite edible," Sturm said in a bare whisper as he chewed arduously. It was edible, though its raw and gummy texture made it worse than tasteless. "Who knows where our next meal is coming from?"

Caramon thought about that for a moment, then lunged as best he could for the next patch that floated by, catching some of the purple-brown vegetation, spotted with grime. Trying not to think about it, the twin chewed determinedly, but he couldn't bear it. With a flash of disgust, Caramon spat the mouthful out.

His brown eyes leveled at Caramon sternly, Sturm chewed on.

After a moment's consideration, Caramon lunged for the kelp again but missed. The vegetation washed by.

The groaning and cries intensified, followed by the booming and splitting sounds of ... what? It sounded like a ship's crash, the noise of wood breaking up, a hull tearing on some unseen reef. The cacophony of sounds rose and fell, echoing spookily.

The haze mingled with drops of rain and seemed to rub up against their faces. The waves diminished so that the sea was eerily calm. All around them was a ghostly gray-white void.

"What can you see?" asked Caramon, his voice hoarse and cracked.

"Nothing," Sturm replied. "And you?"

"Less than nothing."

Suddenly a large mass, a great and formidable cluster of shapes, loomed out of the haze. For a moment, Caramon panicked, thinking a gigantic sea monster was descending on them. Then his vision cleared somewhat, and through his exhaustion, he realized the mass was actually a number of ships and scattered remnants of ships, creaking as they glided through the oddly calm waters.

Sickeningly white, like the bellies of dead fish, the rotting hulks were riddled with gaping holes, their timbers stained with blood, rust, and a yellow-green slime. Strange barnacles and marine life clung to their sides. Tatters of sails hung from the masts. The wind moaned in the rigging. It seemed impossible these ships could float.

"Look!" cried Caramon.

A dark shape glided toward them, the biggest ship of the wrecked fleet. A solitary hooded figure stood at the helm. Three skeletons dangled from a high post, swaying gently. As the ship bore closer, coming within a dozen feet of them, the hooded figure turned and inclined its head, appearing to focus on them.

The hooded figure pointed at Sturm and Caramon. The phantom ship had drawn so close that Caramon could see the figure's eyes, fiery red inside the black holes of its featureless visage. With a bony finger, the hooded ghost—for surely that is what it was, Caramon thought—beckoned.

The ship pulled so close the two stranded friends could have almost reached out and touched it had their arms been free to do so. Stray, rotting beams jutted out from its side. Caramon had to kick away to avoid being struck by one of them.

As the ship passed, pieces of it broke and crashed onto the deck or splashed into the sea. The hooded ghost didn't stir, but its eyes followed them. Caramon felt their terrible gaze on him and Sturm.

Then, as suddenly as it came, the ghost fleet disappeared into the haze. In its wake, the brackish water churned around Sturm and Caramon as the wind picked up and quickly became a howl. A strong current tugged at the warriors' legs. Waves crashed over them, filling their noses and mouths. The strange current sucked them downward.

With his last reserve of strength, Caramon pumped his legs, straining to keep above water. Gasping for air, he realized his friend was faring worse. Sturm was all pretzeled up, almost on top of him, his lungs at the bursting point. Caramon strove to buoy up Sturm as best he could, struggling against the enormous pull of the sea.

Sturm's strength was gone, but the knight didn't panic.

He regretted dying, but the sea had proved a worthy opponent. Death offered a welcome respite. He felt the waves close over his head for what he was certain was the final time, when suddenly the turbulence spent itself and the sea grew calm.

Sturm and Caramon both broke to the surface, choking. The sea still thundered around them, but it was no longer as threatening. The haze had returned as before. The two companions clung awkwardly to the mast that both imprisoned them and kept them afloat. Half-drowned, Sturm barely clung to consciousness. Caramon, exhausted, fought the urge to fall asleep.

Somehow they kept going. By the morning of the fifth day, the two young men had begun to despair. Brine parched their lips. Their faces had burned until the skin cracked, oozing a glistening mucous. Dampness clogged their chests, yet their throats were as dry as tinder.

Still they drifted, clinging together, roped to the mast. The brown waves tumbled over them. In every direction stretched the endless, merciless sea.

Caramon's legs had thoroughly cramped, so that he could barely move them. Sturm's eyes had shrunk into puffed slits. The endless effort to keep their chins above water, had dazed their minds as well as ravaged their bodies.

"If ... if I could only untie these bonds," gasped Caramon, water sloshing into his mouth when he opened it to talk. "You might have a better chance alone."

"I!" declared Sturm, shocked. "I'd never abandon you! It would be dishonorable."

"Anyway," acknowledged Caramon, casting a fleeting glance at Sturm, "I can't budge them, so I guess we're stuck with each other."

A silence grew between them for several minutes. "The mast is a curse," said Sturm at last, his voice grim. "It keeps us afloat, but just barely ... just enough to torture us. Drowning would be preferable." He paused, glancing away. "There! There they are again!"

A pair of aquatic predators had been circling them for a day. Four round, blackened eyes set in a massive forehead poked out of the water now and again, when one of the creatures surfaced to gulp some air. The helpless companions could see the creature's thick, knobby hides and webbed claws. They could also glimpse powerful maws lined with rows of triangular teeth. Although the creatures were huge, broad of back, and at least eight feet in length, they had kept a respectful distance for a day now, circling for hours, diving underwater for long intervals and then returning to circle and watch.

"Vodyanoi ... cousins of the umber hulk," rasped Caramon. "I've heard tales that they existed in deep waters. Why don't they attack?"

"Vodyanoi are cunning," said Sturm in a bare whisper, "but they're are also cowardly. This must be a mated pair. You can bet if they were with a pack, we'd be dead by now. But they know that we're tiring. It won't be long now. All they have to do is wait. It's much simpler than fighting."

Summoning all his strength, Sturm kicked out in the direction of the bulky sea animals. The two vodyanoi opened their huge jaws, let out piercing screeches and dove under the water.

"Don't worry," murmured Sturm, closing his eyes momentarily. "They'll be back."

Sturm didn't think he and Caramon would make it through the day. His stomach felt poisoned, on fire. His legs hung lifelessly, mere dead weight. Once or twice he looked over and saw Caramon, almost asleep, his chin balanced precariously on the bobbing mast. Sturm tried to warn his friend to stay alert, but his parched mouth couldn't form the words.

A shadow flickered across the water in front of Sturm. Looking up, he thought he saw a black dot circling above in the hazy sky, but he couldn't be sure. He thought he had seen that black shape before, too ... yesterday? What was it? Another predator, like the vodyanoi, he guessed. This one from the heavens, waiting for them to die.

There it was again, the cawing that he thought he'd heard before. It seemed to come from the black dot. Was it a giant bird, then, taunting him and Caramon?

Abruptly something plopped in the water almost directly in front of him. It was square, grooved, and several inches thick, a kind of thick, flat bread, floating in the water very near the Solamnic.

Sturm reached out and caught it in his teeth. It was as hard as wood, but it wasn't wood. It was a thick slab of bread. Hungrily he bit down on it, digging his shoulder into Caramon.

The big warrior stirred, easing his eyes open. Sturm let half the bread fall back into the water, nudging it toward Caramon. Caramon had enough wits left to seize it in his teeth, devouring it in several gulps.

The caw sounded again, more distant this time. Caramon and Sturm looked up into the sky, squinting, barely able to see the black speck as it arced over them and vanished from sight.

The thick, hard bread was no substitute for Otik's spicy potatoes, but in their present circumstances, it tasted almost as good.

The warmth of the seawater lulled them. The torpid haze drained their energy. The monotony of the waves drowned their senses.

Trancelike, they drifted aimlessly.

Sturm dreamed of his father and wondered what had become of brave, doomed Angriff Brightblade. One day he would find him and know the answer. For now, the clues were few and far between, like stepping-stones scattered across an endless pond. Whenever Sturm began to step on one of the stones, it turned into a lily pad, and he sank to the bottom.

Caramon dreamed of a warm inn and a comely wench.

Neither of them noticed that the haze had begun to lift, and that the water was losing its muddy brown color.

* * * * *

The kender paced the perimeter of his stone cell in an underground annex of the palace. Tasslehoff Burrfoot seemed to be the only prisoner in this part of the building. Dogz had told him that he was a special prisoner of the minotaur king. This made Tas proud, even if it meant that he was in for some very special torture and inquisition.

Dogz did not adminster the torturing. Once a day, he brought what little gruel the minotaurs permitted Tas to eat. It was disgusting stuff, even to Tas, who like most kender was open-minded about what he ate.

The one in charge, Cleef-Eth, did not adminster the torture, either. It was he who asked the questions between the torturings.

Cleef-Eth demanded to know why Tasslehoff had bought the crushed jalopwort from the minotaur herbalist, Argotz. Cleef-Eth now possessed the crushed jalopwort, as well as the contents of the rest of Tas's pouches, but it appeared what he really wanted to know was why the kender had sought the rare ingredient in the first place.

Tas might have answered if he had happened to know the answer, but only Raistlin knew. In general, the kender always tried to be courteous and helpful. But Tas knew that Argotz had been murdered and that after murdering him, the foul-smelling minotaurs had come after him and Caramon and Sturm and somehow conjured up a magic storm—he must remember to ask Raistlin about the mechanics of the magic storm—which had transported them all to the far eastern rim of the Blood Sea.

So Tas didn't answer the question, and the minotaurs had been torturing him for days now.

Poor dumb, ugly, squalid cowheads. They needed a lot of help with their torture techniques. From Tas's point of view, the minotaur torture masters were pretty confused about the question of how much to hurt him in order to make him tell them what he knew, without hurting him too much or

killing him or incapacitating him. If they killed Tas or inca-
pacitated him without extracting the necessary information,
somebody called the Nightmaster would be very upset.

"Be careful, you fools!" Cleef-Eth mentioned several
times during the torture process. "The Nightmaster has
given strict instructions that the kender must be kept alive
until he talks!"

That meant they couldn't cut out his tongue—which was
too bad, Tas reflected, because that was quite effective as a
torture tool.

After the torture masters had spent a couple of days
punching and kicking him without much result, except for
the bruises and the blood, the kender tried to help out Cleef-
Eth and his lieutenants with more imaginative suggestions.

"Why not hang me up somewhere by my topknot?"
advised Tas.

Cleef-Eth thought that was a good idea, so for an entire
day and night, during which he didn't get much sleep, Tas
hung off the ground from a hook embedded in the ceiling,
dangling from his topknot. His face turned beet red, and he
nearly strangled. Tas had to admit that it really hurt. He
congratulated Cleef-Eth on his excellent torture, but it
didn't produce what the minotaurs wanted to know.

"Cut off my topknot so that I am shamed," suggested
Tas, improvising. "A kender without long hair is a social
leper, sort of like a cowhead without horns."

Cleef-Eth thought that was worth a try, too, so the minotaur torturers snipped Tas's topknot right down to his pate.
Tasslehoff was extremely ashamed—for about five minutes.
After that, he realized the only people who were going to
see his shorn topknot anyway were these smelly minotaurs. He also decided the effect was not entirely unhand-
some, and perhaps he ought to cut off his topknot more
often. All the same, polite to the core, he congratulated the
minotaurs on their torturing ability and their willingness to
try new techniques.

Of course, Cleef-Eth and the minotaur torturers had

some ideas of their own. Tas had to admit that some of them weren't without their merit.

They tried starving him, although Tas detested their jailhouse gruel anyway. The only torture in not eating was that he didn't get to see Dogz, whom he had grown rather fond of. But lately when Dogz brought food, he did so under the watchful glare of Cleef-Eth and consequently didn't risk speaking to Tasslehoff.

The minotaur torturers broke all the fingers of one of Tas's hands, one by one, using a stone hammer on one, bending another back until it snapped, and so on. That hurt plenty. But a kender's fingers, long and slender, are like the bones of a human baby's. They hurt, but they heal quickly. Tasslehoff knew this and did his best to endure the pain honorably, as his friend Sturm probably would have done.

Where were Caramon and Sturm, anyway? Were they dead? During the torture, Tas concentrated on worrying about his two friends. They were probably in need of rescuing. When he got out of his present mess, he would certainly endeavor to find them.

The minotaur torturers tried immersing Tas in freezing ice water. It took three of the horned beasts to hold his bobbing head beneath the surface of a huge tub. They held it under for a long, long time. Tas held his breath for as long as he was able, then couldn't hold it any longer. He had to admit he almost drowned. That might have been the best torture, if he was ranking them according to effectiveness. But still the kender didn't tell Cleef-Eth what the minotaur wanted to know.

Cleef-Eth kept repeating the same questions: "Are you a mage? Why were you seeking these spell components? If you are not a mage, in whose behalf are you working?"

Naturally Tas couldn't answer those questions because it was bound to get Raistlin into a lot of trouble. Poor Raistlin ... although perhaps he wasn't someone you'd want to invite to a party, Tas liked him and knew that the mage wouldn't fare well in this type of situation.

Then suddenly the torture stopped.

For several days, Tasslehoff was left alone. His only visitor was Dogz. The first day after the minotaurs stopped torturing him, Dogz had come down the steps, bringing the kender the first bowl of gruel he had been offered for quite some time. The minotaur put it down gently outside Tas's cell and slid it under the bars with his foot.

Because Tas's right eye was swollen shut and the other one was matted with blood and dirt, and because he didn't feel much like eating anyway, he didn't rush up and grab the gruel and gratefully start to eat. He didn't even look up or say anything to Dogz. So he didn't see how Dogz looked.

His eyes downcast, Dogz slipped away. It was only after the minotaur was gone, hours later, after the kender had decided to check it out, that Tas realized the bowl didn't contain the usual gruel. It was bran meal, cold by now but not all that bad, considering it was cooked by minotaurs. That Dogz!

After that, for several days, Dogz brought hot bran meal, and Tasslehoff slowly got better. His cuts and bruises would heal in time, and some fuzz sprouted where his topknot had been.

He and Dogz got to talking again. "Why did they stop the torturing, Dogz?" the kender asked.

Dogz looked over his shoulder at the steps leading upward. "I don't know if I should be telling you," rumbled the minotaur.

"Why not?" asked Tasslehoff innocently. "You tell me everything else. I already know about your brother, who got killed in a barroom brawl; and your uncle, who was one of the Supreme Council before he was killed in the gladiatorial arena; and your cousin's wife, who got into an argument with a metalsmith, who pulled a knife and ... Hey, did it ever occur to you that your family might be cursed? Everybody seems to get killed." Tas paused, happily licking bran meal off the wooden spoon. He knew by now that he had to stop talking in order to coax a reply from Dogz.

"So why did they stop torturing me?"

"It is because the Nightmaster is sending a high emisarry to interrogate you," rumbled Dogz.

"A what?"

"One of the chief disciples of his cult."

"Oh. Is that good or bad?"

Dogz's face creased in thought. "I do not know," he said honestly, "but it is a great honor for Lacynos to host him. It is rare that the Nightmaster sends one of the High Three all the way from Karthay. I cannot remember the last time."

"Why doesn't he come himself?" asked Tasslehoff.

Dogz emitted a long, low chuckle, showing yellowed teeth. "The Nightmaster rarely leaves Karthay," answered Dogz. "Karthay is his domain."

"Have you ever seen him?"

"Of course not," snorted Dogz.

"Then how do you know he exists?"

Dogz scowled. "That is not funny at all, friend Tas. He is the highest priest of our religion. He is a direct link to Sargonnas, the god we worship."

"Hmm," said Tas. "Sargonnas, consort of Takhisis ..." Tas finished licking the spoon and pushed it and the bowl back under the barred cell.

"Yes," said Dogz enthusiastically. "Faithful servant of the Queen of Darkness. I did not know you were so knowledgeable about the gods of Krynn."

"Oh, I dabble in lots of things. I pick up a little information wherever I go—speaking of which, if this Nightmaster lives on the island of Karthay and never leaves, what is he so busy doing there?"

Dogz hesitated, then shook his head.

A shout came from above. Tas recognized the voice of Sarkis, who was never far away, especially when he had a chance to order Dogz around.

Looking flustered, Dogz grabbed the spoon and empty bowl, then hurried back up the stairs.

* * * * *

One day not long afterward, Dogz brought ordinary, disgusting gruel again. Tas guessed it was a sign that the Nightmaster's high emissary had arrived.

Later that day, a group of minotaurs thundered down the steps to look at Tasslehoff. Apart from a couple of familiar torture masters, they included Sarkis, looking humble and outranked by Cleef-Eth, and a newcomer who was distinct from the others.

Tas studied the newcomer closely. He appeared to be a kind of shaman, young and bulging with muscles, dressed in fur and feathered headgear. His horns were massive, almost brushing the high ceiling.

The others seemed to defer to the shaman, who paced back and forth, cocking his head this way and that at Tasslehoff.

"Look lively, kender," growled Sarkis. "You have an important visitor."

The shaman minotaur looked up, frowning. Cleef-Eth threw Sarkis an annoyed glance.

Always happy for company, Tas did his best to look bright and attractive for the important visitor, which was quite a challenge, considering that he was covered with healing wounds, his clothes were in tatters, and his feet were bare and blistered. He gazed up into the face of the important visitor, who gazed intently back at him.

"We've tried everything on the little nuisance, Fesz," complained Cleef-Eth to the shaman. "He just won't cooperate. I think it best to kill him and be done with it."

"You are not paid to think," rumbled Fesz, almost gently, Tas thought. "If you were, your pay would be very low indeed."

Cleef-Eth snorted but didn't say anything. Fesz turned back to the barred cell. As the kender didn't quite come up to the huge minotaur's chest, Fesz squatted down on his knees and peered directly into the face of the kender.

Tas smelled the minotaur's fetid breath, his foul armpits, his rank strips of furred clothing, but he was too well-mannered to mention any of this just now.

"You are such a handsome sprite of a fellow," purred Fesz, reaching out with his big, sinewy hand to stroke Tas's cheek.

His voice was lyrical and had a soothing effect on the kender. His hand kind of felt good, Tas had to admit.

"You are not our enemy; you are our friend," rumbled Fesz. "I can see that. It's wrong that they have treated you so badly." His head flicked scoldingly in the direction of Cleef-Eth. "Wrong and cruel. These city dwellers have such crude methods. It makes my heart heavy to see that they have inflicted pain upon you. The Nightmaster himself has sent me. I came on his behalf as soon as I learned of your predicament."

Tas was listening. Although the breath was still fetid, the words were lulling. And behind the fist-sized eyes of the shaman, he thought he saw a gleam of kindness that gave him hope.

"I have brought you a restorative, Tasslehoff Burrfoot," rumbled Fesz soothingly. "It will do the job much more considerately than torture. It will make you my friend, and it will make my friends your friends, my enemies your enemies. You have an understandable inclination to act for the cause of good. However, this will put you on my side ... the side of evil."

The huge hands of the minotaur reached a little farther and clutched Tas by the throat, holding him firmly but not too hard; he could still breathe. Tas squirmed uncomfortably as the minotaur pulled him closer. Held not only by the throat but by the shaman's compelling gaze, Tas saw Fesz gesture with his other hand. One of the minotaur retinue hastened forward, carrying an ornamented drinking goblet. Self-importantly, Cleef-Eth grabbed the goblet from the minotaur and stepped up behind Fesz.

Fesz pried the kender's jaws open as Cleef-Eth poured a

greenish gold liquid from the goblet down Tas's throat. Not bad-tasting, Tasslehoff thought. As for turning him evil, Tas felt it was an intriguing idea. It was Tas's last conscious thought.

The kender's head drooped downward as the potion began to take effect. Fesz let him slump to the floor.

Standing, Fesz looked at Tasslehoff Burrfoot with satisfaction. "Put him in my guest quarters," commanded the shaman. "I will deal with him myself. From this moment on, he is one of us."

Cleef-Eth turned to bark orders, but Fesz grabbed him by the shoulder and whirled him around. The shaman struck out at the jailer, hitting him across the face and knocking him down with violent force. Cleef-Eth staggered up from the floor, rubbing his cheek ruefully, but he didn't dare retaliate. Instead, he made a slight, pathetic bow.

Sarkis and the other minotaurs smirked in the background.

"This kender is no mage!" Fesz growled at Cleef-Eth angrily. "Any fool can see that!"

* * * * *

For hundreds of years, the island of Karthay was thought to be abandoned and desolate. Few travelers journeyed there. Those that did risked being greeted by giant insects, swarms of locusts, lumbering umber hulks, and deadly sand creatures who creeped and crawled among its dunes and rocks. Few could survive the howling wind and stinging sand, let alone the harsh, uncompromising heat of the endless days and the bitter cold of the torturous nights on the island.

Hundreds of years ago—nobody knew exactly when—a great city had existed on this island, a fabled city that was also called Karthay. It was the site of magnificent buildings, clean and ordered streets, and a flourishing civilization. It was said to house a great university of higher learning and a library reknowned for its huge store of books.

Then, hundreds, perhaps thousands of years ago, some unknown disaster befell the city of Karthay. Now it lay buried under tons of rock beneath a collapsed cliff face on the south shore of the island. Here and there, broken stone and identifiable pieces of buildings jutted up from the ground. In the collapse of the great city, numerous tunnels and canyons had formed among the rubble, a skein of underground passages, some treacherous with trapped gases, others dotted with sandpits, still others extending safely and uninterrupted for miles.

The inhospitable climate in the haunted ruins made it a congenial setting for the Nightmaster. Although a few unsettling problems had arisen, his plan to summon Sargonnas, to bring the god of vengeance into the world, and to forge alliances with the hostile and evil races of Ansalon was progressing.

The Nightmaster had fashioned his sanctuary in a hollowed-out area of the shattered ruins where once the great library had stood. Of that once great repository of learning, only a few isolated columns and occasional windblown scraps of ancient books remained. Fires ringed the Nightmaster's camp, which was open to the sky.

Never far from the Nightmaster, serving his every whim and learning from his every word and deed, were the two remaining shaman minotaurs of the High Three. Around the perimeter of the sanctuary, at a respectful distance, camped a group of devoted disciples and a small army of stalwart minotaurs who stayed in Karthay for the Nightmaster to command.

On this night, the camp entertained a rare visitor, one who brought the Nightmaster vital information. A scaly creature with tiny wings and an ugly snout, the visitor sat on a broken wall near the high cleric of the minotaurs, sating its thirst on strong, hot spirits after its long journey. Its actual appearance was known only to the Nightmaster and the High Three. The nearby disciples and armed minotaurs, if they endeavored to peer through the darkness, would have seen only a small figure wrapped in a cape and hood.

"I adopted a clever disguise," reported the scaly, snouted creature, its voice harsh and piercing, "and asked everyone that I met in this dull and backward place, but nobody knew where they had gone or why." The creature refilled its stone cup and took a long, satisfying drink.

An acrid, sulfurous smell emanated from the creature and traveled on the wind to the encamped minotaurs. Several of those horned bull-men, notorious for their own stench, exchanged looks.

The Nightmaster, his eyes huge and intelligent, shifted his weight as he listened. Tiny bells jingled whenever he moved. Around his shoulders, he had draped a heavy fur robe. He sighed, waiting for the scaly one to go on.

The wind picked up, shrieking through the ruins, blowing sand and dirt into their faces. The blistering heat of the day had become the harsh cold of night.

"But through my contacts," the creature hissed, "I discovered that one of them had sent a message to a young female, apparently his sister. And this female is on her way here!"

"Here?"

Looking guardedly over his shoulder, the scaly creature leaned over and whispered to the Nightmaster, telling him how the one called Kitiara had received the message and departed immediately. She could be expected to arrive on the island within days. With a ghastly wink, the scaly one assured the Nightmaster that its sources were impeccable, that this news could be relied upon.

Puffed up with arrogant pride, the visitor took another long drink.

With an impassive expression, the Nightmaster watched the creature. "And you think," rumbled the Nightmaster, "that the one I seek is this young mage from Solace—not the prisoner in Lacynos?"

"Yes," hissed the visitor, "and the young mage has disappeared. He and two friends have left Solace. They, too, may be on their way here."

Sighing, the Nightmaster raised his huge head, his horns stabbing upward as he cast his eyes toward the dark sky, searching for omens. The Nightmaster wasn't worried. He, above all, had supreme confidence.

Something was afoot, but it couldn't be anything serious. These were minor irritants. Fesz had been dispatched to deal with the prisoner in Lacynos. He himself would be prepared to greet the young female. The others, wherever they had disappeared to, would be found. In any case, what danger could they pose to the inevitability of Sargonnas?

"You have done well," growled the Nightmaster to the scaly creature.

The scaly one gulped more spirits. He would depart before daylight. Nobody could attest to having seen him. Nobody would be able to say who or what had served the Nightmaster.

Chapter 7
Escape from Ogrebond

Thud.

Raistlin, Flint, and Tanis landed in a heap in the middle
of the floor of a small rectangular, unassuming room with
bleached walls. Although mere seconds had passed since
they leaped off the precipice, time had seemed to stop and
stretch during their fall. All three found themselves breath-
less, dazed, and disoriented. Flint was the first of the companions to stumble to his feet, followed by the half-elf and
the young mage.

No windows or vents broke the smooth stone walls and
ceiling of the room where they found themselves. The only
entrance appeared to be a thick oaken door. Stunned by the
experience of traveling through the portal, Tanis crawled
over and pressed his ear against the door but could hear

nothing.

In the center of the room stood its single item of interest, a huge, gilded, oval piece of glass, shiny and suggestive of a mirror but not a mirror. The oval sat on a wooden base propped up at a sharp angle. At its widest point, the oval's reflective surface curved into a wide indentation, broken in the middle by a needle-thin slit.

Wearing the black gem the Ogress had given him, Raistlin approached the oval, gripping the amulet tightly. He murmured an obscure incantation, followed by a simple command: "Close gate."

The surface moved almost imperceptibly, like the blink of an eye, and the needle-thin slash disappeared. Raistlin removed the amulet from around his neck, wrapped it in some cloth, and stuffed it in one of the folds of his cloak.

"Naturally I'm grateful that we didn't get smashed to bits on those rocks," said Flint, "but where are we?"

Raistlin, occupied with concealing the amulet, said nothing. By the door, Tanis had pulled himself to his feet and was giving the steel handle a fruitless tug.

"It's locked," said Tanis.

"I expected as much," said Raistlin.

"Sealed tight," Tanis continued, squatting to peer through the keyhole. "There's no draft. I can't see much other than a dark hallway and several other doors."

"Outside or inside?" asked Flint, coming over.

"What?" asked Tanis.

"Is the door locked from the outside or inside?"

"Why, it has to be locked from the outside, doesn't it?" Tanis asked, puzzled.

"Don't be too sure," Raistlin cautioned, coming over to inspect the door. He braced himself against the wall, shaking his head as if to clear it. Flint and Tanis exchanged looks. "It seems I am a little wobbly still," explained the young mage.

"It's locked from the inside," declared Flint authoritatively after giving the mechanism of the lock a once-over.

"How can it be locked from the inside? That doesn't make any sense."

But Flint was no longer paying any attention to Tanis. He had taken out one of his long, thin knives and a stitching needle and was poking inside the lock. The diminutive dwarf didn't have to bend over far in order to bring his eyes level with his work. Several minutes passed in silence while he fideled with his makeshift lockpick.

"Too bad Tasslehoff isn't with us," Tanis said. He smiled at the realization that he actually missed the kender. "He'd make short work of that lock."

Flint paused to glare at the half-elf. "That doorknob of a kender would take so long telling you about the time his Uncle Trapspringer was in a similar predicament that he'd totally forget what he was supposed to be doing." The dwarf turned back to his task.

Flint grunted with satisfaction as he heard the click that he was straining to hear. He gave the stitching needle an upward thrust. The door cracked open just a hairsbreadth. "Not to mention the fact that Tas is the reason we've portaled ourselves into this room in the first place!" Flint added righteously.

Raistlin stood up, recovered. "Careful," the young mage warned before sliding open the door and slipping out.

Tanis followed quickly.

"Wait for me!!" cried Flint, hurrying to tuck away his tools and follow.

While the light in the locked room had been dim, the hallway plunged them into nearly total darkness. From one end of the hall, a square of light beckoned—a window. Raistlin rushed over to look out.

Tanis and Flint were right behind the young mage, crowding to gaze over his shoulder.

What they saw was a limitless blue-black sea of wild, choppy waters. The shore was irregular, with sandy beaches in some areas. In others, the water crashed against jagged rocks and awesome cliffs.

Their vantage point was the highest tower of a keep perched on top of a steep hill. A dusty road twisted out of sight. They couldn't help but notice that the road was lined with bodies and skeletons impaled on pikes. On the cracked, withered ground nearby grew mangy scrub bushes and a few gnarled trees.

Directly below the tower, a gatehouse with a spiked portcullis guarded one side of a bridge that spanned a deep gully. Tanis and the others saw that giant bears roamed the gully. Guards manned the gates. Not human guards either, Tanis observed.

Large and animal-like, ridged with hard muscles, the creatures had blunt noses, pointed ears, and beady red eyes. Long, matted hair draped their shoulders. They wore beast skins and fur capes and carried scimitars and spears.

Ogres.

One of the ogre guards turned idly and looked up in their direction.

Quickly they ducked down out of sight.

"The Oracle was right," Raistlin hissed to his companions in a low voice, although they were well out of the ogre guards' hearing. "That is the shore of the Blood Sea. We are inside Ogrebond, in a tower at the top of the keep. Somehow we must get out of here, but to do so means we must fight or evade a small army of ogres, their minions, and evil spirits."

"Great," muttered Flint.

"Let me lead," said Tanis quickly, rising and heading back down the hallway. He turned and gestured. "Let's find a way down."

"I'll go next," said Raistlin, following.

"Happy to go last," muttered Flint.

As Raistlin passed the room from which they had emerged, he took a moment to close the door firmly and try the handle. Satisfied, he waited a moment for his eyes to adjust, then moved on.

Ahead of them, narrow steps curved downward. Feeling the cold, musty wall with one hand as a guide—his other hand was on the hilt of his dagger, just in case—Tanis slowly started down the stairs. Raistlin placed his hand on Tanis's shoulder and followed. Flint did likewise with Raistlin.

They descended for several minutes until they reached a large landing from which led three corridors, each apparently leading to a number of rooms, or at least a series of doors. Vague noises and voices filtered up to the companions from farther below, but they didn't hear anything nearby. Daylight lit the corridors, which seemed, for the moment, uninhabited.

Flint pushed a door open cautiously, revealing a large room barren of decor. The room held a plain bed, a table, a chest, and a cabinet. The bed showed signs of having been slept in recently—probably the night before—but the room was empty. Judging by the silence that reigned, so were the other rooms.

"My guess," said Raistlin, leading them back out into the corridor, "is that these are visitors' quarters. I estimate it to be late afternoon. If there are any visitors, they are busy elsewhere, and we are safe until they return."

"Great," huffed Flint. "All we have to do is wait for nightfall and then pick an ogre to share our bed with."

"Or fight our way out," said Tanis rashly.

At that moment, all three heard a scuffling sound at the far end of the hall. Before any of them could react, they saw a figure emerge from one of the rooms and set something down. Crowding back against each other, the three companions dashed back into the empty guest room.

"Shh!" Tanis said to Flint as they stumbled over one another. Raistlin pulled the door closed behind them.

"What now?" whispered Flint.

Raistlin edged over to the window, taking care not to be spotted. To the west, he saw a broken land dotted with withering grass and dying flora. Far in the distance rose steep hills covered with dark forests.

The keep clung to the side of a jagged, rocky incline.

Ogre guards patrolled along the inner and outer walls below.

"That person down the hall was just a cleaning woman," said Tanis to Flint ruefully, rubbing his foot, which Flint had inadvertently stepped on in the rush.

"How do you know?" snapped Flint. He sat down on the bed.

Tas pointed to his eyes and, with the glimmer of a smile, said, "Elfvision."

Flint let loose a string of oaths.

Before he was through, the door swung open. A small, bulky figure loomed on the threshold, backlit by bright daylight. Instantly Tanis lunged toward the figure, only to be struck hard in the chin by a mop handle. Flint, a step behind the half-elf, wrapped his arms around the head of the intruder. He was bitten on the hand and hurled backward. Raistlin moved away from the window, stepping into the middle of the room.

The newcomer swept into the room, waving a mop and glaring at them.

Both Tanis and Flint retreated a couple more steps. Flint sank back down on the bed. Suddenly struck by the absurdity of the situation, Raistlin chuckled. Indeed the intruder was a cleaning woman—one with thickly corded muscles, a snout like a pig, and long, straggly brown hair. Yet her voice was sharp and intelligent.

"Now tell me who you be and what you're doing here and be quick about it. If your story isn't convincing, you'll be decorating an ogre spear by morning!"

Tanis fingered his sword. Flint rubbed his hand. Both were taken aback at being confronted by a half-ogre, a female of a mixed race that neither of them, in all their long travels, had ever seen. Unquestionably fierce-looking, the woman nonetheless had a merry light in her eyes. Although ugly and bestial by civilized standards, she was dressed neatly in a leather smock and appeared to be reasonably well groomed.

When Tanis shifted his glance over his shoulder at Raistlin, the female half-ogre got a better look at Flint. She squealed with joy and pushed past the astonished half-elf.

The half-ogre thrust her face into Flint's. He leaned away from her, startled and, if truth be told, a little scared. Her breath blew over him like a hot wind. "Garsh! A dwarf! I ain't never seen one—alive, I mean! 'Course, I see all kinds of dwarf skeletons and bones, but it ain't the same as seeing a live one."

The female half-ogre reached out her stubby hands and touched the dwarf's long, full beard. "Garsh, what a pretty beard!"

Flint scowled. His eyes rolled pleadingly toward Tanis and Raistlin.

The half-ogre spun around and faced the other two companions, putting a thick finger to her fleshy lips. "It wouldn't do to let the chief know. He'd kill the dwarf right off and then make me clean this room ten, twenty times to get rid of the stench"—she nodded politely to Flint—"pardon my saying so. And then he'd eat his heart for breakfast."

She thought for a moment. "He'd probably give his innards to the others, but the heart would be his, f'sure. The head, of course, would sit in a position of importance on a spear." She shook her head and made a clucking sound.

Flint blanched.

"Such a pretty dwarf," she peered at him again, batting her eyes. "I don't know but that I have a hankering for 'im." Her face darkened, and she looked conspiratorially at Tanis and Raistlin. "But we must make sure he isn't spotted, or it's death f'sure."

Flint opened his mouth, but Raistlin stepped forward and put his arm around the cleaning woman's shoulders. "Then can you help him ... us ... escape from Ogrebond?"

The female half-ogre's eyes narrowed. "I suppose I could ... and I suppose I would. I don't like these ogres very much, you know. I've been their slave ever since they kilt my father, a poor farmer, and spared me only so's I could clean for them. And let me tell you, for such a loutish lot, these ogres are surprisingly picky about cleaning.

"I'm not one of them, of course. I'm only a half-ogre. My name is Kirsig. What're yours?"

Raistlin made introductions all around, although Kirsig seemed most interested in Flint. "Flint Fireforge," she mused, her eyes shining.

For one of the few times in his life, Flint felt helpless. He looked to Tanis for aid, but the half-elf only shrugged.

"And could you help us arrange to hire a boat to take us across the Blood Sea?" asked Raistlin.

Kirsig clapped her knobby hands girlishly. "The Blood Sea! Garsh, you are a daring band, I can see that! Why d'you want to cross the Blood Sea? It's a terribly risky voyage. You have to skirt the Maelstrom and know your seamanship. Your captain must be bold and skilled, and he'll be sure to demand a pretty purse."

"We'll pay as much as we can," answered Tanis warily, "Do you know such a captain?"

"If he can be found," replied Kirsig coyly, her face dark with secrecy, "but"—she paused—"I cannot leave the keep until after midnight, when my duties are done. You can stay here, but you'll have to be careful. The chief, his band, the legion that guards the keep … any of them might appear outside this door. They get confused easy, y'know," she said, winking conspiratorially, "and sometimes wander about the keep, looking for their weapons or shoes.

"Tonight the chief's entertaining a tribal delegation from the Vale of Vipers. They'll be staying just above you, on the top floor. You dare not make a move until everyone inside the keep is asleep. If you escape"—she corrected herself—"*when* you escape, you'll have to lie in hiding until I can locate the captain and make the arrangements."

"Are you certain … ?" asked Raistlin tentatively.

Kirsig laughed lustily. "Oh, don't worry. He's a capable one, more than capable."

"How—how will we escape?" stammered Flint. He was reluctant to draw attention to himself, yet the question loomed in his mind. Kirsig turned to regard him solicitously. As Flint stared, she reached out a hand and touched his beard, stroking it.

"Escape, yes!" she said excitedly. "That is the problem, and we shall solve it. We'll teach those dumb ogres a lesson." She lowered her voice, motioning Raistlin and Tanis to draw closer. "But there's only two ways out of Ogrebond. One is if you're dead—that's the sure way—and the other—" She hesitated.

She blabbers more than Tasslehoff, thought Flint.

"Yes?" prompted Tanis.

"The other," Kirsig whispered, "is worse."

* * * * *

They had to confer quickly, for time was wasting and Kirsig would be missed if she stayed away from her housekeeping chores too long.

Raistlin told Kirsig about their quest. The young mage explained about his brother, Sturm, and Tasslehoff being missing, and even the portal they had used to get here. Kirsig's eyes bulged at the mention of the minotaur isles. She had never been across the Blood Sea, which she knew all about from folk tales, and indeed had never been anywhere except the Ogrelands. But recently, she told Raistlin, some bull-men had visited Ogrebond and parleyed with the chief.

"What about?" Raistlin wanted to know, keenly interested.

"How should I know?" Kirsig said. "I'm not custodian of the secrets around here. All I can tell you is that those minotaurs smell terrible and leave their quarters in disgusting condition. Filthy cows!" She spat. The spittle landed near Tanis's feet. The half-elf took a diplomatic step backward.

According to Kirsig, the only way out of Ogrebond, without fighting your way through the front gate, was through the sewage channel. If they were lucky, said Kirsig, their visit and escape would remain a secret. Nobody would even suspect that outsiders had been in the keep.

Tanis made a face at the thought of the sewage channel.

"Go on," urged Raistlin, sensing that Kirsig had more to say.

"I pour all the slops and dregs down there, and worse— if you know what I mean. I know where the tunnel comes out, down near the bay, a place where the guards can't see you. The only thing is—" Again she hesitated.

"What?" demanded Tanis.

"The sewer is haunted with the spirits of the dead. Ghosts and ghoulies. Everybody says so. It will be dangerous to pass through. You could die."

"We'll take that chance," Raistlin said quickly.

"Then stay in this room and keep quiet," Kirsig said, giving each of them, in turn, a stern look. "I'll be back after the stroke of midnight. By then most of 'em inside the keep are drunk on grog or in dreamland. You'll be safe here, but don't stick your noses out of this room."

She took a last, fond look at Flint, letting her fingers slip slowly and reluctantly away from his gray-flecked beard. His eyes remained frozen. "Such a pretty dwarf," Kirsig said before picking up her bucket and mop. She opened the door a crack, peered outside, then slipped through it without another word.

After the door closed behind her, Tanis waited several moments before whispering to Raistlin. "Do you think we can trust her?"

The young mage slumped on a chair. He nodded.

Tanis seemed satisfied.

"But—" began Flint feebly.

His two companions cast him an amused glance. "Surely she wouldn't betray her special new friend," Tanis said.

Flint scowled, flushed beet red, and fell silent.

* * * * *

At dusk, the three companions heard loud noises from the lower floors, harsh voices raised in laughter and shouting, a volley of oaths building to a tumult, then joined in an ogre chorus:

> "Steel peg, ice pick, fire thong, ho!
> Sliver the heart of friend or foe!
> Blood in the eye—yo!
> Ogres one and all!"

Such carrying-ons continued until long after the moons rose, causing Tanis to worry that the revelry might last through the night.

Finally heavy-footed clomping echoed in the hallways, followed by the sounds of shoving and arguing, armor and heavy garb dropping to the floor; and then, at last, relative stillness, punctuated by guttural snoring. From the room's lone window, Tanis saw the battlement guards change shift.

At last the trio heard a quiet shuffling. The door slid open, and there stood Kirsig.

"Follow me!" the female half-ogre grunted, beckoning.

Keeping to the shadows, they followed her down the stairs, hearing the groans and breathing of sleeping ogres on all sides as they descended three flights. Through half-open doorways, they could see feet propped up on bedposts and an occasional glint of metal hanging from wall hooks. But no one challenged them. Just in case, Flint and Tanis held onto their weapons tightly.

On the main floor, the three companions had to pass through a huge, high-ceilinged room where the remains of the evening's banquet—goblets and animal bones and the like—lay where they had spilled on the huge oaken table and tiled floor. The walls were hung with vivid tapestries of gory battles. The fire had nearly sputtered out. Only embers remained.

A throne set on a dais reigned over one end of the table, and on the throne lay a gigantic, muscular, yellow-brown ogre, his feet stretched across one armrest, thoroughly drunk and asleep. His mottled skin was covered with bumps and bruises. He was snoring with his snout open. A thick band of silver, decorated with green jewels, stretched tightly around his forehead, the only conspicuous sign of his stature.

"Arrast, the chief," whispered Kirsig, pointing. "Don't worry. He drank so much grog, he'll be in a stupor till morning."

As if he heard himself being discussed, Arrast stirred slightly and turned over on his side, his face set against the back of the throne. He lifted his head momentarily, gave a coarse bellow, then resumed his snoring.

Not entirely reassured, remembering what Kirsig had said earlier, Flint hurried past the sleeping chief of Ogre-bond.

At the far end of the huge room, a square grating covered a deep, dark pit sunk into the floor. Although Flint peered down it, he could see nothing. Slithering and scratching sounds drifted up from far below. The fetid stench that wafted upward was enough to make the dwarf momentarily lose his balance.

"Games pit," said Kirsig, grabbing him by the elbow.

"Black willows," said Raistlin grimly.

Tanis nodded.

"Yes," agreed Flint, although he didn't have the slightest idea what "black willows" were, and as he hurried past the dark pit, he told himself he had no desire to find out.

Through a small archway and down narrow stone stairs to a lower level they descended. This was the dungeon, a fact made plain by the damp, rotting odor, the debris of bones and broken weaponry, and the piles of straw discolored by streaks of dried blood. The walls held flickering sconces that offered only dim light.

Kirsig pointed ahead. Tanis and Raistlin followed Kirsig closely, with Flint straggling behind. They entered a large musty room. Two dark corridors lined with cells branched off to the right and left. Even at this hour, faint moans and cries emitted from the recesses, the sleep of the occupants disturbed by who knows what manner of nightmares.

"I wish we could do something to help them, poor devils," Tanis whispered to Raistlin.

"First we must rescue ourselves," Raistlin replied.

"There!" pointed Kirsig, indicating a large vent in the far corner of the floor of the room.

They hurried over to it. Although Tanis and Flint easily loosened the grate covering the vent, they had difficulty lifting it aside. Kirsig and even Raistlin bent to help. At last its weight shifted, and they were able to slide it away.

When Kirsig straightened up, she found herself eye to eye with a hulking, dull-orange ogre guard. Opening its mouth, the creature barked something at them in a language that none of the three companions from Solace understood.

They only understood the word "Kirsig" and made a guess at the rest of the obviously hostile message.

Tanis lunged at the creature, swinging his sword, but the ogre guard was twice his height and, despite appearances, no slow-witted oaf. The ogre guard swung his arm up in the air and batted the sword away, knocking Tanis against a wall, stunning the half-elf. With his knife, Flint made a game stab at the guard, but the ogre's reach was long, and worse, he held a thick, spiked club. The ogre brought his club up in an arc, then down, aiming at Flint's head. The dwarf dodged aside, but the club caught him on the shoulder, smacking him to the ground.

Raistlin took a step backward, his face masklike. He began to chant in a low voice, anxiously feeling in one of his pouches for the components he needed to throw a spell.

The ogre noticed the young mage and advanced cautiously. His yellow eyes gleamed, and a spotted tongue darted in and out between jutting, blackened teeth. With taloned hands, he reached out for Raistlin.

Suddenly the ogre's eyes went slack, and he crashed

forward. Raistlin had all he could do to jump out of the way or be crushed. From the ogre's back protruded a long, thin dagger, trickling black blood.

Raistlin stared. Flint and Tanis got up groggily and gazed at the unpredictable Kirsig.

"I keeps one handy," said the female half-ogre, proud but shy. She put her foot on the ogre's back and pulled out the dagger, wiped it clean, and stuck it back inside her leather skirt. "You would, too, if you worked at Ogrebond and had to mingle with ogres!"

Tanis congratulated her on her bravery.

It was hard to tell in the dim light, but Kirsig appeared to blush. "No time for that," she said briskly. "Down we go!"

One by one, the three companions lowered themselves down the vent. Using the fallen ogre's spear as a lever, Kirsig managed to replace the grating.

"Good luck!" Kirsig called after them.

Left alone, she dragged the body of the ogre guard over to a corner and hurriedly piled straw on top of it, concealing it as best she could.

* * * * *

The foul liquid they found themselves in shone in the dark with iridescent silver and purple streaks. Bubbling foam, spongy globules, and floating chunks of things that stank of disease and death eddied around them. Scavenger fish darted at the garbage, their scaly sides brushing against the companions' churning legs. A giant snake lay belly up in the sewage, part of its awesome length submerged, two man-sized bulges in the portion of its white, swollen stomach that bobbed on the surface.

Weird, faraway cries rent the dark tunnel. Ancient corpses had beached on outcroppings along the walls, their dusty bones giving off a kind of eerie light. The companions could hear but not see the rats skittering along the thin, narrow ledge that ran along the tunnel sides.

Tanis kept a firm grip on Raistlin's wrist. "Are you all right?" the half-elf asked both his friends.

Flint bobbed along on the other side of Raistlin. The sewage channel was only about six feet wide. Their feet could almost touch the irregular, debris-strewn bottom, but not quite, and Flint had to kick himself upward at intervals to keep his chin above the slimy water.

"I'm fine. Don't worry about me," said Raistlin tersely.

Flint grunted his reply. He was fine, too, if you call half drowning in a grimy, disgusting, ogre sewer tunnel fine.

The stream of garbage flowed around them, tugging them in an easterly direction which, as Kirsig had said, was toward the shore of the Blood Sea. The current pulled at them with surprising strength. They had all they could do to hold on to one another and stay afloat.

"Hang on," warned Tanis, tightening his grip on Raistlin. "The channel must run down a slope. We're going to be picking up speed."

Flint had one hand clamped on Raistlin's shoulder as the three of them began to be carried along with the current at a faster and faster pace. Nausea as much as terror gripped the companions. They whirled along, past all manner of garbage and dead things wedged in crevices or stuck on outthrust stones.

The cries they had heard earlier now picked up in intensity and became almost deafening. The tunnel angled and took a downward dip, so that Tanis, Flint, and Raistlin were pitched forward. The current accelerated still more, and they were tossed this way and that, struggling for control.

Floating bodies—some ogres, some too sodden to tell— bumped up against them in the horrible flow.

The fearsome cries rose to a din as the tunnel took a sharp curve. The current tossed Flint into a stone wall. The dwarf cried out in pain, clutching at his leg. Raistlin managed to stretch out and grab him by the collar.

Whirling downward, the trio spun by a horribly disfigured creature clinging to the ledge. It might have been human once. Now it was one of the undead. A long tongue flicked out at them, running over teeth that were sharp and supernaturally elongated. The nails on its hands had become razor-sharp claws. It clung to the ledge with one mottled, dessicated limb, and with the other leaned toward them, making a gesture with its clawed fist that was at once threatening and pathetic.

Tanis raised an arm, managing to ward off the creature, pushing aside the outstretched arm of the undead thing. It opened its unclean maw and screamed futile gibberish at the three companions as they shot past it, eluding its grasp.

Choking on the stench and the sludge, they were borne by the torrent, hurtling down the dark, fetid tunnel as if riding a water chute. Finally, after what seemed an eternity, Tanis, Flint, and Raistlin shot out into startlingly bright moonlight that illuminated a shallow cove lined with rocks and filthy debris.

Tanis helped Raistlin to his feet. With their arms around one another, they staggered along the shore of the cove to a sheltered area away from the sewage outlet. Flint was nowhere to be seen. After several minutes, Tanis began to wonder what had happened to Flint. He picked his way back and found the grizzled dwarf sitting on a rock, drenched, splattered with muck, furious, and in pain.

"What is it?" asked Tanis wearily.

"My leg," gasped Flint. "I can't put any weight on it. I think it's broken."

Tanis hurried to examine him. Sure enough, there was a fracture in the right limb, which had already swelled and was turning purple.

With Flint complaining all the way, Tanis flung the dwarf across his shoulders and carried him from the cove, setting him down gently next to Raistlin.

Although the young mage was plainly worn out, his face covered with grime and small cuts, he found a broken tree limb nearby, tore strips from his robe, and did the best he could to approximate a tight splint on Flint's leg.

"Just my luck," said Flint sulkily, wincing as Raistlin wound the bandaging.

"We should have left you to the lacedon," said the young mage with uncharacteristic wry humor.

"The what?" asked the dwarf.

"The ghoul back there," said Tanis. He was lying on the sand, covered with slime and dirt, but he was too exhausted to care. "Kirsig was right about there being undead creatures in the tunnel."

"Of course, they'd like you better if you were dead. They feed on corpses, you know," said Raistlin dryly, finishing with the splint. Unceremoniously he curled up against a rock and within minutes was asleep.

Flint grumbled something unintelligible.

Their little cove was sheltered by a horn of rocks. Beyond that, the dark and forbidding Blood Sea stretched to the horizon. Light from the two moons, Lunitari and Solinari, speckled the black water with silver. They could hear nothing but the crash of surf and the lapping of waves.

For hours, Tanis and Flint waited for Kirsig, shivering. At one point, thinking Flint hadn't said anything in a long while, Tanis looked over and realized that the bone-weary dwarf had fallen asleep as well, sitting up against a rock with his broken leg stretched out in front of him. With a sigh, Tanis settled in for the night watch.

* * * * *

It was an hour or so before dawn when Tanis caught sight of a small craft wending its way across the cove. Kirsig was sitting on one of the forward seats, but someone else was pulling the oars. Tanis roused Flint and Raistlin.

As the boat pulled up next to them, Kirsig jumped out, followed by the other occupant of the boat, a tall, well-proportioned black-skinned man with a gleaming bald pate. He was bare-chested, wearing only a thick breechcloth and high-strapped sandals. A fine bone necklace curved around his muscular neck, and a small jeweled knife hung from a loop on his waist.

"I'm sorry I took so long," explained Kirsig hurriedly. "I had to go to town and hunt up Nugetre. Then I had to pack my things. ..." Suddenly she stopped and stared, wide-eyed. "Garsh, what happened to the pretty dwarf!"

She rushed over to Flint, who remained sitting against the rock, and knelt down to examine his leg solicitously. The dwarf scowled.

The one called Nugetre was standing with his hands on his hips, staring at Tanis and Raistlin, grinning as he sized them up.

"Kirsig ..." began Tanis.

"What do you mean, you had to pack your things?" Raistlin asked Kirsig pointedly.

The female half-ogre turned to Raistlin. "Well," she huffed, "I had to kill one of the ogre guards. I couldn't very well stay there, could I? So I'm coming with you!"

"But—but—" stammered Raistlin.

"A woman on such a voyage?" Tanis said.

"If you ask me—" began Flint.

Nugetre silenced them all with an outburst of loud, lusty laughter.

After a long pause, Tanis asked Kirsig, "What does he find so funny?"

"What I find funny, half-elf," said Nugetre, eyeing the three of them scornfully, "is that more than half of my crew are female. And they meet the standards I set just as well as the men do."

"I've known Nugetre for years," said Kirsig hastily. "He used to buy food from my father to take on his crossings. He's one of the best seamen around and is willing to take us across the Blood Sea."

"For a fee," reminded Nugetre, wagging a finger at the female half-ogre.

"Besides," added Kirsig enthusiastically, "you're going to need some help with this dwarf ... medical help, I mean.

I've picked up a few tricks over the years. They won't cure the plague, but they should lessen the pain and speed the healing of that broken leg."

Flint looked helplessly at Tanis and Raistlin. Tanis and Raistlin looked at each other.

"Okay," Tanis said resignedly.

Kirsig and the three companions all squeezed into the boat, and the muscular Nugetre began to row with an easy rhythm. Within minutes, they were out of the cove and hundreds of yards from shore. They could barely glimpse the shadowy shape of Ogrebond atop the steep, rocky hill.

A pale rosy light had begun to show in the sky as they reached Nugetre's ship.

Chapter 8
The Broken Man

Something grabbed at Sturm. Weakly the Solamnic looked up, his vision blurry. He felt himself being lifted.

The next thing he knew, as if experiencing it through a haze, Sturm was lying in the bottom of a small wooden boat alongside Caramon. His friend's clothes hung on him in tatters; encrusted sores and bruises covered his body. What skin remained intact had been baked a deep bronze-red by the sun. Sturm stared at the young warrior, whose eyes remained closed. With relief, the young knight noted that his companion breathed steadily. Then Sturm, too, passed out.

A gnarled old fisherman named Lazaril had scooped them out of the sea, cut their bonds, and dumped them into his boat.

Now the fisherman, bent and wiry, regarded them, his hand on his chin, thinking. Lazaril had been hoping to catch a stringer of eels this morning to sell later in the day at the open market in Atossa, a city on the north coast of Mithas. But if he worked it right, these two humans would fetch more than a dozen stringers of eels.

They looked terrible, though—possibly near death. He ought to clean them up as best he could. He took off his leather vest and put it on the smaller one, whose shirt had been torn off. And he made an effort to wash their faces and rinse their wounds. They had a good many of them, but Lazaril could fix them up. They were in no condition to resist. Perhaps their ship had sunk or been raided by pirates. That was unlucky for them, but a lucky break for Lazaril.

The two companions woke up briefly, choking when Lazaril poured some spring water down their gullets, then force-fed them some dried fish. The larger one, the first one he had fished out of the sea, looked up at him with questioning eyes, swallowing hungrily but dazedly before once again losing consciousness. The other one seemed in worse shape. Lazaril couldn't get more than a few bites down his throat.

Working quickly, the fisherman did some hurried, makeshift mending of their clothes and daubed their skin with a folk balm to soothe the blistering. A little touch here, a little remedy there, and the two half-drowned humans looked almost normal. Well, not quite, but almost.

"You're missing your true calling, Lazaril," the old fisherman said to himself admiringly, chuckling. "You should have been a practitioner of the healing arts."

The fisherman grabbed the oars and pulled strongly, making headway against the slight wind, and within an hour, the boat came into view of the small harbor of Atossa.

Neither of the two companions had regained consciousness. That would be too much to expect. As they approached the harbor Lazaril pulled a tarpaulin over the two unconscious figures so that none of his competitors

would spot his unusual cargo. On the main pier, the old
fisherman spotted a ragamuffin and gave the boy a copper
to run and find the minotaur who served as harbormaster.

The small harbor bustled with trade and activity. Human
pirates and mercenary brigands rubbed shoulders with the
hulking beast-men who ruled the island. Pitiful slaves—
mostly human, but a smattering of other races as well—
shouldered cargo, watched over by minotaurs who strode
the docks imperiously and, when the slightest occasion
warranted, wielded their whips viciously.

A strapping minotaur with fierce eyes and jutting horns
came marching up the boardwalk, the ragamuffin behind
him hurrying to keep up. Lazaril gave the boy his copper
and shooed him away officiously. The minotaur folded his
arms and waited, a stern, impatient look on his bestial visage. Lazaril gave him a sly, toothy grin.

Lazaril knew this one by sight, although until now he
had always been anxious to give the harbormaster of
Atossa wide berth. This was Vigila, appointed by the king
himself. All fishermen, and any other harbor regulars,
knew him for his brutality and iron command of the small
harbor. It was he who dispensed justice on the docks, collected the king's tithe—keeping a portion for himself—and
maintained the necessary quota of slaves. It was with him
that Lazaril must bargain.

With a modest flourish, the fisherman pulled aside the
tarpaulin, revealing the two humans. He looked up at Vigila expectantly.

"What?" asked Vigila, sneering. "You have caught a
couple of human carp, old fisherman. Of what interest are
they to me?"

Lazaril swallowed and forced a toothy grin. "Your excellency," he began, not sure how to address the harbormaster,
"their wounds are quite superficial. I believe these are very
strong humans who, if they were brought back to health,
would make excellent slaves. They are weak now, but they
just need food and water to regain their strength. Then they

could be worked hard—worked hard until their deaths. That would be of some interest to you, would it not?"

Vigila snorted savagely, his eyes seeming to bore through Lazaril. "Throw them back in the water, old fisherman. Stick to your usual catch. Hook something that you can at least put on your plate for supper." The low rumble that came from his throat might have been a chuckle.

Lazaril summoned his courage, and again came the sly smile. "I believe this one"—the fisherman patted Caramon's shoulder—"could be trained for the games. He could be a gladiator; he has the girth of one. Although I will gladly sell him to you at a special price for a gladiator. Think of how pleased the king would be if you gave him a gladiator who had been plucked from the sea. It would be another distinguishing mark in your career."

Vigila looked thoughtful. The idea clearly appealed to the harbormaster, Lazaril saw.

"Humans never last long in the games," the minotaur said contemptuously.

"But," pursued the fisherman, silently congratulating himself on his tact and bargaining prowess, "they are very entertaining to watch, even when they lose."

Caramon and Sturm stirred slightly, then lifted their heads. Each wondered, not for the first time in recent days, where he was. After days adrift in a savage sea, neither could make sense of the scene before him.

An old fisherman with carrot-colored hair was standing bowlegged in his boat, talking in a low voice to a huge minotaur, who towered over him. The minotaur wore a leather skirt and a variety of straps and belts. He carried a huge, rough-hewn stick. A figure of some authority as he stood on the pier, the bull-man appeared to be haggling with the fisherman.

But their brains were so clouded and the discussion between the fisherman and the huge minotaur so seemingly muted and far away that Caramon and Sturm couldn't make out the words.

The harbormaster glanced over at the two companions, saw their heads lifted pitifully toward him, and saw them slump over again. The old fisherman nodded and beamed encouragingly.

"Here, old fisherman," grumbled Vigila, reaching into one of his pockets and throwing Lazaril a handful of coins. "I will take this human wreckage off your hands. Maybe I can freshen them up. Maybe not." The harbormaster turned and signaled for a cart.

Another minotaur, far down the pier, cracked a whip. Two human slaves began pulling a large wooden-wheeled cart toward the harbormaster.

Lazaril scrambled to scoop up the coins, some of which, the old fisherman was dismayed to notice, had fallen into the scummy harbor water and sunk down out of reach, out of sight.

While Lazaril scurried, Vigila flexed his muscles, leaned over, and picked up Caramon and Sturm, one powerful limb gripping each of them around the chest. Too weak and confused to struggle, Caramon and Sturm felt themselves fly through the air as Vigila lifted them up and tossed them into the cart. They landed, sprawled over each other.

A whip cracked, the human slaves reversed position, and the cart moved away down the pier.

"Hey! These are all coppers!" complained Lazaril as the old fisherman counted the coins he had picked up and realized he had been cheated. "That's the slave price, not the gladiator price!"

The old fisherman took a step up the ladder toward the pier. That was his second mistake. His first had been raising his voice in anger.

Vigila turned back to him, his eyes bulging with fury.

Lazaril froze. "But this is not the gladiator price," the old fisherman whined softly. He wanted to retreat to his boat. He wanted to go back out in the middle of the ocean and catch his daily string of eel. But his foot dangled uselessly in the air as he missed the rung of the ladder.

Vigila lowered his head and charged at the fisherman, impaling the old man on his sharp horns. Lifting his head up into the air, the harbormaster bellowed angrily and then spun around several times before he finally lowered his head once again and flicked the body off so that it sailed far out over the water.

Lazaril twitched and thrashed as he flew through the air, then landed heavily in the water and lay still. Gulls dove to peck at the old fisherman's body.

The ragamuffin messenger, who had taken refuge behind a barrel, crawled forward to pick up a few of the coppers the fisherman had dropped. He didn't give Lazaril's corpse a second glance. Such outbursts of violence were not at all uncommon in the harbor of Atossa, and were to be expected from Vigila. Those who noticed at all paused only briefly, then resumed their buying and selling, their arguing and fighting, as if nothing had happened. Nobody stared.

It would not have been wise to stare.

* * * * *

At the same time that Tasslehoff Burrfoot was being tortured in his cell in the minotaur capital of Lacynos, Sturm Brightblade and Caramon Majere were being locked up in a dungeon not thirty miles away, in the smaller enclave of Atossa.

Relieved to be rescued from certain doom in the Blood Sea, Sturm and Caramon didn't put up any fight. In truth, they had no energy and little will to do so.

Tossed into a filthy cell, one of dozens in an underground prison in Atossa, the two companions crumpled to the stone floor. They slept all the rest of the day and ensuing night, and when they awakened, they ate ravenously. Minotaur guards dished out bowls of meat and water from huge buckets they carried from cell to cell. Despite the unappetizing color and aroma of the meat, Caramon and Sturm did not complain. Never had either of them been so hungry.

By the second night, they were able to sit up and talk to each other. Although their clothes hung in shreds on their grimy bodies, which bore numerous marks of their ordeal, Sturm and Caramon were able to call on large reserves of youth and strength. They were rebounding miraculously.

"From what I have been able to overhear, and from the obvious nature of our captors, I believe we are on the island of Mithas," Sturm told Caramon as the two conversed in low voices late that night. "Somehow we were transported on the *Venora* thousands of miles from the Straits of Schallsea to the far fringe of the Blood Sea. Whoever accomplished that incredible feat took Tasslehoff prisoner for some reason and tossed us overboard, left for dead." Sturm paused, thinking back to their days floating in the torpid, turbulent Blood Sea. "Whatever our fate here, we are fortunate to be alive. The Blood Sea does not relinquish many castaways."

"And what do you think," asked Caramon slowly, "about the fate of Tas?"

Sturm shook his head sadly.

On their third morning in the cell, two brutish minotaurs came to stare at them. One of them wore official-looking insignia and listened as the other talked in a low growl, pointing back and forth between Caramon and Sturm.

"See how quickly they recover from their wounds. They are very powerful fighters. If we permit them time to mend and build their strength, they will entertain us in the games. If they don't work out as gladiators, we can always throw them into the slave pits."

Caramon stared at them indifferently. He felt weak and beaten and couldn't make much sense of what they were saying anyway. What did it matter which he was destined to be, a minotaur slave or a doomed gladiator, here, thousands of miles from Solace?

Sturm rose and thrust his face between the bars, glaring at the two minotaurs. "I would gladly fight either of you right now," said the young Solamnic angrily, "if you would let me out of here but for a moment! I will never be a slave, and as for your gladiator games—pah!" He spat in their direction.

In an eyeblink, the minotaur with the insignia back-handed him, catching Sturm across the face before the Solamnic was able to pull it safely behind the bars. He was knocked backward, his lip bleeding. Sturm continued to glare at the ugly horned creature.

"That one is quite foolish," rumbled the important minotaur, "but we shall cure him of his foolishness." With a huge, hairy hand he rubbed his chin, looking at the two companions. "Feed them well for a few weeks, and then we shall see how strong they are.

"Let that one"—the minotaur pointed to Caramon—"help with the feeding and emptying the slops. It is reward," he said with a smirk, "for holding his tongue. Unlike his friend, he shall have the opportunity to stretch and build his muscles, and when it comes time to fight for his life, perhaps he will live a little longer."

* * * * *

The next morning the companions were awakened rudely by the minotaur guards. One held a sword at Sturm's throat, while the other beckoned Caramon outside the cell. The guard handed Caramon two huge buckets of meat and water and instructed him to deliver a portion to each of the prisoners in the cells that lined the dark, dank corridors heading off in four directions—north, south, east and west.

Faltering under the weight of the buckets, the warrior realized how much he had been weakened by his experience at sea. The minotaur guards laughed at Caramon as he struggled to lift the buckets, then stumbled off along his designated route. One of the minotaur guards returned to his post, while the other trailed behind Caramon, brandishing a sword to make sure the ridiculous human did as he was instructed.

For three hours thereafter, Caramon walked the corridors of the prison, ladling rations into troughs outside the prisoners' cells. From inside, the prisoners could stretch out their hands and cradle the food and water to their mouths.

The prisoners were minotaur as well as human, the twin was surprised to discover. Despite their humiliation at being prisoners, the minotaur captives stared at Caramon with bitter contempt. Though he brought them the food and water they desperately craved, Caramon knew they regarded humans as an inferior race.

Most of the prisoners were renegades, pirates, or worse. Some were too tired or sick or wounded to even respond when Caramon dished out their food. In at least one instance, Caramon felt certain that the prisoner, crumpled forlornly in a corner and covered with crawling insects, was long dead. He told the minotaur guard, who was always nearby, watching him. The guard expressed indifference but took a closer look and made a notation in a leather-hided book that hung at his side.

At the far end of one of the dim corridors was an isolated cell, several hundred feet from its nearest neighbor. This was the strangest case of all. An abject figure was strapped to the inside wall, held erect, unable to sit or lie down. His body seemed broken. His head drooped. He had to muster all of his strength in order to look up as Caramon came tottering along with the buckets of meat and water.

Caramon could see very little inside the dimly lit cell, but he could make out that the man's head was oval-shaped, his eyes tiny black holes. Pus and blood oozed from his shoulders and back, as if some vital appendage had been torn from his body. He didn't look as though he could even be alive, hanging there, yet, looking up at Caramon, he managed a curious, brave grin.

Caramon wondered how the broken man could get loose to eat his meat and drink his water. Putting the buckets down, the warrior hesitated.

"Go on," growled the minotaur guard, several feet behind Caramon. "We lets him eat a little now and then. Otherwise he can look at it and smell it as it goes rotten. It's all part of the accommodations here."

Caramon took his time measuring out the meat and spooning some water into the man's trough. As he suspected he would, the minotaur guard had turned away idly and walked a few paces down the corridor. He was no longer watching closely.

"Why are you chained?" whispered Caramon softly.

"So I do not kill myself," said the broken man. "I would prefer death to subjugation."

"Why are you here?".

"I am being interrogated," answered the man in a curiously amused tone.

"What did you do?"

"I am not one of them. That is enough."

Caramon turned.

"Wait!" whispered the man. "Are you one of the new humans?"

Caramon looked astonished. He glanced at the minotaur guard. The bull-man was paying no attention. His back was to them, and he was clanging his sword idly against the corridor walls.

Caramon leaned toward the broken man. "What do you mean?"

"Are you one of the humans plucked from the sea?"

"Yes," said Caramon wonderingly. "How could you know about that?"

"Shh. Not now. Another time."

The minotaur guard turned, bored with waiting. "Hey, you, don't dawdle! Hurry up!"

With a nod of his chin, the chained man waved him on. Reluctantly Caramon followed the minotaur. His shoulders and arms ached from carrying the heavy buckets.

* * * * *

Although they weren't watched closely, Caramon and Sturm chose to talk only at night, whispering in the dark. Caramon told Sturm about the strange man chained in his cell and how he seemed to know about the humans "plucked from the sea." Sturm thought about it, but he couldn't figure out how the prisoner could have known about them. He must be mistaking them for others, the young Solamnic surmised.

Wistfully they talked about Solace and their friends, Tanis, Flint, and Raistlin, Caramon's twin.

They wondered about Tasslehoff and why the minotaurs who had sailed up to the wreck of the *Venora* had wanted to keep the kender alive. Considering possible reasons, Sturm said that if Tas were indeed alive, he would make a very poor slave, and he wouldn't fare much better as a gladiator against minotaur opponents.

"Oh, I don't know about that," disagreed Caramon with a broad grin. "If they let Tas improvise with his hoopak, he'd stand a fighting chance."

They both had to chuckle at the thought of Tas brandishing his hoopak against one of the hulking bull-men.

Sturm realized that it was the first time either of them had smiled or laughed for over a week. "How long do you think it has been," he asked Caramon, "since we were betrayed by the captain of the *Venora*, and delivered to this part of the world?"

"I've lost track of time. I'd say ten to twelve days."

"That sounds about right," said Sturm dispiritedly. "Do you think Raistlin and the others are looking for us? Do you think we'll ever get out of here?"

Caramon looked over at his friend, surprised at the glum tone. In the darkness, he could see only an occasional reflection from Sturm's eyes. This time, it was the twin who was feeling optimistic. He reached out and touched the young Solamnic on the shoulder. "Trust in the gods," Caramon said.

"Yes," repeated Sturm. "Trust in the gods."

They slept as best they could on the stone floor, their backs against each other for warmth.

Four more days and nights passed with agonizing slowness. At times they heard other prisoners cry out. Other times they heard what sounded like dead bodies being dragged out.

Once the important minotaur with the insignia came back to gaze at them again. This time he was with a bony human slave dressed in rags and wearing thick sandals. The minotaur said nothing but simply stared, arms folded, appraising them. The look on his face was impassive. The human slave fawned and slavered at his feet, muttering incomprehensibly. The minotaur stroked his head like a dog. Finally the minotaur turned on his heels and left. The human slave loped after him.

This time Sturm held his tongue during the inspection, having decided to conserve his anger until he had a real chance to fight back.

Caramon was the fortunate one. Once a day he was let out of his cell and given the task of lugging the buckets of meat and water to the other prisoners. The exercise reinvigorated his muscles, and each day the buckets seemed lighter, the chore easier.

The routine was always the same: Two guards would let him out, then one of them would retreat to the guard post near the entrance of the dungeon, while the other would accompany Caramon on his rounds, hovering nearby.

There were at least a dozen armed minotaurs stationed at the guard post every hour of the day and night. Rushing them would be suicidal. There seemed little opportunity of escape.

On the second day of his new task, Caramon had seen the broken man again. It was obvious the man had been tortured during the night. His shoulders and back were bleeding profusely. He hung limply in his bonds, unconscious. Again Caramon whispered to him, but this time he got no response.

The minotaur guard yelled at the Majere twin to hurry up.

The broken man had been in little better condition the next day.

On the fourth day, the oval face had looked up and the mouth twitched but the words that came out were babble to Caramon's ears. The man spoke in a foreign tongue, not the common speech. And after speaking in a delirious rush, the man's head fell limp.

Caramon and Sturm talked about the broken man again that night. Most of the other captives were obviously scum who would be familiar types in any prison population. However, this one aroused Caramon's sympathy and curiosity. But the two companions could reach no conclusion as to who the broken man might be or how he might have known of their coming.

On the fifth day, the chained man was stronger, somehow revived. He seemed to be waiting for Caramon and motioned him to come closer. The twin looked over his shoulder at the minotaur guard, who waited far down the corridor, seated on the floor with his back to the wall. The minotaur was growing careless. After all, Caramon was unarmed and had no prayer of escape.

"It is being arranged," whispered the broken man, summoning all his strength.

"What?" asked Caramon, puzzled. He made a great show of slowly ladling out the meat and water in case the minotaur guard was watching. The warrior edged closer, so that his face protruded through the bars. "How do you know about me and Sturm? And what is being arranged?"

"I have spoken to my brothers. We can get you out."

Caramon's heart beat rapidly. "Why me? Why not you?"

"I am trapped," the broken man said pathetically. "My cage is never unlocked, except for interrogations and beatings—and occasional feedings." He nodded toward the trough. "But my people know about you and your friend. I was told of your coming. They will help you."

"Why me?" repeated Caramon.

"Because you are not a minotaur," the broken man said. "Because you were sent. But most importantly"—he managed a weak smile—"because it can be done."

Daring another glance over his shoulder, Caramon saw that the minotaur guard's chin had dropped down on his chest. He was nodding off. That gave Caramon precious extra moments. "How do you communicate with your people?" asked the twin. He had to be suspicious, yet admittedly he was drawn to this courageous prisoner.

Painfully the broken man brought a hand up as far as it would go against the straps holding him, pointing to his head. "Telepathy."

Caramon looked up. "Telepathy?" he repeated dubiously.

The broken man nodded. In spite of himself, Caramon wanted to believe him.

"What about my friend? What about Sturm?"

There was a long moment of silence. "You will have to leave him behind," the broken man said grimly.

"I can't do that!"

"You will have to leave him."

"When?"

"Tomorrow."

A scuffling behind him told Caramon that the guard had scrambled to his feet and was coming this way.

"Hey!" came the by now familiar growl. "What are you two talking about?"

Caramon grabbed the buckets and whirled around, coming face-to-face with the minotaur. The Majere twin caught a breath. "Just like all the others," he said with what he hoped was an edge of annoyance. "He's complaining about the food."

The minotaur guard looked at Caramon suspiciously, then raked the broken man with a glance. Satisfied, he gave Caramon a shove down the hall. The warrior stumbled, then regained his footing, and continued along the corridor without a backward glance. He could hear the minotaur guard shuffling after him.

"So he don't like the food, don't he?" the minotaur guard grunted. "Well, we only lets him eat as a reward, and something tells me he's gonna be all tied up today!"

* * * * *

Later that night, Sturm and Caramon talked over what had happened. Neither of them understood it, nor did either think it was possible to escape.

"Anyway," said Caramon stubbornly, "I wouldn't go without you."

"You have no choice," Sturm replied solemnly. "We have no choice. If one of us is free, the other has hope. I would go if it were me."

"Would you?" asked Caramon skeptically.

"Yes," lied Sturm.

Caramon thought long and hard. "If by some means I do escape, I vow to return and get you out."

Sturm clasped his friend's hand warmly.

* * * * *

The next day, as usual, the minotaur guards came to let Caramon out at mealtime. The Majere twin hoisted the two heavy buckets of meat and water and began his regular tour, traveling up and down the dank corridors of the prison cell block. He was careful to follow his customary routine so that the minotaur guard, who watched over him halfheartedly from a dozen yards behind, wouldn't grow suspicious. Caramon had no idea what to expect, but he was determined to stay alert to every possibility.

After Caramon had been carrying the food and water to prisoners for over two hours, the guard began to lag farther behind, confident that his charge was performing his duties adequately.

By the time Caramon came to the far end of the corridor where the broken man was sequestered, the minotaur guard had dropped well behind. He squatted on the floor, idly stabbing at some vermin that darted across his path.

Caramon felt his stomach turn when he saw that the broken man had been beaten and tortured anew. His wounds were streaming with blood. It seemed as though his back had been shredded open. His face was covered with black and purple bruises.

The warrior dropped the two buckets, spilling the contents, and rushed forward, pressing his face through the bars.

The chained man raised his chin ever so slightly, but his eyes were puffed shut. His head twisted in Caramon's direction.

Down the corridor, the minotaur guard, seemingly oblivious, stabbed at another creature on the floor.

"What—" began Caramon in a shrill whisper that he had to suppress before it turned into an angry scream.

"Business as usual, my friend," gasped the broken man, his voice cracked and weak.

"Why do they torture you so?"

"I am not one of them. That is enough."

Caramon lowered his head, filled with pity and shame. In doing so, for the first time he caught a glimpse of the man's feet. His long legs tapered into birdlike claws. The Majere twin opened his mouth in astonishment.

"There is no time for further explanations," gasped the broken man. "Hurry! Set those buckets on top of one another to the right of the door. No ... there! Steady. Keep them balanced. Now climb on top!"

Caramon looked dubious.

"Hurry!"

Without having any idea why, Caramon did as he was told. He began to mount the stacked buckets. A glance over his shoulder told him that the guard was still distracted by his little game of stab the vermin.

"What about you?" Caramon asked, hesitating.

"If I am lucky, I will be permitted to die."

Then Caramon heard a rough sliding of stone. He looked up and saw a massive brick being shifted out of place in the ceiling over his head.

"Stretch your hands up!"

As he did so, Caramon caught a last glimpse of his savior. The broken man's face glowed with momentary triumph before his chin dropped to his chest.

Rough, strong hands pulled Caramon up.

* * * * *

The massive brick slowly slid back in place.

Caramon could see nothing but darkness and a dim, moving shape. He was prodded into a low, flat tunnel. The burly Majere twin had to half crawl, half crouch as he tried to scurry along. Whoever—whatever—was ahead of him turned every dozen yards or so and shrieked at him in an inhuman language. It was a high-pitched, barking noise that had the effect of urging him forward even if Caramon had no idea what it meant.

The person or thing scuttling with ease along the low tunnel stayed so far ahead of him that Caramon couldn't distinguish any of its features.

Rocks scraped Caramon's head and back. Roots and cobwebs brushed across his face. His joints hurt from the bending.

"Hey!" Caramon whispered. "Who are you? Where are we going?"

The shape up ahead stopped for a moment, turned, and shrieked something at Caramon, then kept going, seeming to pick up speed. It was all Caramon could do to keep the shape in sight as it lurched and twisted ahead of him in the dim tunnel.

Once or twice they came to places where the tunnel forked, and if Caramon hadn't kept the figure in view, he wouldn't have known which way to go. He realized he could never find his way back, even if for some reason he chose to return to the prison.

After an hour of this arduous progress, the tunnel began to slope gradually upward. Caramon followed the shape ahead of him as it found footholds, clung to roots, and scratched for purchase. Aching from the unaccustomed exertion, the warrior wished they could take a moment to rest.

Finally, almost without warning, Caramon felt the ground slope up steeply under his feet. Clawing upward, he burst out of the ground into bright sunlight. It had been so long since he had seen the sun that he was momentarily blinded. Before Caramon could adjust his eyes and take stock of his rescuer, a burlap sack was dropped over his head, someone pulled the drawstring at his feet, and he fell over.

But he didn't strike the ground, because in the same instant, Caramon had the distinct sensation of being caught, lifted off the ground, and borne aloft.

* * * * *

The minotaur guard who had failed the simple responsibility of keeping watch over Caramon was executed the next morning.

The minotaur with the important insignia came back down to the dungeon and, with his fawning human slave hopping along at his side, he retraced Caramon's movements. He walked up and down the corridors, looking and thinking. He stopped in front of the cell where the minotaur guard said he had last seen Caramon. He looked at the miserable inhabitant of the cell, barely clinging to life, and he gazed at the walls and the floor and the ceiling.

Although he was a very intelligent minotaur, he couldn't for the life of him figure out how the human, who was being nurtured toward a glorious future as a gladiator, had escaped. Where could he go?

He and his minotaur aide took out their frustration on the other human, the one called Sturm. They beat him bloody, demanding to know how his companion had gotten away. They may have beaten Sturm a little too hard, because the human's face became so swollen that he wouldn't have been able to say anything even if he wanted to. In any case, he couldn't have told much, because Sturm had absolutely no idea where Caramon had gone or how he had escaped.

After beating him, the minotaur officer decided that the one called Sturm probably knew nothing or he would have talked, and that the best thing to do, considering, would be to nurse Sturm back to health all over again, favoring him with the best food and water.

If they were lucky, they would still get one gladiator out of all this trouble.

Then, heaving a deep sigh, the minotaur dictated a communique to his fawning human slave. The communique would be sent to the capital city of Lacynos, to the king himself. Unpleasant though it may be, it was his duty to report such an unusual occurrence as an escape from the prison of Atossa.

Chapter 9
Tanis Keeps A Log

Captain Nugetre made his living hiring out the Castor to carry cargo, people—whatever he was asked, no questions asked—throughout the Eastern seas. Tanis, Raistlin, Flint, and Kirsig attracted little attention from the crew when they boarded that morning.

Anticipating an eventful voyage, Tanis decided to keep a log, requesting and receiving paper for that purpose from the captain's supply.

FIRST DAY

Tempestuous winds and murky weather greeted us as soon as we lost sight of the shoreline. The reddish sea deepened in color to a muddy brown, a portent of dangers ahead.

Captain Nugetre gathered myself, Flint, Raistlin, the half-ogre Kirsig, and his own first mate—a tall, broad-shouldered woman with a cap of straight blond hair, who goes by the name of Yuril (she reminds me of no one so much as Caramon, for she is a strapping physical specimen)—in his cabin for a look at his maps and a discussion of the route.

Although Nugetre is an arrogant man, it seems from the attitude of his crew that he has earned their liking as well as respect. Certainly Kirsig speaks highly of him, mostly as a result of his contacts with her father. His cabin is a modest affair, containing a plain writing desk, a cabinet of charts and maps, and a small hammock.

Once we were all present, Captain Nugetre began by warning us that there could be no guarantee that we would arrive safely at our destination, the far minotaur isles. "I have chanced the Blood Sea as often as any seafaring man," the captain declared, "but I never forget that it is a risk, a deadly one. Your reasons had better be worth gambling of your lives."

Flint started to say something, but Raistlin cut him off. The dwarf's broken leg was bound in neat wrapping, but his face was green and had been ever since he was dragged aboard the ship. The choppy waves that we have experienced since setting sail have confirmed his misgivings about sea voyages and aggravated his suffering.

Raistlin assured the captain that we had no intention of turning back. To emphasize his point, he set a bag of gems and coins on the captain's desk. Their value was substantial. Flint sat up, his eyes wide. "Double that," said Raistlin pointedly, "if we make the crossing within ten days."

Kirsig had already told Nugetre that we needed to make all possible speed, and the captain outlined his unusual tactic for meeting Raistlin's deadline.

Other ships' captains steer well clear of the Outer Reach of the Maelstrom at the center of the Blood Sea. It is the wisest course, for when a vessel is caught in its mighty undertow, it is sucked into the ever tightening rings of the whirlpool, and finally down into the dark red waters that churn feverishly where once stood *the great city of Istar.*

Nugetre proposed to head directly for the outer ring of the Maelstrom, and to ride its current without giving in to the choking waters. Once it had carried us near enough to the minotaur isles—a distance of some three hundred miles—the Castor *would fight free of the deadly pull.*

"That is the only way we can make the distance inside of ten days," the captain concluded. "Otherwise, because of the currents and the prevailing winds, it is a journey of several weeks. Safer, but slower by far."

"Have you ever attempted this before?" asked Raistlin intently.

"No," answered the captain flatly.

A heavy silence thickened the air after his reply. "But it can be done," spoke up Yuril unexpectedly. "I sailed with a captain once who did it. The voyage was terrible. Not only did we have to battle the current, but also the perpetual storm that reigns over the Maelstrom. Death beckoned at every instant. We lost several good sailors in the heavy squalls. But the captain was determined to ride it out. He turned the ship at precisely the right instant, and we broke free. The strategy did indeed save time."

Curious, I asked her what had happened to that captain. Why did she now sail with Captain Nugetre?

"Pah," Yuril replied. "My former captain lost his life on land, in Bloodwatch. He was a genius aboard ship, a dolt in other respects. Imagine besting the Blood Sea, only to be stabbed to death in a common barroom brawl." She paused and squared her shoulders, staring at each of us in turn. "I have been sailing with Captain Nugetre for two years now. He has the skill and courage necessary. With these, it can be done."

She stabbed her finger at the map laid out on the desk, showing where the ship would enter the Maelstrom, and where, if luck was with us, we would be expelled.

Yuril said the Outer Reach of the Blood Sea was approximately three days away, assuming steady breezes and no problems.

"How long will we be in this ... Maelstrom?" asked Kirsig a bit plaintively.

"Two days and two nights," replied Yuril, "if we stay on course."

Raistlin seemed to be pondering the map. I waited for him to make the decision.

A woeful-faced Flint whispered to me, "Don't you think we should consider the slower and safer method? We really have no proof that Sturm, Caramon, and Tas are in imminent danger."

Raistlin shot him a reproachful glance. Flint looked down, tugging at his beard.

I knew my old friend was no less concerned about the others than Raistlin and I were. I patted him on the back, whispering, "It will get us off this ship sooner." Then I spoke up in favor of the plan.

Raistlin nodded agreement, and Kirsig surprised me with a hug. I didn't dare look at Flint again, for I knew that the dwarf, embarrassed at his earlier remark and annoyed to be stuck in the middle of a sea voyage—with a broken leg to boot—would be glowering at me.

By nightfall, strong gales buffeted the Castor. Darkness blanketed the waters. The sea was cold and black and roiling. No stars graced the night sky. We are three days away from the suction of the Maelstrom, so it may have been my imagination already to feel the gradual, quickening pull.

SECOND AND THIRD DAYS

Frequent strange calms broken by heavy winds, hail and rain. We have sighted no other ships in this section of the sea. Even during the calms, our ship is being drawn in a northerly direction.

Did I describe the Castor?

A two-masted pentare, it is, with two sails and oar ports that are left unmanned except during calms. The crew numbers about two dozen, at least half of whom are female. They are all human and regard Flint and Kirsig, particularly, with some wonderment, even though I believe they have seen ogres before in their travels.

Some of the sailors are black-skinned, from remote northern islands, and I peer at them with equal curiosity. The women, especially, for they are beautiful to look at, yet well muscled and obviously seaworthy. They dress in leather and sandals and can climb the masts and rig the sails as well as any seaman.

They speak mostly in their own harsh-sounding vernacular, although almost all of them also speak Common.

None of the crew carry weapons, and so far we have had no cause to resort to any. There is a small armory aft, in which are stored swords, crossbows, ballista bolts, oil, some armor, and the ship's supply of brandy.

Yuril moves among the crew easily, barking commands that they hasten to carry out. She oversaw the building of four extra side rudders, crude in their design, shaped almost like giant flippers. According to Captain Nugetre's plan, they were attached to either end of the ship just below sea level. When we enter the treacherous perimeter of the Blood Sea, they will act to steady the Castor and, we hope, guide it during the worst of the buffeting it will surely receive from the Malelstrom.

With the extra rudders come an elaborate system of ropes and gears fastened to blocks of wood hammered into the deck. Two sailors volunteered to dangle off the side of the boat, plunging their heads below crashing waves in order to securely attach the additional rudders. They received extra rations that night and the cheers of their comrades.

Captain Nugetre presides over everything, his head held high. He says very little, and it is almost as if Yuril is in command. But he chides her when she is slow and laughs loudly when she barks an insult in reply.

Apart from the main deck and the captain's cabin, the Castor has a small galley with fresh water and food supplies, an aft and bow castle, the oar bay and lower deck, crew quarters (which the crew uses in shifts) and a cargo hold. As far as I can tell, we are carrying no cargo other than food, repair supplies, and the array of weapons already mentioned.

Near the cargo hold is a one-room brig, which has been empty of occupants since we left Ogrebond, and a small mate's cabin *where Yuril sleeps—if and when she sleeps. She seems to stalk the deck at all hours. When the captain himself sleeps, she is his eyes and ears.*

Fortunately, four small cabins serve for passengers—one each for Raistlin, Flint, Kirsig, and myself. They are spare, with a hammock, bench, window chest, and table in each.

By choice, Raistlin has been spending much of his time in his cabin alone. I suspect young Majere is collecting his strength for the ordeal ahead. The few times that I have seen him on deck he has seemed preoccupied. Surely he is worried about Caramon's well-being.

Flint has spent most of the first three days in his cabin as well, but not by choice, for he is somewhat immobilized by his bad leg. I'm not sure, what with his dislike of bodies of water, that he isn't happy to be so restrained, but it is hard to tell with Flint. Even in the happiest of states, he is perpetually grumbling.

Kirsig has cared well for Flint's leg. The swelling has gone down, the discoloration faded. It turns out that she does know some useful healing skills. I think my friend will be walking again by the time we reach the Outer Reach of the Maelstrom.

Kirsig refuses to leave Flint's side, doting on him shamelessly. She strokes his hair and beard, calling him her "pretty dwarf." The more firmly he tries to cast her off, the more tightly she clings to him.

Others on board are not so harsh in their attitude toward the half-ogre. Yesterday (day two) one of the sailors fell from a high turret and opened a nasty wound. Blood gushed from his side. Kirsig was summoned on deck, and she went to work with naught but a stitching needle, neatly closing the wound. Up till then, I'd say that Yuril had regarded the female half-ogre with amused indifference. Now I notice that she goes out of her way to greet Kirsig in the morning, addressing her with respect.

FOURTH DAY

The water has turned as foreboding as the skies. Dark blood-red is its color here in the OuterReach of the Blood Sea. The waves heave in great swells.

Raistlin explained that the color of the water stems from the reddish soils of the fertile fields that once surrounded the city of Istar. Since Istar was destroyed in the Cataclysm, the Maelstrom that flows in its place constantly churns up those soils, coloring the water red, giving the Blood Sea its name, and reminding all of the fate of the fabled city entombed beneath it.

Overhearing him, Captain Nugetre scoffed and said the color of the sea came from the blood of the thousands trapped and drowned when the gods wreaked their will on the city of Istar.

Flint is up and hobbling about now; his leg is getting stronger. He joined us on deck at midday when a commotion spread over the ship. Sailors stood in clusters, pointing excitedly, arguing about the omens of the sea and sky.

One of the crew, a stout, manly veteran, insisted that dragons have been spotted in the skies over the Blood Sea in this vicinity. Challenged by his fellows, he admitted that he never sailed this close to the Outer Reach before and that these were stories he heard in taverns in Bloodwatch.

The others jeered at his admission, but I noticed that Raistlin had listened to him carefully, a thoughtful expression on his tense face. "Dragons!" snorted Flint. "Next we'll be hearing about genies who grant three wishes!"

By midafternoon, we found ourselves in the grip of a strong current that pulled us northwesterly. Captain Nugetre's instructions were to lay off any drag, take the sails down, and glide with the current. The first shift of crew took positions along the rails, in small groups assigned to one of the anchors or the oars or the extra rudders. But they were under orders to do nothing for the time being, to let the ship be sucked along the Outer Reach.

The *Castor* was swept along in a gradually accelerating curve. The skies above had darkened so that it was difficult to say whether it was night or day, based on the evidence of our eyes. Thunder exploded in the air, lightning flashed, and a stinging rain attacked us intermittently.

Captain Nugetre manned the helm of the ship. We all watched him as he stood in the aft castle, tossing the wheel back and forth *violently, trying to correct the movement of the ship and keep it from being drawn into the Tightening Ring. Whatever else the crew was supposed to be doing, we all stole glances at the captain, knowing that beyond the Tightening Ring lay the Nightmare Sea and the place where Istar slept beneath the vengeful Blood Sea, the Heart of Darkness. No seafarer is known ever to have ventured beyond the Tightening Ring and made it back to tell his story.*

I noticed that Kirsig ran to assist Yuril, whose job it was to move from post to post, calming the sailors. The half-ogre bounced alongside the taller, more muscular and handsome woman, making for an odd contrast. She amused the sailors with her half-comical presence yet did as much as Yuril to maintain discipline.

Flint and I dashed to vacant oar ports, ready to lend our muscle if the need arose. I have to say that Flint has bravely swallowed his fear of the sea and, although his face turned white in this instance, he stood ready to help in whatever way he could.

Raistlin clung to a center mast, buffeted by the growing winds but determined to stay and watch whatever developed.

FOURTH DAY: EVENING

A deepening of the darkness let us know night had fallen, and with it came the full horror. The skies erupted with thunder, the sea seemed afire with bolts of lightning, and the heavens poured icy, slanting rain. The waves rose to a towering height, then dashed violently over the decks. At one point we heard screams, and later we learned that one unlucky sailor had been swept overboard.

The ship listed crazily, and in the blackness of the night, there was no sure way to steer the Castor's course. The wind howled behind us, in front of us, all around us, impossible to reckon with. Yuril had relieved the captain and was at the helm when the worst began. She was soon joined by Nugetre; the two of them strained to keep the wheel from spinning dizzily. They shouted and cursed at each other and at the elements, linking arms around the wheel, desperate to steady the ship.

The continuous gusts of wind drove icy sprays into the ship fore and aft. Some bailing was necessary. The worst of it was that with the storm, the bailing, and the uncertainty, no real rest or food was possible all night. Both shifts worked alongside one another, weary, chilled to the bone, and filled with dread.

I argued with Raistlin, insisting that our goal would be better served if he were safe below deck. He refused to listen. However, in the early morning, when the storm abated somewhat and several of us hurried to catch some sleep, I saw that he was slumped at his post.

Kirsig hastened to help the young mage to his cabin below. Flint and I followed not long after, shivering in the wind and spray. From my cabin, I could hear Raistlin muttering and tossing in a restless sleep.

We all slept fitfully, cognizant of the ship's erratic movement and our own building fear.

FIFTH DAY

Day and night the weather worsens, and our peril increases. After a brief respite, the storm returned in full fury. Huge waves crashed into the ship, and violent rain soaked us to the skin. We were deluged by water. We had to shout into each other's ears in order to be heard over the deafening thunder. Though Nugetre remained at the helm, I couldn't imagine his efforts had any effect. The Castor seemed lifted and flung like a cork in the surf. We lurched drunkenly from the attack of the Blood Sea.

The seething chaos did not let up. In the late afternoon, Captain Nugetre, his red-rimmed eyes burning, announced that we had crossed over into the Tightening Ring. Now, he said, it was mandatory that we break the grip of the current and somehow lead the Castor east and north, back to the Outer Reach.

Otherwise we would be sucked into the Maelstrom.

Nugetre banished Yuril from the deck, sending her below to get some rest. Until then, she had refused to let anyone spell her in her duties. Alone, he held the tiller until full evening. I shall *always remember how, while he was steering that day, he sang out some lusty sailor's song that I had never heard out of anyone else's mouth. His brazen confidence as he struggled with the ship seemed to infect the other sailors, who didn't flinch from their posts despite the brutal elements.*

The captain ordered some of his crew to the oars on the port side and others to raise the smallest sail. Shouting orders and encouragement, Nugetre and his sailors somehow managed to wrestle the Castor back to the Outer Reach.

Raistlin reappeared on deck at midday. Obviously still fatigued, his face wan, Raistlin still gave off an aura of excitement. I could see that his strength and determination had been renewed. How long, I asked him, do we have to endure this?

"My guess is that we have gone some hundred and fifty miles," answered the young mage, "That means we have another hundred and fifty to go before we try to break free of the Outer Reach and come out in the Northern Blood Sea."

"Another night and day," estimated Kirsig, who had come up behind the Majere twin.

"Where's Flint?" I asked her.

"Over there." The female half-ogre pointed proudly to one of the masts, where Flint sat, drenched with water, his face glum but resolute as he held tight to one of the ropes that restrained the rudders.

FIFTH DAY: EVENING

A night that took us to the limits of our endurance. The wind shrieked as it turned the seascape into a black haze of blinding spray. Thunder boomed without interruption, and at one point, volleys of lightning hit the deck, toppling a secondary mast and crushing the neck of the unfortunate sailor beneath it. We had to tie ourselves to pegs and poles in order to avoid being washed into the churning waters. No one slept. Even momentary rest was made impossible by brutal interruptions—a lightning flash, the peal of thunder, stinging rain, or something hard flung into our faces by the incessant wind.

Still Captain Nugetre and Yuril clung to the tiller.

SIXTH DAY

Two of the crew have been lost in the struggle with the Blood Sea. The rest of us, facing the prospect of a never-ending tempest, almost long for surrender to the wrathful Maelstrom.

Raistlin stayed in his cabin for most of the day, exhausted. Flint, his eyes pouchy and his eyebrows sodden, was sent below by Yuril, who noticed his dazed behavior.

At midday, the storm entered a brief lull, the type we knew would bring a fearful escalation in its aftermath.

In the relative quiet, we heard moaning, screaming, and cackling borne on the wind. The ship began to spin crazily with a frightening speed that was worse than anything we had experienced thus far.

The crew members, nearly hysterical, stood and pointed at the churning waters. I could see nothing, but they babbled about horrors—grinning faces, clawed hands, and wicked horns—pushing at the ship, causing it to pitch and spin.

Yuril shouted at them to return to their posts. Captain Nugetre himself looked stricken with horror, but his was not imaginary.

"We've gone too far! We're into the Tightening Ring, approaching the Nightmare Sea!" he cried, his face twisted with apprehension. "Man the oars! Throw the anchor! Make ready—"

His voice was almost drowned out by the rising clamor. A red mist swirled up from the sea, flowing onto the deck and through the portholes. Small red impkins, with leathery, batlike wings, barbed tails, and twisted horns, formed out of the vapors and swarmed up the masts, pulling on the rigging and loosening ropes. Like the Blood Sea itself, their skin was dark red, their jagged teeth a gleaming white.

Giggling, screaming, and ranting, they unleashed panic on the ship.

Some of the men rushed to grapple with the imps, but the captain screamed at them. "You fools, they are illusions!"

Illusions they may have been, but in the next instant, I saw two of them grab one of the sailors and heave him overboard.

I spotted Raistlin standing on the steps that led to our cabins. He bent his head, moved his hands, and uttered some incantation. To my astonishment, the impkins vanished, although the red mist lingered. In the next instant, the young mage sank back out of sight. Few had noticed what he had done.

In the meantime, the storm resumed its fury.

Flint fought his way over to me, looking as frightened as I had ever seen him. "What should we do?" he shouted.

For a moment, I was uncertain. "There!" I cried. We saw Yuril and a couple other sailors struggling to unloose the heavy, claw-shaped anchor, a task made all the more difficult by the fierce wind and rain. We dashed over and found ourselves next to Kirsig, who forced a grin as she threw her bulk into the task.

Beneath us, I could feel the oars begin to pull, but I also heard several of them snap against the force of the current and the waves.

The ship pitched wildly, rocking back and forth, throwing several of us, myself included, to the deck.

"Now!" shouted Captain Nugetre.

Finding our footing, we managed to heft the anchor over the side. The thick rope unspooled so rapidly that one of the sailors tossed a bucket of water on it so that it wouldn't burn. For several minutes, it dropped through blood-red water, coming almost to the end of the reel before finally reaching bottom.

Yuril uttered a cry of astonishment. "Never have I heard of such depths!" she exclaimed.

As Captain Nugetre had expected, the anchor temporarily stabilized the ship. But because of the wind and storm, the Castor tore at the anchor rope, threatening to break free.

Flint stood by, one of his stout hatchets at the ready. When Captain Nugretre shouted "Now!" the dwarf slashed downward, cutting the anchor rope in one clean blow. The pent-up momentum of the ship was such that it practically leaped several hundred feet through the air, breaking the grip of the suction.

At the same time, Yuril and I had made our way to the sailors in the aft section who had the extra rudders at the ready. Just as the ship splashed down, before it was caught in the current again, we released the makeshift rudders. Looking over the side, I could see them fall into the water, forming flippers at the rear of the boat.

"Now!" Captain Nugetre shouted again over the din of the storm.

I could feel the oar crew pull in unison, and this time the boat, with a momentum of its own, surged in a northeasterly direction. Working the oars with every available sailor, the crew held the Castor to its northeasterly course, propelling it farther and farther from the dangerous core of the Blood Sea.

SEVENTH AND EIGHTH DAYS

The worst was over. Now our course lay across Firewater toward Mithas and Karthay. The sailors celebrated their victory over the Maelstrom, looking strangely wild, with salt caked on their lips and wreaths of seaweed in their hair.

Captain Nugetre gave orders to break out a ration of brandy for each of us by way of reward.

Damage to the ship was surprisingly slight, considering the battering we had taken. One mast and a number of oars had been broken. Debris tossed about by the storm had rent some of the sails, even though they had been rolled up. Kirsig was useful at stitchery, and I happen to know a little needlework myself. Together we worked at mending the sails. The men gladly tore the shirts off their backs to provide crude patches.

A few of the sailors roamed the deck, taking care of the gashes in the vessel, none of which were major.

Flint set his mind to fashioning a new makeshift anchor, which would have to serve until the next time the Castor made port. Gathering pieces of lead and other soft metal from around the ship, he melted everything down over a huge pot and was able to hammer out a mottled sinker that Yuril pronounced satisfactory. The new anchor was set in place of the old.

The waves continued high and choppy. The water had cleared

only slightly; it was still that unsettling rust color. Though fixing up the Castor *and keeping it on track demanded hard and constant work, all of us felt great relief.*

A fair wind blew at our backs. A sun that grew hotter each day shone overhead. A haze formed in the sky and refused to go away.

EIGHTH DAY: EVENING

Raistlin has been staying in his cabin during the day and pacing the decks at night. Flint and I both realized that he hadn't told us everything that occupied his thoughts.

This night, a black, starless night that held no cheer, I found him on the foredeck, standing and staring out over the choppy waters. Hearing me behind him, he turned and offered a slight smile—small encouragement, but enough to embolden me to interrupt his reverie.

"You must be very worried about Caramon," I ventured mildly.

To my surprise, the young mage raised an eyebrow, as if this was the furthest thing from his thoughts. "Caramon," he said to me with his usual brusqueness, "can take care of himself. If he didn't die back in the Straits of Schullseu, I feel quite certain that we shall find him somewhere in this forsaken part of Krynn. He is more likely to rescue us than it would be for us to rescue him."

"But I thought," I began, "that we came all this way because you believe that he was taken prisoner by minotaurs."

"Yes ... partly," said Raistlin. He started to say something else, then paused, perhaps to gather his thoughts, perhaps simply to pull his cloak about himself more tightly to ward off the chill in the air. "Yet," he continued after a moment, "there are more important things to consider, apart from the fate of my happy-go-lucky brother. There is the reason why he was taken and the use of the rare herb, jalopwort." His tone was very solemn. In the darkness, I couldn't gauge his expression.

I leaned closer, thinking to draw the mystery out of him. "What is it then, Raistlin?" I asked. "What spell have we been pursuing across these thousands of miles?"

He turned toward me, peering at me intently. Seeming to consider my question, he took a moment before replying. "The spell that I came across can be cast only by a high cleric of the minotaurs. It is a spell that would open a portal and invite into the world the god of the bull-men, Sargonnas, servant of Takhisis."

Now it was my turn to be silent, to consider. As an initiate magic-user, Raistlin believed in the gods of Good, the gods of Neutrality, and the gods of Evil, of whom Takhisis was supreme. While I had seen both good and evil in my life, about the gods I was not as certain as the young mage. Sargonnas was a god of whom I knew little.

Perhaps sensing my reserve, Raistlin turned away with a sigh. "That is not the end of it," he said. "This spell can only be triggered during certain conjunctions of the moon and stars. The effort required to arrange it is extraordinary. It can only mean that the bull-men have a goal important enough to require the aid of Sargonnas. Morath thinks—and I concur—that this must be a plan to conquer all of Ansalon."

"But the minotaurs could never do it alone no matter how many they are or how well organized," I objected.

"True," said Raistlin, "but what if they forged alliances with unlikely allies—the evil races of the sea or the ogres, for example?"

"They are an arrogant race," I protested, "one that would never forge alliances."

"That may not be true," said Kirsig, stepping out from the shadows. The half-ogre had a way of creeping up on people, but Raistlin held an odd liking for her and did not seem perturbed by her presence, nor by the obvious fact that she had been listening to us from the shadows.

"That may explain something odd that has been happening at Ogrebond for the last several months," Kirsig went on.

"What?" asked Raistlin with interest.

"Delegations—galleys—of minotaurs have been visiting in order to parley with the different ogre tribes. It is most unusual. Before then, I never heard of any friendship between the ogres and minotaurs. Usually, in fact, it was quite the opposite: deadly enmity."

"Do you see what I mean?" Raistlin said to me, turning and clasping his hands over a rail, staring at the dark water and even blacker sky. "Caramon's fate is the least of my worries!"

NINTH DAY

In the early morning, one of the sailors thought he spotted something moving under the water alongside the ship. Everybody sharpened his guard, knowing that in these strange waters, it could be anything.

At noon, the creature was spotted again—a huge, gray, slithery shape that seemed to be following the Castor. *Our progress lagged in the hot, hazy weather, and the creature mimicked our speed, seeming almost lazy in its sinuous movements. The creature remained so far below the surface that we could distinguish very little about it except that it was every bit as large and long as the ship itself.*

By late afternoon, the curious creature had been pursuing us for a dozen miles without surfacing. This lack of action lulled us into complacency. Some of the Castor's *sailors were belowdecks while others dozed at their posts when suddenly the thing reared its head and attacked.*

I was amidships when I looked up to see a long, bulging, serpentine body bearing down on us.

Instantly I knew what it was: a nudibranch, or giant aquatic slug, rare in these parts. I fell back behind a storage box just in time, for the slug crashed its gaping maw into the stern and simultaneously spewed out a thick stream of corrosive saliva.

The Castor *jolted backward. Everybody standing was flung to the deck, everybody sleeping stunned awake. One of the sailors had had no time to dodge the acidic spittle. She screamed and rolled on the deck, burning in pain. Another failed to see the nudibranch fast enough and was swallowed whole.*

Those who witnessed the attack yelled for help, and their comrades came running, bearing weapons that seemed puny in comparison to the nudibranch's immense bulk. Captain Nugetre raced up from below, shouting orders. Yuril had been at the tiller.

Now she crouched next to me, gazing in horror at the rampaging thing.

As we watched, the giant slug lifted its ugly, tentacled head so high that we could see its dead white underbelly, then smashed downward into the deck, using its body like a battering ram. Wood and splinters flew in every direction. The nudibranch was half on the deck, half in the sea. The ship listed dangerously.

For several minutes, the giant slug's head disappeared out of sight below the deck. Gruesome slurping noises and the screams of sailors caught in their quarters signified the creature's bloody feeding frenzy.

"Flint!" I cried suddenly.

"Hush!" said the dwarf. "I'm right behind you."

So he was, and Raistlin and Kirsig, too. All watched with amazement as the giant slug reared its head again and smashed back into the ship. The deck sloped steeply. With each battering from the nudibranch, the Castor listed more dangerously.

"It's eating its way through the ship," said Raistlin.

"They will eat anything," said Yuril, "Plants, carrion, garbage—anything."

As we watched, one of the sailors, a black-skinned woman with short-cropped hair, whooped and leaped on the back of the giant slug, stabbing downward with a sharp sword.

But the nudibranch had a thick, rubbery hide, and the formidable blade barely caused a wound. The nudibranch paused in its attack on the Castor and, with surprising agility, managed to twist its head around, grab the brave sailor in its mouth, mangle her, then toss her body into the ocean several hundred yards away.

Without working out a plan, Flint, Kirsig, Yuril, and I rushed the creature and stabbed at it, landing some ineffectual blows. Other sailors joined us. The giant slug twisted and thrashed, knocking down several sailors, covering one of them with burning spittle. All we could do was harry it and do our best to stay out of the creature's reach.

I saw Raistlin at the far end of the boat, working at something. He turned and called out to Flint.

The dwarf hastened to him. Together they bent over and began to drag an object toward us and the giant slug. When two other seamen hurried to help them, Raistlin left Flint and ran over to the tiller, where Captain Nugetre was busy trying to keep control of the listing ship. Raistlin conferred briefly with Nugetre, who nodded at what the young mage was saying.

I could see now that Flint and the sailors were dragging the anchor toward us. Kirsig, Yuril, and I raced over to help them lift it up. Then, at a signal from Flint, we thrust it at the head of the giant slug.

As Raistlin had hoped, the nudibranch—not known for its intelligence—opened its mouth wide for what we were shoving in its direction. We released the anchor at the last moment and scurried to safety.

An almost surprised expression crossed the slug's rudimentary face as Captain Nugetre turned the wheel hard away from the creature. The sudden movement caused it to slide backward off the deck into the sea. Flint's anchor took it swiftly down into the murky depths until we could no longer glimpse any evidence of it other than the explosion of bubbles that rose to the surface.

The attack had left the Castor sorely in need of repair. Three sailors were dead, as we were reminded by the blood staining the deck, and Flint had to take up the task of creating another anchor from scrap metal.

TENTH DAY

Captain Nugetre says we are no more than half a day from the coast of Karthay, even at the slow pace we must now maintain. The Castor is a crippled ship. Only round-the-clock bailing shifts keep us afloat, a strain on the crew, which has been halved by our experiences. Flint, Raistlin, Kirsig, and I pitch in.

Although the journey across the Blood Sea has been as fast as anyone could have hoped, the captain says that he isn't sure that the fee makes up for the damage to his ship and crew.

"I will not take the chance of making the landing at Karthay," Captain Nugetre announced. "I won't incur any further risks. I will give you a small boat to row to shore. Consider yourselves fortunate at that."

Despite Kirsig's best entreaties, Captain Nugetre has refused to budge from his position.

Raistlin paid him his double fee and didn't press him about the landing. The captain has more than kept his part of the bargain, Raistlin said, thanking him.

Kirsig announced her intention to come with us. Flint tried to talk her out of it—unsuccessfully. She insisted that she wouldn't abandon her "pretty dwarf."

More of a surprise was that Yuril announced her desire to join us. Captain Nugetre raged at her, but to no effect. The first mate said that she owed us her life—at least twice over—and that she intended to help us fulfill our quest. The captain seemed saddened as well as angry at her decision. Not for the first time did I get the idea that these two at some time had been more than captain and ship's mate to each other.

Three of the sailors, all female and more loyal to Yuril than to Captain Nugetre, said they would come along as well.

That made eight, and the furious Nugetre had to promise us two small boats in order to land us ashore.

Chapter 10
The Evil Kender

The potion worked wonderfully. Most assuredly, Tasslehoff Burrfoot had been changed into an evil kender. There could be no question about that. From his former topknot to his toes, Tas was thoroughly evil.

The minotaur guards weren't so sure they didn't like Tas better the way he was before, before Fesz, the shaman minotaur and the high emissary of the Nightmaster, had fed him the potion that perverted his true kender nature.

Of course, they couldn't be called Tasslehoff's guards anymore, not strictly speaking. Glorying in his new evilness, Tas had been upgraded from prisoner to honored guest of the minotaur king. He occupied privileged quarters on an upper floor of the palace, a spacious room of plush and velvet with a balcony overlooking the sprawling, seedy city of Lacynos.

Across the hall was another privileged guest room, even more privileged and roomier, that had been set aside for Fesz, who needed to be close to Tas on account of their growing friendship and frequent consultations.

A small number of minotaur guards still stood outside Tas's room in the hallway. They were ordered to keep Tas from leaving the premises without escort or authorization, but they were also ordered not to act like guards. Instead, they were to act friendly and do the kender's bidding, and they dared not disobey.

The evil kender was ten times the nuisance that the good kender had been—that is, if anyone would have called Tas "good" in the first place. Worse than a nuisance, in the unanimous opinion of the minotaur guards, Tas was downright ... well, evil.

Since the guards were his to order around, Tas made sure they were kept busy attending to his every whim. And Tas had plenty of whims, one for every minute of the day, it seemed.

In his evilness, Tas had decided that he would like to take three hot baths each day at strictly appointed intervals. It was hard work, even for the minotaur guards, to organize the baths and heft the hot water buckets up the several flights of stairs leading to the privileged guest quarters three times a day.

And woe betide them if the water wasn't hot enough. If it wasn't, Tas would throw a terrible tantrum, hitting them over the head with the empty bucket or poking them in the eyes with a curtain rod, the best poking weapon he had at his disposal. Or he would curse them with an amazing litany of taunts. Some of the guards could barely restrain themselves, having to take insults and orders from a kender. But take it they did, and after the hitting and poking and taunting, they usually had to slink out and start all over again, praying to get the bathwater hot enough next time.

Because he was a bit bored being cooped up all day, every day in his privileged quarters, Tasslehoff also decided that he wanted the room redone and painted in more pleasing colors. He didn't like its present off-white, but it was very difficult for Tas to decide precisely which color, or colors, the room ought to be.

First he ordered two of the guards to repaint his room a deep indigo blue—by sundown. Afterward, staring at the deep indigo blue that covered the floor, walls, and ceiling, Tas almost fell asleep. So he decided that deep indigo blue was a tad too lulling.

He ordered the same two guards to repaint the room a bright crimson—by sundown of the next day. The guards grumbled and swore, especially because Tas poked at them, swatted their heads, and berated them as they slaved to meet the deadline.

Bright crimson kept the kender wide awake at night. So Tas decided that the floor could stay crimson, if it was covered with some rugs—he wouldn't be noticing the floor much at night anyway—but the walls ought to be some substantial color, like orange, while the ceiling ought to be some profoundly evil color, like midnight black.

The same two minotaur guards, because they had done such a good job the first two times and also because they had done such a bad job the first two times, were selected to repaint Tasslehoff's room again.

All the minotaur guards complained bitterly among themselves about Tasslehoff. No matter why or when they entered the kender's quarters, they were likely to be struck by some flying object or tackled from behind or tripped by wire strung across their path. Insults—the worst insults Tas could think of, comparisons to dumb cows and dull-horned bulls—poured out nonstop. Food was rejected and tossed in their faces.

Dogz, the only minotaur who managed to avoid being poked or insulted, sadly remembered the good old Tasslehoff, before he had turned evil.

"Tasslehoff Burrfoot is a valued minion of the Night-master," Fesz had declared. And the minotaur guards dared not disagree.

To Fesz, Tas's hostile and agressive behavior was proof positive that the kender had turned evil. And if his obnoxious behavior wasn't evidence enough, Tasslehoff also had proved extremely cooperative in telling Fesz a great deal about the thin, intelligent mage from Solace who had sent him to Southern Ergoth to obtain the rare jalopwort from a minotaur herbalist.

Tas also told Fesz all about his good friends, Flint and Tanis Half-Elven, and his Uncle Trapspringer, and the time he, Tas, had almost captured a woolly mammoth single-handedly. He told him about poor Sturm and Caramon, probably carcasses picked over by spiny fish at the bottom of the Blood Sea by now. It was good riddance to bad rubbish, because they were honorable and pure and wouldn't fit in with the kender's new way of looking at the world as something to be stomped on and mashed and conquered.

Indeed, the kender loved to talk about his friends—"ex-friends," he sometimes corrected himself. He especially loved to talk about the dwarf, Flint Fireforge. So much did he love to talk about Flint that occassionally Fesz had to put his arm around the kender and gently steer him back to the subject of Raistlin Majere, the enemy of the minotaur race and therefore, Fesz reminded him, an enemy of Tas's.

Raistlin Majere was the one who interested Fesz the most. This human who was studying to be a mage, and who had wanted the jalopwort because of a spell he had stumbled across in some ancient text.

"Oh, Raistlin is very smart, you bet," Tas told Fesz. "A pretty good mage, considering that he hasn't taken the Test yet, but don't ask me what the Test is, because it's something very secret, and although I know more about it than practically anybody else, it ties my tongue just to try to explain it. If Raistlin's figured out where the jalopwort went—meaning, where I am, here in Minotaurville—then he's probably on his way here right now. He'll want the jalopwort back, and probably he'll want to rescue me, too—hah! Probably Tanis and Flint will be coming with him. Boy, Flint will get a big kick out of how evil I am before I kill him!

"But you're right, Fesz. Raistlin is the real threat. I think you and I better start to figure out how to trap him and choke him and stab him and then maybe do something really evil to his dead body, like—I don't know. You've got more experience than I do in this sort of thing. What do you suggest?"

Whenever the kender got really excited, as he was now, he paced the room, bouncing up and down with an unmistakably wide, wicked leer. It made Fesz feel pleased. Furthermore, it was usually an appropriate time to give the kender another dose of the potion that would keep him evil as long as Tas kept drinking it.

Tas had been extremely cooperative and very evil for about a week now. Fesz had written down everything the kender said that related to Raistlin and the jalopwort, and dispatched the essence of what he learned across the channel to the Nightmaster on the island of Karthay. Even though the kender was evil, he was still insatiably curious about everything. He begged Fesz to reveal how he managed to communicate with the Nightmaster.

One afternoon, feeling rather fatherly toward Tas, the shaman minotaur escorted the kender into his quarters to show him where he lived.

"Hey, how come you have a bigger room than I do?" asked Tasslehoff, looking around indignantly. "You've got nicer paintings and bigger windows, too—and two windows! I love the color combination you've chosen—a simple brown and dark green combination, like trees and leaves. It reminds me of a forest, in fact. Those stupid minotaur guards have had me all confused with crimson and blue and orange. When I get back, I'm going to give them a piece of my mind."

Fesz put his arm around the irrepressibly wicked kender with whom he was feeling more and more of a kinship and led him to the windowsill. On the sill sat a large round jar of unusually corpulent bees with unusually long stingers. They swarmed inside the jar, buzzing noisily.

"These superintelligent bees bear my messages to the Nightmaster," said Fesz intently, watching Tas's reaction. "They can fly great distances, and they relay messages through telepathic means. Of course"—he gave Tas a sly wink—"they have other nasty uses, but they are most useful for quick and reliable communication."

For once in his life, Tas was caught speechless. His jaw sagged. He had never heard of such creatures in all his travels.

With a flourish, the shaman minotaur unscrewed the top of the jar and let the bees rise into the air. They hovered momentarily a few inches above the jar before collecting into a swarm and buzzing up and off in an easterly direction.

"Wow!" exclaimed Tas, "When I was coming back from Southern Ergoth, I sent a magic message to Raistlin—that's probably how he knows where we are—but all I had was this dumb old bottle that I had to throw into the ocean, and who knows whether it sank to the bottom of sea? If I had bees like that, I could … except where would I put them? I don't think it would be a good idea to carry them in my rucksack in case the jar broke, and—"

Pleased with the kender's ceaseless flow of information, Fesz wrote this new tidbit down as Tasslehoff rattled on. It would be part of his next report to the Nightmaster.

By now the minotaur shaman had a quite thorough description of Raistlin Majere and the half-elf and the dwarf who would likely be accompanying him. He had a sense of the young mage's flaws and weaknesses. Disguised assassins—minotaurs would be too conspicuous—would be dispatched to Solace in the event that Raistlin was still there. But if Raistlin was on his way to the minotaur isles, the Nightmaster would be forewarned and ready.

This Raistlin was not a genuine threat, Fesz felt certain, but it couldn't hurt to be vigilant.

On the eighth day of the kender's evil transformation, Fesz entered Tas's quarters, looking puzzled. He was carrying a parchment bearing a message he himself had transcribed. It was a message from the Nightmaster, delivered to Fesz by the superintelligent bees.

Always happy to see his friend, Tas bounced up and down, greeting him with an elaborate salute he had devised. Then he snatched the message from the shaman's hands:

> *Have captured a lone female on the shore. She is well armed, obviously a warrior. She refuses to tell me her name or how or why she has come here. We are holding her for sacrifice. I suspect she is the one we have been awaiting. Ask the kender if he knows who she is.*

> *The Nightmaster*

"The bees brought this message today," said Fesz, his bullish brow knit in thought. "Do you have any idea who this woman could be?"

Tas didn't have to think about it for very long. "Why, it must be Kitiara!" he exclaimed. "Although how she got to Karthay so fast is beyond me."

"Who is Kitiara?"

"Kitiara Uth Matar," said Tasslehoff. "Didn't I tell you about her? Well, I tend to forget her about half the time because she's only Raistlin's half-sister. No pun intended, but if she's here now, that must mean that Raistlin contacted her, so he can't be very far behind...."

Fesz scribbled it all down as fast as he could.

* * * * *

Fesz and Tas became such good friends that sometimes, in the late afternoons, they would get into a cart pulled by human slaves and travel to various sites around Lacynos. These amiable trips always put Tas in a talkative mood, Fesz discovered—not that it took much to do that—and the shaman minotaur learned more and more about the aspiring mage, Raistlin.

Naturally these two were always followed by one or two minotaur guards, who kept some distance behind them not only out of a sense of protocol, but also because they didn't want Tasslehoff throwing stones at them or otherwise harassing them.

On these trips, Tas got to know the entire city. He especially liked the evil, smelly places, like the slave pits and the arena of games.

A number of slave pits were scattered around the city. They were deep holes carved out of the ground for use as primitive living quarters for the thousands of slaves who carried out the day-to-day labor of Lacynos. During the daytime, only about one hundred slaves might occupy these pens—those too ill or too young to work. Their numbers swelled to seven hundred or so in each pen at night, when those slaves who were still alive after a hard day's toil returned.

The ranks of slaves consisted mostly of persons captured by minotaur pirates, sold by professional slavers, or condemned to a period of indenture for criminal offenses. There was an occasional luckless elf or dishonored minotaur, but nary a kender. In Lacynos, Tas observed, humans predominated as the oppressed race.

Dozens of minotaur guards lined the perimeter of each pit. The only access was a wide ramp, up whose slope the slaves marched, six or seven abreast, every morning, then down again at nightfall. To guard against an uprising, several retaining walls rimmed the pit. These could be collapsed, dropping tons of earth onto any rebellious mob.

Tas was very impressed by one slave pit that he visited.

He praised the ingenuity of the setup and asked a lot of questions.

"If I ever go back to Solace," he told Fesz, adding quickly, "not that I really want to, because I'm having such a good time here in Lacynos. But if I do ever go back to Solace, I think it would be a fine idea to have a slave pit just like this one in the middle of the town. Teach 'em all a lesson. Of course, Solace is up in the treetrops, and speaking technically, I'm not sure that you can build a pit up in the trees, so that is a minor problem I'll have to work out. But I sure do love these slave pits!"

The kender stood on a walkway, peering down into the pit at a throng of slaves, some of them obviously ill or wounded, lying curled up on the ground, others pushing and fighting. He saw a broad-shouldered human wearing some tattered Solamnic regalia shove his way proudly through the milling population. At the other end of the slave pit, he saw a female cleric on bended knee tending to one of the fallen slaves.

One of the minotaur guards got too close and Tasslehoff raised his elbow, accidentally knocking him over the railing of the walkway and down some fifty feet to the bottom of the pit. The slaves scurried out of his way as he hurtled downward, landing with a sickening crunch.

"Oops! Pardon me," said Tas, looking up at Fesz sheepishly. "I was just wondering what a minotaur would sound like, landing on his head after falling a long way down."

The indulgent Fesz returned the kender's evil smile.

The arena of games was spectactular as architecture, even if the games were a mite boring, to Tasslehoff's taste, as a spectator sport. Thousands of slaves had toiled under the whip to build the huge stone structure with its high walls, imposing entryways, and comfortable viewing galleries. Many thousands more had died in the barbaric competition in the packed dirt arena, a twice-monthly event that drew the entire city's population, so rabid were the minotaurs about their national sport of watching one gladiator pitted against another in a fight to the death.

Tas and Fesz spent one sunny afternoon in a private box reserved for the king and his guests near the floor of the arena, directly opposite the ramp entrance, which ascended from the catacombs that served as a waiting room for the gladiators.

One human scum was fighting another human scum. Both were dressed in skimpy clothing and carried fierce-looking weapons. Both were quick and muscular.

For the life of him, Tas couldn't tell them apart. He could barely keep his bleary eyes open as their ruthless combat went on for what seemed like hours.

Cheering, jeering, shouting minotaurs and human pirates packed the coliseum. The atmosphere was festive. Wives and children accompanied some of the bull-men. Everyone applauded his champion wildly. Many had placed bets.

One of the human gladiators dodged the other's thrust, smashed him in the face with his shield, and stuck him through the neck with his long sword. The audience roared, demanding that the loser be beheaded. The victorious human obliged, then pranced around the arena, pleasing the crowd by holding aloft the head dripping with blood.

"By the way," said Tas, yawning, "that reminds me. I sure would like to have my hoopak back. It's the only real weapon I carry, and besides, it's got sentimental value."

"Where is your hoopak?" rumbled Fesz solicitously.

"It was with my rucksack," explained Tas, "until everything I owned got confiscated. I sure would like it back."

"Would you like the whole rucksack back?" asked Fesz.
"You bet."

Fesz said he didn't see any harm in that. Tas grinned.

They spent the whole next day at the shipyard. Tas found it very interesting. He could plainly see that the minotaurs were busy preparing for a big war or something. Piles of lumber littered the wharf. Hundreds of human slaves, overseen by grim-faced, weapon-flourishing minotaurs, streamed over the scene like ants, wielding tools such as adzes, saws, and drills.

"At night," explained Fesz, "the work continues. Torches illuminate the construction. We need to be ready for Sargonnas when he is brought into this world."

Tas nodded. He already knew all about what Fesz and the Nightmaster and the kingdom of minotaurs were planning. Fesz had been telling him bit by bit, just as Tas had been telling Fesz about Raistlin Majere.

The jalopwort was part of an obscure spell that the leading shaman of the minotaurs intended to cast to open a portal and invite the evil god into the material world. Sargonnas would lead the minotaur kingdom in its obsessive goal to conquer and oppress the inferior races of Ansalon—that is, everyone who wasn't a minotaur.

From what Fesz had told Tas, the spell was scheduled to be cast when the sun, moon, and stars formed a special configuration in the skies.

"Very soon," Fesz had hinted. "Very, very soon."

Naturally Tas, being evil himself, was excited about the coming of an evil god and was hoping to make the acquaintance of Sargonnas. That was one of the reasons why the kender was working so hard developing his friendship with Fesz.

"Are you sure the minotaurs can take over the whole world without any help?" asked Tas innocently, a concerned and thoughtful look on his face. He looked around the shipyard with all its war galleys nearing completion. They were pretty impressive, but there were a great many humans and dwarves and elves and kender and gnomes and sundry other races over on the mainland. Maybe the minotaurs had been stuck on these remote isles for so long they didn't have any idea of the enormous opposition they would face.

"Very sensible of you, Tas," said Fesz, lowering his voice to a soft rumble and looking over his shoulder cautiously. "No. Although we are a mighty race, we need and seek allies. We have made tentative pacts with the ogres and with their aquatic cousins, the orughi. We have made diplomatic approaches to the trolls, although they are such a disorganized race, and to certain tribes of barbarians. There are also certain other, uh, elements that you would not be familiar with—I am not at liberty to discuss them, but they will be very important to our combined force as the invasion plans unfold."

"What about kender?" asked Tas, a trifle put out. "Don't you think kender might be able to contribute something?"

"Why, of course," said Fesz, somewhat disconcerted. "I don't know why I left out kender. Kender might be very helpful, if they are all more or less like you. We know very little about kender, you see, and up until now, we hadn't considered them in our thinking."

Tas puffed himself up. "I may be able to intercede with the kender race," he said, "After all, I am a figure of some renown in Kendermore. Or at least I was a figure of some renown last time I was there, which was, oh, ten or twenty or thirty years ago, before my period of wanderlust. My Uncle Trapspringer is a figure of much, much greater renown, it goes without saying." Tas frowned as something occurred to him. "Although I'm not sure that Uncle Trapspringer will want to throw in with us, because he's rather crotchety about his friends. He's not too friendly with his enemies either." The kender thought a moment, then brightened. "But since I haven't been back there in quite some time, it's more than possible that Uncle Trapspringer isn't living in Kendermore anymore and won't pose the least problem!"

"Well," rumbled Fesz considerately, "I'll be sure to let the Nightmaster know all about the kender race and their, uh, potential."

"Tell him it was my idea," said Tas, beaming.

Fesz nodded and wrote it down.

When they got back from the shipyard, Dogz was waiting for them with a communication from the king. Dogz handed the message to Fesz, but he wouldn't even look at

Tasslehoff. The minotaur averted his eyes, as if he were ashamed of his kender friend.

Over Fesz's shoulder, Tas read the message:

Two humans captured near Atossa. One of them escaped by inexplicable, perhaps magical means. Might he be this Raistlin you are seeking? Report immediately to the Supreme Circle.

The King

Fesz looked questioningly at Tasslehoff.

"Well," said the kender, "I don't know. I don't think it could be Raistlin. The note says two humans. Raistlin's only one human, not to mention Flint's a dwarf and Tanis is an elf—well actually a half-elf, but he doesn't like to be reminded of his human heritage. So I don't think it could be Raistlin."

Fesz knitted his bullish brow.

"Hey, wait a minute!" added Tas excitedly. "Maybe it's Sturm and Caramon. They're two humans. They're supposed to be dead, and I don't think they know any magic, but maybe Raistlin taught Caramon some tricks when they were kids together or something. I bet that's who it is. Oh, boy! Sturm and Caramon are alive. I wonder which one escaped?"

"Sturm and Caramon," rumbled Fesz. "Those were the two humans who were thrown into the Blood Sea."

"That's right."

"Supposing they were still alive," wondered the shaman minotaur. "Why would Raistlin have taught Caramon magic when they both were children?"

"I don't know," responded the kender. "Except maybe because they're twin brothers."

"They're brothers!" Fesz practically shouted. Even Dogz gave a start. Fesz had to lower his voice and struggle to maintain a calm tone. "You never told me that Raistlin has a brother!"

The kender shrugged. "You never asked me. Besides, I thought Caramon was dead, didn't you? Does it matter if Raistlin has a brother? I told you he has a sister, didn't I? Well, actually a half-sister, if you want to get—"

"Wait!" Fesz put up a hand, then, with a great weary sigh, took out his quill pen and began to scribble something on a scrap of parchment. He paused, thought of something, and looked down at Tas. "Before we go on," he said with an extraordinary effort at patience, "does Raistlin have any more sisters or brothers whom we haven't talked about so far?"

"No," Tas said petulantly, confused as to why Fesz seemed so upset. "At least not any that I've heard about."

"Only Kitiara and Caramon."

"Yup."

Fesz wrote something else down hurriedly, then stuck the note in a pocket.

"I wonder which it was, Sturm or Caramon ..." murmured Tasslehoff.

"We must go to Atossa and find out," declared Fesz.

Tas broke out into a huge, happy grin.

"After I make an appearance before the Supreme Circle," added the shaman minotaur hastily.

"The Supreme Circle ... wow!" exclaimed Tasslehoff. "I've never met a whole circle of supreme anything before. I can hardly wait!"

From behind him, Dogz clamped a huge, heavy hand on the kender's shoulder.

"I am truly sorry, friend Tas," said Fesz with obvious sincerity, "but I must go alone. The Supreme Circle would not be pleased if I brought a kender."

* * * * *

Around the large, round oaken table in the palace's main hall sat eight grim-faced, bull-horned minotaurs—nine, if you included the king, who had journeyed from his main residence in the southern city of Nethosak for this emergency conclave. While the others merely looked displeased, the king's bestial countenance bristled with murderous anger, which he was barely able to keep in check. The king had other important things to do and didn't appreciate this interruption in his schedule.

Clockwise from the left of the king, the eight members of the Supreme Circle included Inultus, who commanded the minotaur military and civil police. He was swathed in emblems and badges proclaiming his rank. Next to him sat Akz, whose nickname was Attacca, but no one dared utter it to his face. He was the leader of the minotaur navy. Akz detested Inultus, and vice versa. They were known enemies but were forced to cooperate on policy matters for the greater good of the kingdom. Akz wore nothing across his broad muscular chest. His only garb was a jeweled leather strap girding his powerful loins.

Next to Akz sat the oldest among them, a furrowed minotaur with tufts of gray-white hair called Victri, the representative of the rural minotaurs who tilled the land and maintained isolated government farms throughout the few fertile sections of the isles. Although most self-respecting warriors held the agricultural minotaurs in contempt, they were vital to the economy and stability of the isles. Furthermore, Victri had served on the Supreme Circle the longest. Everyone knew his reputation for honor and wisdom. Quite apart from that, Victri was a ferocious fighter who had distinguished himself in battle. Dressed like a tiller of the land, Victri wore more clothing than any other member of the Supreme Circle, including a heavy shawl that draped his brutish shoulders.

Next to Victri sat Juvabit, a historian and scholar in a society that did not much value scholarly pursuit. Although he was an intellectual by minotaur standards, Juvabit looked indistinguishable from the rest, with his ugly snout, curved horns, and cloven hooves. The only thing that hinted at his stature was a tassel, woven from thin gold strands, which he wore dangling from one shoulder. It signified the Order of the King, the nation's highest accolade, and Juvabit was the only one in the room to have earned it. If anything, that made Juvabit even more insolent than the others, confident in his belief that his fellow members of the Supreme Circle were dullards and that not only was he smarter than any of the others, but he could hold his own against any one of them in hand-to-hand combat.

Next to Jubavit sprawled Atra Cura, his bulky form spilling out of the big wooden chair he sat in. Atra Cura's job was to monitor the human and minotaur pirates who roamed the nearby seas, to extract a percentage of their plunder for the king—and a percentage of that percentage for himself—and to keep the rival pirate factions in line. It would not be inaccurate to say that Atra Cura himself was the fiercest, most murderous pirate of them all. Alone among the minotaurs of the Supreme Circle, he was dressed flamboyantly in bright hues decorated with magnificent gems. Atra Cura flaunted conspicuous weapons, with several sabres and knives tucked into his garb.

The lone female, Kharis-O, was the designated leader of a nomadic band of female minotaurs called the Apart Clan that scorned males and lived outside the cities. The Apart Clan, which had followers in each of the main minotaur isles as well as most of the lesser ones, rarely interacted with the more organized sectors of the society, yet nobody doubted their loyalty to the minotaur race. They could be counted on in times of war, and their fierce battle prowess was every bit the equal of the male warriors. Nothing in Kharis-O's exceptionally ugly face hinted at femininity. Indeed, she offered no concession to her gender in her clothing. She wore tight leather leggings beneath a short leather skirt, and thick, hobnailed sandals. She sat glowering at everyone around the table but said nothing.

The last two members of the Supreme Circle were Bartill and Groppis. Bartill was the head of the architectural and construction guilds, and therefore one of the most powerful minotaurs in the realm. Everyone had to be careful to curry favor with him.

Groppis, inevitably Bartill's ally in a debate, was the keeper of the treasury, every bit as vital in the hierarchy as Bartill. It was Groppis who collected taxes, stashed plunder, and kept a strict accounting of the government wealth, doling out stipends according to autocratic decisions.

The ninth was the king himself, in his fourteenth year of rule. The king exhibited the arrogance of his office and the physical superiority to match. In order to retain his rank, the king met his strongest challenger annually in one-on-one combat in the coliseum arena. For fourteen years, the present king had maintained an adamant grip on his position, ramming, stabbing, piercing, or strangling to death with his bare hands any and all comers. The thin silver band set with small diamonds that he wore around his forehead as a symbol of his reign would be passed on to the next king only if and when he was ever bested.

The king and the eight other members of the Supreme Circle glared at Fesz, demanding to know how the Nightmaster's plans were progressing and whether the unusual news from Atossa meant any kind of setback.

"I will go to Atossa myself in the morning," replied Fesz firmly, "and from there to Karthay to assist the Nightmaster in the final preparations."

"Is this human who escaped the mysterious mage you have been seeking?" asked Akz, the leader of the navy. "I do not intend to mobilize my fleet unless I have absolute assurances that nothing has interfered with the Nightmaster's plans to bring Sargonnas into this world."

"We have lavished great resources on the Nightmaster and his effort," noted the keeper of the treasury, Groppis.

"As for me," put in Atra Cura, the pirate representative, "of course I believe and trust in the Nightmaster, but some of my loose federation of followers are independent-minded, and will require more than my word to go on."

The others nodded and murmured in agreement.

Fesz took a long moment to reply, placing his hands on the table and lowering his eyes to gaze at them from beneath hooded lids. His eyes were deep, his expression furious, yet he managed to calm himself and took a deep breath.

"I am one of the three chosen shamans of the Nightmaster," said Fesz in a low, ominous rumble, "and I do not need to reply to each of your individual craven anxieties. Your petty fears do dishonor to all minotaurs and to your status as members of the Supreme Circle.

"The Nightmaster has informed you that he will cast a remarkable spell to bring Sargonnas, the Lord of Dark Vengeance, into the world. Much expense and preparation has gone into that spell. And everything will happen according to plan when the heavens are in conjunction four days from now, in early nighttime when the stars are at their zenith."

There were gasps from several of the members of the Supreme Circle. Until now, the Nightmaster hadn't revealed the precise timetable of the spell. Fesz's mention of the exact date and time had had the intended effect of making all the worry and opposition among the assembled leaders disappear.

"What about this escaped prisoner?" asked the king.

"I do not believe he is the human called Raistlin," Fesz answered respectfully, "but I will stop in Atossa on the way to Karthay and make certain."

"Where is this Raistlin, then?"

"That I do not know," admitted Fesz. "Perhaps he isn't coming after all. Perhaps we have overestimated him in our minds. In any case, I don't think Raistlin Majere is anything but a minor annoyance, a mosquito on the arse of a woolly mammoth."

The eight members of the Supreme Circle chuckled at Fesz's use of an old minotaur adage.

The king looked satisfied. "What about the kender?" he

wanted to know. "Is he still under the effects of the evil potion?"

Fesz nodded. "Most assuredly he is," rumbled Fesz, "and he has proved quite helpful as an ally. I plan to take him with me to Atossa and Karthay. I hope to persuade the Nightmaster that he might play a role in the ritual."

The king looked skeptical.

"Do not fear," the shaman minotaur said smoothly. "Before I depart, I will be sure to double the dose of his potion."

Chapter 11
The Ancient Kyrie

Although he bounced and jostled inside the sack, which withstood his repeated efforts to tear a hole in it so that he could see out, Caramon didn't sense he was in any immediate danger.

The Majere twin guessed he was being transported a great distance away from the minotaur prison, although who his rescuers were and why they had taken him remained a puzzle. As glad as he was to be free of the minotaurs, Caramon fretted about leaving Sturm behind, and he realized that he was someone else's prisoner now. In effect, he had traded one captivity for another.

His uneasiness wasn't relieved, over the course of the next two hours, by the distinct impression that he was being swept through the air. Caramon could feel no hard surface beneath or on either side of the burlap sack. The only noises that reached his ears sounded like nothing so much as the steady beating of wings and the occasional caw of a giant bird.

Somewhere in the back of his mind, the young warrior seemed to remember having heard a similar cawing once before.

Eventually Caramon had the sensation he was descending from a great height, a descent that ended with the burlap sack, with him still curled up inside, bumping and scraping along rocky ground. Moments later, someone tugged the sack open. On wobbly legs, Caramon stepped out.

A spectacular sight greeted him.

He stood on a ledge in a high-walled canyon that wound out of sight to his left and right. The sides of the canyon were honeycombed with dozens of caves stretching as far as the eye could see. And perched in front of the caves, as if to greet him, were hundreds of an ancient and wondrous folk whose remote civilization few humans ever had been privileged to glimpse.

A welcoming committee of these fantastical "bird-people" stood with Caramon on the ledge. They were a mix of hawk and human, walking upright on long, sinewy legs that ended in birdlike talons. Huge feathered wings sprouted from their backs and attached to their arms and hands. With growing excitement, Caramon thought, Why, they look just like …

… like the broken man back in the prison cell. These were his people! Those terrible wounds on his back and shoulders, Caramon now realized, must have been where the minotaurs had ripped off his wings.

The bird-man nearest Caramon was the one who had rescued the Majere twin from captivity. He was taller than Caramon, and leaner. His bronzed face, quite human in appearance, was fiercely handsome. Rather than hair, flowing golden feathers grew from his head. Fine brown pinfeathers covered his chest. He wore no clothing other than a waistcloth of leather.

"Who are you?" Caramon asked his rescuer.

"In your language," the bird-man said with pride in the common tongue, "I am Cloudreaver."

Caramon fumbled for the proper words. "What are you?"

Cloudreaver frowned and stepped aside, gesturing with his wings to one of the bird-people behind him. His pebble-black eyes watched Caramon haughtily.

Following Cloudreaver's gesture, Caramon saw an elder whom he had not noticed at first. Others grouped protectively around this venerable bird-man who shuffled forward on clawed feet to meet Caramon. In spite of his odd gait, he moved with dignity and grace.

The elder bird-man's feather hair was silver white and streamed down to his chest. Many year of exposure to the sun and elements had darkened and lined his face. In spite of his apparent age, muscles rippled across his chest and in his sinewy legs.

Slightly bent over, his head cocked to one side, the elder bird-man approached Caramon with a glimmer of warmth in his clear yellow eyes. "We are the kyrie," explained the elder, his speech clipped but precise. "I am Arikara—in your tongue, Sun Feather, leader of the people who inhabit the skies."

"Kyrie?" questioned Caramon.

Sun Feather cocked his head, peering at Caramon. "A proud and long-lived folk," the kyrie leader said softly. "You have not heard of us?"

Caramon glanced at the hundreds of feathered kyrie who gazed at him from the high safety of their respective aeries. They murmured amongst themselves; some of them pointed at him. Raistlin may have mentioned the kyrie once. His twin read so many books, it was hard for Caramon to keep track. The burly warrior shook his head from side to side in response to Sun Feather's question.

"That is to be expected," said Sun Feather, placing a huge wing over Caramon's shoulder and leading him gently toward a shelter dug out of the canyon wall.

Caramon hadn't spotted the cave before, perhaps because the hide that draped the entrance was the color of sandstone and blended in with the canyon wall. Some of the other kyrie followed, including Cloudreaver, another elder whose face was dotted with sun spots, and two females, one young, another older, both dresed in leather skirts and vests decorated with quills and beads.

The entrance opened onto a spacious cave that vaulted upward into a high dome. Dried grass and twigs covered the floor of the tamped-down earth. A central fire pit, filled with heated rocks, gave off warmth. Weapons and cooking utensils hung from pegs in the walls. Animal furs, more than sufficient to ward off the desert night cold, were stacked near the threshold.

Sun Feather took aside the two females and gave them some instructions in a language that Caramon could not decipher.

Cloudreaver bade Caramon sit near the fire pit. The other elder, whom Cloudreaver introduced as Three Far-Eyes, sat opposite their visitor. Cloudreaver took a place next to Three Far-Eyes.

Sun Feather sat down next to Caramon, moving gingerly. He picked up a stick and prodded the ground with it. It took Caramon a moment to realize he was outlining a rough map. "Centuries ago the kyrie inhabited many of the islands of Ansalon," Sun Feather told Caramon. "We migrated around the world, never content to stay in one place. Our long flights over the oceans were made possible by a magical device called the Northstone. Because we grew to depend on the Northstone, we lost many of our natural instincts, including the ability to navigate. Then we lost the Northstone, and it fell into the possession of our dire enemies, the minotaurs."

The female kyrie hovered in the background, apparently

busy with preparations for a meal. Now the older one circled behind the three male kyrie and Caramon, distributing stone mugs of a pale, flecked liquid. Caramon cupped his in both hands, sipping eagerly. The warm broth was like nothing Caramon had ever tasted before—rich, flavorful, and instantly nourishing. He could feel it course through his body, refreshing him and sating his hunger.

The kyrie leader's face hardened with bitter memories as he continued his chronicle. "Gradually we gathered here," Sun Feather related, "most of us on the island of Mithas, other clans scattered on nearby islands. Although we can still take long, soaring flights, we no longer cross the oceans. Without the Northstone, we are stranded in this part of the world. We live here"—he gestured broadly—"as best as we are able, as peaceably as we are allowed."

Caramon had countless questions he wanted to ask. He sputtered out two: "What do you want with me? Why did you rescue me from the dungeon in Atossa?"

Cloudreaver answered before Sun Feather could. "I saw you and your friend nearly drowning in the Blood Sea. I did what I could to alleviate your plight."

Caramon's eyes widened. "So that was you!" he exclaimed. "You dropped some kind of bread to us."

"It was my own ration," said the kyrie mildly.

Impulsively Caramon reached across and clasped the kyrie's hands. "You saved our lives," the Majere twin said warmly. "Then you risked your own to help me escape from prison." The young warrior spoke passionately, his words heartfelt. "I owe you more than I could ever hope to repay."

Cloudreaver looked a little uneasy at Caramon's effusive display of emotion. Sun Feather beamed. "Cloudreaver is my son," said the kyrie elder proudly. As Caramon gazed at the bird-man who had gone to such lengths to rescue him, Cloudreaver lowered his eyes. All the earlier traces of arrogance had vanished.

"I have two sons," added Sun Feather. "My firstborn …"

His voice faltered. "My firstborn, Morning Sky, is the one who was ... with you ... being held prisoner in Atossa." He bent his head sorrowfully.

Caramon didn't know what to say. Finally he had learned who the broken man was. Bowing his head, he was overcome with emotion at the realization that the man was Sun Feather's firstborn, Morning Sky. Did Sun Feather know how close his son was to death? How Morning Sky had been tortured and abused by the minotaurs? Did Sun Feather know how brave and resolute his son was? How, even in his brief conversations with Caramon, he had shown no fear of his fate?

Silence settled over the room, then was broken by the plaintive weeping of one of the females.

"We know how the minotaurs are treating Morning Sky," said Sun Feather softly. "We know that he has been tortured to the point of death. We have little hope of ever seeing him free, among us, again."

It was as if the leader of the kyrie had read Caramon's mind. Noticing the warrior's questioning glance, Sun Feather pointed to his head, and Caramon remembered what the broken man had said about telepathy.

"But why couldn't you have freed your son instead of me?" asked Caramon earnestly.

"My son is chained constantly," replied Sun Feather in an even voice, "except when he is permitted to eat. Otherwise he would kill himself. The minotaurs know that about kyrie, even if they know little else about our kind. It is a disgrace for a kyrie to be captured alive."

Caramon drank from his cup of broth. It didn't seem right. He was free, while Morning Sky was being tortured and beaten in prison. "Maybe," the human warrior ventured, "if we were to storm the dungeon ..."

"It would be suicide for all involved," put in Three Far-Eyes, speaking for the first time. The old one's face was somber. "We are a courageous people, but we are not foolhardy."

"What about the tunnel?"

Cloudreaver scoffed. "The tunnel is tight and narrow. It would take hours to squeeze even a small attack force into the prison through the tunnel, and there would be no fast way out. We would have a dozen guards to contend with, as well as the chains and bars of my brother's cell. We have thought about all of this. We have discussed it, argued about it, and come up with nothing."

The kyrie frowned, a shadow darkening his face. "No, there is no way out for my brother. He is doomed."

From the other kyrie came murmured assent. Caramon sat silent for a long time. "Why do they torture him?" the young human from Solace wondered aloud.

"We have pitted ourselves against the minotaurs for hundreds upon hundreds of years," answered Sun Feather. "Over time, we have gathered in these and other mountain enclaves, living far away from the minotaur cities. Although we roam the valleys, foraging food and hunting small animals, we always retreat here. While the bull-men are adept in land battle or at sea, they are oafs when it comes to exploring the mountains. They cannot climb the high peaks to drive us out. To them, we are an alien presence in the midst of their homeland. To us, they are a scourge upon the earth. As they are determined to hunt and destroy us, so too are we sworn to kill them whenever they cross our path.

"In recent months," Sun Feather continued, "minotaur contingents have penetrated our territory and become more intrepid in locating our aeries. The bull-men have successfully raided some of our smaller outlying settlements, vanquishing our warriors, butchering scores of our women and young. It is said that, in some instances, they have been aided by scaly flying creatures who scouted the terrain in advance and carried weapons and supplies."

"Dragons?" It was Caramon's turn to scoff. "Everyone knows there are no dragons in Ansalon. That is nighttime talk for children, for fables."

"Not dragons," Cloudreaver cut in vehemently. "Flying creatures of a type that has not existed before this time."

Caramon looked skeptical.

"Of course we have no proof," said Sun Feather. "There are no surviving eyewitnesses. The minotaurs kill every kyrie and burn everything, leaving only scorched earth. They rarely take prisoners." He paused, allowed himself a sip of hot liquid, and continued, choosing his words carefully and controlling his emotions. "My son, Morning Sky, is one of the exceptions. He was captured at an outpost that he commanded. They realized he is of high rank, possibly noble lineage. From him, they demanded information about our number, our customs and rituals, the whereabouts of our sanctuaries."

This soliloquoy seemed to have exhausted Sun Feather, whose face sagged and shoulders drooped. He put down his cup of broth, then clasped his hands together and nodded to Cloudreaver.

"They have not tortured any information out of him," spat Cloudreaver, "nor will they get any, no matter how devious their cruelty. Morning Sky will expel his final breath without telling them so much as his name."

Caramon looked into Cloudreaver's pebble-black eyes, grim and fatalistic, like his brother's, the broken man's. Sun Feather reached over and touched his son on the wrist. The older female kyrie came over and whispered something in Sun Feather's ear. The elder kyrie nodded.

"And what about you, my son?" asked Three Far-Eyes gently, breaking the silence. "What is your name? What is your story?"

Caramon told them, leaving nothing out. The trip to Southern Ergoth, the magic storm, the capture of Tasslehoff, his and Sturm's trial at sea, their imprisonment. Although the kyrie were exceedingly interested in the role the minotaurs played in Caramon's curious saga, they could add little to the mystery of why the minotaur kingdom would be so preoccupied by a single kender, much less the herb, jalopwort.

"Except," pointed out Three Far-Eyes, "do not forget one thing. Jalopwort is common on Mithas and Karthay, but quite rare, if not altogether absent, from other parts of the world. And like other things on Mithas, the minotaurs define it as their own, sacred, with certain ritualistic uses."

Sun Feather nodded sagely.

Time passed. Now the young female kyrie—her face strikingly beautiful, her red hair flecked with gold— brought out cups and bowls, setting them before Caramon and the others.

Following the example of the kyrie, Caramon dipped his fingers into a basin of cool water, then washed and dried his hands. From the serving bowls, he chose an assortment of nuts, berries, and greens. The older female appeared behind his shoulder and ladled several small cubes of raw red meat onto his plate.

After some minutes, during which they all ate hungrily, Cloudreaver spoke. "A sentinel stays in the tunnel at all times," the young kyrie said, returning to the topic of his brother. "He watches over Morning Sky, hoping against hope for some change in his circumstances.

"We speak to him only a little, always furtively. It would not be wise to take chances. When Morning Sky is able, he speaks to us. Even if the minotaur guards overhear a few words, they do not understand our native language, so they think it is delirium. That is how we were able to tell Morning Sky about the two humans who had been captured and brought to the prison. After talking it over with him, we decided to risk liberating you."

"Why?" asked Caramon thoughtfully.

"For one thing, I saw how you behaved toward my brother," answered Cloudreaver.

"You saw me?"

"I was in the tunnel. That close to my brother, I could see through his eyes, through the walls of stone. My heart beats with the same rhythm as his. My head shares his thoughts.

I listened to your words and saw and believed you to be a good and compassionate human."

Caramon was silent. He was thinking about his own brother, Raistlin. Wasn't it that way between him and Raist? That they could see with each other's eyes sometimes? That their hearts also beat as one?

"We do not have much experience with humans," interjected Sun Feather diplomatically. "I myself have never before been face-to-face with one in my three hundred years of life on this earth."

"Three hundred years!" exclaimed Caramon. The young warrior knew that dwarves and elves were long-lived, but already Sun Feather had lived more than three times the span that Caramon would in his time.

"Yes," admitted Sun Feather, chuckling. "I am old and past my prime. When I am gone, it will be up to Cloud-reaver—"

"Father!" cried Cloudreaver, bringing up his arm and making an angry gesture.

The female kyrie looked upset. Three Far-Eyes dropped his glance. Sun Feather looked chastened.

"Cloudreaver is right," the leader of the kyrie said in a low voice. "It is not right to speak of Morning Sky as if he is already dead. Morning Sky is the firstborn and blood heir to the leadership. But—" His voice broke.

Three Far-Eyes hastened to change the subject. "Most of the humans we know of," said Three Far-Eyes softly, "are brigands or slaves. But our legends tell us that humans can be intelligent and sensitive and loyal. Besides, we felt that it was worth the risk to bring shame down on the bull-men. They will be greatly dishonored by news of an escape from their prison at Atossa."

"Won't they punish Morning Sky?" worried Caramon.

"They will never execute my brother," said Cloudreaver grimly. "They will keep him alive as long as they can."

After the meal was over, the female kyrie brought out pipes, chewing tobacco, and a bowl with thick, cut-up pieces of some kind of gummy root. Cloudreaver chose a long-stemmed pipe, filled it with some substance from a pouch, and puffed on it contemplatively. Three Far-Eyes chewed on tobacco. Sun Feather reached for the root, and Caramon politely followed suit.

Outside, darkness had fallen and quiet reigned. Inside the cave, the elder female moved about the room, reaching for a half-dozen small spheres set into the wall, which by her touch were magically lit and cast a pale blue light.

Caramon chewed on the root meditatively. It had a mild, pleasant taste. The day had been a long and arduous one. His body ached, and his mind as well.

As he chewed, a tingling sensation flowed through his body. Caramon felt his muscles relax. His mind floated free. No longer did he feel weary and sad.

His thoughts flitted to Raistlin. He wondered where his twin brother was, and whether Raist had any inkling of where Caramon was.

He worried about his brother. Kitiara had pounded it into his head that it was his job to worry about his twin brother, although Caramon knew that at this moment, Raistlin was probably worrying just as much about him. Caramon sincerely hoped he was a good representative of the human race for those kyrie who, like Sun Feather, had never met a human before. Surely Raistlin would have better understood the situation and been a more impressive representative of humankind.

Caramon wondered about Tasslehoff. Poor Tas. Likely the kender was dead. What could the minotaurs have wanted with him? Something obscure and unpleasant, Caramon felt sure. Tas wasn't in the prison, nor was he in Atossa, or surely the kyrie would have taken note of him, Caramon thought. Kender do not tend to blend in to the background.

The young warrior looked around at the kyrie in the cave, nodding at him. He wondered if they could read his thoughts. At that moment, he felt almost as if he could read theirs. He sensed their profound despondency over Morning Sky, and at the same time, their stubborn resiliency as a people. They were a remarkable race. He felt proud to be in the company of the ancient kyrie.

Caramon's mind wandered to Sturm. Sturm wouldn't be so comfortable here, high up in the mountains, eating a fine repast and chewing this agreeable after-supper root—not if his friend Caramon was the one who had been left behind in prison.

The minotaurs might not take out their frustration on Morning Sky, Caramon realized with a jolt. But they might—probably would—torture Sturm.

"I must go back," declared the human from Solace suddenly, startling the kyrie by breaking the harmonious silence that had prevailed in the cave. Caramon set his jaw. "I must go back and rescue my friend Sturm."

The faces around him were disapproving. "That would not be wise," said Sun Feather.

"Foolish," said Cloudreaver, putting down his pipe.

"I—I—" Caramon faltered. He didn't possess the eloquence of his twin. "I must go back," Caramon repeated. "Sturm Brightblade would surely try to rescue me. No risk would deter him, not a hundred, a thousand, minotaurs. He'd consider it his honor-bound duty. I can only try to do what he would, under opposite circumstances."

"But how can you get inside the prison?" asked Three Far-Eyes sympathetically. "And, what is more important, how would you get out?"

Caramon had no ready reply. He addressed Cloudreaver. "You say you keep a sentinel in the tunnel at all times?"

"Yes," responded Cloudreaver. "Day and night."

"Then I will hear his reports, watch, and wait. I will seek my opportunity. Even if nothing changes, I must still try something."

Everyone kept silent. Caramon looked at Sun Feather, waiting for the leader of the kyrie to speak. The elder's face was unreadable.

"I will go with the human!" said Cloudreaver unexpectedly.

Sun Feather appeared shocked. "You cannot, my son! Already you have taken too many risks. You have not only your own future but also the future of the entire race to consider."

Cloudreaver's eyes were hard, stubborn. "I will not take any risk that you wouldn't take yourself—if you were not old bones." Although Cloudreaver's words struck his father with the force of blows, Sun Feather's eyes shone with unmistakable pride. "I admire this Caramon," said Cloudreaver. "I should like to help his friend as I helped him."

Caramon reached over and clasped Cloudreaver's hand. This time the kyrie put his other hand on top of Caramon's in a gesture of solidarity.

Three Far-Eyes spoke up. "If Cloudreaver goes, others with the appetite for fighting the minotaurs should have the opportunity to go with him. The human should be brought to the Warrior Society."

Cloudreaver looked grateful for the words. Although Caramon didn't know what the Warrior Society was, the fervor in the old bird-man's voice surprised him.

For long minutes, Sun Feather stared at Cloudreaver as father to son. "You must do what you feel you must do," Sun Feather said heavily at last. The leader of the kyrie sighed. "But you must do nothing rash—and you will not be doing anything tonight. Agreed? So, it is time to sleep, and in our sleep to dream the things we hope to do."

Taking the signal from Sun Feather, Three Far-Eyes and the young female kyrie left the cave. Cloudreaver hesitated and gave Caramon a friendly nod, then he, too, left. Sun Feather placed a winged arm on Caramon's shoulder as the Majere twin rose to leave.

"You will sleep here," said Sun Feather. He gestured toward the corner, where the older female kyrie had lingered and was setting up a thick pile of furs.

"But this is your dwelling," protested Caramon, "and I have brought you nothing but heartache."

Sun Feather shook his head. "You have brought nothing that was not here before you arrived," said the elder kyrie, "and as long as you stay among us, I wish that you would take this cave as your place to eat and sleep. It is cold in the mountains at night, and you are not as accustomed to the conditions as we kyrie."

Caramon opened his mouth to object, but Sun Feather raised a hand. "I am welcome anywhere among my people," the leader of the kyrie said, "and will not want for a place to eat and rest. And some nights I like to have the excuse of the open sky." His dark face wrinkled into a smile. "Even though I am old bones."

Caramon didn't protest further. In truth, he was happy for the comfort of the cave.

* * * * *

For the next several days, Caramon lived as one of the kyrie in their cave city among the sheer cliffs that girdled the high valleys in the far north of Mithas.

Taller and leaner than Caramon, Cloudreaver could easily carry the warrior, grasped in his taloned feet, while flying from plateau to plateau. Everywhere he went, Caramon was an object of curiosity among the kyrie, though he was invariably greeted with warmth. While the females, especially, gossiped and chattered about him in their kyrie tongue, most of the bird-people switched to Common in his presence. They overwhelmed him with their hospitality. Many of them already seemed to know the story of his escape, and his connection with Morning Sky.

Some of the kyrie caves were huge and able to house dozens of families, Caramon noted, while some isolated families chose to camp in sunlit hollows at the base of cliffs. The occasional wood beams or ladders Caramon noticed had been borne through the sky from miles away,

Cloudreaver told him. Wood didn't grow at this altitude
and was quite a luxury, and therefore a measure of status.

The tough, clever kyrie had devised ingenious ways of
surviving in a region that was hot and parched by day, cool
and dry by night. Rainwater was precious. What little that
fell was diverted into holding pools at the bottom of the
canyons, with only a small supply kept high near the cave
cities where moisture evaporated quickly due to the constant onslaught of sun and wind. The kyrie had dug irriga-
tion canals and built dams from the rocky ground, the
canals deep to reduce the amount of water exposed to the
sun, and narrow so they could be covered during cold
nights.

Jackrabbits, cottontails, mule deer, and rodents provided
the kyrie with meat. These were hunted daily by males to
whom that duty had been delegated. While not a farming
people, each kyrie family kept a small garden fed by irriga-
tion. The garden supplemented their diet of meat with cac-
tus fruit, nuts, beans, and seeds. On forays into the valleys,
they collected wild grains. A lean, lithe race, the kyrie ate
little—only one full meal a day.

Caramon asked Cloudreaver about the magical blue orbs
that he noticed everywhere, which provided illumination
inside the caves at night. As Cloudreaver explained it,
many of the kyrie had modest magical skills. As a people,
they were especially reknowned for their ability to communicate with and cast spells over animals. But the magically
inclined among them who were most revered were those
who could predict or alter the weather. In any case, the
blue-light orbs were a very simple spell, Cloudreaver said.

While the men took charge of hunting, the women occupied themselves with pottery-making, leatherwork, and the
etching of shells. Whereas humans tended to carry their
belongings in pouches and rucksacks, many of the kyrie
had small baskets slung at their sides. These might contain
anything from dried fruit to family artifacts to small
weapons. The traditional weapon, which didn't fit into a

basket, was a curved club, carved of wood, called a stryker. Many of the males who went off hunting carried bows and arrows as well as their strykers.

Caramon noticed there was a steady coming and going of the young males. They flew magnificently, these young, strong kyrie, like great eagles, covering ground rapidly, beating their huge wings. Some arrived fresh from hunting, the carcasses of animals slung over their shoulders. Others were obviously scouts and messengers.

The scouts and messengers reported directly to Cloud-reaver. Some of them pointed at Caramon, speaking rapidly in the kyrie tongue. Some of the young bird-men looked at him haughtily, as Cloudreaver once had, and Caramon guessed they were arguing with Cloudreaver in their native language.

Although Caramon pressed Cloudreaver to learn what they were saying, the son of Sun Feather was evasive. Caramon figured that was his royal prerogative, but he was anxious about Sturm and wanted to know what, if anything, the kyrie had reported about the Solamnic. More than once Cloudreaver asked the human warrior to remain patient.

After four days among the kyrie, Caramon, well rested, leaner, and tougher, was still far from patient.

"Where is Atossa from here?" Caramon asked Cloud-reaver, standing on the ledge where he had first arrived.

Cloudreaver pointed south. "A hundred miles."

"I could return there and take a turn as sentinel in the tunnels," pressed Caramon.

Cloudreaver put his hand on the shoulder of the anxious warrior. "No, my friend," he repeated. "Soon. Your friend is still alive. My brother is still alive. But you must be patient. We must wait a little longer for something to happen."

That night, Caramon was in the cave that Sun Feather had ceded to him, lying on his back, ready for sleep, when Cloudreaver came for him.

Caramon started as the son of Sun Feather entered. His

kyrie friend was strangely daubed with paint, ornamented in beads and shells. Cloudreaver brought out a blindfold. Although Caramon felt uneasy, he let the kyrie tie it around his eyes so that he couldn't see where he was being taken.

Then Caramon felt the by now familiar sensation of being lifted up and borne through the air, but only for a short distance this time. When the blindfold came off, Caramon was in another, larger cave with about a dozen male kyrie who were garbed and decorated like Cloudreaver. Some of them he remembered meeting. Others he had never seen before.

They sat cross-legged in a circle. As Caramon, guided by Cloudreaver, joined the group, one of the male kyrie got up and came over to him, daubing his face with ash-gray, zigzag lines and draping him with ceremonial feathers and jewelry. This kyrie Caramon knew to be Cloudreaver's friend. His name was Bird-Spirit.

The bird-men linked hands and began to chant in the kyrie tongue. Caramon was seated between two kyrie he did not know. Looking around, he realized that Cloudreaver was gone. The kyrie gripped his hands. Although the young warrior had no idea what the kyrie were chanting, Caramon felt himself drawn into their solemn ritual.

The chanting continued for a long time. In spite of himself, Caramon felt himself being lulled to sleep. When he jerked his eyes open, he saw that the others, too, had closed their eyes. The kyrie were deliberately trancelike. Someone had lit sticks of incense, and a pungent odor, accompanied by curls of smoke, filled the cave.

All of a sudden the chanting stopped, and Cloudreaver appeared from a dark corner, carrying a large, heavy wooden box. This he carefully placed in the center of the circle. All eyes followed his every movement as the kyrie leaned over, opened a latched lid, and pulled out—Caramon caught his breath—a rare sea dragon.

The sea dragon was large, resembling a giant turtle with a lizardlike head, a thick dark shell, webbed toes, and massive, paddlelike flippers. Caramon knew that these ferocious creatures, not true dragons, were legendary for attacking ships. Rarely were they caught alive. Although it could breathe either air or water, it couldn't survive long without being immersed in water. As large and fierce-looking as this one was, it moved its head and tail ponderously outside its element.

Cloudreaver held it up and made a show of handing it to Bird-Spirit, who sat opposite Caramon in the circle. The head of the sea dragon thrashed, its powerful jaws snapping at the air. For long minutes, Bird-Spirit held the sea dragon over his head, chanting and murmuring while the savage creature did everything possible to twist out of his grip and lunge at him.

Bird-Spirit handed the sea dragon back to Cloudreaver, who passed it on to the next kyrie, and so on around the circle until Cloudreaver brought the huge creature to Caramon. The others watched him intently. Close up, the sea animal was revolting. It shrieked and thrashed, lashing out with its jaws. Fearful, Caramon hesitated for just a moment, then reached out and took the sea dragon from Cloudreaver.

Following the example of the others, Caramon held the sea dragon above his head, keeping silent while the other kyrie chanted for him. The Majere twin held the creature aloft until his arms ached, then lowered it, returning the sea dragon to Cloudreaver.

Cloudreaver met Caramon's eyes and passed the sea dragon on to the next kyrie.

After the sea dragon had gone around the circle, the chanting rose as Cloudreaver held the creature down in the center. He pulled out a long, sharp knife, and as the creature flopped around, trying to escape, Cloudreaver plunged the knife into the animal's back again and again, penetrating the shell.

Bird-Spirit rushed forward with a bowl, collecting the sea animal's spew of blood and body juices.

After some time, the creature lay still. One of the kyrie lifted its body back into the box and dragged the box off to one side.

Again Cloudreaver turned to Bird-Spirit first, this time offering the knife to his friend. Bird-Spirit took the knife and cut himself across the top of the forearm, a gash that dripped blood. Cloudreaver caught some of the blood in the bowl, then took the bowl from Bird-Spirit and passed it around the circle.

One by one the others cut themselves and dripped their own blood into the bowl containing the vital juices of the rare sea dragon.

When the knife came to Caramon, he looked up and met Cloudreaver's eyes once more. Without knowing why, but trusting the rituals of this good and honorable race of bird-people, Caramon cut himself on the forearm. Inexperienced, he cut himself rather deeply, and after blood spurted into the bowl, he had to grip his arm to stem the flow.

Cloudreaver was the last to cut himself.

Everyone kept silent now. The chanting had stopped. Nobody moved.

Kneeling in the center of the circle, Cloudreaver was the first to drink from the bowl. He started forward to hand it to Bird-Spirit, then had a second thought. The son of Sun Feather, the brother of Morning Sky, the heir to leadership of the kyrie turned and brought the bowl to Caramon Majere.

If the truth were known, Caramon was sickened at the thought of drinking the mixture, but he had come this far. He would do what was asked of him. Gripping the bowl with both hands, he put the slightly warm liquid to his lips and gulped some down.

Glancing up, he saw approval in Cloudreaver's eyes. Around the circle, he saw nodding faces.

Around the circle the bowl went.

Caramon was not the only warrior to be sickened that night by the sea dragon ritual. Within minutes of drinking the mixture of blood and sea dragon juices, he had rushed outside to vomit repeatedly in the darkness.

Afterward, with a wry grin, Cloudreaver told Caramon that that was no dishonor. Caramon had purified himself, and now he would be considered one of them, an honorary—for he was not a kyrie—member of their Warrior Society.

Chapter 12
The Pit of Doom

Early in the morning, before leaving for Atossa, Tasslehoff drank a double dose of the evil potion. He said he was beginning to like the taste of it—milky, a tad sweet—and it was not a problem for Fesz to coax it all down.

Because of his familiarity with the kender, Dogz was assigned to go along on the journey from Lacynos to Atossa, and from there to Karthay. His mission: to guard Tas.

"Well, let's call it safeguarding," Fesz was overheard by Tas to say to Dogz.

Dogz was disgusted with how Tasslehoff was behaving lately, which was less like a kender and more like a just plain evil person. The huge minotaur tried to beg off the assignment, but Fesz insisted that Dogz accompany them.

"He thinks you're his friend," said Fesz wisely, adding,

"Besides, I command it."

In half a day, the three of them covered the distance to Atossa, riding in a royal coach drawn by a team of sleek black horses. As much for display as for protection, a troop of fully armored minotaur soldiers thundered alongside, stirring up clouds of dust. The road was rocky and full of bumps, and both minotaurs and the kender were tossed up and down repeatedly in their seats.

Outside the windows of the coach, Tasslehoff glimpsed barren desert. Between the noise and the dust and the sweltering heat and the boring scenery, it really wasn't a very agreeable journey, Tasslehoff thought. Although he did enjoy being bounced up and down in his seat more than Fesz and Dogz did.

They arrived at midday, to be greeted with much pomp and circumstance. The delegation saluted Fesz in the manner to which a high dignitary was entitled. The welcoming minotaurs observed Tas with obvious curiosity. Dogz stood scowling in the background.

A minotaur with showy insignia, attended by a human slave, made a big show of fawning over Fesz and inviting him to a lunch in his honor. But Fesz, already in a foul mood because of the hot, noisy, thoroughly unpleasant journey, brushed past the other minotaur, insisting upon seeing the human prisoner—the one who had not escaped—right away.

"Yes, right away! Or heads will roll!" added Tasslehoff in a voice that brooked no argument.

* * * * *

"That's him," rumbled Dogz. "He's one of the humans from the ship." He added, almost guiltily, "I guess we should have killed him right off, instead of throwing him overboard."

"Of course you should have," said Tas, somewhat sulkily. "Now look at all the bother he's caused. If you had asked me, I would have said, 'Kill him and be done with it.' Don't put off until tomorrow what you can do today—especially when it comes to killing, I always say. Of course, I wasn't really evil at the time, so maybe I wouldn't have said 'Kill him and be done with it' exactly, but in retrospect, Dogz, you're absolutely right."

"What's his name again?" asked Fesz, cocking his head and observing the human.

They were standing in front of Sturm Brightblade's prison cell. Sturm sat on a chair facing them, his hands tied with rope behind the chair. The Solamnic was somewhat bruised and bloody, probably signs of recent beatings. But the minotaur guards had obviously tried to freshen him up to make him look presentable for the unusual visit from this high emisarry of the Nightmaster.

Sturm glowered at them. He was surprised and initially relieved to see Tasslehoff, but the kender hadn't greeted him, maintaining an aloof demeanor. Sturm watched, puzzled, as Tas whispered in conspiratorial conversation with the minotaurs. The kender was certainly acting peculiarly. The young Solamnic couldn't catch Tas's eye.

What was he up to?

One of the minotaurs, Sturm noted, was the oddest specimen he had laid eyes on yet. Hulking and large-horned, this one was obviously some dignitary or high priest. The bull creature was dressed in feathers and furs and moved with solemn, dignified purpose.

Sturm had the distinct impression Tas was acting as the minotaur's sidekick or aide.

"Sturm Brightblade," said Tas, spitting contemptuously the way he had seen some of the minotaurs do. "He thinks he's a Solamnic Knight, but he's not really—just another sad case of misguided ambition, if you ask me. It's a long story, and I'm not sure you want to go into it, but as far as I can figure it out, it all started with his father—"

"Let me see him more closely," growled Fesz, interrupting.

Behind them, the minotaur guard hurried to oblige. The door slid open, and Tas and Fesz stepped inside the cell.

Dogz waited outside the cell, feeling indifferent to the whole situation.

Fesz approached Sturm, studying him with a frown on his face. Tas did likewise, hoping that Fesz noticed how well he imitated the minotaur's every movement. The kender stuck his face right up next to Sturm's, cocking his head just as the minotaur shaman did.

Having already learned that it was a mistake to react impulsively in this prison, Sturm decided to remain silent, assess this latest development, and watch for some inkling of what game the unpredictable kender was playing.

"A big mistake," said Tasslehoff scornfully. "Obviously they've been torturing this fellow, which is a monumental waste of time. He'd die rather than break his code of honor. The same goes for Kitiara, if I haven't mentioned it before. Waste of time to torture her. Only in her case, it has nothing to do with honor. It's just plain pigheadedness. When we get to Karthay, we can tell the Nightmaster, if he hasn't figured it out for himself. Which he probably has, being the Nightmaster and all."

Sturm listened carefully. What was this kender babble about Kitiara, Karthay, and someone called the Nightmaster?

"It's especially a waste of time to torture Sturm if all you're going to do is punch and kick and occasionally cut him up a little. Sturm comes from a long line of Solamnic traditional nonsense, and he doesn't respond to ordinary physical torture the way some humans might. Now, if it was up to me, I'd do something a little more imaginative."

Fesz had moved past Sturm to pace the cell behind the prisoner. The shaman minotaur inhaled deeply, his nostrils flaring. He tilted his horned head. Fesz had already forgotten Sturm. He was memorizing the still-lingering scent of the other human, the one called Caramon, the brother of Raistlin.

Tasslehoff reached into his pouch, rummaging for something. He pulled out a small pair of scissors. With the other hand, he grabbed one end of Sturm's long, drooping mustache.

"This is what I'd do," he cried triumphantly, slicing off the end of Sturm's mustache. Sturm winced but said nothing, glaring furiously at the kender.

"Yes!" Tas held the tuft of brown hair in the air, proudly displaying it to Fesz. "Now, that's what I call torture! These Solamnics are very proud of their mustaches. Oh, very proud indeed!"

He leaned back toward Sturm with an exuberant grin. "I've wanted to do that for a long time," the kender taunted the young Solamnic. "Yes, a very, very long time! You think you're so high and mighty just because you can grow a long, droopy mustache. Well, I could, too, if I wanted to. I could grow a mustache longer than a topknot. I—"

"I would like to see where the kyrie is held," rumbled Fesz, cutting Tas off, "and where the other human was last seen before he disappeared."

"Yes, your excellency!" said the guard, hurrying to escort them. Grabbing the kender by the shoulders, the guard steered Tas out of the cell. The evil kender twisted under the minotaur's grip, shrieking over his shoulder at the tight-lipped Sturm.

"And I suppose you think we came all this way just to see you, Mr. Droopy Mustache! Hah! It just so happens that we are on our way to Karthay, where we are going to rendezvous with the Nightmaster and do a great, big, important magic spell that will bring Sargonnas into this world. And did I mention that none other than Kitiara Uth Matar is there already, being held prisoner, so we've got more important people on our schedule to torture than you. ..."

The minotaur guard led the way down a corridor. Fesz followed, prodding Tas in front of him.

It was Dogz who paused to gaze at Sturm. The minotaur rubbed his chin ruefully, thinking he really ought to have

killed the two humans the first time he encountered them.
Next time he would know better. Now he was up to his
thick, bull neck in things he didn't understand. With a sigh,
Dogz trailed after Fesz, Tas, and the minotaur guard.

Sturm was left with half a mustache to ponder what was
going on.

* * * * *

The three minotaurs and Tas headed toward the far end
of one of the dim corridors, where a sole prisoner was kept
behind bars, manacled to a side wall.

This prisoner, Fesz explained to Tasslehoff on the way,
was a kyrie, one of the fabled bird-people who lived in
remote, mountainous areas of Mithas. The kyrie were
sworn enemies of the race of minotaurs, rarely seen in captivity.

"Your former friend, Caramon, was a trustee who
brought food and water to the other prisoners," noted Fesz.
"He was last spotted outside the kyrie's cell. Then he vanished without a trace—like magic."

If he was talking about Raistlin, Caramon's twin brother,
Tasslehoff said sagely, then they'd have to take into account
all sorts of possibilities—invisibility spells, time travel,
even escape disguised as a scurrying centipede. But since it
was Caramon, the kender was certain that magic had had
nothing to do with it.

"This Raistlin must be a very powerful mage," rumbled
Fesz, impressed.

"Yes, very powerful," agreed Tas, adding mentally to
himself, although he isn't really a mage—yet. Aloud he
added, "As powerful as they come. I wouldn't even dare to
guess how powerful, because even while I was taking the
time to guess, Raistlin would probably be learning a new
spell or two and becoming even more powerful!"

When they arrived at the cell of the kyrie, Tas was cha-
grined and disappointed. Except for his legs, which were

decidedly birdlike, the prisoner didn't look much like a bird-man. The kyrie had been beaten severely, and his arms hung limp at his sides. A pathetic sight.

A slight twitch told Tas that the kyrie was alive, but just barely. From the looks of him, he might as well have been dead.

When Dogz leaned over and whispered to Tas that the ugly-looking, infected scars on the kyrie's back were where his wings had been ripped off, the kender exploded.

"What?" Tasselhoff exclaimed, turning on the dungeon guard and aiming several sharp kicks at the bull-man's knobby kneecaps. "I get one of the only chances of my life to sneak a peek at a kyrie, and you have to bully the man practically to death and tear his wings off! Why, without his wings, he's practically human-looking—hardly worth the trip to Atossa! You could at least have waited until—"

Fesz pulled Tas away from the astonished guard, whose first impulse was to bash the kender over the head until he thought better of it.

The guard retreated up the corridor. Dogz followed him, calmly explaining in a low voice that the kender had been taking an evil potion at the behest of the shaman and such behavior was to be expected, even sanctioned.

After Fesz soothed Tas, the shaman slowly paced the width of the corridor. He peered at the abject kyrie, then studied the inside and outside of the cell, his eyes roving slowly over the floor, the walls, and the ceiling. He knelt, and with his huge, muscular hands, he felt the solidity of the stone floor. He ran his fingers along the cracks in the side wall. He cocked his head, closed his eyes, and listened for unaccustomed sounds. Then he opened them again, a frown creasing his bull face.

"We did all that, too," said the minotaur guard to Dogz sourly, from where he stood farther up the corridor. "We didn't turn up anything either."

The shaman jerked up his horns, which barely cleared the ceiling. Fesz shot the guard a withering glance. Realizing that he had been overheard, the guard lowered his eyes and stared at his feet.

Fesz stepped back, inviting Tas to take a look.

The kender was eager to prove himself. He had been watching Fesz carefully. First Tas stared at the kyrie. Then he examined the inside of the cell, his eyes darting around suspiciously. It was hard to see much in the dim light. Then he looked around the corridor outside the cell. He knelt down on the stone floor and felt for anything unusual. He ran his fingers along the walls. Like Fesz, he cocked his head, closed and opened his eyes, strained to listen.

He thought he heard a rustling sound somewhere.

"Did Caramon leave anything behind ... even the slightest hint of a clue?" asked Tasslehoff.

"Nothing," mumbled the minotaur guard from farther up the corridor. "Just the two buckets of food and water that he had been carrying. They were overturned, almost empty."

Fesz watched the kender carefully.

Tas paced around in a circle, coming back to a position in front of the cell. He glanced at Fesz. He looked at the kyrie again. Slowly he raised his eyes to the ceiling, which was even higher than Caramon Majere was tall—but not by much.

About two buckets and an armspan higher, Tas guessed.

"I think—" began Tas.

"Yes?" Fesz asked eagerly.

"I think," the kender declared in a loud voice, "that the thing we ought to do is punish Sturm Brightblade!"

"Punish Sturm Brightblade?" Fesz repeated. The emissary of the Nightmaster sounded puzzled.

"It's a matter of principle," explained Tasslehoff, even louder. "The principle being that Sturm must have known that Caramon was going to try to escape, and since he refuses to give us the slightest cooperation—"

"We've already done our best to torture it out of him," offered the dungeon guard from up the corridor.

"Your best!" the kender exploded. "You have the temerity to tell me you've done your best?"

Dogz snorted but held his tongue. Although the minotaur guard wasn't a very fast learner, he realized that he ought not to say anything else.

Turning to Fesz, Tasslehoff asked, with great solemnity, "Are there any minotaur methods of execution that are truly special?"

Fesz pondered the question, delighted that Tas had turned his imagination to such worthwhile pursuits. "Well," answered the shaman minotaur slowly, "the Pit of Doom is a particularly cruel spectacle, one that I myself—before spending my time on Karthay, in devotion to the Nightmaster—always enjoyed watching."

"The Pit of Doom?" mused the kender. Tas liked the sound of it.

"A dance of death around hellish holes of fiery liquid," the shaman minotaur explained briefly. "A demise made all the more humiliating by the fact that it is staged for the entertainment of hordes of spectators who watch from a gallery."

Tas's eyes widened. "The Pit of Doom!" he exclaimed with glee, practically shouting, "That's it! That's the punishment that I would like to see meted out to that snooty Solamnic!"

"The only difficulty," rumbled Fesz, "is that we must get to Karthay in three days."

"Three days!" repeated Tas loudly, clearly enunciating and emphasizing every word. "So why can't we stick old Sturm in the Pit of Doom tomorrow morning and set sail by midday?"

"I don't see any reason why not," agreed Fesz, "but we must hasten to make arrangements."

"Good," said the kender. "I would consider it a personal privilege to watch Sturm get his just deserts. Also, I have an abiding curiosity about all pits, whether of doom or just plain—"

Fesz was already in motion.

With a pitying backward glance at the kyrie and a hasty look up at the ceiling, Tas hurried after the shaman minotaur.

The broken man twitched.

Dogz snorted.

As Tas passed the minotaur guard, he paused and gave him a hard kick in the shins.

* * * * *

The next morning one hundred bull-folk crowded the small semicircular gallery that rose along one side of the Pit of Doom.

Snorting and stomping, the minotaur audience made its impatience known as they awaited the arrival of the officials, without whom the duel to the death—between the local champion, a merciless bull-man named Tossak, and the human prisoner, the Solamnic, Sturm Brightblade—could not begin.

In ceremonial procession, a dozen functionaries and prison authorities accompanied Dogz, Tasslehoff, and Fesz as they entered the arena and took their seats in a privileged section of the gallery. The spectators craned their necks to gawk at the unusual sight of a kender sitting next to an emissary of the Nightmaster. As befit the occasion, Tas sat up straight, scowling as fiercely as he could.

At the suggestion of the evil kender Tasslehoff Burrfoot, Sturm had been told the night before that he would be thrust into a deadly competition the following day. He took the announcement impassively.

On the bright side, his bonds were untied and he was given the very best food and a pallet to sleep on. The minotaurs promised he could fight with the weapon of his choice. After considering the options they showed him, Sturm chose a long, thin, double-edged blade with a chiseled hilt. Whatever happened in the fight to come, Sturm vowed that he would give a good account of himself.

Battered and weary from his torture and imprisonment, the young Solamnic tried to make sense of the situation. He tried to fathom why Tas would be cooperating with these minotaurs. Could it be possible that the kender truly was allied with them? As weak as he was, Sturm lay awake half the night thinking without coming to any definite conclusion.

In the morning, his hand drifted, in its customary fashion, up to his mustache to tug on it thoughtfully. The Solamnic felt only thin air. Ruefully Sturm rubbed his cheek, remembering the kender's glee as he snipped off half the young man's moustache. Sturm flushed, suddenly very angry, his determination to fight and fight well strengthened.

Within the hour, Sturm stood at one end of a tunnel, gripping his sword tightly. At a signal from a minotaur keeper, he started down the narrow passage. As he moved toward the entrance to the pit, he felt the first rush of warm air.

Entering the staging area, Sturm saw what his keeper had described as the Pit of Doom. It was actually a large bowl, superheated by some kind of subterranean geothermal source. The underground source had broken through to the surface in the base of the bowl, which consisted of molten lava that bubbled and seethed, occasionally belching out great bursts of searing gases. Islands of black rock jutted up from the fiery red liquid, connected by bridges that arched high over the lava pit. A fall from them would mean certain death.

Rising from the lava, the heat scalded Sturm's skin. As he looked around the pit, he had to shield his eyes from the brightness and intense heat.

Scanning the crowd in the gallery on the other side of the pit, the Solamnic saw no sign of Tasslehoff amidst the rows of seated minotaurs. Shouting and jeering assaulted his ears, even as the aggregate smell of the minotaur crowd overwhelmed his nostrils.

Directly opposite from Sturm, another tunnel opened into the arena, its entrance shrouded in shadow. As Sturm watched, a horned figure loomed in the darkness, filled the opening, then emerged into view.

Sturm guessed his opponent to be at least seven and a half feet tall. His horns, which added another two feet to his height, were waxed and shiny.

White-blond hair streamed down to his shoulders, and thick fur covered the exposed parts of his hide. Two large rings pierced one ear, while his massive chest rippled with muscle.

On one hand, he wore a mandoll—an iron gauntlet, of the unique type prized by minotaur champions, with spikes on the knuckles and a dagger blade along the back of the thumb. The other hand gripped a heavy clabbard with a sharp, saw-toothed edge.

"Tos-sak! Tos-sak! Tos-sak!" chanted the crowd.

"Sturm! Sturm! Sturm!" squeaked one voice, its high pitch distinguishing it from the minotaur crowd. Sturm recognized it as belonging to Tasslehoff.

Tossak acknowledged the crowd with an arrogant nod. Then the huge minotaur glared in Sturm's direction, flared his bestial snout, and emitted a fierce bellow of challenge.

With a speed and agility that took the Solamnic by surprise, Tossak charged toward him, nimbly leaping from island to island of black rock until he arrived at the bridge that led across to Sturm.

Again the minotaur champion bellowed his challenge, waving and stabbing his clabbard in the air for emphasis.

"Tos-sak! Tos-sak! Tos-sak!" chanted the crowd.

Dizziness swept over Sturm. The blasting heat, the thundering crowd, and the bellowing minotaur warrior all combined to throw him off balance. Sturm shook his head to clear it. Then the Solamnic surprised everyone by how quickly he moved—away from Tossak.

Vaulting across an island of black rock, Sturm planted himself on another bridge that gave him a clear view of Tossak yet kept him safe from immediate attack. Knightly tenets included prudence, Sturm rationalized, and in this instance, that meant buying some time while he figured out the best way to fight the huge beast-man.

Watching the human's retreat, Tossak snorted angrily, pawing the ground with his cleft hooves.

"Sturm! Sturm! Sturm!" chanted Tasslehoff.

Sturm risked a glance into the crowd. There, near the crowd's center, sat the kender, wedged between two minotaurs, one of them the same one he had seen Tas with yesterday, the furred and feathered shaman.

Tas waved gaily at Sturm.

Before Sturm returned his attention to the arena, Tossak made his move, once again leaping across the dark islands of rock, seemingly oblivious to the heat that engulfed the pit and burned Sturm's eyes.

Again the bull-man came to a stop just short of Sturm, on the far side of the bridge from Sturm. Again he thundered his challenge.

Once again the Solamnic turned and sprinted in the opposite direction, hopping over rock islands and sprinting across bridges until he was as far away from Tossak as he could get and still be in the arena.

The heat was sapping Sturm's energy. Drenched in sweat, the Solamnic fought to stay alert. Below him, the hot lava bubbled and belched at the bottom of the pit.

"Tos-sak! Tos-sak! Tos-sak!"

"Sturm! Sturm! Sturm!"

By now, Tossak felt certain that his opponent was a coward. The minotaur champion rolled his eyes and shrugged his shoulders, drawing another cheer from the crowd. He turned and sauntered in Sturm's direction, taking his time traversing the rock islands and bridges, until he came within striking distance of the Solamnic, just across a short rock bridge.

Again Tossak brandished his weapon in the air, shouting and gesticulating.

The crowd erupted in a thunderous cheer ...

... at which point Sturm charged across the bridge, his sword leveled before him, pointed straight at the minotaur.

All Sturm could think about was how slowly his legs seemed to be moving, how heavy the sword felt in his hands, how soon nothing would matter anymore because he would be dead. The Solamnic was hardly in the best of condition to be fighting a minotaur to the death. After days of hanging on to life at sea and more days of harsh treatment in the Atossa prison, Sturm felt as if he were wading through a lake choked with weeds.

For the moment, he had the advantage, though. Not expecting the charge, distracted by the din of the crowd, and not quite believing what Sturm was doing after his previous apparent cowardice, Tossak failed to react to his opponent's charge until the last possible instant.

Then, almost as if by reflex, the minotaur swung his gauntleted hand and caught Sturm's blow. The sound of Sturm's blade striking the iron gauntlet rang throughout the arena. The knight's weapon was knocked to the ground and went skittering across the bridge, teetering on the edge.

Sturm dove after it as Tossak, in earnest now, pursued him. Sturm reached the sword just in time to twist around and swing it upward, slashing one of Tossak's thighs.

The minotaur screamed with rage and backed up slightly, but only for a moment. Then Tossak lunged forward and, with his gauntleted hand, grabbed the sword from Sturm, wresting it from the Solamnic's grip and flinging it over the side of the bridge into the pit, where it sank into the fiery liquid.

The crowd roared its approval.

Tossak wiped blood from his leg, tasting it as he eyed Sturm. Advancing on the Solamnic, he swung his heavy clabbard. Sturm scrambled away from the edge of the bridge as he desperately sought an opening.

The minotaur champion swung his clabbard hard in a half-circle, coming just inches from Sturm's forehead. When Tossak swung once more, Sturm ducked under the blow, then came up in a low tackle that dropped Tossak to the bridge, knocking his clabbard down. Before Tossak, more astonished than hurt, could react, the Solamnic had managed to kick the weapon to the side of the bridge where it slid off into the fiery pit.

The crowd rumbled with excitement.

Springing to his feet, Tossak howled in fury and humiliation as he stomped toward Sturm, who was half-stumbling backward.

A heavy blow swatted the Solamnic across the face, knocking him down. A kick sent him rolling. He caught himself at the edge of the bridge just in time. Sturm tried to regain his footing but Tossak was right beside him. The minotaur clamped a heavy hand on one of Sturm's ankles and lifted him up, dangling the young Solamnic over the edge of the liquid fire pit.

Squirming, windmilling his arms futilely, Sturm looked down and saw nothing but heaving, molten lava.

Intense heat washed over Sturm.

Tossak raised his head triumphantly, showing off his dangling prize to the crowd. His bestial countenance cracked open in a leering grin. He filled his lungs and let loose an ear-splitting bellow.

The crowd roared back.

The minotaur fighter lifted his gauntleted hand and triggered the dagger concealed along the back of his thumb. The sharp, curved blade flicked open. Tossak cocked his arm and moved to deliver the piercing blow that would end the life of his impotent opponent.

* * * * *

Tasslehoff had been watching the duel with enormous fascination. But something was missing from the event, he felt, something that would even the odds, as it were. The kender squirmed in his seat, impatiently awaiting some unexpected turn of events.

Tossak held Sturm aloft with one massive hand, dangling him over the edge of the bridge, ready to drop him into the Pit of Doom. As the huge minotaur opened the deadly piercing blade on the thumb of his mandoll gauntlet and gestured to the crowd that Sturm was going to meet his demise, Tas noticed a flock of shadows flying across the arena.

The rest of the crowd noticed at the same time.

So did Tossak.

* * * * *

A curved club, expertly aimed, struck Tossak in the arm that held Sturm, while another, this one spiked with thorns, smashed into his face.

Clawing at his fresh wounds, Tossak dropped Sturm.

Sturm fell, hurtling towards the fiery lava. But a figure swooped under him and caught him. The dazed Solamnic felt himself borne upward.

All was chaos and outraged shouts.

Standing agape, Fesz was profoundly shaken. It could only be seen as a bad omen, this second escape by a human, and this one so close to the time chosen by the Nightmaster for the coming of Sargonnas.

Tas hopped around, his eyes popping at the spectacle. "There he is!" he shouted to Dogz and Fesz, pointing to a muscular figure with long brown hair who was clutched in the talons of one of the kyrie. "That's the guy I was telling you about—that's Caramon!"

A minotaur guard dashed toward the raiding party and brandished a forepann, swinging the two-handed trident in a wide circle, hoping to hit one of the despised bird-people.

Two spiked clubs struck him simultaneously. The minotaur toppled over and, with a horrible scream, sank into the lava pit as the bird-people rose into the sky and soared out of the arena.

Blood streaming from the wounds that would leave his visage forever carved with scars, Tossak stood on the bridge, shaking his gauntleted fist at the sky.

* * * * *

On Karthay, the Nightmaster was growing concerned about the increasing number of bad omens.

He had already discerned that it was a waste of time to torture the human female. Furthermore, he wasn't particularly interested in torturing her.

He had far more significant plans for her. She would serve as bait for the other humans reported to be in the area. Failing that, she would be useful in the spell that would bring Sargonnas into the world, useful as a sacrificial victim.

The young female had proved to be a handful ever since she had been spotted skulking around the perimeter of the Nightmaster's camp in the volcanic ruins of the once fabled city of Karthay.

Somehow, though she was barely half the size of an average minotaur, the human female had held her own against them, running one of the minotaurs through the neck with her sword and cutting off the hand of another before being captured. Dragged into camp shouting insults, the slender, dark-haired female had refused to tell the Nightmaster anything about herself or her mission.

It was only through his excellent network of spies and assassins that the Nightmaster discovered she was the half-sister of the young mage Raistlin of Solace—Kitiara Uth Matar. And if Kitiara was on Karthay, Raistlin Majere wouldn't be far behind.

Kitiara was being held within sight of the Nightmaster's camp in a makeshift cell, a large cage of slatted wood brought from Lacynos to hold animals. At first, she was a raging nuisance, continually hissing and spitting at the minotaurs who stood guard over her. The Nightmaster hadn't fed Kitiara for several days now, and she was beginning to quiet down somewhat.

It was not Kitiara Uth Matar who worried the Nightmaster.

It was the feeling, like a stone in his heart, that something was going terribly wrong. First there was the kender and his two human companions who had bought the crushed jalopwort from the renegade Argotz. Argotz had been dealt with, and the kender was captured and turned into an evil partner. Fesz vouched for the allegiance of Tasslehoff Burrfoot and was on his way to Karthay with him.

The two human companions were supposed to have drowned in the Blood Sea, yet somehow they had survived and turned up in the prison in Atossa. Unfortunately the Nightmaster had found out about that too late. By some method so mysterious that the prison officials still hadn't figured it out, one of the humans had managed to escape. This was Raistlin's twin brother, Caramon. That was bad enough.

Now came the news that the other human had escaped, too—by a startling method. Condemned to die in the Pit of Doom, the other human, a would-be Solamnic Knight named Sturm Brightblade, had been rescued at the last moment by an airborne assault of kyrie. Despite the best efforts of the minotaur soldiers, the kyrie had escaped to the north, to their hidden stronghold in the mountains.

According to the message sent by Fesz, the evil kender Tasslehoff Burrfoot swore he had seen Caramon Majere directing the audacious daylight rescue operation.

The two humans, Caramon and Sturm, must have forged some kind of alliance with the bird-people, dedicated enemies of the minotaurs.

That, the Nightmaster reflected, was truly disturbing.

Reports of these developments had made the Supreme

Circle uneasy. The orughi were proving skittish about committing large numbers of troops to the command of the minotaurs. The ogre tribes had said outright that they would not participate in the drive to enslave the world until they had seen evidence of the existence of Sargonnas.

Other promised allegiances were also shaky.

The Nightmaster stooped to the ground and sifted gray volcanic ash through his fingers. He was surrounded by a petrified city, with steps that led nowhere, columns that supported nothing. A long table and a chair stood near a flickering fire. A shelf held books as well as beakers of spell ingredients. The room was more an arrangement of furniture than a room, with no walls, doors, or ceiling. It stood in the middle of the ruins, open to the black, forbidding sky.

This part of the anicent city had once been the entrance to the great library. Now it was nothing but cold volcanic rock.

The night wind stirred the Nightmaster's feathers and bells. He looked over at the human female in her wooden cage. Even without having eaten for several days, Kitiara was fueled by energy and restlessly paced her cell.

The Nightmaster looked over at his two highest-ranking acolytes, the two members of the High Three who had remained behind when Fesz journeyed to Mithas. They huddled together, sleeping sitting up, draped by one blanket.

Minotaur soldiers patrolled the perimeter of the camp.

Sighing, the Nightmaster looked up at the sky, the two moons, and the stars.

Three more days, two more nights.

Only a few hours remained before dawn. A couple more hours of numbing cold, and then, after sunrise, the merciless heat would return. The Nightmaster was worried, but he retained his faith in Sargonnas. Wrapping himself in his cloak, the Nightmaster lay down on the cold ground and slept soundly.

Chapter 13
The Isle of Karthay

The damaged Castor had limped back to the mouth of the bay and was about to enter the open sea. Watching the boat from shore, Tanis adjusted the sack slung across his back, a small store of provisions provided by Captain Nugetre. Nearby stood Flint, shifting his weight from foot to foot, trying to stretch out the soreness in his leg without anyone noticing. But Kirsig watched the dwarf solicitously.

Yuril, plus the four other sailors from the *Castor* who had decided crewing on a disabled ship was not to their taste, worked near the water's edge, dragging their two small boats up onto the beach. Tanis hoped they hadn't traded one bad job for worse.

Standing apart from the others, his back to the sea, Raist-lin surveyed the terrain.

The narrow strip of rock-strewn beach gave way to low sand dunes. Beyond these, the land began rising and breaking up into a maze of ravines and plateaus. As far as the eye could see the terrain looked barren and uninviting.

Although it was only midmorning, the sun burned hot and bright in the sky. A dry wind stirred up the sand on the shore. Tanis felt the grit invade his throat.

A hand brushed the half-elf's arm. It belonged to Raistlin. The young mage had a disconcerting habit of moving around so quietly it was difficult to keep track of him.

Raistlin didn't seem dismayed by the tough, broken landscape. "I judge that we have about a two-day journey inland before we reach the ruins of the dead city," said the mage to Tanis in a low voice. "Do you think Flint's leg will hold up?"

"His leg is much better," replied Tanis. "The old dwarf will probably outlast all of us."

Both men looked over to where Kirsig hovered around Flint, apparently offering a poultice for his leg while the dwarf grumbled and attempted to shoo her away. But not too strenuously, Tanis noticed. He and Raistlin exchanged a grin.

When Tanis turned back, his momentary good humor faded. "The question I have, Raistlin, is where are we headed? You haven't told us very much about the spell that you say will open a portal to let this evil god, or whatever it is, into this world."

Raistlin caught not only the impatience but also the hint of skepticism in Tanis's voice. "Surely in the land of your mother's people you learned something about the old gods," the young mage answered, knowing that any reference to Tanis's divided heritage risked offending the half-elf. Raistlin saw that his words had hit their mark, for color rose in Tanis's cheeks.

"I can't vouch for whether the spell I uncovered will open a portal, or whether the old gods such as Sargonnas are more than mere fairy tales," the mage continued brusquely. "I do know that the spell seems to be ancient and powerful magic. And I know that if there is any chance of Sargonnas entering this world, it behooves us to try to prevent it."

"What about Sturm, Caramon, and Tasslehoff? Are they somewhere on this island?" Tanis asked. "Aren't they the reason we came all this way?"

"I can't wave a magic wand to see if they're here or not," snapped Raistlin, "but you heard what Kirsig said about the minotaurs forming alliances with other races. If, as I suspect, the minotaurs are caught up in their age-old visions of conquest and are trying to bring Sargonnas into the world to help them, it wouldn't matter where Caramon and the others are. We're all in dire jeopardy."

Raistlin paused, taking a deep breath. Visibly calmed, he continued. "The jalopwort was just one of the ingredients necessary for the spell. The magic also calls for the sacrifice of a victim amenable to Sargonnas. My guess is that may be the reason why Caramon, Sturm, and Tas were brought to this part of the world. One of them may be the intended offering.

"We don't have much time. The spell can only occur during certain conjunctions of the sun, the moons, and the stars. These conjunctions occur not twice in one hundred years, and the next is only three nights away.

"Now let me show you a map I copied from an antique atlas in Morath's library."

Tanis waited, convinced. With Flint and Kirsig, who had overheard the tense discussion and joined them, the half-elf looked at a scrap of parchment that Raistlin had produced. It was covered with squiggly lines and geographic symbols. Yuril and the other sailors came hurrying up, and the small group gathered round the young mage.

"I think the spell will be cast somewhere in or near the ancient ruins of the city of Karthay," said Raistlin. "The city was destroyed by a volcano during the Cataclysm and buried under tons of ash and lava. It is a sacred site of the minotaur nation." He pointed to an area on the map marked as a mountain range. "Sargonnas is the god of deserts, fires, and volcanos," he added.

"Based on this map, I think we can get there in time, but the journey promises to be dangerous. Anyone who does not relish that prospect should feel free to stay here and wait for us." At this, Raistlin looked up, not at Flint, but at Yuril and the female sailors.

Yuril and her small band had apparently already discussed the risks. "I have a debt to repay," spoke the sinewy sailor, "and my friends here are no strangers to adventure. I speak for us all when I say we cast our lot with you." Yuril delivered her statement proudly, one hand on the hilt of the short sword she wore at her waist. The muscles stood out on her bronzed forearms.

We are fortunate to have her and the others, thought Tanis.

"This dead city," Flint spoke up, "will probably be well guarded, and Sturm and Caramon and that damnable kender along with it. What do you plan to do once we get there?"

"I don't know," admitted Raistlin. "I won't know until we see how many soldiers are guarding the area. Between us," he added, looking at Tanis, "we should be able to come up with a plan."

Tanis felt his heart constrict as he thought once more of the missing Kitiara. He turned away from the group, pretending to scan the inhospitable terrain.

* * * * *

Following Raistlin's map, they picked up a trail along a river that had long ago flowed to the sea from the Worldscap Mountains. Now it had dried up, leaving only cracked, sun-baked earth.

The river route led them down one side and up the other of countless ravines and gashes in the earth. When they could, they kept to the dusty riverbed. Other times, they followed the dry river from paths above, proceeding single-file on narrow ridgetops. All day they stuck to their course, making such slow and uncertain progress traveling up and down and then doubling back that Tanis was left confused as to what, if any, headway they were making. Pausing as they reached one of several plateaus, the half-elf was glad to see that the Blood Sea had receded into the distance while a range of towering peaks had drawn somewhat nearer.

The land appeared empty—empty of greenery, animals, indeed of all life. The wind gusted at the higher elevations, strong and dry, howling into their faces and driving grit into their eyes and throats. The sun glared overhead, creating ovenlike heat that reached into all but the deepest recesses of the rocks. Whenever they plunged abruptly downward and briefly luxuriated in cool shadows, they felt a hint of something worse—the bitter chill of the territory at night.

By late afternoon, the small group was exhausted and dispirited. Raistlin and Tanis headed the column, in effect sharing leadership. Flint and Yuril brought up the rear. Trekking along the bottom of a ravine, the companions trudged along in silence, no longer so confident of the path they had chosen.

All of a sudden Raistlin and Tanis rounded a bend to find a sheer wall that loomed before them with no possibility of being scaled. To both their left and right stretched fifty vertical feet of smooth rock. Once again the group had no option but to turn back and retrace their steps.

By the time Flint and Yuril had climbed out of the ravine and Raistlin had made another sighting of the dry, winding riverbed below, the sun was sinking out of sight. Tanis felt the first chill as darkness began to settle over the land. He saw Flint sink down to the ground, his face lined with sweat and dirt. Immediately several of the sailors followed suit.

Next to him, Raistlin peered at the parchment map, turning it around in his hands, trying to decipher which was the best route.

"The old river keeps splitting off and changing direction," the young mage said wearily.

"Your map must be a hundred years out of date," said Tanis, "Who knows how many rockslides and earthquakes have come along since then?"

Raistlin frowned at him.

"I don't think any of us can go much farther today," said the half-elf softly, indicating the group that had collapsed on the ground behind him.

"I told you," said the mage sharply, "that if we don't get to Karthay inside of two days, there may be grave consequences."

"Perhaps there will be enough light from the twin moons later tonight to permit us to cover some ground," said Tanis diplomatically. "But right now it would be best for us to stop to eat and rest. Besides, I thought I spotted some ant-lion pits during the day, and we wouldn't want to stumble into one in the dark."

Flint had come up behind them. "Ant-lion pits?" said the dwarf worriedly. "I agree with Tanis. Let's make camp for the night."

Raistlin hesitated.

"There'd be more shelter down in one of the ravines," added Flint, "but we'd also be more vulnerable to attack." Tanis nodded.

With a heavy sigh, Raistlin gave in. His pale, tense face suddenly showed a deep exhaustion. Tanis felt quite certain that the young mage couldn't have lasted much longer.

Everybody was happy with the decision.

As night fell, the temperature continued to drop. Now the wind cut into them bitterly. They made camp behind a line of boulders. Although the boulders afforded them only meager protection from the biting wind, they did offer another advantage, Flint noted. "In the dark, any attacker will find it hard to distinguish which is stone and which is flesh," the dwarf said, "and we will appear to be twice our actual number."

Yuril volunteered to go prowling for wildlife for supper, but Tanis declined her offer. "It's growing too dark," Tanis explained. "If anyone should hunt, it is I, with my nightvision. But even if I caught anything, we couldn't cook it. Raistlin and I agree that we shouldn't light any fires until we are sure of our bearings. On this high plateau, it might be a beacon to whoever—or whatever—else is on this part of the island."

The small group huddled together on the leeward side of the boulders. Tanis walked from person to person, sharing the provisions he carried—small portions of meal bread, dried fruit, and half a cupful of water for everyone. All day they hadn't come across one spring or stream where Tanis could have refilled his canteen. When he reached Flint, Tanis noticed that Kirsig wasn't at the dwarf's side as usual.

"Where's Kirsig?" the half-elf asked anxiously.

"Don't bother about her," the dwarf snapped. "She scurried off somewhere after you gave your speech about the fires. Now at last I've got some peace and quiet."

Alarmed at this news, Tanis gazed out over the darkening plateau but could see no sign of the female half-ogre. Despite his protestations, Flint also peered nervously into the gathering night. Just then Kirsig trotted into sight holding a bulging bag.

"Hello, dearies. You weren't worried about me, were you?" she asked, pinching Flint's cheek. "I just thought that since we didn't have much in the way of victuals with us, I'd go see what I could dig up. And dig I did!" She held the bag up triumphantly.

"Smagroot," Kirsig proclaimed. She held out the sack, insisting everybody take some of its contents. Tanis reached in and grabbed the smallest sample he could find. The smagroot was green, fleshy, and moist, with a texture a little like an uncooked potato. Tanis nibbled on one end of the root. It tasted sweet and soothed his throat with welcome moisture as he swallowed.

"Best thing in the world if you're stuck in a desert, my daddy always used to say," Kirsig babbled as she dispensed the smagroot.

Raistlin had come up next to Tanis and taken some. "I have read of smagroot," said the young mage, eagerly tasting the exotic root. "The plant is also called desert balm and has saved the lives of many travelers stranded in dry parts. But I am surprised that anybody could find some and dig it up in the dark." Looking over at Flint, Tanis saw that the grizzled dwarf was beaming the way a teacher does when his prized pupil performs well.

The smagroot momentarily lifted the gloom that had settled on the travelers with nightfall. Everybody ate their fill, and Kirsig still had half a bag left for the next day. After "dinner," each member of the group worked at making himself comfortable for a night of restless sleep on cold, hard ground. The night was black. Clouds hid the stars. "I'll take the first watch," Tanis volunteered.

"I would like to take the first watch," announced Raistlin, surprising Tanis and Flint. "I'm not ready to go to sleep," the mage explained, "and I could use the solitude to clear my thoughts."

Tanis hestitated a moment, then shrugged. After several minutes of tossing and turning, however, he found himself unable to sleep. He propped himself up on one elbow, then sat up. Staring across the space of the camp, his eyes adjusted to the dark so that he could see more than just the auras supplied by his normal nightvision.

Raistlin leaned up against a boulder, staring up at the sky. Hair fell across his face, and the young mage appeared lost in thought.

Tanis jumped as a loud rumble broke the silence, then had to smile when he realized it was only Flint's snoring, augmented this evening by Kirsig's. In between the rumbles, a sandpapery noise, like that of a small nocturnal animal scuttling across the ground, reached his ears.

Tanis jerked up his head. Raistlin, he saw, did the same.

The sandpapery whisper had grown louder, until it seemed not to come from the ground but from the sky above. Looking up, Tanis saw nothing before he felt a heavy weight drop onto his shoulders, accompanied by the sensation of being smothered. He attempted to call out a warning but only succeeded in inhaling what felt like a mouthful of feathers. When he tried to reach for the knife in his belt, Tanis found he couldn't move his arms, which were pinned to his sides. Sharp talons pinched into his neck.

Muffled sounds coming from outside his feather cocoon indicated the others were caught in the same predicament. Suddenly, from over his head, rang out a clear, melodic voice, speaking in Common. "These are not bull-men. They appear to be like you and your friend."

The feather cocoon opened, and a torch flared in Tanis's face, blinding him for an instant. Tanis felt himself caught up in a bear hug.

"Tanis Half-Elven! I didn't know if I'd ever see you again. And Raistlin, brother mine!"

Now it was the mage's turn to be enveloped in Caramon's muscular frame.

Raistlin smiled broadly. "We expected to find you a captive, not a captor, Brother," the young mage responded, "but as I told Tanis, I trusted we would find you somehow, alive and well."

The twins stood side by side, Caramon's strong arms draped across the slender shoulders of his brother. In the flickering light of the lone torch, Tanis marveled, not for the first time, at how the Majere twins could be at the same time so alike, yet so dissimilar. At this moment, the difference was heightened by the leather thong with feathers attached that encircled Caramon's head, and the feathers that seemed to sprout from his shoulders but were no doubt just sewn to his tunic.

Looking around in the wavering light cast by the torch, it seemed to Tanis that those who accompanied Caramon also sprouted feathers. Tanis squinted. The half-elf couldn't be sure, but these tall beings—they stood at least a head taller than Caramon, who was himself more than six feet—appeared to have wings instead of arms!

Joining him, Flint looked suspiciously at the newcomers and broached the obvious question. "Aren't you going to introduce us to your friends, or at least tell them that they needn't regard us as enemies?" the dwarf asked Caramon, looking at the feathered creatures nervously.

Caramon grinned broadly. "I apologize. But there is no need to be alarmed." He gestured toward the half-dozen figures who had arrived with him—indeed, who had carried him and Sturm in flight. "These are my friends, the kyrie, a noble folk and sworn enemies of the minotaurs. They rescued Sturm and me from the dungeon where we were imprisoned on the island of Mithas."

He turned slightly to indicate the kyrie nearest Raistlin. "Cloudreaver, this is my brother Raistlin, and my friends Flint Fireforge and Tanis Half-Elven from Solace. The females I do not know," Caramon added, casting a jaundiced eye at Kirsig and then an altogether more favorable glance at Yuril and her fellow sailors. "Though I shall be happy to make their acquaintance," he finished, with an obvious wink at the statuesque Yuril. She didn't return his gesture, but neither did she turn away.

"So where is Sturm?" demanded Flint, unwilling to relinquish a lifetime of skepticism about strange races simply on Caramon's say-so. "And though I'm not sure I really want to know, what about Tasslehoff?"

"I am here," came a hoarse voice from outside the circle of light cast by the torch. The kyrie, Bird-Spirit, stood aside to reveal Sturm struggling to his feet. Much to his embarassment, the Solamnic had fainted soon after the kyrie landed at the companion's camp. Only a day and a half had passed since he was rescued from the Pit of Doom. Sturm hadn't had a chance to fully recover from his lengthy ordeal of being shipwrecked, imprisoned, beaten, and almost killed in a duel. He limped into view.

Flint stared. In the dim light, Sturm's face looked oddly lopsided. "What did you do to your mustache?" the dwarf demanded, incredulous.

"Never mind his mustache. Can't you see the poor thing isn't well?" Kirsig scolded, hurrying to Sturm's side. "C'mon, dearie, let me help."

Far too well mannered to recoil at the grotesque appearance of the female half-ogre, Sturm did look questioningly at Flint.

"Aw, don't worry about her. She's all right," the dwarf said gruffly. "And she's not half bad at healing."

Raistlin spoke up. "She's considerably better than that, Sturm. Kirsig has proved invaluable during our voyage at sea and our experience thus far on land." Yuril and the sailors murmured their assent. Her face flushed with pleasure, Kirsig took Sturm's hand and led him over to her pack.

"What are you doing here?"

The question, directed to each other, sprang from Caramon's and Raistlin's lips at the same time. In spite of the cold night air, in spite of the grim surroundings, the twins had to grin at one another.

"I suspect that the stories we have to tell each other are long ones. Perhaps first we should build a fire to warm our bones during the telling," suggested the kyrie called Cloudreaver.

"We didn't build a fire for fear it would reveal our presence," Tanis explained.

"Do not worry," Cloudreaver assured him. "We have scouts roving the skies over the island. To the west is a harsh desert wasteland, and to the far north, a mountainous tropical forest. The only minotaurs that we have spotted are camped at the base of Worldscap Peak in the ruins of the dead city of Karthay. It is two or three days from here by land, but only several hours of flight for a kyrie."

The kyrie carried a small amount of firewood and tinder with them. By the time a fire blazed up, everyone's spirits had improved. The motley company gathered around the flames.

Kirsig heated water to brew a special tea for Sturm who, in the improved light, looked pale and weak. Caramon, on the other hand, appeared to be leaner but more rugged, still a strapping specimen. Yuril, sitting across the campfire from the young warrior, obviously thought so.

While Sturm sipped his tea, Caramon related the tale of treachery aboard the *Venora*, the magic storm, being transported with Sturm and Tas across thousands of miles to the Blood Sea, the abduction of Tas, and being cast overboard. Of his and Sturm's long, painful sojourn at sea, Caramon said only a few terse words. It was when he began talking about their imprisonment at Atossa that Raistlin sat up and appeared to grow particularly interested.

"At first the minotaurs seemed to have taken us prisoner just to make us slaves or to have us fight as gladiators for their amusement," said Caramon.

"But after the kyrie rescued Caramon, some high-ranking minotaurs came around asking questions," put in Sturm, speaking quietly. "They knew your name, Raistlin—and Kitiara's, too—and mentioned someone called the Nightmaster. The strangest thing is that Tas was with them and seemed to be helping them."

"Tas?" Flint asked, disbelieving. "I never thought the little kender was a hero, but casting his lot in with the minotaurs who held you captive—maybe they just dragged him along, under some threat, to make you think he was helping them. To break your spirit."

"Nobody was forcing Tas to do anything," Sturm replied bitterly. "He volunteered instructions on the fine points of torture. Indeed it was Tasslehoff Burrfoot who cut off my mustache!" Sturm paused, controlling his anger. "Far worse, it was Tas who suggested that I be made to fight a duel to the death in the Pit of Doom.

"From what I overheard before our friends, the kyrie, rescued me, I think the minotaurs are holding Kitiara prisoner somewhere on this island. That is why we came here, not even knowing that you were in the vicinity."

"We try to track any unusual troop movements by the minotaurs," Cloudreaver added. "Several months ago, we observed them setting up a camp in the ruins of the old city of Karthay. Now it seems every week more of the bull men arrive there."

Raistlin had grown agitated, standing up and pacing as Caramon, Sturm, and Cloudreaver told their story.

"The Nightmaster must suspect that we're already here," cut in Raistlin. "That is not good. And now we know that they are holding Kit captive. That is even worse news. What you don't know, Caramon, is that the minotaurs have gathered here to cast a powerful spell to bring one of their evil deities into the world. And that spell calls for the sacrifice of a non-minotaur."

"Who is this Nightmaster?" Flint wanted to know.

Tanis had been about to ask the very same question.

"He is their high shaman," answered Raistlin. "The Nightmaster is the one who would cast the spell to open the portal for Sargonnas."

Caramon and Sturm looked bewildered. Briefly Raistlin filled them and the kyrie in on everything that had happened to him, Tanis, and Flint—the magic message he had received from Tas, the visit to the Oracle and the trip through the portal to Ogrebond, the escape from Ogrebond with Kirsig, their eventful trip across the Blood Sea, leading up to their arrival on the isle of Karthay.

"The reason we came here," explained the young mage, "is that I stumbled across an ancient spell in one of my library searches. The spell intrigued me, and I had already sent Tasslehoff off to buy a rare component for it, jalopwort, before I realized the full import of what I had done. The spell that is being prepared would invite the evil Lord of Dark Vengeance, Sargonnas, into the material world. With the help of my Master Mage, I investigated further and came to the conclusion that the spell would be cast on the island of Karthay by the Nightmaster of the minotaur nation.

"Kirsig tells us that the bull-men are forging alliances with the ogres and other nefarious races. I fear that this is part of their scheme to introduce Sargonnas into our world and to set in motion events that would mean the conquest of Ansalon."

"Sargonnas," hissed Cloudreaver.

"Then you have heard of him?" queried Raistlin.

"Kyrie legend tells of a Sargonnas, a giant red condor who wreaked havoc on our people many generations ago. It communed with one of our weakest-minded nobles, who betrayed into the condor's possession our nation's most sacred artifact, the Northstone, which enabled the kyrie to navigate between all the islands and land masses of the world instead of being confined to this small pocket, in perpetual war with our enemies, the minotaurs," Cloudreaver explained. "If Sargonnas is hoping to return, that is very bad news for my people. We will help you in any way that we can."

For a moment, everyone was silent, the enormity of the task before them weighing on the group. What do we do next? was the question on everybody's mind.

"We can't do anything until the morning," Tanis answered the unspoken question, "so let's try to get some rest."

* * * * *

Now the group consisted of eight humans, plus a dwarf, a half-elf, a half-ogre, and six kyrie. Other kyrie were scouting parts of the island, but only one had arrived at their camp by morning, making seven. Raistlin was buoyed by the news that the kyrie could fly the others to a place near the Nightmaster's encampment in the ruined city in two shifts. First the kyrie would fly Raistlin, Tanis, Caramon, Sturm, and Yuril, then they would return and, after a short period of rest, do likewise with Flint, Kirsig, and the sailors.

Even with the time necessary for two round trips, the journey would take much less time than an overland march. The companions would arrive at the edge of the ruined city of Karthay one day before the conjunction of the heavens that, Raistlin gauged, was vital for the spell of Sargonnas.

Flint, who had already weathered the Blood Sea, was in no hurry to be swept aloft by the feathered bird-men, no matter how noble or friendly they were with Caramon and Sturm. "I don't mind waiting behind with all these females," said the dwarf. "I don't mind a bit. First I'll watch you all go for a sky ride, and if you don't fall or crash or get burned by the sun, then don't worry, I'll be sure to follow."

"I hate to leave you behind," said Tanis.

"Don't worry," joked Flint. "I've got Kirsig to watch over me."

Tanis smiled. "Yes," granted the half-elf. "I think she is giving Lolly Ockenfels some stiff competition."

"That's the last time I try to hold a civil conversation with you, Tanis Half-Elven," Flint exploded, turning beet red. "No respect! You show me no respect!"

Flint continued sputtering while Tanis and the others took off.

* * * * *

The kyrie had had time to fashion harnesses out of leather and rope for their passengers. The bird-men's strong talons would grip these and carry the humans aloft. It wasn't the most graceful way to fly, suspended from the shoulders, legs dangling, Tanis decided, but it would have to do.

A kyrie named Heart of Storm carried the half-elf, his huge wings beating steadily for several hours as the land passed below. At times, Tanis could glimpse the others nearby, but at other times the formation of kyrie couldn't be seen in the banks of clouds. Tanis felt fortunate to be suspended by Heart of Storm's shadow, for once again the sun was blazing in the sky, radiating intense, dry heat.

As they approached Worldscap, the kyrie tightened their formation and flew lower. Cloudreaver, who was carrying Caramon, made a wide sweep westward and glided to a landing on high ground overlooking the ruined city to the east and the inactive volcano of Worldscap to the north. Gently Heart of Storm lowered Tanis to the ground. The kyrie rested only a moment, waiting while Tanis and the others removed their harnesses, before taking off to get the ones who had been left behind and complete the first round of their mission.

The dead city, only a few miles away, looked like a gray, pock-marked moonscape. From this distance, the companions could see no evidence of habitation—only broken towers and miles of lava-encrusted ruins. Farther north, Worldscap loomed, a dark, ominous specter casting its shadow on the ruins of Karthay.

Raistlin broke the awed silence of the group as they looked out over the scene. "Yuril, you and Sturm wait here for the rest of the company," directed the mage. "Caramon, Tanis, and I will scout the immediate area to make sure that there are no minotaurs in the vicinity and perhaps to forage some food for supper."

Sturm clasped each of them in turn on the shoulder. Yuril nodded coolly. When they filed away down a trail, she began to sharpen her sword on a stone. Sturm, still less than his vigorous self, lay sprawled on the ground nearby.

Even this far from the city, black ash dotted the rocks and ground. A half-mile down the trail, the hardened path forked. Raistlin stood rubbing his chin as he considered the two possibilities, both sloping gradually downward.

"This way," said Caramon, pointing.

"No," said Tanis, indicating the other path. "This way."

"I'll go that way," said Raistlin, selecting the one that Tanis had picked out, "and you two try the other path."

Both Caramon and Tanis looked aghast at the idea of Raistlin setting off on his own, but neither of them could figure out what to say. The mage stared at them coolly.

"Well?" he demanded.

"Don't—don't you think we should stick together?" Caramon stammered.

Tanis nodded his agreement with Caramon.

"It would be better to check out both directions," said Raistlin. "You aren't worried about me, are you, Brother? I got this far without your help."

"No," said Caramon softly.

"Only ..." said Tanis.

"Only what?" asked Raistlin, glaring.

"Only," said the half-elf, "we should agree to meet back here inside of two hours."

"Agreed."

"And call out if you see anything," added Caramon.

"Of course," Raistlin said testily.

With misgivings, Tanis and Caramon watched Raistlin set off down one fork of the path. Then they sighed in unison and started off along the other trail.

The two of them had some luck. Caramon killed a fat snake, which could be cooked up in a stew, and Tanis found some edible nuts on a stubborn bush that clung to the rocky ground. They saw no signs of minotaurs or any other enemy. After an hour of exploring along the trail, they turned back. For more than an hour, they waited at the designated place without any sign of Raistlin. Concerned, Tanis and Caramon hiked back up to where Sturm and Yuril waited, hoping the mage had returned in their absence. But Raistlin wasn't there either.

Just then the other kyrie arrived carrying Flint, Kirsig, and the rest of the sailors. Flint was a whiter shade of pale and cursing a blue streak. Kirsig had never had a more exciting time, she averred. The female sailors took it all in stride. They were veterans at travel, and if the Blood Sea hadn't killed them, why, they weren't likely to die during an airlift from the kyrie.

"Did you happen to see my brother Raistlin from above?" Caramon asked Cloudreaver anxiously.

"No," said Cloudreaver, frowning. "Isn't he here with you?"

"No," Caramon replied with agitation. Angrily the warrior twin kicked a rock. "I should have known better," Caramon muttered. Gloomily he sat down on a rock.

Flint looked at Tanis questioningly. The half-elf shrugged. "Caramon's right," said Tanis somberly. "We should have known better."

Cloudreaver went over to Caramon and squatted on the ground next to him. "Is your brother safe? Did he wander off somewhere? What do you suspect?"

"I suspect," Caramon said miserably, "that my dear brother has sneaked off to try to do something about this Nightmaster on his own. I only hope he doesn't get himself killed."

"Well," prodded Flint, "Raistlin said the big spell was going to be cast tomorrow night. In the meantime, what's the plan?"

There was a general awkward silence.

"I had the idea," said Tanis with some slight embarassment, "that Raistlin had something in mind. Unless he comes back, we'll have to guess at what it was—or think of something ourselves."

"He won't be coming back," said Caramon dismally.

"Then we must act accordingly," said Cloudreaver with authority. The kyrie divided up his warriors, sending half of them to rove the skies, spy on the ruined city, and, if possible, make contact with the other kyrie who were scouting the island, urging them to rejoin the main group. Three of the kyrie would stay behind and take up guard and camp duties.

"We must return by nightfall," Cloudreaver advised Bird-Spirit, who was chief among the scouts, "or by morning at the latest. Tomorrow, whatever the strategy, we must mount an attack."

Kirsig, Yuril, and the sailors started setting up the camp. Flint, Sturm, Tanis, and Caramon, watching the others dutifully go to work, looked at each other sheepishly. Trying to forget their worries about Raistlin, the companions pitched in.

Chapter 14
The Nightmaster

Several miles off the eastern tip of Karthay, in the sea near Beakwere, hundreds of orughi had begun to gather. Their gray, thickly muscled shoulders stuck out of the water, while their webbed feet flapped below the surface. Their upturned faces showed high foreheads, blunt noses, pointy ears, beady eyes, and stringy golden hair slick with wetness. Some carried battle-axes and daggers, while others bore the iron boomerangs with long metallic cords called tonkks.

The orughi looked to the west. Because they were an amphibious species, they could swim for days on end without tiring. Now the orughi treaded water, waiting to see some manifestation of Sargonnas.

Some miles away, on the other side of the point and farther out into the Land Ho Straits, beneath a blanket of haze waited a fleet of warships manned by ogres sent to seal the alliance with the minotaurs. There were only dozens, not hundreds, of ships, but each was there as a representative of an ogre tribe, each answerable to a chieftain of that despised race. At a signal, they would mobilize. Now their warships rocked in the waters almost peacefully, awaiting the time.

The ogres kept their distance from their watery cousins, the orughi. They held the thick-witted, web-footed orughi in contempt and would not join with the water-bred ogres unless Sargonnas decreed it.

Even now the appointed commander of the ogre fleet, Oolong of the Xak clan, watched the distant orughi horde through his eyescope. Oolong Xak sighed with disgruntlement, scratching his lice-ridden scalp and running his grimy fingers through long, matted hair. Any upstanding ogre would be embarassed to be allies with the orughi in a war, yet the minotaurs had almost talked the ogres into it—lured them with promises and trinkets. But Oolong Xak was not the only one among them whose doubts would not be allayed except by the final proof of Sargonnas himself.

Scores of miles away, in the palace in the city of Lacynos on the island of Mithas, the eight minotaurs of the Supreme Circle and their king awaited the great spell with varying degrees of enthusiasm, impatience, and skepticism.

The king of the minotaurs sorely desired the conquest of Ansalon as a means to impress his subjects with the scope and vision of his power. The king had invested troops and money in the careful plans of the Nightmaster; success would be a validation of his wisdom.

His only wholehearted supporter was Atra Cura, the bloodthirsty representative of the minotaur pirates. Any war was a good war for Atra Cura and his confederation of followers, who stood to gain much from the chaos that would inevitably occur along the lanes of the Blood Sea.

Dozens of war galleys stood at the ready in the harbor of Lacynos, and many dozens more were in various stages of completion across the bays and harbors of Mithas. Akz, leader of the minotaur navy, had driven his slaves ruthlessly to meet the deadlines, although he was of a mixed mind, more or less indifferent, to the grand intentions of the Nightmaster. Akz was not an overly religious minotaur, and he had been around long enough as a member of the Supreme Circle to see war plans come and go.

Still, no one had ever dared try to summon Sargonnas into the world before. That took boldness and ambition, Akz admitted to himself. But if the spell did not attain its end, then so what? The galleys could be used for another future enterprise. Akz was in no hurry to sacrifice his ships and trained forces on a wild-eyed, long-range war unless it could be said that the gods themselves approved of it. Therefore Akz would not lift a finger to act unless Sargonnas decreed it.

Although Inultus, the commander of the minotaur military, hated Akz, they always agreed on questions of war. Inultus, too, was happy to commit his legions of trained soldiers … if Sargonnas decreed it. Otherwise, Inultus did not see any reason to enter into an historic and highly distasteful pact with the ogres and orughi in order to launch the most significant attack on the continent of Ansalon in the annals of the minotaur race.

Two other members of the Supreme Circle had unquestioned loyalty to the king and backed his policies despite personal qualms about allegiances with the ogres and orughi. Victri, chosen leader of the rural minotaurs, would gladly fight in any war decreed by the king, yet he nurtured misgivings about this one and secretly hoped the Nightmaster would fail. The great scholar and historian, Juvabit, also voted with the king, whom he had known through family ties dating back to his youth. But the rational Juvabit distrusted the mystical Nightmaster and his obsessive cult. So Juvabit, too, privately wished the Nightmaster would be unsuccessful.

Groppis, keeper of the treasury, held no opinion other

than that he wished the whole thing hadn't cost so much money to this point—almost as much as he wished the mapped-out campaign for the future conquest of Ansalon was budgeted at less.

That left the sole female, Kharis-O, leader of the nomadic minotaurs, and Bartill, head of the architectural and construction guilds.

There was nothing duplicitous about their expressed views. Both were on record against the alliance, the planned war, and the grandiose schemes of the Nightmaster: Bartill, because he was always preoccupied with his own projects and need for money; Kharis-O, because she represented separatist clans and was herself exceedingly contrary. Regularly she voted against the majority, and regularly she lost.

However, like Bartill, Kharis-O was fully prepared to go to war. A minotaur was loyal unto death, and honor required that both act in accordance with all the decisions of the Supreme Circle.

The eight members of the Supreme Circle had been summoned by the king to await the coming of Sargonnas.

The eight waited in the main hall of the palace. Some drummed fingers on the large oaken table. Some paced the room, snorting with irritation when they brushed shoulders with each other. Some lay their horned bull heads down on the oaken table, snoring gutturally.

Tomorrow night would be the time.

* * * * *

The sanctum of the Nightmaster was perfectly fascinating, Tasslehoff Burrfoot had to admit.

Crumbling walls dotted the dry, broken land. Here and there a few columns, all that was left of the temples of the fabled city, slanted toward the sky. Tumbled masonry lay everywhere. A broken statuette or two stood among the rubble.

Fissures, the result of earthquakes that had rocked the once-great city, zigzagged across the ground, contributing to the eerie landscape. Gray and black ash, some hardened into a brittle crust, blanketed everything.

The Nightmaster watched Tasslehoff as the kender picked his way across part of the dead city, plucking up an occasional ash-covered object and stuffing it in his backpack. Tas turned, saw the Nightmaster observing him, and waved, bounding back in his direction.

"Isn't the kender ... interesting?" asked Fesz, for lack of a better word. The shaman was standing at the Nightmaster's elbow. "I trust you agree that it was a good idea to bring him here. Tasslehoff has been very helpful with information about all of his former friends, and he begged to accompany me."

"You're certain that he is evil?" rumbled the Nightmaster, tilting his head to peer at the approaching kender with his big bull eyes.

"He drinks a double dose of the potion every day. And he has given me no cause to doubt him."

"What is that strange wooden stick across his back?"

"It is called a hoopak, my lord," replied Fesz. "The kender says it is an invincible weapon." The shaman minotaur cracked a jagged smile. "I don't see any harm in indulging his childishness."

The Nightmaster cast a sideways glance at his disciple. Fesz was in line to succeed him. In some ways, he was the Nightmaster's most shrewd and trusted disciple, but in other ways, the Nightmaster knew, Fesz was the most guileless, the most trusting of minotaurs.

"What about the human, Sturm?"

"An incident that does dishonor to all minotaurs," agreed Fesz, "but Tasslehoff cannot be suspected. Sturm was within moments of losing the duel, and Tas was cheering as loudly as the rest of us. No minotaur was more upset and angry at the rescue than Tasslehoff himself. He insisted that several of the guards be put to death as punishment for allowing the Solamnic to escape! Why, he asked to execute one himself. Of course, we couldn't allow that because of the High Laws, but the fact remains, he asked."

The Nightmaster seemed to ponder this information. Then, with a shrug of his shoulders, he turned back to his room without walls that had once been the entrance to the great library. As he moved with animal grace, feathers rustled in the wind and the bells draping his immense shoulders and horns jingled.

"Hullo, Nightmaster!" Tasslehoff chirped after him.

The Nightmaster didn't turn around to acknowledge the kender's greeting. The high shaman sat heavily at his long table, while the other two members of the High Three hastened to bring him spellbooks and components. These he arranged in front of him, inspecting and comparing them, while making notes with a quill pen.

"Kind of standoffish, isn't he?" asked Tas.

"The time is near," rumbled Fesz solemnly. "The Nightmaster is concentrating all of his attention on the task at hand. I must go to him, Tasslehoff, and help him with the preparations."

Fesz turned and crossed over to the long table, where he took his place with the other two high acolytes of the Nightmaster. As the Nightmaster bent to his calculations, the High Three stood behind him, careful not to interrupt but quick to do his bidding each time he growled an instruction.

Tas shrugged and skipped over to where Kitiara was imprisoned in her wood-slatted cage. She looked a tad gaunt and unbathed, he thought to himself. He noticed that Dogz, sprawled on a blanket nearby, was watching him intently.

"So, Kit," said Tasslehoff, nonchalantly, "how'd you get to Karthay so quick? I'm impressed. I bet it was something magical, wasn't it?"

Kitiara looked at him stonily.

"Well, tell me this, then. How'd you get captured so easily? I thought Caramon was the only stupid Majere."

She glared at him and bit off the words. "How many times do I have to tell you? I'm not a Majere!"

Tas shrugged. "Well, half a Majere, then. Probably the half that got captured." He chuckled at his own jest.

"In case you haven't noticed, this place is crawling with minotaurs. How was I supposed to know that?"

Tas cut her off. "Hey, I hear you're going to be sacrificed when the time comes—tomorrow night, Fesz tells me—so if you have any messages you want me to give to Raistlin if I ever see him again, you might want to tell me now."

With all the strength she had left, Kit hurled herself futilely against the side of the cage. The slats shuddered, and the kender backed up a safe distance. Kit pressed her face against the slats and snarled in Tasslehoff's face.

"I don't know what mischief you're brewing, Tasslehoff," hissed Kit, "but if I ever get out of here, I'll wrap my hands around your treacherous little neck and squeeze the life out of you!"

"Well, I'm sorry that you're taking that attitude," said Tas in a hurt tone, "because we are such old and dear friends. Besides," he added mischievously, "I wonder if you're not just a little bit jealous. Admit it, you wouldn't mind being evil for a while yourself. ..."

Kit stared daggers at him.

Tasslehoff backstepped toward Dogz, grinning. The kender turned and looked at the minotaur, who eyed him ruefully.

"Now what's the matter with you?" asked Tas, plopping himself down on the ground next to the minotaur who was supposed to be guarding him.

"Nothing, friend Tas," said Dogz, picking up some dry ash and letting it sift through his fingers. He avoided Tas's eyes.

"Nothing, friend Tas," mimicked Tas in a singsong voice. He glanced around, estimating there were about a dozen minotaurs surrounding the perimeter of the Nightmaster's encampment. They carried all manner of weapons—double-edged axes, studded clubs, throwing spears, and barbed whips. Dozens more roamed farther out.

By contrast, none of the High Three were armed, nor was the Nightmaster. Only Dogz carried a broadsword, katar, and chain flail.

Dogz lowered his voice to a soft growl. "Sometimes I wonder about you, friend Tas," said the minotaur.

"Wonder what?"

"If you are really a friend to all these people—first, Sturm. And now this female, Kitiara. The way you treat them."

Tas patted Dogz on the shoulder. "Well, I got turned into an evil kender, right?" Tas reminded Dogz. "I'm just doing my best to act like one. Sure, they used to be my friends. But that was when I was good —well, pretty good—most of the time, anyway. Now I'm evil. And if I betray them, I'm just doing my job in the evil category. You ought to be proud of me."

"Yes," said Dogz hestitantly.

"The way I look at it," Tas expanded, lying back on the ash-covered ground, clasping his hands behind his head, "I'm a kind of honorary minotaur nowadays. Didn't you tell me once that might makes right and the minotaur race was going to conquer the world someday, and all that stuff?"

"Yes," replied Dogz once again.

"Well, I'm just proving my loyalty to the minotaur nation. If you had a choice between betraying your nation or betraying your friends—oops, I mean used-to-be friends—which would you do?"

The minotaur dipped his huge horns, and when he looked up, his eyes were huge and sad. His fetid breath nearly overwhelmed Tas. "I don't know. Betray my friends, I suppose," he added slowly, obviously confused.

"Aren't you looking forward to the time when Sargonnas comes into the world?"

Dogz looked over to where the Nightmaster sat reading

his spellbooks. Behind him, the High Three stood purposefully.

"Yes," said Dogz.

"Well, see? So am I," said Tas triumphantly. He patted Dogz's shoulder. "Don't worry so much, Dogz," added the kender. "It'll put wrinkles on your snout." Tas yawned exaggeratedly. "Now I'm going to catch some much-needed rest."

The kender closed his eyes. A moment later, he opened one to monitor Dogz's reaction.

Dogz had sat up and was cleaning and polishing his weapons with a faraway look. Like Tasslehoff, the minotaur used to have clearly defined friends and enemies—take kender, for instance. Dogz used to loathe kender, even though he had never met or seen one. When he had first encountered Tasslehoff aboard the *Venora*, he didn't even want to touch him. He regarded Tas as worse than an enemy, as one of the lowest beings on the scale of creation.

But after taking Tas prisoner and spending a good deal of time with him, Dogz had grown fond of the quirky little kender. He admired his pluck and bravery under torture, his sense of humor in dire situations. From conversations with Tas, he had learned a lot about Solace and the kender's friends—especially the gruff dwarf Flint Fireforge and Tas's Uncle Trapspringer—and he had come to think of them as his friends, too.

Dogz had plenty of relatives, but he didn't have that many friends. Friendship was an entirely new concept to him, and Tas was responsible for teaching it to him.

Then Tasslehoff had been turned evil by Fesz, and he had changed. He became demanding, less fun to be around. Maybe the evil Tas would help bring Sargonnas into the world, but Dogz wasn't sure that he didn't like the old version of the kender better.

Dogz sighed. He bent to scrape some dirt off his katar, a long blade on an **H**-shaped hilt, oiling and polishing the unusual dagger as he thought long and hard about the subject of friendship.

Twenty yards away, in her wooden cage, Kitiara paced restlessly. Her watchful eyes missed nothing. She strained her ears to pick up scraps of conversations around her as the words drifted to her across the broken ground. Kit wasn't the world's greatest fan of kender, but she definitely liked Tasslehoff better the way he had been before.

The Nightmaster had mentioned Sturm, so apparently the Solamnic was still alive. And the other day, Kit had heard him speak of Caramon and Raistlin, too. It was clear they were all somewhere in this vicinity and that the Nightmaster feared their intrusion.

That thought brought a lopsided smile to Kit's face.

The sun had reached its highest point. The land baked and cracked under its intensity. The thick-skinned minotaurs seemed oblivious to the conditions. Dogz methodically cleaned and oiled his weapons. The minotaur guards on the perimeter passed in and out of Kit's sight on their appointed rounds.

The Nightmaster continued to sit at his long table, sorting and sifting ingredients for the monumental spell he would cast tomorrow night.

One of the few benefits of Kit's cramped cage was that the wooden slats over her head kept out the worst of the sunlight. Her gaze flicked over to the traitorous kender. His eyes were closed. Tasslehoff Burrfoot appeared to be sleeping peacefully.

* * * * *

As the Nightmaster labored over his spell, he thought back to his moment of ephiphany five days before—one day before the human female was captured—when at last the timing of the spell had been confirmed and Sargonnas had revealed himself to the minotaur.

He had been up on the mountain plateau, at noonday, with the colored glass prisms, crystals, and silver shards of mirror scattered around him. In them he was reading the movement of the stars and the sun, reckoning their positions in the heavens in relation to the two moons, and coming to the conclusion that all the externals were right.

Suddenly he spied a ripple in one of the reflective surfaces. Glancing around rapidly, he saw flickers and ripples in the pieces of shiny cut glass. As the Nightmaster watched in wonderment, the flickering and rippling took shape, so that each fragment of glass held a piece of the face of the God of Dark Vengeance.

A terrible, fearsome, obscure face, misted with red, stared at the Nightmaster through brooding black eyes.

Then all of a sudden, flickering in the pieces of glass, the image of Sargonnas vanished.

His eyes drawn skyward, the Nightmaster beheld a great red condor with black plumage, a wingspan that seemed to blanket the sky, and a curiously small, naked head. Fire licked at the tips of its wings.

Greetings, Nightmaster, servant of evil.

The red condor had seemed to speak inside the Nightmaster's head with a silky, enticing voice. Tongues of flame darted from the corners of its beak.

Greetings, Sargonnas, God of Dark Vengeance, ally of Takhisis.

The Nightmaster had never felt so powerful—nor so humbled—as then, when Sargonnas had first spoken to him.

Your plan is known to me. For centuries, I have waited for someone with your audacity and courage. For centuries, I have plotted to enter the material world and wreak havoc with my powers. For centuries, I have been foiled. Have you taken every precaution with the spell? Are you ready for the time?

Yes, Lord.

Are you watchful of deceit? Treachery?

Yes, Lord.

Are you worthy?

I trust, Lord.

Do not fail me. Do not dare to fail me, or you will learn that my vengeance reaches everywhere.

With that, the red condor had shimmered in the sun, then evaporated as if it had never been there.

The Nightmaster sank to his knees, turning his head, dazed. The conversation with Sargonnas had taken place entirely in his mind. Looking around, he could see the minotaur guards standing idly at their positions. They had neither heard nor seen Sargonnas.

The same was true of the two members of the High Three, who hadn't noticed anything out of the ordinary—until now.

One of them had come running up to the Nightmaster. "Are you all right, Excellency?" the young, bulging bull-man asked solicitously.

The Nightmaster hadn't answered immediately. The young shaman had struggled to help the Nightmaster to his feet.

"Are you all right, Excellency?"

The voice this time belonged to Fesz. Standing behind the Nightmaster, the shaman had stepped forward and tapped him on the shoulder.

Jolted back to the present, the Nightmaster was confronted by one of the officers of the minotaur troops. He stood in front of the Nightmaster, who had been lost in thought at his long table in the middle of the dead city. The Nightmaster blinked, eyeing the horned soldier in front of him, and growled a reply to Fesz.

"Yes, of course I'm all right."

"I bear news," said the minotaur soldier. "The companions who landed on the south shore of the island have been joined by a host of kyrie."

"Kyrie," grunted the Nightmaster. "How many?"

"At least six, maybe as many as fifteen," replied the soldier, adding smugly, "probably all members of the Warrior Society. But we can handle that number easily. We could handle ten times that number."

"Yes."

The minotaur soldier hesitated.

"Yes?"

"They are marching in this direction. They seem to know precisely where they are headed."

"Why do they march? Why do the kyrie not fly them here?"

"We are puzzled by that, too, Excellency," replied the soldier. "It may be that there are too many of them to be carried by the kyrie, or that they must rest up after coming from the mountains of Mithas."

"Pah!" snorted the Nightmaster so vehemently that the minotaur soldier drew back a step. "The kyrie do not tire so easily. There must be another reason, which we will soon learn."

The minotaur soldier sounded less complacent. "Yes," replied the soldier in a chastened rumble. "We estimate they will be here by midday tomorrow."

"Good."

To the surprise of the minotaur soldier, the Nightmaster didn't seem the least bit annoyed by this intelligence. Indeed he seemed refreshed and returned to his work, writing vigorously in the margins of the book he had been studying.

The Nightmaster looked up. This time he did sound irritated. "Yes? Is there something else?"

"N-No, Excellency," stammered the soldier, then turned to go.

Good, the Nightmaster repeated to himself. The humans—from reports, accompanied by a dwarf and an elf—were on their way, and the kyrie had joined them. That last was unexpected. It would require some adjustment to his plan, but there was still time.

Behind him, Fesz and the other two members of the High Three nodded to each other. They trusted in the wisdom of the Nightmaster.

Behind them, Tas slept … with one eye open.
Behind him, in her cage, Kitiara crouched, listening.

* * * * *

Day became night.

Tasslehoff awoke with a start, realizing that he had drifted off. Hours had passed.

The Nightmaster's sanctum buzzed with activity. Fesz and the other two shaman minotaurs were busily packing objects into small crates and rucksacks. A half-dozen minotaur guards had moved in closer and appeared to be waiting for orders. The Nightmaster, his long table swept clean of spellbooks and components, stood in the center of the camp, pointing and giving instructions.

The Nightmaster was dressed in full ceremonial garb, with clusters of feathers and bells hanging from his horned head like streamers, a dark red cloak thrown over his hulking shoulders.

"Hey, what's going on?" asked Tas good-naturedly as he strolled up to Dogz, who was busy packing his own belongings.

Dogz turned to the kender. "The Nightmaster says it is almost time," he said solemnly. "We are going to move to a new encampment during the night in order to conceal our whereabouts from the humans and kyrie who advance upon our location."

Tas digested this information. "Good idea," the kender said enthusiastically.

Spotting Tas, Fesz hurried over. The shaman's eyes glittered with excitement. "The Nightmaster has given permission for you to come with us," said Fesz. "You don't know what a rare privilege this is, for one of your race. Usually the only persons who are present at the spellcasting are the Nightmaster himself, the High Three, and the victim to be sacrificed. But he feels that a kender, a representative of a race known for its luck and good fortune—especially an evil representative—can only be agreeable to Sargonnas."

Tas's eyes darted to Kitiara. The female warrior was standing stock-still in her cage, eyes wide, one ear pressed against the wood slats, listening.

"I'm flattered," said Tasslehoff, puffing up with pride. "More than flattered, really. I'm bowled over. For whatever little part I am designated to play in the great drama to come, I am truly grateful. Indeed, I should like to personally inform the Nightmaster of my deepest gratitude."

The kender had already started toward the Nightmaster when Fesz grabbed him by the collar and pulled him back. "I don't think that this would be a good time to talk to the Nightmaster, when he has so many other important matters on his mind," said Fesz, lowering his voice.

"Oh," said Tas. "Good thinking."

The kender watched as two guards moved toward the slatted cage. They pulled Kitiara Uth Matar, kicking and screaming, out the door and proceeded to put chains on her legs and bind her arms with rope behind her back.

"If you think I'm going to let you sacrifice me to some stupid god of darkness—not to mention allowing some damnable kender come along and watch the entertainment—then you're in for a rude awak—"

The minotaur guards shoved a gag into Kitiara's mouth, cutting her off in midsentence. Tasslehoff regretted that, because he was curious to find out how in the world Kit thought she was going to be in a position to rudely awaken anyone, unless it were Sargonnas.

The Nightmaster had heard Kitiara's outburst. His back stiffened. Now he wheeled, enraged, and stalked toward the female warrior from Solace.

The Nightmaster spat angrily in Kitiara's face, losing his customary composure. "Spawn of slime! You are not fit to mention the name of the Lord of Dark Vengeance! You are not fit to exist in the same world! Soon you will die, and in death you will trade places with Sargonnas. You will be condemned to his world, while he will pass through the portal to our material plane!"

Fesz, Dogz, and the others stared, taken aback by the Nightmaster's vehemence. Hesitantly the minotaur guards finished blindfolding Kitiara, who continued to struggle futilely.

Tas was about to say something inappropriate when a new, unexpected voice sang out in the darkness.

"I expect the spell would be enhanced if your victim of sacrifice was less reluctant to die for the pleasure of Sargonnas!"

Raistlin! That was Raistlin's voice! Tas would recognize it anywhere, even here in the middle of this desolate place. Kit ceased struggling, indicating that she, too, recognized the voice of her half-brother.

But where was he? Raistlin was nowhere to be seen.

The guards gripped their weapons nervously. Dogz unsheathed his broadsword, his eyes darting around anxiously. The High Three grouped together, ready to cast a spell if need be.

At the sound of the voice, the Nightmaster had spun toward it but saw nothing. Tas could see the huge bull eyes of the high shaman, and he was surprised to see in them not fear or uncertainty but a glint of relief. It was as if the Nightmaster had anticipated this.

"Is that you?" rumbled the Nightmaster. "Are you the one they call Raistlin—the half-brother of this unruly female?"

"I am Raistlin," said the voice.

Tas looked all around, but for the life of him, he couldn't figure out where Raistlin was hiding.

"Show yourself, then."

There was a low, dry chuckle, followed once more by the seemingly disembodied voice: "I think not."

The Nightmaster remained silent for several long moments. Tasslehoff was about to say something when the Nightmaster rumbled silkily, almost in a purr, "I understand." He gestured broadly. "You have made yourself invisible in order to penetrate the ring of troops. Bravo! I was wondering how you might do it. Are your companions far behind?"

There was a momentary hesitation from Raistlin. "I came alone."

"Good."

"Let my sister go. I will take her place."

Tasslehoff heard a muffled scream and turned around to see Kit trying to tear herself from the grip of the guards. The minotaurs looked a little uneasy to be in the presence of a voice that didn't seem to be attached to a body.

"Capital idea!" shouted Tasslehoff. "Hello, Raistlin. It's me, Tasslehoff! Did you get the magic message bottle?"

"Yes," said the Nightmaster, glancing over his shoulder and scowling at the kender. "It is a capital idea. But how do I know that you will keep your word?"

"How do I know you will keep yours?"

The Nightmaster pondered Raistlin's question. Fesz came over and whispered something to him. "Ah," said the Nightmaster. "Allow me to introduce Fesz, my senior disciple and the shaman of highest standing under me. Go to him, and he will bind your hands. After you have done that"—he signaled to the minotaur from Lacynos—"Dogz will take Kitiara to the perimeter of the camp and let her go. You have my word."

Dogz grabbed the ropes that bound Kitiara. The two guards, who seemed happy to be relieved of their role, stepped away.

"Fair enough," came Raistlin's voice, and as the words were spoken, Raistlin's slender form materialized beside Fesz. The shaman grabbed him roughly and lashed rope around his hands, pinning them behind his back.

Weakened by the effort of sustaining the invisibility spell that had carried him past the minotaurs guarding the dead city, the young mage fell to his knees.

Tasslehoff bounded over to him.

The Nightmaster nodded to Dogz, who picked up

Kitiara, slung her across his shoulders, and started off across the clearing. Soon the two of them were swallowed up by the darkness.

"Raistlin!" cried Tasslehoff. "I knew you'd come—that is, if you got the magic message bottle. You did get it, didn't you?"

A hand grabbed Tas's shoulder, roughly pushing the kender out of the way. The Nightmaster stepped into his place, leaning close to the young mage, blasting Raistlin with his rancid breath.

"So this is the mighty Raistlin," rumbled the Nightmaster.

Raistlin didn't say anything. Instead, he stared unflinchingly into the Nightmaster's eyes.

"This human is nothing next to you, Nightmaster," said Fesz contemptuously. "He refuses to even fight for his life!"

"Keep him tied!" commanded the Nightmaster. "If he wants food and drink, give it to him. But don't underestimate him. Guard him carefully.

"Now let us decamp quickly! I don't want to take the chance that he wasn't telling the truth when he said he came alone!"

The minotaurs hurried to obey.

Tasslehoff got up slowly from the ground. The Nightmaster's every utterance should be worshipped, he knew, but even so, the evil Tas thought the high shaman could stand to learn some manners. Rubbing his shoulder ruefully, the kender thought of his good old hoopak. ...

*   *   *   *   *

Dogz hadn't gone very far when one of the minotaur soldiers came running to catch up with him.

They were in a different part of the dead city, near the ruins of a portico, the remains of a wall and tumbled masonry.

"From the Nightmaster," said the soldier handing Dogz

a message scribed on parchment.

Kill the human female, said the message. It was written in the Nightmaster's unmistakable scrawl.

Dogz hesitated. The human bundle slung over his shoulders tried to scream and kick, without much success. The huge minotaur put Kit down on the ground and rested one of his cleft hooves on her to keep her from rolling away.

"I must speak to the prisoner," said Dogz. "Wait for me."

The soldier backed away into the shadows.

Dogz looked around. Nearby stood a broken column. He dragged Kit over to it, took a length of rope from his side, and wrapped it firmly around her, tying her to the broken column. Then he removed her blindfold.

Her eyes looked at him questioningly.

"I have been ordered to kill you," rumbled the minotaur simply.

Kit's dark eyes stared, defiant.

The minotaur looked around till he spotted a large stone block, then went over to it slowly and sat down. The order to kill the human female disturbed him—first of all, because the human female had been a friend of the kender Tasslehoff before the kender became evil, and second, because the Nightmaster had given his word that the human female would be allowed to go free.

Both reasons bothered Dogz equally, and the minotaur sat there for a long time, pondering. Finally he got up and approached the human female. "I will not kill you tonight," he said simply.

He moved to put the blindfold back on her. "I am not going to take you back to the Nightmaster," he explained. "I will leave you here until we return. Then I will decide what to do."

Kitiara struggled furiously against her bonds, trying to speak.

Dogz paused, considering. "If you try to scream or shout, I will smash your head in," he said. Then he took off her gag.

"I—I—I don't care about myself," stammered Kitiara in a choking voice.

The minotaur waited.

"It's Raistlin," she said. "He's my brother. Can you do anything to help him?"

The minotaur started to replace the gag.

"Wait!" she cried softly.

There was a pause as the minotaur regarded her with scorn. "Raistlin is to be the victim," said Dogz. "It is Raistlin's honor to bring Sargonnas, the god of the minotaurs, into this world." Again the minotaur started to replace the gag.

"Then never mind Raistlin," Kit said desperately.

Dogz halted.

Kit's thoughts whirled. She recalled overhearing the conversation between Dogz and Tas about friendship and betrayal. That gave her an idea. It might be Raistlin's only chance.

"You're … you're friends with Tasslehoff, right?"

"Yes," said Dogz warily.

"Then give him something for me."

She told him what it was. His eyes widened.

Dogz backed away from Kit, then turned and kicked at the cold, ash-covered ground. He stood there for several minutes as Kit watched him, knowing that she had struck gold. Strange as it seemed, the minotaur regarded himself as a friend of Tas's.

Slowly Dogz lowered the gag. Kitiara told him where the item was. He searched her body and found it, a tiny thing that nobody had found when searching her before and that no one would notice if Dogz carried it. Dogz tucked the small object into his belt, then brusquely raised the gag and fastened it firmly over Kitiara's mouth.

His eyes stared into hers as he replaced the blindfold.

He found the minotaur soldier and ordered him to stay behind and guard Kit with his life.

Then Dogz sprinted off to catch up with the Nightmaster and his entourage.

Chapter 15
The Attack

By dusk, so many kyrie had arrived at the camp that Tanis lost track of their ever-increasing numbers. Twenty, perhaps two dozen, the half-elf guessed. The winged people flew in and reported in their own tongue to Cloudreaver, then milled around looking at the humans and others. Some flew away again. Others brought out weapons for sharpening.

The odds were getting better, Tanis told Flint. The dwarf, a frown on his face, wasn't entirely convinced. He was impatient for Cloudreaver to share the information gathered from his scouts.

Flint and Caramon went over to talk to the kyrie warrior. "Do we know yet where Kitiara is being held and what we're up against in terms of troops?" Flint asked, speaking in Common out of deference to the kyrie.

The others, including Tanis and Sturm, had drifted over behind them. Cloudreaver stood and addressed the companions intently.

"My scouts flew over the ancient city and saw many dozens of minotaurs camped throughout its ruins, almost all of them soldiers, all of them heavily armed," the kyrie warrior reported. "The high shaman's quarters are near the center of the ruined city, exposed to the open air but well patroled. A human female is being held in a cage in the Nightmaster's camp. There is a great deal of activity in the camp, obviously preparations for something. My scouts do not dare fly too close for fear of being detected. One of my brothers thought he saw a little person, neither human nor minotaur, scampering about, but he could not be sure."

"That blasted kender," muttered Flint.

"What about my brother?" Caramon looked questioningly at Cloudreaver.

"As yet," Cloudreaver replied grimly, "there is no sign of the mage."

"So we know Kit is imprisoned near the center of the old city," said Tanis. "We also know that she's well guarded. How many are we now ... twenty, thirty?"

No one volunteered an immediate reply. Tanis looked around the group. Brave but tense faces stared back at him. Everyone realized the numbers heavily favored the minotaur forces.

Cloudreaver shrugged. "Perhaps Bird-Spirit will know something more about the camp when he returns," Cloudreaver said encouragingly. "He is not only my chief of scouts, but an expert tactician when it comes time for battle."

"Whatever the odds, we have to attempt a rescue tomorrow," Sturm said. The other companions murmured their agreement.

"Yes," assented Cloudreaver in a solemn tone. "Tomorrow."

Almost involuntarily, everyone glanced upward. Already the sun had disappeared from the sky. A rosy twilight would precede the cold night.

"I suspect we'll have our fill of fighting tomorrow," Flint said grumpily. "Best thing to do is make sure we're ready." With that, the old dwarf pulled out his battle-axe and whetstone. The rest of the group settled down to similar preparations for battle.

* * * * *

Winging his way back to the temporary camp, something below caught Bird-Spirit's attention. He circled around and backtracked to get a better look. A minotaur soldier was rolling around near a large hole in the ground, apparently fighting, but what was he fighting with? Bird-Spirit risked dipping down for a closer look.

The bull man, at least seven feet tall, was dwarfed by the creature it fought—a hulking, four-legged armored monster with a raised crest on its back, taller than the minotaur and almost twice again as long. The bizarre creature moved low to the ground on four horny paws, striking out repeatedly at the minotaur and snapping at him with its jaws. The creature had knocked the minotaur to the ground and was keeping him from getting up with its vicious assaults.

Waving a forpann, the minotaur attempted to stab the creature with the trident part of his weapon. If he was successful, he could use the weighted net to pin down the beast and finish the kill. Off balance and dodging the creature's attack, however, the minotaur was having trouble landing a blow. Each jab of the creature's claws drew more blood.

Fascinated, trying to determine what the thing fighting the minotaur was, Bird-Spirit dropped farther, hovering just above the fray.

The minotaur managed to jump up and hurl himself across the beast's back. Holding on with one hand, the minotaur stabbed the creature under its crest, where its plate of armor stood out from its back. With a keening cry, the creature leaped several feet into the air, just beneath the hovering kyrie.

Only then did Bird-Spirit realize what the creature was. It was a bulette, sometimes called a land shark, a voracious predator so rare that neither Bird-Spirit nor any other kyrie that he knew of had ever seen one.

From the small basket dangling at his side, Bird-Spirit pulled out what looked like a bundled vine.

Below him, the minotaur's momentary advantage had evaporated. The bulette had managed to twist around in midair, landing squarely on the minotaur's shoulders. The bulette began to slash at the bull-man's legs and back with its clawed feet. At the same time, powerful jaws fastened around his neck.

Just at that point, Bird-Spirit swooped down and threw the tanglenet over the bulette. Consisting of a rare plant called choke creeper, the tanglenet quickly enveloped its target, pinning it down in a living constraint. Whenever the bulette tried to move, the plant constricted, its rubbery tendrils wrapping tightly around the brute monster.

Bird-Spirit doubted whether the tanglenet would have been as effective against the bulette if the savage creature hadn't been wounded. It also helped that the bulette, preoccupied with its own fight, hadn't noticed the kyrie until it was too late.

The kyrie warrior dropped to the ground and cautiously approached the bulette. The monster neither thrashed about nor cried out. It remained exceedingly still, as if dead, regarding Bird-Spirit with malevolent yellowish eyes that chilled the kyrie's blood. Neckless, the bulette's head jutted out from beneath its collar of armor, ending in the ferocious, pointed jaw that resembled nothing so much as that of a giant snapping turtle.

The tanglenet continued to weave around the bulette, immobilizing the creature's head, binding its armored, blue-green body and limbs ever more tightly. Off to the side, the minotaur twitched in his death throes. His blood drenched the desert ground, staining it red.

Bird-Spirit knew that the voracious bulette attacked and consumed anything in its territory, burrowing underground when it wanted to rest, breaking to the surface when it detected vibrations that meant new prey was nearby. No person or creature stayed in the locality of a bulette by choice.

Like all kyrie, Bird-Spirit possessed magical knowledge from the ancient world, a body of knowledge that predated by centuries the magic of the three moons and included the ability to communicate with any animal. Despite misgivings about the bulette, the bold kyrie decided to try to talk to the monster.

"I mean you no harm," Bird-Spirit said, speaking in the universal animal tongue. "I wish to speak with you about why I am here—and about the minotaurs who are swarming over this island."

The creature continued to stare at Bird-Spirit in silence. Finally it responded.

"I do not care about you or your petty interests. My interests concern keeping my stomach full. Those stupid bull-men who deny their animal heritage and hold themselves above us are of no concern to me."

Not only was the bulette malicious but it was also thickheaded, thought Bird-Spirit.

"Right now I would think that one additional interest you might have would be to see that the wound on your back is tended to." Bird-Spirit had noticed that a green slime, probably the bulette's blood, was oozing steadily from the wound inflicted by the minotaur. "With my healing skills, I will take care of the wound if you will simply hear me out."

Suspiciously the bulette answered, "Although I am your prisoner, you would find it hard to kill me, kyrie. Even so, it would appear I have few alternatives."

"Minotaurs from Mithas have established an outpost on this island. As you must know, the bull-men either exterminate or subjugate all who stand in their way. This does not bode well for you or any of the other creatures on Karthay." Bird-Spirit paused to make sure the bulette was listening.

"We kyrie have our own reasons for wanting the minotaurs off Karthay as soon as possible, but we are too few to overwhelm them. Only a small group of kyrie warriors, a handful of humans, a dwarf, and an elf make up our company. We would benefit greatly if a skilled general such as yourself, and those animals you chose to command, fought at our side."

Bird-Spirit calculated that an appeal to the bulette's inflated opinion of itself would be useful. He was right. If a great, hulking, beady-eyed monster could be said to puff up with pride, the bulette did.

However, the monster almost immediately reverted to its thickheaded posture. "I need neither kyrie nor anyone else to destroy the minotaurs. If I cared to do such a thing, I would do it myself, slowly, one by one, over a period of time. Why should I join with you?"

Bird-Spirit had no doubt that the bulette was probably right. Left to its own devices, it could eliminate the minotaurs on its own, given enough time. But Cloudreaver, Caramon, and the others couldn't wait for that eventuality.

"If you ally yourself with us, we promise to cede this island to you and the other animals as your domain for the next one thousand years. As the leader in battle, you no doubt would be recognized as the supreme chief of the island," Bird-Spirit added. He couldn't read the effect of his appeal in the bulette's cold, blank eyes. "And then there is the matter of your wound, which through magic I am able to heal."

The bulette remained impassive. Bird-Spirit waited patiently. The wound continued to secrete green slime.

"My injury first," the monster finally said. "Then we can discuss who might join us in a battle against the minotaurs.

The bull-men have no friends among the creatures on this island. Of course," it seemed to chuckle, "neither do I."

* * * * *

In order to dress the bulette's wound, Bird-Spirit had to cut the creature free from the tanglenet first, slashing the chokeweed near the base of its stem, then dissecting the tendrils in as many places as possible. Later he used some of the pieces to make a sling to hold the monster so he could carry it back to their campsite.

It took all of Bird-Spirit's strength to lift and transport the huge creature. Caramon, Tanis, Sturm, Flint, and the rest looked on in horror as the kyrie deposited the land shark in their midst just after dusk. Although the creature appeared docile, it lumbered sullenly to the edge of the camp and stared out into the desert distrustfully.

Cloudreaver greeted Bird-Spirit when he saw him return with the land shark. The two kyrie stood apart and talked together briefly in their own language. Then, beaming, Cloudreaver brought his friend forward to join the others.

"What good is such a creature to us?" asked Caramon.

"The minotaur camp is well defended. We are greatly out-numbered. We need allies wherever we can find them," Cloudreaver explained. "There is no more fearless fighter than a bulette. According to Bird-Spirit, this one has promised to summon other land creatures to come to our aid and has told us as well about a mountain lair of rocs that he feels can also be entreated to join our cause. I will send Star Twin to communicate with the rocs and seek their help."

"Rocs!" Flint exclaimed. Although Flint was a hill dwarf, not a mountain dwarf, he was still well versed in the repu-tation of these huge birds of prey, which resembled over-grown eagles, with wingspans of up to one hundred and twenty feet. Mountain dwarves who mined in remote regions sometimes were attacked by rocs defending their nests.

"There never was a roc who helped a dwarf, or vice versa," Flint said vehemently.

Caramon looked pleadingly at Tanis, who interceded to calm the dwarf. "Cloudreaver is right—we need help. If Bird-Spirit can capture a bulette, then perhaps Star Twin can tame the rocs for us." Tanis looked at the half-ogre, who as usual was standing not far from Flint. "Kirsig and I will do our best to keep the rocs out of your way and keep you out of theirs."

Kirsig, who was taking the subject of rocs and dwarves very seriously, crossed her arms in front of her chest and nodded emphatically.

"When can we expect our unusual allies to join us?" asked Sturm. Since his rescue from the Pit of Doom, the Solamnic had come to have a deep respect for the kyrie and saw no reason to question the wisdom of their unorthodox plan.

Bird-Spirit cocked his head in the direction of the bulette, appearing to listen for a few moments. "The message has gone out. The morning should bring new friends. The best thing to do is wait. We should rest until then."

Following his own advice, the kyrie squatted down, closed his eyes, and went to sleep almost immediately. Or at least he seemed to. After a minute, Bird-Spirit opened one eye. "Wake me to stand guard if necessary," he added before closing his eyes again.

"I rested today while you scouted," Yuril stated. "I'll take first shift and wake someone when I get tired."

Yuril scooped up a blanket from the ground and strode over to sit against a large tree at the edge of the forest cover where they had made camp. The others began moving off to find a comfortable place to sleep. Several kyrie and the rest of the sailors from the *Castor* had already begun to bed down.

"I, uh, have to sharpen my sword and get my other weapons ready for tomorrow," Caramon mumbled to no one in particular. "I guess I'll go keep Yuril company."

Sturm and Tanis exchanged looks. "Just remember that one of you is supposed to be standing watch," Tanis called out after him.

In truth, Caramon had been preoccupied with the where-abouts of his twin ever since Raistlin had disappeared earlier in the day. He didn't think he could fall asleep even if he tried. Yuril, however, proved to be a soothing presence.

* * * * *

Flint also slept, but not well. His dreams were filled with the rustlings and movements of great wings swooping down on him. Kirsig, who sat up to keep watch over the dwarf, had to pull the blanket he had thrown off back up around the old dwarf's neck several times.

When he finally woke the next morning, Flint saw that the sounds disturbing his sleep had been real, only they were produced by curious land animals rather than denizens of the air.

On the southwestern edge of the campsite stood the bulette. Behind it, in the early dawn light, the desert ground appeared to surge and buckle. Flint looked closer. "Great Reorx!" he exclaimed. Dozens of giant, low-slung insects, their backs covered by hard, black, jointed shells, their heads ending in a pair of small but effective-looking mandibles, covered the desert floor.

"Horax."

"What?" Flint asked the kyrie who had come up next to him.

"They live underground and grow to be almost as long as we are tall. They attack in packs," the kyrie explained. "Luckily I've never had the misfortune to run into them. I've heard they crush the life out of you with their curved pincers."

Seeing Flint's jaw drop, the kyrie added, "Don't worry. They're taking orders from the bulette, and the bulette's on our side—for the time being."

"Their pincers are powerful, all right," piped up Kirsig, who had joined them. The half-ogre seemed to have a useful store of information about any given subject. "My daddy said they could really be a nuisance if they got into underground tunnels you were using. They don't much like sunlight, usually. I trust they can put up with it for a few hours during the attack."

All of the companions, the kyrie, and the sailors had risen now and were staring at the strange horde of animals—the bulette, the packs of horax, and in the rear, odd rock formations that shifted and moved. Flint rubbed his eyes wonderingly.

"Kirsig," he whispered, tugging on the half-ogre's sleeve. Flint pointed beyond the horax.

The reddish-brown rocks had shifted again, revealing themselves to be not inanimate stones but the knobby hide of a gigantic reptile. Flint gauged the monstrous serpentine creature to be nearly two hundred feet from the end of its long, whiplike tail to the tip of its pointed, fanged snout. The behemoth appeared to rest flat on the ground, its flipperlike feet splayed out on either side of its scaly body.

What Flint had taken for caverns in the rock were actually the creature's eye sockets, which were recessed so deeply you couldn't glimpse its eyes. The monster idly lashed its tail across the ground, flattening several rock outcroppings.

"The greater hatori, and a very ancient one by the size of it," whispered Kirsig. "It can't have had much to eat on this island over the past decades, and a hungry hatori is a hungry fighter, as my daddy always used to say."

The bulette glared first at the kyrie and their friends, then out over the army it had assembled. While none of these killer animals had any love for each other, they had even less for the minotaurs, who were known in the desert world as wanton, arrogant bullies.

The bulette had communicated the arrangement proposed by Bird-Spirit and Cloudreaver. The animals would fight together for one day, and the kyrie would cede desolate Karthay to them for one thousand years. Because of the presence of Kit, and presumably Raistlin, in the ruined city, the creatures were under strict orders not to harm any humans or other races, only minotaurs. These they could kill according to their whim.

A sudden gust of wind nearly knocked Flint down. The wind continued gusting, blowing blankets and packs around the campsite. With a sinking feeling, Flint looked up. Just overhead hovered four rocs, two adults and two smaller ones, probably their adolescent offspring. Sharp black eyes regarded the assembled company. With their muscular bodies, sleek, bulletlike heads, and immense wingspans, each roc was as big as a vallenwood. Their glossy brown and yellow plumage and strong, curved beaks shone in the rays of the rising sun.

*   *   *   *   *

Toth-Ur paced restlessly in front of his tent. The afternoon sun beat down on him, matting his glossy black fur with perspiration. The Nightmaster and his retinue had departed safely for the volcano's summit. Apparently everything was in order, but uneasiness dogged Toth-Ur's steps. Zedhar hadn't returned from his scouting mission the previous day. The commander debated sending out a search party for him, but with his troops' numbers already diminished by the contingent that accompanied the Nightmaster, Toth-Ur was reluctant to do so. The high shaman had warned him to be vigilant today ... especially today.

His tent was pitched near the western perimeter of the ruined city of Karthay, near a crumbled parapet. Hands on his haunches, Toth-Ur surveyed the barren, desolate landscape. A few soldiers stood off to one side, ready to do his bidding.

Suddenly a giant shape burst from the ground, not ten feet in front of the commander's tent, springing straight up into the air, then coming down heavily on a minotaur soldier's back. A quick thrust of its jaw snapped the bull-man's neck.

Before the other soldiers had time to do much more than unsheath their swords, one horax after another was streaming out of the hole made by the bulette. Everywhere the astonished Toth-Ur looked, strange, horrible animals were pouring out of holes in the ground and attacking his small army from all directions.

The minotaurs couldn't stand their ground, for the savage animal force had attacked in their midst. Some died on the spot. Others stood and fought, though swords and spears merely glanced off the insectoids' chitinous shells. Others retreated to better fighting positions.

The bulette was on a rampage, leaping and smashing and snapping minotaurs with impunity.

The packs of horax were blood-crazed. It took two or three of the creatures to overwhelm a single minotaur. One would fasten its mandibles around each leg just above a hoof, crushing the bones. A third horax would jab the minotaur's soft body parts after the soldier fell to the ground. Then all would stop and devour the victim.

To the south approached an even worse nightmare. The very desert seemed to be on the move against the minotaurs. The greater hatori had emerged and was slithering backward toward a contingent of minotaurs bravely standing their ground. It whipped its bony tail back and forth, knocking down a half-dozen soldiers at a blow, mercilessly mashing them into the ground.

To the north, the giant rocs swept down from the clouds, their wings almost blotting out the sun. They circled out of spear range while the bull-men tossed everything they could think of in their direction. Then, before reinforcements could arrive, each of the rocs hurtled toward the ruins and snatched up huge chunks of ash-encrusted stone, dropping them on two or three minotaur soldiers at a time and crushing the enemy. Kyrie flew with the rocs, giving orders to the giant birds.

Everywhere the minotaurs struggled to regroup. Turning away from a fight was unthinkable to a minotaur, but the attack by this army of monstrous creatures unnerved them. Their eyes goggled. Their responses were disorganized and ineffective. Toth-Ur had never seen, never dreamed, anything like it. The minotaur commander gave the order to fall back.

* * * * *

Sturm, Flint, Kirsig, Yuril, and the other sailors from the *Castor* hunkered down behind the hatori, dodging spears and tesstos, the barbed clubs favored by many of the minotaurs.

While in hand-to-hand combat with a seven-foot tall brute wielding a katar, Sturm heard Yuril cry out. With a final lunge, the Solamnic stabbed the minotaur soldier through its stomach, then stepped out of the way of the falling beast. He turned to find Yuril.

A short way off, the female first mate stood looking down at the crumpled form of one of her fellow sailors, which lay next to the beheaded body of a minotaur. "It's Dinchee," she said, looking up at Sturm with moist eyes. "We—we sailed together for many years." Yuril kicked the headless bull-man in the side, then raced back into the fight. Sturm thought about pulling the sailor's body to the side for burial later, but before he could, two hairy, cleft hooves materialized in front of him.

The Solamnic looked up just in time to parry the downward swing of a two-handed sword. The powerful blow cracked his sword in two. The minotaur's nostrils flared as it raised the sword again. Sturm fumbled with the dagger at his belt. Desperately he pulled it free and flung it. It clove into the stomach of the beast, who doubled over. Sturm reached up and pulled the knife sharply upward, then out, disemboweling the bull-man.

* * * * *

The commander of the minotaur army had retrenched inside the perimeter of the city. But his soldiers were in disarray, and the enemy appeared to be all around and above them, swirling and attacking.

A runner approached Toth-Ur. "A band of kyrie, an elf, and a human have penetrated the inner city and are near the Nightmaster's camp, where the human female was being held prisoner."

With an oath, Toth-Ur shouted "Follow me!" to a small band of soldiers and stormed off in the direction of the old library.

* * * * *

The plan had been for the desert creatures and rocs to engage and occupy the perimeter forces, while Caramon, Tanis, Cloudreaver, Bird-Spirit, and the other kyrie would pierce the Nightmaster's enclave, rescuing Kitiara. By now it was almost sundown, but nobody had been able to locate Kit—or Raistlin, for that matter.

Side by side, Caramon and Tanis had fought toward the high shaman's campsite, driving away the few minotaur soldiers who had remained behind to guard it. But when they reached the cage that the kyrie said had held Kit, the cage was empty.

Dangerous though it was, without any flanking support, Bird-Spirit offered to fly quickly over the interior of the ruined city to look for her.

Before he could take off, a shatang, a barbed throwing spear, clattered into their midst. Caramon turned just in time to duck away from the downward stroke of Toth-Ur's studded club. The commander bore down on the Majere twin, slashing at him with the tessto in one hand, a clabbard in another. From the grunts and clanging swords around him, the young warrior surmised that his friends were also engaged in pitched fighting.

The kyries' primitive stone weapons would have put them at a definite disadvantage against the tempered metal of the minotaurs, except that the bird-men were able to lift into the air in an instant, slashing at the minotaurs with their talons while changing the angle of their attack, disconcerting their opponents, whose sword thrusts often went awry.

One of the minotaur soldiers launched a barbed spear that caught Cloudreaver in the wing. With his other hand, the kyrie warrior jerked the weapon out, then stabbed it into the gut of the soldier who had moved too close, pressing his advantage.

Caramon, who had only a sword to work with, began falling back in the face of Toth-Ur's formidable two-handed assault. Suddenly a startled look came over the commander's face. His weapons dropped to the ground. Clutching madly at his back, the huge minotaur crashed forward. Yuril leaned over and put her foot on the bull-man's back, pulling out her sword with a smooth movement. She wiped it nonchalantly on the ground, then touched it to her forehead in Caramon's direction.

"Glad to be of service," she said with a fleeting smile before running off.

* * * * *

As Sturm, Flint, and Kirsig passed through a tumbled-down colonnade, a minotaur who had managed to elude the hatori and the horax jumped out at the dwarf, whirling a tessto. Flint ducked but fell to the ground, cracking his head. Dizzily the dwarf watched as the soldier straddled him, his club upraised.

Kirsig uttered a banshee yell, then threw herself full length at the soldier, tackling him. Flint scrambled away, shaking his head to clear it. Looking back, the dwarf saw the minotaur stumble under Kirsig's surprise assault, then recover. The bull-man snatched up the half-ogre in one hand, then, with the other, bashed her head in.

Too late, Sturm made it to the minotaur, planting a sword neatly between his two horns. The ever-game Kirsig was dead.

* * * * *

"My hero."

Flying with Tanis, Bird-Spirit had spotted the human female tied to a broken column in a nearby part of the city. A lone minotaur stubbornly guarded her, but between them, the kyrie and the half-elf had made short work of the dogged soldier.

Exhausted from struggling against her bonds and frustrated at not being able to take part in the battle she had been observing from a distance, Kitiara greeted Tanis testily.

"You have a bad habit of rescuing me," she said as the half-elf untied her. She looked with wide eyes at Bird-Spirit, who grinned back at her. "Only this time I guess I needed a little help," she added grudgingly.

"You're welcome," replied Tanis, knowing this was as close to a thank-you as he would ever get from Kitiara Uth Matar.

Kit, to his eyes, looked starved and grimy. The half-elf quickly pulled a dried stick of jerky from a pouch and handed it to her. Kitiara gobbled it hungrily. Watching her, starved and grimy though she was, Tanis was struck anew by her hard beauty.

Caramon came running up and gave Kitiara a big hug. Sturm was close behind, and Yuril behind him.

"Where's Raist?" Caramon asked.

Bird-Spirit shook his head. Tanis countered, "Where are Flint and Kirsig?"

"The half-ogre is dead," Sturm said grimly. "She died bravely. Flint is okay." He waved his arm. "He's over there—fighting."

Kit had been rubbing her wrists and ankles. Already she looked refreshed and ready for action. She pointed to Worldscap. "Raistlin was here, but he volunteered to take my place as the Nightmaster's sacrifice. I think they're up there. We don't have any time to lose." Night was falling. "But how can we get to the summit in time?"

Cloudreaver and three other kyrie had landed in the meantime. "We can fly up there in a matter of minutes," said the kyrie warrior.

Kit looked dubious. Tanis assured her that it was possible.

"Sturm," ordered Caramon, "find Flint and tell him and the others to pull back. Leave the minotaurs to the animal army. Get out of this ruined city and meet us back at last night's camp."

"But—" protested the Solamnic.

"There's no time. We don't have enough kyrie to fly all of us," Tanis interjected, "and someone has to warn Flint."

Sturm nodded and raced off.

Cloudreaver grabbed Caramon in his talons and took off. Bird-Spirit took Tanis. The two other kyrie trailed, carrying Yuril and Kitiara.

They soared toward Worldscap.

The furious fighting was left behind. Tonight the bulette, the hatori, and the rocs would feast.

Chapter 16
The Spell of Sargonnas

According to legend, Worldscap had last erupted during the Cataclysm. Raining volcanic death on Karthay, it wiped the city and its people from the face of the earth. Karthay had been uninhabited ever since, until the Nightmaster with his flock of disciples had arrived to make their secret preparations for bringing Sargonnas into the world.

Worldscap stood like a huge jagged tooth on the edge of the city, where it presented a formidable barrier to the north and west. Its slopes were furrowed by deep ravines and impenetrable clusters of hardened lava. The Nightmaster and his acolytes had spent months carving a swath to the summit, a black and barren crater.

From a distance, it looked as though the top of the mountain had been lopped off. Numerous steep-sided cinder cones dotted the unusually broad bowl. Everywhere were signs of volcanic activity, including lava bombs, molds of tree trunks, and giant groundsels engulfed by hardened lava. Mud pots bubbled. Jets of steam and gas whistled from cracks in the ground.

One oval-shaped depression in the crater was larger and more volatile than the rest. This was the heart of the volcano, crusted over with dried lava. Its center consisted of a plug of rock that had solidified deep down in the volcano's vent.

The Nightmaster believed that under the oval-shaped depression lay the original volcanic crater, whose eruption had precipitated the collapse of the peak into the core of the mountain. And underneath the original crater waited the fire fountain that could re-ignite volcanic activity. For weeks, the Nightmaster's followers had been working with the minotaur troops to dig out the vent.

From his camp on the ash-covered terrace of the dead city's once-great library, the Nightmaster regularly hiked to a mountain plateau west of Karthay to read his signs. But the spell to summon Sargonnas would be cast here, on the summit of Worldscap, in the heart of the volcano.

Everything had been prepared. The acolytes and a select number of minotaur soldiers had been camped on the summit for days, setting up the makeshift laboratory, the rows of ingredients, the charms and stones and dead creatures, the scrolls and books that the Nightmaster would need during the casting of the spell.

After long hours of labor, the cap had been dug out of the original volcano and the mouth of the fire fountain breached. The span of the mouth was roughly a dozen feet. Deep down, one could glimpse fiery orange lava, seething and bubbling.

The soldiers had built a wooden scaffold near the edge of the mouth, with a dozen stairs leading to a platform overlooking the fiery fountain.

The stars had glided into conjunction. Day was turning

into night.

All was ready when the Nightmaster and his group crested the summit. Wearing ceremonial furs and feathers, with bells jingling as he moved, the Nightmaster strutted proudly toward the oval-shaped depression that housed the volcano's original crater. He walked between a double line of his acolytes and soldiers who had gathered in formation to greet him.

Trailing the Nightmaster were several armed minotaurs and the High Three shamans. Following them was a young, thin human in a dark robe, who stumbled as he was prodded forward by the sullen Dogz, and a kender without a topknot who chattered enthusiastically about the glorious spectacle of evil he was about to witness.

* * * * *

"Tell me, Raistlin, how you divined that I was going to cast this ancient and generally forgotten spell? Satisfy my curiosity. You know you are going to die anyway."

The Nightmaster bent over Raistlin, leering triumphantly.

The young mage sat in stony silence on a rock near the lip of the crater, his arms bound behind him, his feet also tied tightly with rope. Yet Raistlin refused to let defeat show in his face. Instead, he offered the Nightmaster an enigmatic smile with his reply.

"It was completely by chance. It was only a torn page in a yellowed spellbook that caught my eye. I knew that the spell had something to do with minotaur rituals. That much was obvious. And there was a citation of Sargonnas, the Lord of Dark Vengeance. But I had no hope of assembling the spell components, and beyond that, I cared little.

"Then my friend, Tasslehoff Burrfoot"—here Raistlin nodded in the direction of the kender, who was bounding back and forth between members of the High Three, trying to help them mix potions and ingredients but mostly getting in the way—"happened to make mention of a minotaur herbalist located on the island of Southern Ergoth. A minotaur herbalist ... that aroused my curiosity. I asked a kender friend of Tasslehoff's who sometimes sold herbs, roots, and other items to me about certain peculiar ingredients that were mentioned on the torn page of the yellowed spellbook.

"One of these ingredients was crushed jalopwort, and the kender assured me that the minotaur had a supply available. Along with my brother and a friend, Tas volunteered to travel to Southern Ergoth to purchase the jalopwort."

Here Raistlin paused, glancing around. The pale of evening had settled in, promising a crisp night, with the stars clear in their formations.

The acolytes and troops had retreated to the edge of the summit, well away from the staging area. Silent and grim, holding their weapons aloft so that the steel and embroidered gems glinted under the twin moons, the small force of soldiers stood back from the Nightmaster, Raistlin, and the others.

Dogz took a position near the Nightmaster, guarding Raistlin.

"Even then, I would not have thought too much about it," the young mage continued. "It is part of my business to be interested in exotic herbs and rare spells. Except then my brother, his friend, and Tasslehoff vanished. And before they vanished, Tas sent me a magic message bottle that told me all about the strange execution of the minotaur herbalist.

"The person who brought me the message bottle added some curious details about the missing ship and its treacherous captain. After completing his job, it seems the captain was also killed in a manner that appeared to me to be distinctly magical."

Raistlin's eyes glittered with intelligence as he spoke.

"After that, it was mostly guesswork. I went back to the

crumbling spellbook and read and studied the partial spell. I discussed my conclusions with—" here he paused—"let me call him a learned advisor.

"Through these efforts, it gradually dawned on me that the jalopwort was just a small part of a magical undertaking grander than anything I had suspected, that this ambitious spell had to involve minotaurs at the highest level, and that the spellcasting that was being planned would, if successful, bring Sargonnas, god of the minotaurs, into the material plane. The most logical place for such a rite would be here, near the ruins of Karthay, the last known place on Krynn where the Lord of Vengeance showed his wrath of fire."

"So you did get my magic message bottle!" chirped Tasslehoff. The kender had bounded up behind Raistlin. "I'm glad it wasn't wast—"

The Nightmaster grabbed Tasslehoff, whose habit of idle chatter was beginning to irritate him, and rather roughly shoved the kender under one arm, blanketing his mouth with a huge hand.

Raistlin looked at both of them coolly.

"Yes," purred the Nightmaster while Tas did his best to get loose from the high shaman's smothering grip. "Tasslehoff sent you a magic message bottle. You and he are old friends, right? So how do you like the new, improved Tasslehoff—to whom one of my disciples has fed a potion and turned into an evil kender? He has been most useful to us so far"—here the Nightmaster gave Tas a hard squeeze—"and I trust he will continue to be useful to us in the future."

Raistlin glanced at the struggling kender, then returned his gaze to the Nightmaster. "So that is how you did it," said Raistlin. "A potion."

"Do you doubt it?" rumbled the Nightmaster. For a moment, the Nightmaster lifted his arm away from Tas's mouth.

"It's true," said Tasslehoff, wrinkling his face into what

he hoped was a fierce-looking sneer. "I'm incredibly evil now. Quite a change, huh?"

The Nightmaster clapped his arm back around the kender's mouth, and Tas resumed his struggling.

"I would have thought," Raistlin said blandly, "that a potion would not have any long-term effect."

The Nightmaster smiled. "You're quite right," he rumbled. "Dogz!" Dogz approached him, and he handed the kender over to Dogz. "Give Tasslehoff his double dose—now!"

Dogz looked at the Nightmaster, then quickly looked away. For an instant, his eyes met Raistlin's. Then Dogz nodded to the Nightmaster.

The Nightmaster returned his attention to Raistlin. "I am grateful to you for reminding me."

With Tas protesting, Dogz led the kender off to a far corner of the spellcasting area, where a small table was set up. Raistlin saw Dogz set the kender down by the shoulders, swirl something in a beaker, and tip the contents into the kender's mouth. After that, Raistlin observed, Dogz watched Tas for several minutes until the kender's head drooped down and he was slumped peacefully in the chair.

All around them, preparations for the casting of the spell had reached their zenith. Fesz and the other two shaman minotaurs were tossing handfuls of components culled from jars and beakers into the dug-out crater. After hundreds of years of dormancy, the volcano had begun to hiss and sputter. A faint orange light spilled forth from the mouth of the fire fountain.

Dogz trotted back in the direction of Raistlin and the Nightmaster.

"I would have considered the kender for a sacrificial victim," rumbled the Nightmaster, "if kender were not such an insignificant race. Sargonnas would much prefer a human, and a young mage such as yourself will, as you might guess, improve the spell greatly." Here he paused and studied Raistlin closely.

"I am so ignorant of the customs of humans. Tell me why you are not wearing the robes of white, red, or black."

"I have not taken the Test," said Raistlin, "and I have not yet chosen the color of the robes that I will one day wear."

"If you were a black robe," mused the Nightmaster, "we would be on the same side. You would worship Sargonnas as I do."

"I know very little about Sargonnas. That is one of the reasons why I came."

"You came to rescue your brother," the Nightmaster said with a sneer.

"Partly," answered Raistlin, "and partly because I am interested in all the orders of magic—black, white, and neutral."

"Really?"

The High Three had finished their preliminary work. Dogz was standing back, arms folded, in the shadows. Fesz came over and interrupted.

"Pardon, Excellency," said Fesz, "but we are ready."

The high shaman gave him a nod. Fesz turned away.

The Nightmaster leaned over Raistlin, his fetid breath hot on the mage's face. The high shaman examined the young mage from Solace with fresh interest. Raistlin didn't flinch under his gaze.

"So," rumbled the Nightmaster, "that is why you volunteered to take your sister's place ... because you wanted to observe the spell and to encounter Sargonnas himself—as you surely will, since you will be the victim who makes possible his entry into this world!"

Raistlin waited a long time before replying. "Partly," is all he said.

The Nightmaster reared back and struck Raistlin across the face, bowling him off the rock that served as his chair. Blood streaked down Raistlin's face. For good measure, the Nightmaster kicked the young mage hard in the side as he lay on the ground. Still Raistlin did not cry out.

Dogz watched, his arms folded, his face impassive.

"Guards!" called the Nightmaster. Two armed minotaurs broke rank with the others on the perimeter of the area and came running over. "Bring this pathetic human over to the crater and hold him until I am ready for him!"

The soldiers picked Raistlin up and dragged him over to the crater's edge, so near to the mouth that the heat from below blasted him.

The High Three lined up across the crater at an angle from Raistlin.

The Nightmaster donned a crimson cloak and marched up the dozen steps to the top of the scaffold. There a stand held a massive tome.

Raistlin shook his head to clear it from the blow by the Nightmaster. He was only slightly dazed. Although he was held tightly by the soldiers, the young mage could twist around and glimpse Tasslehoff behind the High Three, still slumped on his chair.

Atop the scaffold, the Nightmaster lifted his horned head, took a deep breath, and gazed skyward.

Cold gripped the summit, though no wind stirred. The clouds that blotted out the sky on previous nights had disappeared. The stars shone like beacons.

Not only could Raistlin feel the intense heat of the volcano, but now he also could clearly hear the bubbling of the fiery orange liquid as it gradually welled to the surface.

The Nightmaster began to read from the tome in an ancient minotaur dialect, his guttural voice rising steadily in volume.

The High Three started to murmur in the background.

Raistlin could make out almost none of the words, only an occasional invocation to Sargonnas.

As he chanted the spell, the Nightmaster moved his powerful arms in a strange, graceful manner, weaving intricate hand language in the air. His cloak swished behind him. The small bells draping his sharp, curved horns jingled a musical accompaniment to his every movement. His deep bull voice, growling out mysterious phrases, contrasted eerily with his balletlike motions.

Thunk! Flying out of nowhere, an object struck the throat of one of the minotaur guards, hitting him with such force that he immediately let loose his grip on Raistlin, clutched at his throat, and fell to the ground, dead.

Before anybody could react, another object flew in from the periphery of Raistlin's vision, this one even bigger. It was Tasslehoff Burrfoot.

Tas leaped from the shadows onto the back of the other minotaur holding Raistlin. He was doing his best to choke and pummel a creature who was three times his size and six times the weight of the kender. He was doing a pretty good job of it, however, because the kender had landed so high on the minotaur's back that the creature couldn't reach far enough behind to get his hands on Tas.

But it was only a couple of seconds before Fesz sprinted over and jerked Tas to the ground. Although Tas got right up, he was moving groggily. Fesz easily latched on to his collar and lifted the squirming kender several feet into the air.

"You shame me, kender!" boomed Fesz, shaking Tas so violently that the kender started to hiccup. "You, whom I believed and trusted—you, whom I turned evil—you, whom I honored with the great privilege of attending the coming of Sargonnas—you—you—"

The shaman minotaur was livid with anger and disappointment.

Meanwhile, the minotaur soldier recovered his balance. Indeed he had never lost his hold on Raistlin.

The young mage could think of no spell which he could unleash without the use of his hands. Still bound and tied, Raistlin could do little but intently watch the scene unfold.

"Great privilege"—hiccup—"pfooey!" Tasslehoff spat into the smelly bull face of Fesz. "You cowheads wouldn't know honor from"—hiccup—"cow dung. I've had it with your cave breath, your exalted horns that any dumb ox could grow"—hiccup—"your smelly wardrobe, your barnyard manners"—hiccup, hiccup ...

Tas was practically purple from being shaken so violently.

Suddenly a thunderous roar stilled both of them. Everyone looked up to the top of the scaffold, where the Nightmaster, who had been momentarily forgotten in the melee. With his fists clenched and his jagged teeth bared in a snarl, the Nightmaster personified rage.

"Silence!" screamed down the Nightmaster. "You are interrupting the spell!"

"But—" rumbled Fesz plaintively, "but the kender—"

"Be done with him," commanded the Nightmaster. "Throw him into the crater!"

"Yes," said Fesz meekly.

"No!" roared a different voice.

Raistlin, who had been looking up at the Nightmaster, turned his head just in time to see Fesz clutch at his throat. Embedded there, so deeply that the shaman couldn't budge it, was a dagger with an H-shaped hilt, Dogz's well-polished katar. Fesz dropped Tasslehoff, who landed with a thud. Then the shaman minotaur unceremoniously keeled over, quite dead.

From the scaffolding, the Nightmaster shouted, "Seize him!"

Dogz didn't even try to run away, nor did he resist when several soldiers surrounded him, pointing their spears and swords threateningly. In truth, the minotaur couldn't have said why he did what he had done—the unthinkable, treason—except that he liked the kender, Tasslehoff Burrfoot. Especially now that Tas seemed to be back to his old self. Dogz had reacted out of an instinct that he didn't know he possessed—the instinct of friendship.

Dogz sank to his knees.

The kender got up from his.

Hiccup.

Thoroughly pinioned by the remaining minotaur guard, Raistlin was trying to think of a spell he could manage in this desperate situation when Tasslehoff's hiccup suggested one: the invisibility spell that Raistlin had used to get past the minotaur guards earlier that day. It wouldn't do Raistlin much good now, but if he could pass it on to someone else.... It wouldn't last for long, but long enough for Tas to get away. The young mage concentrated. Behind his back, he moved his fingers underneath their bonds.

Raistlin murmured the words to the spell, substituting Tasslehoff's name and throwing all of his focus and energy in Tas's direction.

With a soft popping sound, the kender vanished.

The Nightmaster, who had been preparing to cast a bolt of lightning at Tasslehoff, cursed himself. "Fool! I'm a fool!" he raged. "I should have thought of that." The high shaman leaned over the scaffold railing and shouted to the soldier who was holding Raistlin. "Put a gag around his mouth and make sure the mage can't speak. Then bring him up the steps and give him to me."

The guard hurled Raistlin down on the ground and bound his mouth roughly with a dirty strip of cloth. Then he began to drag Raistlin toward the scaffold steps.

The Nightmaster leaned over the railing in the opposite direction and yelled at several of his disciples who stood outside the line of minotaur soldiers. "The kender is invisible! Find him and kill him!"

Four of the minotaurs burst into the staging area, then stopped, confused. After a moment, they began stalking around, bending and peering suspiciously at thin air.

Hiccup.

Every time the soldiers heard a hiccup, they whirled and raced to another spot, lunging for something that wasn't there, colliding with each other.

The Nightmaster leaned over the railing toward the High Three, who had been reduced to the High Two with Fesz's death, and shouted, "Continue! The spell is almost completed!"

The two shaman minotaurs, taken aback by the unexpected death of Fesz, successor to the Nightmaster, had stopped their chanting. They appeared to be confused. But the murderous look the Nightmaster wore was enough to galvanize them into action. Once again they took up their supportive roles in the spell, intoning the required phrases.

The Nightmaster returned his attention to Raistlin, who was just then being yanked to the top of the steps by the armed minotaur. The high shaman grasped the young mage's arm, ordering the soldier to rejoin the forces below. The minotaur soldier gladly did so.

Raistlin couldn't move his arms or legs. His mouth was sealed so tightly he could barely breathe. The Nightmaster brought him to the edge of the scaffold, dangling him over the edge.

From this vantage, the volcanic pit seemed about to overflow with liquid fire. The heat seared the young mage's face.

"Mark it well, mage," hissed the Nightmaster, "for soon you will be swallowed up by the Lord of Volcanoes!"

With a muscular spin, the Nightmaster hurled Raistlin into one corner of the scaffold. The high shaman turned back to the massive magic tome and picked up where he had been forced to break off.

Hiccup.

Down below, the Nightmaster's acolytes scurried to track the hiccuping and catch the invisible kender. They missed again and again.

The Nightmaster blocked out the sounds. Nothing could stop him now that he was so close. Again he began to rumble in an ancient dialect. Again he moved his arms, weaving the powerful spell.

Crumpled in the corner of the platform, Raistlin felt defeated. With his sensitive hearing, he could hear the hiccuping below. The young mage wished that Tas would go for help, or escape, or at the very least stop hiccuping.

The Nightmaster turned a page.

Hiccup.

The hiccups were fewer and farther between now, like thunder after a storm has passed. The minions of the Nightmaster had given up. They had no idea how to catch an invisible kender. Those who were searching for Tas grouped together off to one side, distracted by the sight of the Nightmaster above on the scaffold, resuming his display of spellcasting.

Hiccup.

A minotaur soldier felt his sword being pulled from its sheath. He grabbed at the hilt just in time and wrested it back after a tug-of-war with something invisible. The minotaur swatted at the something and missed. One by one, each of the soldiers around him swatted and missed. Then a soldier unsheathed his sword and swung wildly, cutting off the ear of the minotaur standing next to him.

Hiccup.

The noise sounded close to where Dogz knelt on both knees, guarded by a knot of minotaur soldiers. The soldiers started at the hiccup, but couldn't tell precisely where it had come from. A couple of them moved away from Dogz, gripping their weapons and sniffing suspiciously. That left three watching the turncoat.

On the scaffold, the Nightmaster turned another page, continuing to read aloud the mysterious phrases of long-ago magic in his deep voice.

"Psst, Dogz! It's me, Tas!"

Dogz's mournful eyes widened, more concerned for the kender's sake than he was for himself. The three guards stood a couple of feet away, their backs to him, watching the Nightmaster. They hadn't heard Tasslehoff.

With his eyes, Dogz showed that he had heard.

"Hey, I want to thank you for killing Fesz! That was a swell thing to do. What a friend you are! Of course, I would have done it myself long ago if only—"

With his eyes, Dogz tried to tell the kender that he ought to get away from him—far away from him—before the armed guards turned around.

"Say, Dogz, you wouldn't happen to have a small dagger or anything—"

"Fesz," rumbled Dogz as softly as he could.

One of the guards heard him. He turned and stared suspiciously at Dogz, who shrugged. The guard came over and poked around in the air with his spear, hitting nothing.

Hiccup.

The minotaur guard rammed the butt end of the spear into Dogz's gut. Dogz doubled over, gasping for breath.

Atop the scaffold, the Nightmaster turned the final page. He took a moment, breathed deeply, and pulled some dried leaves and other ingredients from small pouches he carried, flinging them out over the volcano.

A mist of particles rose from the crater, spreading out and filling the air above it, tinting everything orange-red. The mist was dry and hot.

"The jalopwort," the Nightmaster growled, nodding in Raistlin's direction, "and the last of the other ingredients called for by the spell."

Raistlin, backed up against one of the corner posts, stared straight ahead, impassive. The moment the Nightmaster turned back to the tome of spells, he resumed his desperate effort to saw through the rope by rubbing it against the wooden corner of the scaffold.

Hiccup.

On the ground, something invisible was trying to pull the katar out of Fesz's neck. Nobody was paying the slightest attention to the dead shaman, so Tas was able to put his foot on Fesz's head and pull with both hands. Nobody noticed when the katar slid out of the minotaur's body and disappeared under Tasslehoff's tunic.

Fortunately Tasslehoff had finally gotten over the hiccups.

Unfortunately he had only a few minutes of invisibility left.

As carefully and quietly as he could, the invisible Tas crawled past the minotaur guard stationed at the foot of the scaffold. Up the steps, one by one, on his hands and knees, he crept toward Raistlin.

The mage heard the odd scraping and rustling sounds on the steps behind him and froze. Even as he did so, he felt the sharp edge of a blade begin to saw through the ropes that tied his hands.

Glancing over his shoulder, Raistlin saw Tasslehoff, one step from the top, gradually turning visible. He shook his head violently to warn the kender, but, intent on his task, Tas wasn't looking at Raistlin's face. Even if he had been looking, the kender wouldn't have had the slightest idea what the mage was trying to communicate.

The Nightmaster heard a noise at his feet.

Looking up, Tas saw the Nightmaster reaching down for him.

Faster than a dart eel, Tas withdrew the katar and rolled to his left. He came up on the floor of the scaffold, stabbing forward and down. The katar sank into the Nightmaster's cleft right hoof.

The high shaman of the minotaurs howled with pain and yanked out the katar, dropping it over the side of the scaffold. Bellowing with fury, the Nightmaster ripped a strip of cloth from his cloak and wrapped it around his foot, which was streaming blood. Then he jerked his head up, nostrils flaring, looking for Tas.

As close to panic as a kender gets, Tasslehoff had frozen, trying to decide whether to stay or run, when he saw the bulging eyes of the Nightmaster fasten on him. "Uh-oh," he murmured and instantly made the decision to run.

But it was too late. The Nightmaster covered the short distance between them in an eyeblink, snatching the kender up in one huge hand. With a deafening roar, the high shaman whirled and hurled Tas far out over the mouth of the volcano.

Down, down Tas fell, toward the liquid furnace ...

... only to be caught up by something that swooped beneath him.

The Nightmaster gaped in astonishment as a kyrie warrior plucked the kender from the air with its talons. The kyrie soared up and past the shaman, then back down to the ground, where he deposited an equally astonished Tasslehoff Burrfoot a short distance away.

Running from one side of the scaffold to the other, looking down, the Nightmaster saw that a small group of kyrie and humans had engaged his minotaur force in battle. Several of the minotaurs were lying on the ground, dead or wounded, while others had retreated, bunching together behind mounds of dead lava, lobbing spears and arrows at the intruders.

The Nightmaster could pick out the human female, Kitiara, among the attackers, but he looked in vain for his two shamans, who had left their posts and vanished in the confusion.

At the foot of the scaffold, the Nightmaster saw a muscular, brown-haired human challenging the sole guard, swinging a sword against the polearm wielded by the minotaur. Although sorely pressed, the guard was doing a good job of protecting his position, using his superior bulk to ward off blows and deny the human access to the scaffold.

Momentarily stunned by what he saw, the Nightmaster stumbled backward on his hobbled foot. All of his careful planning, spoiled by a kender, some kyrie, and a handful of pitiable humans! That thought fueled his insane rage.

The high shaman stepped forward and raised both arms to the skies. He shouted out a magical command. His right arm swept downward.

A dozen brilliant balls of fire exploded on the ground near the group of humans and kyrie. Tongues of red flame briefly lit the scene.

Two minotaur soldiers who had been fighting the invaders were instantly incinerated. One of the kyrie, the Nightmaster noted with satisfaction, twisted on the ground, its wings aflame. Another kyrie bent over his unfortunate comrade, trying to smother the flames.

Chuckling at their futility, the Nightmaster prepared to launch another spell.

Then a noise behind him reminded him of Raistlin Majere.

* * * * *

Down on the ground, Tasslehoff hopped and leaped to avoid the balls of fire that sprang up all around him. He wondered about the unusual bird creatures that seemed to be fighting on the side of Caramon and, he was pleased to note, Tanis and Kitiara.

"Hi, Kitiara! How'd you get away?" the kender yelled as he ran to one side, then crawled on his hands and knees through some smoke, apparently looking for something.

He noticed that Kitiara only scowled back at him briefly before thrusting her sword into the side of a charging minotaur. She backed away into a patch of smoke and darkness, trailed by some of the bird-people. Why was Kit always in such a bad mood? Hadn't he greeted her nicely?

The smoke filled Tas's eyes with tears. He groped along the ground, finally laying his hands on what he had been searching for. Before he could get up, he felt a foot come down hard on his hand.

Tas looked up, then grinned with relief. "Hello, Tanis! Boy, is it great to see you and Caramon and Kitiara. Where's Flint?"

The half-elf stared down at him quizzically. "Whose side are you on, Tasslehoff?" he asked sternly.

"Why, Tanis," said Tas, genuinely hurt. "What a question to ask! I'm on your side, of course. Aren't you on mine? It's just me and Raistlin against all these minotaurs, and we sure could use some help."

Tanis eyed the kender closely, then slowly lifted his foot. Tasslehoff grabbed his hoopak, then accepted Tanis's hand and rose to his feet. Tas rubbed his hand ruefully.

"You wouldn't happen to have an extra sword, would you?" the kender asked plaintively.

Tanis shook his head, but he pulled a dagger out of its sheath and handed it to Tas hilt first. "Here," the half-elf said.

The kender took it eagerly. The knife would do. Meantime, he had his precious hoopak back.

The half-elf smiled at him. "Sure I'm on your side ... if you're on mine. There have been some strange rumors about you lately."

"Have there?" asked Tas, grinning broadly. "Well, I've had a heck of a time. First we got betrayed by the captain of the *Venora*—I didn't like him much, anyway. I called him 'Old Walrus Face.' Then this big, incredible storm came along, only it wasn't really a storm but—"

Three minotaurs, carrying studded clubs and swords, crashed through the smoke, attacking them.

Tanis swung fiercely, blocking their charge, then raced off in one direction. Tasslehoff ran off in the other.

*   *   *   *   *

One of the kyrie had fallen in the bombardment of fire balls. Another had dragged his comrade off to one side and been separated from the group.

Tanis had disappeared.

The others were gathered near a small embankment. A group of minotaur soldiers harried them. Kitiara and Yuril, their backs against a rock, lashed out with their swords at two of the bull-men. Cloudreaver and three other kyrie warriors fought nearby, fending off several minotaurs with curved clubs.

One of the minotaurs closed in and stabbed his sword at Yuril, piercing her side. Instantly Kitiara swung around, slicing off the arm of the attacker at the elbow. The minotaur fell back, clutching his limb to stem the flow of blood. His fellow soldier shoved him out of the way, then lunged at Kitiara while she was still off balance.

At least Kit thought he had lunged, but when she stepped nimbly aside, the minotaur continued to fall forward onto his face, dead. A small knife protruded from the back of his neck.

She just managed to glimpse the kender as he dashed away.

Yuril slumped, and Kitiara grabbed her by the shoulders. "Can you make it?" she asked. Yuril nodded weakly and lost consciousness.

* * * * *

Tasslehoff couldn't find Dogz.

The minotaurs had dragged the traitor off to the perimeter of the staging area, where one bull-man soldier, removed from the rest of the action, nervously supervised the prisoner. Dogz sat in anguish, lost in his own world, staring at his feet. Suddenly he heard a solid thunk. He looked up to see the minotaur soldier drop to his knees, clawing at his throat, then topple face forward into the dirt.

Tas sauntered into view.

"It's all in the wrist," he boasted. "Not every kender can throw a hoopak as good as me. Why, I'd venture to say hardly any kender can throw a hoopak as good as mc. Well, maybe Uncle Trapspringer can, but, after all, he's the one who taught me!"

In the midst of the noisy, smoke-enshrouded confusion all around them, Tas quickly untied Dogz.

Dogz didn't move. "You came back, friend Tas," he said, his voice missing its usual booming resonance.

"I owed you one, didn't I?"

"It is good to see you the way you were before ," said the minotaur. "So the human female's antidote did work."

* * * * *

The minotaur soldier showed himself to be stubborn, savage, and battle-wise. Caramon couldn't get past him. The bull-man held a long polearm with a crescent blade at each end of its shaft. Again and again the young warrior tried to slash forward, but the minotaur kept him busy dodging the heavy weapon, which he twirled like a baton.

It seemed like a standoff until Tanis came running up, bringing his sword to bear alongside Caramon's. The half-elf slashed, while Caramon kept up his stabbing attack. Their weapons rang against the polearm.

For the first time, Caramon saw a hint of panic in the soldier's eyes. The minotaur stumbled and retreated a few steps. All his moves were defensive now, and Tanis and Caramon pushed their advantage. The minotaur was obviously tiring from the attack and couldn't last much longer.

* * * * *

On the scaffold, the Nightmaster turned to confront Raistlin Majere.

After Tasslehoff had cut the rope binding his hands, the young mage had worked fast, managing to pull the cord off his legs. Now, eyes intense, he stood there, pale and sweating, poised like an animal ready to spring.

"Things are not going very well … are they?" Raistlin said in a low, purposeful voice.

The Nightmaster had been thrown off balance by the nightmare sequence of events. But now the figure before him, the human who had somehow divined his plans and conspired to wreck them, renewed his sense of purpose. The high shaman of the minotaur race stared down at the much shorter Raistlin. He noted with satisfaction that the puny human didn't have any weapon.

"The spell has been spoken," rumbled the high shaman. "All that remains is the sacrifice. And I see that you are still here, Raistlin Majere of Solace. It occurs to me that there has been enough interruption and delay. The time for you to die is now. Sargonnas awaits!"

Raistlin had edged around as the Nightmaster spoke. Now he lunged—away from the high shaman, toward the tome of spells that rested on a stand. He snatched up the book of magic, holding it before him.

The Nightmaster stopped, hobbling toward Raistlin, surprised. "What is this, mage?" the shaman minotaur said with a sneer. "Do you think you have time to learn a spell in order to defeat me? Or are you simply intending to use my spellbook as a shield?"

Raistlin whirled and tossed the spellbook far out over the mouth of the volcano.

"No!" shouted the Nightmaster, lunging futilely after the book. "No-o-o-o!"

Just as the minotaur turned his back on Raistlin, Tanis and Caramon reached the top of the scaffold. They hurled their weapons at the hulking figure. Two swords rammed into the Nightmaster's back. The high shaman of the minotaur race teetered on the edge of the scaffold for a second, then lost his footing and fell forward into the fiery crater.

Caramon and Tanis embraced Raistlin.

The young mage glanced questioningly toward the continued fighting below.

"Kit is fine," explained Caramon quickly. "So is Tasslehoff. We're doing our best to hold them off!"

"There is no more time," said Raistlin tersely. "We have to hurry!"

Caramon and Tanis saw that already a red cloud was billowing out of the mouth of the volcano. Like a whirlwind of fire, it grew and swirled. They had to turn their faces away from the searing heat.

A sound like the hooves of a hundred thousand horses accompanied it.

Caramon glanced down briefly at the pool of orange fire whose huge waves splashed upward before Raistlin yanked him away. Caramon and Tanis were pushed back down the scaffold steps by the young mage.

* * * * *

"Kitiara's antidote?" asked the kender blankly.

"I exchanged it for your usual double dose," said Dogz solemnly.

"Yeah, well, I've been meaning to talk to you about that. That potion never tasted very good, but this last time was even worse ..."

The kender stopped suddenly. He heard a strange noise, like rolling thunder, quite different from the battle sounds he had been hearing. Tas looked up at the scaffold. It stood empty. A firestorm spewed from the mouth of the volcano, swelling over the scene.

"Uh-oh," Tasslehoff gulped. "We'll talk about all that later. Right now we'd better get out of here." He tugged at Dogz, who hadn't risen from where he was sitting.

"I'm not going," said Dogz.

"You're not what?"

"I'm not going," repeated Dogz. Now he stood, leaned over, and put his hands on the kender's shoulders. Dogz looked into his friend's eyes. "I have disgraced my race," said the minotaur. "I have disobeyed orders. I am dishonored."

"What?" sputtered Tas, looking around wildly. Minotaurs ran past them, throwing down their weapons and screaming. Through the confusion of smoke and fire, he couldn't see any of his companions. "What do you mean? You saved my life! You're a hero in my book!"

Dogz squeezed Tas's shoulders. His eyes were moist. "Go, friend Tas," said Dogz mournfully. "Save yourself. I am not worth saving. I am dishonored." He sat back down.

Tasslehoff was about to hurl a reply when one of those huge, feathered creatures swooped down and picked him up. The creature joined several other bird-people in flight. Each appeared to be carrying a human in its talons.

The kyrie veered away sharply and then up. They had

just risen above the smoke and fires when they heard a tremendous explosion. Twisting around, Tas and the others could see a colossal plume of red fire bursting from the mouth of the volcano. The plume hovered in the air, forming into a shape that looked very much like a giant condor. For several minutes, the condor rained fiery death on everyone who still remained on the summit of the volcano. After several minutes, the condor dissipated, the plume withdrew, and the volcano became quiet once again.

Sargonnas had come and gone.

Epilogue

The hundreds of orughi waiting off the coast of Beakwere slowly came to the realization that the spell hadn't worked. Sargonnas wasn't coming—not this time. Their beady eyes disappointed, the orughi turned away from Karthay toward the smaller, even less hospitable islands where they dwelled. They swam northward, their hundreds of muscular, webbed feet stroking the water, churning up a mile-wide trail of foam in their wake.

The ogres in their warships near Land Ho Straits also recognized that the time had passed. Oolong Xak, commander of the ogre tribal fleet, gave the signal for dozens of warships to turn back—back toward Ogrebond and the continent of Ansalon. At least, Oolong Xak thought with a sigh, the ogres hadn't cemented any alliance with the contemptible orughi. It was bad enough that the orgre chieftains had consented to join with the minotaurs. The bull-men had led everybody astray with their pipe dream of Sargonnas.

Back in the palace in the city of Lacynos, the eight mino taurs of the Supreme Circle accepted the news of the Night-master's failure with varying reactions.

Of one thing, everyone was certain. This turn of events deeply compromised the king of the minotaurs. After he heard the news of the calamity, the king immediately left the Supreme Circle to return to his residence.

Although Atra Cura had supported the king, this policy blunder didn't reflect badly on the minotaur pirate leader. In fact, it reinforced his vainglorious belief that the king was slipping and that he, Atra Cura, was the logical successor to the throne—perhaps as soon as next year.

The leader of the navy, Akz; the commander of the mino-taur military, Inultus; the scholar and historian, Juvabit; the keeper of the treasury, Groppis; and the construction guild-master, Bartill—these five council members lingered in the hall long after the startling announcement that the Night-master had been killed. They tried to outdo one another with their claims that privately each had foreseen the flaws in the arrogant high shaman's plans.

Before departing, Victri, leader of the rural minotaurs, spoke eloquently about the patriotism that flamed in every bull-man's breast, and how, despite occasional setbacks, the minotaur kingdom would one day overrun all of Ansalon.

As for Kharis-O, leader of the nomadic minotaurs, she glowered at all the others and left without uttering a word.

* * * * *

On the island of Karthay, the companions regrouped back on the high ground where they had camped the night before the attack on the ruined city.

The minotaur forces had scattered. Those remaining on

the volcano summit had been burned to death by the plume of fiery mist that had briefly flared from the crater. After the fighting ended, the army of sand and rock creatures who had helped the companions defeat the minotaurs had returned to their burrows and caves.

Kirsig's body was carried back to the camp by Flint. By himself, the dwarf dug a simple grave in a spot where the ground wasn't too hard. He stuck the sword she had carried into the fresh mound, leaving it for all to see.

"Kirsig called herself a cleaning woman and a healer," the dwarf proclaimed over her burial place. He tugged on his beard, then looked at the ground. "But those of us who fought alongside her know that she had the true, unwavering heart of a warrior. And we shall miss her," he added, brushing away rare tears.

Two of the sailors from the *Castor* and three of the kyrie warriors had been killed in the attack, including Bird-Spirit. It had been Bird-Spirit who was incinerated on the summit of Worldscap.

Sturm grieved for the kyrie who had rescued him from certain death at the Pit of Doom.

Cloudreaver grieved for his friend. True, Bird-Spirit had died in battle, an honorable death for any kyrie. But his body had been left behind on the mountaintop when the volcano erupted in its fiery shower of death. "Our dead are always burned on a pyre above the ground," Cloudreaver told Sturm sadly. "But the ashes are supposed to be scattered to the four winds. The lava will have buried Bird-Spirit's body. In death, he will never be free."

Where she had been wounded, Yuril's side felt sore, a soreness that would remain with her for the rest of her life. But she was recuperating and would live. Caramon tended to her during her convalescence, bringing her hot tea and palliatives by day, blankets at night.

Watching them, Flint grumbled plaintively to Tanis, "Reminds me of Kirsig—he's acting just like a female." Tanis merely nodded, admiring Caramon's tenderness.

The kyrie continued to perform their long scouting flights. One day one of them returned and reported to Cloudreaver that a ship, the *Castor*, hovered off the southern coast. Hearing that, Yuril and the two surviving sailors conferred, then announced that they had decided to head back to sea. Astonished, Caramon tried to talk Yuril into staying with the companions.

"No," laughed the tall, strong seawoman. "You don't understand, do you? Captain Nugetre is a difficult man, but the sea is where I belong, and he knows that. You are reunited with your brother. Now I must rejoin the sea."

Raistlin and Tanis bid Yuril good-bye, vowing their eternal gratitude. Flint shook her hand and the hands of the other two sailors solemnly. Kit embraced Yuril. Caramon, after sulking briefly, planted a kiss on her lips that lasted so long Tasslehoff had to tap him on the shoulders.

Three of the kyrie carried the female sailors back to the sea vessel that awaited them.

Four kyrie returned—the three who had gone to meet the *Castor*, plus a messenger from the island of Mithas.

A sentinel had reported from the dungeon in Atossa. Morning Sky was dead. The broken bird-man, Cloudreaver's brother, had perished without revealing anything to his cruel captors.

Cloudreaver wept when he heard the news.

"You must go back," the kyrie messenger told Cloudreaver. "Sun Feather calls you. He says to tell you that you are heir to the leadership now."

Cloudreaver collected his warriors of the sky together, announcing that they would return to Mithas immediately. The companions gathered to say a sad farewell to the ancient people who had helped save them and stop Sargonnas.

"We will meet again," said Raistlin solemnly.

"I trust that we will," said Cloudreaver.

Sturm gave Cloudreaver a stiff but heartfelt hug.

Caramon stepped forward, uncertain of what to say or

do. He had grown close to Cloudreaver in this short time. He doubted he would ever forget his kyrie friend.

Cloudreaver looked at the human. He lifted up Caramon's arm and pulled up his sleeve, finding the scar from the Night of the Sea Dragon. The kyrie touched the scar with two fingers, then brought the two fingers to his lips.

"Warrior," said Cloudreaver. "Brother."

"Warrior," repeated Caramon. "Brother."

The kyrie flew off in a glorious rush of giant feathered wings.

* * * * *

It had been seven days since the attack on the ruined city and the defeat of the Nightmaster, two days since the departure of the kyrie.

There was a listlessness about the companions. Although some of them were bruised and nursing wounds, none of them was so badly hurt that he, or she, couldn't move on. Nevertheless, the seven companions lingered on the high ground overlooking the dead city, where in the distance they could still glimpse the smoldering peak of Worldscap.

Tasslehoff had been trying to convince everyone that he had never been truly evil in the first place. It was all a fabulous charade, the kender insisted.

Nonetheless, Sturm had been giving Tas a wide berth. Privately he believed that the evil kender had nearly gotten him killed in Atossa. Nobody could convince the Solamnic otherwise. And not everybody was certain he should try.

This late afternoon, as suppertime approached, Flint saw Tas and Sturm arguing together vehemently. Unexpectedly the dwarf doubled over, clutching his sides with laughter. Sturm demanded to know what Flint found so funny.

"Ken—ken—kender without a topknot!" sputtered the dwarf. "Solamnic with only half a mustache!"

Everybody joined in the laughter—all except Sturm, who didn't see what was so darned funny.

Tas laughed the longest. When he finally regained control of himself, he turned serious. "You believe me, don't you, Raistlin?"

"Yes, I do," said Raistlin simply.

"See! Raistlin believes me!" cried the kender, beaming.

"My brother is very wise," said Kitiara as she built a fire to cook the evening meal, "but he has a soft spot for kender."

"What do you think, Kitiara?" demanded Sturm, hoping for an ally.

"I've told you," answered Kit. "He was evil, until Dogz substituted my vial of leucrotta saliva for his evil potion. If it wasn't for Dogz, Tas would still be evil—and maybe we'd all be dead."

Tas listened respectfully. He liked this version of what happened because it made Dogz out to be a hero, and Dogz had been his friend.

"Leucrotta's saliva?" Sturm repeated, confused.

"It acts as an antidote to love potions," cut in Tanis, "and Kitiara figured that if it acted as an antidote to love potions, it might have the same effect on an evil potion. I guess it did, because Tas is here and he's not evil anymore."

"The big expert on love potions," muttered Flint, rolling his eyes. He handed a big pot to Kit and indicated that she should go for water.

Tas wore a big grin to prove to everybody he wasn't evil anymore.

"Well, maybe," said Sturm doubtfully.

"Is that possible?" asked Caramon of Raistlin.

"Possible," said his brother noncommittally.

"I keep meaning to ask," said Tanis, "if you were hunting a leucrotta with Uncle Nellthis, Kit, how'd you get to Karthay so fast?"

The others looked up to hear the answer. But Kitiara had left to get the pot filled for cooking.

When she returned, they were already discussing a new topic—the familiar debate of the last week: Where should they go and what should they do next?

For eight days, they had camped on the ridge, burying the dead, seeing friends head for home, and delaying their own agenda.

"I'll tell you what I'd like to do," said Caramon boldly. "I'd like to return to Mithas and help Cloudreaver and the kyrie go to war against the minotaurs. I'd like to avenge the death of Morning Sky!"

"I'd like to go back to Mithas, too," agreed Sturm. "I'd like to have another crack at that gladiator, Tossak, now that I'm feeling fit."

"Is there much treasure in those minotaur cities?" asked Kit.

"Sure!" exclaimed Tas.

"I don't know," said Tanis thoughtfully. "I miss Solace, but now that we're this far away—on the other side of the world, really—it seems to me that we should take advantage of it and explore the land and meet the people. What do you think, Raistlin?"

The wind had picked up. Night was coming on, with its attendant chill. Lunitari and Solinari were beginning their ascent.

The young mage smiled thinly. "We can't stay here forever. And there's no easy way home. So I say let's vote in the morning. Whatever the vote, let's act on it and leave here."

They were interrupted by the sounds of some sort of ruckus. The companions looked over to where Flint stood by the fire. An appetizing smell wafted from the big pot. The grizzled dwarf glared at them while clanging the side of the pot with a big wooden spoon.

"Talk, talk, talk!" fumed the dwarf. "Let's eat!"